*Gripping Novels of Crime
and Detection*

SIGNET DOUBLE MYSTERY:

THE COPPER FRAME

and

A ROOM TO DIE IN

The Copper Frame

and

A Room To Die In

by ELLERY QUEEN

A SIGNET BOOK

NEW AMERICAN LIBRARY

PUBLISHER'S NOTE

These novels are works of fiction. Names, characters, places, and incidents are either the product of the author's imagination or are used fictitiously, and any resemblance to actual persons, living or dead, events, or locales is entirely coincidental.

SIGNET TRADEMARK REG. U.S. PAT. OFF. AND FOREIGN COUNTRIES
REGISTERED TRADEMARK—MARCA REGISTRADA
HECHO EN CHICAGO, U.S.A.

SIGNET, SIGNET CLASSIC, MENTOR, PLUME, MERIDIAN AND NAL BOOKS are published by New American Library, 1633 Broadway, New York, New York 10019

FIRST PRINTING (DOUBLE ELLERY QUEEN EDITION), AUGUST, 1981

3 4 5 6 7 8 9

PRINTED IN THE UNITED STATES OF AMERICA

THE COPPER FRAME

CAST OF CHARACTERS

chapter 1

LIEUTENANT TED SAXON was surprised when a radio call came into headquarters from Car One. Car One was the police chief's car, and it was taking his father and two other police officers to a county law-enforcement officers' meeting at Rigby. By 8 P.M., when they call came in, it should have been nearly there, beyond the twenty-mile range of its broadcast band.

Nevertheless, the message was quite clear. The voice from the speaker said, "Car One to Control. Can you read me, Control?"

Lifting the microphone from its bracket on the radio panel, Saxon said, "Control to Car One. I read you fine. What's up?"

The voice said, "This is Sam Lennox. That you, Ted?"

"Yes."

"We're on Route Sixty, five miles out of Rigby. The chief and Lieutenant Burns have both been shot by a suspect we stopped. I'm rushing them to Rigby Memorial Hospital. Description of suspects's car: new Chevrolet two-door sedan, gray with blue top, New York License IUL-053. No description of suspect because it's dark and he started firing before the chief and Burns got close to him, then took off. Last seen thirty seconds ago heading south on Route Sixty toward Rigby. I fired after the car and believe I hit it a couple of times, but I didn't give chase because I can't leave the wounded men."

Ted Saxon had been too busy jotting down the pertinent data to think of anything else while Lennox was speaking. But now it registered on him that his father and one of his closest friends had been shot.

He said huskily, "I'll get it right out, Sam. How bad are they hit?"

The patrolman's voice came over the radio with an edge of bitterness. "Vic's only nicked, but your dad's hit bad. I'll phone you from the hospital. Car One to Control, over and out."

"Control to Car One, roger," Saxon said mechanically.

He phoned the Rigby police first, to have a road block set up. Then he contacted the sheriff's office and the state police by radio. As the Iroquois radio communication system was linked to both, he was able to relay the information to them simultaneously.

Then there was nothing to do but wait.

Ted Saxon was a younger image of his father, with the same wide shoulders and hipless frame, the same wide-mouthed face sprinkled with freckles and the same sandy red hair. The only difference was that usually there was a smile on the younger man's face, whereas Chief Andy Saxon seldom indulged in any expression at all.

Peering outside, the lieutenant saw that the night was pitch black and the air was filled with tiny flakes of falling snow. By the thermometer bracketed just outside the door and angled so that it could be read from indoors, he saw that it was twenty above zero.

Christmas weather, he thought. In ten more days it would be Christmas. A box of cigars for his dad was already wrapped and hidden at the back of his closet. He wondered if the old man would ever get to smoke them.

Sam Lennox phoned at eight-thirty. "I'm calling from Rigby Memorial, Ted," the patrolman said heavily. "I'm sorry, but your dad was D.O.A."

For a few moments Saxon couldn't speak. It was too hard to adjust to the thought of his indestructible father being dead. At sixty-two Chief Andy Saxon still had been sturdy as an oak and twice as tough. For thirty years he had run the Iroquois Police Department with an iron hand, fair and impartial, but as demanding of perfection as a Marine drill sergeant.

Eventually Saxon managed to ask, "How's Vic?"

"Just a bullet singe on the right biceps. They patched him up with a Band-Aid. We're starting back now. I'll give you the details when we get there."

Saxon hung up and sat staring into space. He had been closer to his father than most Iroquoisans were aware from their reserved relationship in public. Though Andy Saxon's public image was that of a remote, unapproachable man, his son knew the hidden side of his character that made him capable of both warmth and compassion. Vaguely, Ted could recall a house always filled with laughter before his mother died, when he was ten. And though the laughter stopped the night his father stonily returned to the house half an hour before the visiting period at the hospital ended, the house remained, if not as gay, at least one of warmth and security.

A single parent, striving to fill the roles of both father and mother, often develops a closer relationship with a child than two parents possibly could, and this had been the case between Andy and his boy Ted.

Sam Lennox and Vic Burns got back from Rigby at nine-thirty. They came in stamping the snow from their galoshes and brushing flakes from their overcoats, both making a to-do of it in an obvious effort to outwait each other in approaching the desk.

Finally Lennox conceded defeat and moved his thin, lanky frame forward. His eyes briefly touched Saxon's before shifting to gaze past his left shoulder.

"Sorry, Ted," he murmured. "Twenty, twenty-five years ago it would never have happened, but I guess I'm getting old."

Despite his grief, Saxon felt a twinge of sympathy for the veteran patrolman. After twenty-eight years on the force, Sam Lennox was not, by a country mile, quite the police officer he had once been. The gradual-

ly increasing redness of the veins in his cheeks and
nose suggested the reason. Long ago a younger man
with Sam Lennox's drinking habits would have been
bounced from the force by Andy Saxon. But discip-
linarian that he was, even the hard-bitten chief couldn't
bring himself to rob a veteran of so many years of his
pension. For the past two years Lennox had been
relegated to the relative sinecure of the chief's driver.

Saxon said, "I'm sure it wasn't your fault, Sam. The
old man was still fast as a whip, so if he was caught flat-
footed, it must have happened too suddenly for anyone
to save him."

"It did," Vic Burns said, coming over to the desk.
"The chief and I had just stepped from the car when the
guy started banging away. The chief was down and I
had a numb arm before I could reach for my gun."

Lieutenant Vic Burns was a stocky, open-faced man
of about Saxon's age: thirty. A former member of the
Buffalo Police Department, he and Ted had met at the
F.B.I. school in Washington three years before, where
they had taken an instant liking to each other. It was
Ted Saxon who had talked him into transferring to the
Iroquois force.

"Just how'd it happen?" Saxon asked.

"It must have been a setup," Burns said. "The guy
must have been some old con with a grudge against the
chief. It was in the paper that your father planned to
attend the county law-enforcement officers' meeting, so
anyone could have known he'd be on Route Sixty
about that time. Sam says he followed us clear from the
out-skirts of Iroquois."

Saxon glanced at Lennox, who said, "I could see his
lights in the rear-view mirror. I didn't think anything
of it until afterward, because the way the roads and the
weather were, nobody was passing anybody else."

"That's why we stopped him," Burns said. "All of a
sudden he cut around us, nearly putting us in the
ditch, and gunned off at about sixty. With road conditions what they were and visibility cut by falling snow,
that was about thirty too fast for safety. The chief

told Sam to give him the siren. I guess that's what the guy wanted, because he pulled right over. When Sam parked behind him and the chief and I got out, the shooting started. Then he took off again."

Sam Lennox said, "I tumbled out and emptied my gun at his taillights. I think I hit him a couple of times, but it didn't slow him down."

"Neither of you got any glimpse of the man's face?"

"My headlights were on the back of his car," Lennox said. "But he had on a hat with the brim turned down. It all happened too fast. He just leaned out the driver's window and started shooting, then took off. All I know is it was a man."

"Sure he was alone?"

"Unless someone was crouched on the floor," Burns said. "There was only one head showing."

At that moment a radio call came from the state police. The wanted car had been found, abandoned on a side road off Route Sixty only a mile from the murder scene, with three bullet holes in its trunk. The dispatcher added that a report had been received from the Buffalo police that the car had been stolen in Buffalo earlier that day.

When the state-police dispatcher signed off, Saxon said heavily, "I guess it was a setup, all right. He must have had a getaway car planted in that side road."

"Or an accomplice waiting for him in one," Burns suggested.

Belatedly Saxon remembered that Vic Burns had been wounded, too. Glancing at him, he saw a singed area on the upper right sleeve of his overcoat. There was a tiny hole in the center of the area and another a couple of inches behind it where the bullet had come out. The exit hole was ringed with dried blood.

In a tone of apology Saxon said, "I haven't even asked how you are, Vic."

"Don't worry about me," Burns said. "It's only a nick about an eighth of an inch deep."

"How do you know it wasn't you the gunman was after?" Saxon asked. "You got shot, too."

Burns said, "We thought of that. But the item in the paper didn't mention me. I decided to go at the last minute."

Sam Lennox said diffidently, "Want me to take over the rest of your trick, Ted? You probably don't feel much like sitting here all alone."

Saxon shook his head. "Thanks, but I'd hang around anyway to hear what reports come in. I'll be all right. What about Dad's body?"

Burns said, "We phoned the coroner. He's having the autopsy performed at Rigby Memorial instead of shipping the body back here. You'll have to contact whatever funeral director you want to pick it up when the coroner's through with it."

"Okay. I'll call Alstrom in the morning," Saxon said. "Thanks for stopping in, fellows."

chapter 2

AFTER BURNS AND LENNOX LEFT, police headquarters became oppressively silent. At 11 P.M. a radio call came from the state-police barracks reporting that the killer's car had been towed in and dusted for prints. There had been none because the interior of the car had been wiped clean.

At eleven-fifteen Saxon was standing with his arms resting on the counter, simply waiting for time to pass, when Emily Vane came in, her cheeks bright from the cold and her face smiling. In his preoccupation over the death of his father, Saxon had forgotten that she was coming by. When Emily worked the three-to-eleven trick at the Iroquois General Hospital on the same nights he worked the desk from four to midnight, she always stopped by to while away the last forty-five minutes of his duty with him, after which he drove her home.

Kicking the snow from her boots, Emily slipped off her coat. Under it was her white nurse's uniform. She untied her headscarf and hung both on a wall hook near the door. She was a slim, attractive girl of twenty-five with dark, wavy hair worn to her shoulders, big pale-blue eyes, and a milky Irish complexion.

"Coffee ready?" she asked brightly, moving toward the counter. Then she saw his expression and her smile faded. "What's the matter?"

"Dad was killed tonight," he said quietly.

Her eyes widened and her face lost color. "Oh, no! I'm so sorry, Ted."

"One of the hazards of police work," he said bitterly. "He was shot on his way to the county law-en-

13

forcement officers' meeting at Rigby. We don't yet know by whom, but it may have been some ex-con with a grudge."

He told her what he knew of the affair. When he finished, she reached across the counter to lay her hand on his. "I know how much he meant to you, Ted. I was pretty fond of him myself. I wish there were something I could do."

"You can make the coffee I forgot to make."

They had finished their coffee and Emily had washed the cups by the time Saxon's relief came on. Then there was the delay of repeating what had happened to Jack Dow, the relief desk man, and listening to his words of sympathy. It was twelve-fifteen before they got away from headquarters.

They made little conversation as Ted drove Emily home. He was conscious of her silent tenderness as she sat snuggled up against him. The three-room apartment Emily shared with Julie Fox, another nurse, was at the northeast edge of town. Julie was already in bed asleep when they got there. Sitting on the sofa in the tiny front room, they conversed in whispers so as not to disturb her.

Lying in the crook of his arm with her head on his shoulder, Emily said, "We'll have to postpone our plans, of course, but I don't want you to have to worry about it. I'll take care of contacting everyone."

They had planned to be married December twenty-first; the reception hall was already reserved and the invitations had gone out. Emily's parents had made reservations to fly from Seattle on the nineteenth, only four days away.

Saxon said, "Dad wouldn't want us to delay our wedding on account of him. He was pushing me to set the date six months ago. I think he was afraid I'd let you escape."

"I know, Ted. I'm proud of the way he approved of me. But we just can't go ahead now. The whole town would be shocked. We'll have to leave plans indefinite until some time after the first of the year."

"I suppose," he said gloomily. "But the old man wouldn't agree with you. He'd tell the town to go soak its collective head."

Raising her lips, she kissed the edge of his chin. "Maybe, but he wouldn't want the townspeople thinking badly of you, either. You'd better go home now. We'll talk again tomorrow."

At the door she didn't press against him and tighten her arms about his neck as she usually did when they said good-night. She merely cupped his face in her hands and stood on tiptoe to give him a gentle kiss on the lips. It struck him that Emily was remarkably gifted in adjusting her moods to his. She knew instinctively that at this moment he neither needed nor wanted any demonstration of the passion of which she was extremely capable.

The next morning Saxon awoke to an oppressive sense of loneliness. Without the presence of his father at breakfast, the big old house was entirely too quiet and empty. He had a sudden urge to get out of it. After breakfast, instead of merely phoning the Alstrom Funeral Parlor, he drove over there to make arrangements. Afterward, about 10 A.M., he stopped by police headquarters to see if there had been any developments. There had not been.

Lieutenant Art Marks, big, cumbersome, and plodding, was on the desk. At forty-five Marks wasn't the oldest man on the force by several, but he was second highest in seniority, his twenty-four years of service being exceeded only by Sam Lennox's twenty-eight. He had been a lieutenant, the highest grade on the Iroquois force aside from chief, for nearly fifteen years.

After expressing his sympathy, Marks said, "The mayor's looking for you, Ted. He phoned your home, but there was no answer."

"I'll run upstairs to see him," Saxon said. "Know what he wants?"

"Probably just to say he's sorry about your dad."

The police station was on the ground floor of the city hall, with its outside entrance facing the alley. A second door, used only in the daytime when the city hall was open, led into an inner corridor. Saxon took the corridor to the front stairs and started to climb.

It took him fifteen minutes to reach the top because the big, open stairway was the main artery of traffic in the city hall and people were always moving up and down it. He was stopped a dozen times by city-hall employees, councilmen, and citizens with business in the building, all of whom wanted to express their condolences.

Eventually he managed to work his way to the second floor and the mayor's office.

Benjamin Foley, after twenty-four years as mayor of Iroquois, was now in the unenviable position of being a lame-duck mayor. In the previous November elections he had finally met political defeat at the hands of a younger man, and the new mayor was scheduled to take office January second.

A plump, affable man of sixty-five, Foley had shown no bitterness at being turned out to pasture after nearly a quarter of a century in harness, but Saxon suspected he was deeply hurt. The loss of income meant nothing to him, Saxon knew, since the position of mayor was only a parttime job paying fifteen hundred dollars a year, and Foley was a shrewd lawyer with a thriving practice. But Ben Foley sincerely loved his small city, and he had been under the impression that it returned the love. It had been a blow to his pride to have a whopping 70 per cent of the electorate turn against him after his many years of service.

When Saxon entered the always-open door of the mayor's office, Ben Foley glanced up from the letter he was reading, then got to his feet and stretched his right hand across the desk.

"I was utterly shocked to hear about your dad, Ted. The town's going to miss him."

"Thanks, Ben," Saxon said, dropping into a chair. "Dad always regarded you as his closest friend."

Foley lit a pipe. When he had it going, he said, "The chief and I were a team, Ted. I don't think I'm bragging when I say the two of us are responsible for Iroquois's being the clean town it is today."

"I've heard Dad say the same thing," Saxon agreed.

Foley reflectively puffed on his pipe. "You'd be surprised at the pressures public officials such as your dad and I are subject to, Ted. Particularly in a tourist town like ours. There are always some businessmen eager to attract more tourists by letting things open up a bit. You know what I mean. They want the police to wink at a little illegal gambling, or maybe a red-light district."

"*Some* businessmen?" Saxon said dryly. "I'd say the majority in this town. Isn't that what won Adam Bennock the election?"

The mayor grinned a little sourly. "Harness racing isn't illegal, Ted. Maybe if Adam can live up to his campaign promise and get the new track put here, it will make the town grow."

"Then why'd you fight him on the issue?"

"Because I don't think a growing town is necessarily a better town. Take a look at what we already have. No one's starving here. Most of our businesses are small, but they all seem solvent enough for the merchants to buy new cars every year and belong to the country club. We have fine schools, an excellent hospital, and the best beaches between Buffalo and Erie. There's nothing even approaching a slum district. I think it's a pretty nice place to live as it is. But maybe I'm an old fogey."

"No," Saxon disagreed. "I'm not too hot about a harness track here, either. It's bound to bring in a different tourist element from the one we're used to."

"It's not just the track that worries me," the mayor said, puffing on his pipe and finding that it had gone out. He felt for another match, struck it on the underside of his desk, and got the pipe going again. "There are always racketeers looking for a ripe town to pluck. Particularly a tourist town, where there's a ready-made clientele for gambling and vice. Your dad and I always managed to keep that breed of vulture out of Iroquois, but now he's gone, and I'm leaving office too. Frankly, I'm worried about the town's future."

"Because you think the new race track might be an opening wedge for racketeers?"

"Uh-huh. You know who's behind that promotion?"

"Sure," Saxon said. "The Upstate Harness Racing Association."

"That's just a corporation name."

"Well, I saw the names of the directors in the paper, but I don't recall any of them. None were familiar."

"Of course not," Foley said. "They're all out-of-towners. They're just names, too. The money behind them was put up by Larry Cutter."

Saxon's eyes widened. "The racketeer who was run out of Saratoga Springs last year for running a wide-open casino?"

"Uh-huh. Know where he is now?"

"Sure. We get the Buffalo intelligence reports on the movements of known racketeers. He's living in Buffalo, but he's not operating there and he's not about to. The Buffalo cops are just waiting for him to make a wrong move so they can pounce."

"He won't make any wrong moves within the city limits of Buffalo," Foley said. "If you were a racketeer with a lot of expensive gambling equipment in storage and a cadre of idle hoods on your payroll, what would you do?"

Saxon said slowly, "I guess I'd look for a friendly town where the officials would let me resume operations for a cut of the take."

"Exactly. And what could be a nicer place than Iroquois? Only twenty-five miles from Buffalo, yet in another county. Cutter would have all greater Buffalo to draw on for casino patrons, and still would be out of the jurisdiction of both the Buffalo police and the Erie County sheriff's office." The mayor frowned down at his pipe, which had gone out again. He decided to give it up and set it in a ash tray.

Saxon said, "If you knew this, Ben, why didn't you mention it during the campaign?"

"Because I found it out only yesterday. Your dad told me."

"Dad knew?" Saxon said in surprise.

"Uh-huh. He was tipped off by the Buffalo intelligence squad yesterday morning. I'm surprised he didn't mention it to you."

"We didn't see much of each other yesterday," Saxon said. "I came on duty at four and he left at five. The desk was pretty busy for a while, so we didn't have a chance to talk."

The mayor leaned on his arms on the desk and stared into Saxon's face. "There's a reason other than offering sympathy that I sent for you, Ted. If Larry Cutter is planning to move into Iroquois, he has to get two people on his side first: the mayor and the chief of police. I don't know much about Adam Bennock. Maybe he's as honest as Abe Lincoln. But just in case, I'd like to make sure we still have a chief of police as incorruptible as Andy Saxon."

Saxon raised his eyebrows. "If you're thinking of me, I appreciate the compliment, but the city council appoints the chief of police."

"Permanent appointment, sure. But according to the city charter, the mayor is empowered to appoint an acting chief in the event of the permanent chief's disability or death."

"What good will that do?" Saxon asked. "Bennock swept in a majority of council seats with him. After the first of the year, they'll appoint whoever he wants."

"You don't understand politics, and you also underestimate your popularity," Foley said. "You're not just Andy Saxon's son. The whole town knows you're the best cop on the force. And certainly the best fitted for chief. Who else has a degree in criminology?"

"Nobody. But Art Marks has fourteen years' seniority over me as a lieutenant and seventeen over me in total time on the force."

The mayor made a dismissing gesture. "Art Marks would probably be Bennock's choice, if Bennock does make a deal with Larry Cutter, because Art is unimaginative enough to do as he's told. But everyone in town knows Art hasn't the capability to be chief. He might possibly be accepted if I appointed him now, but the town would explode if the new council kicked you out as acting chief once you're actually serving in the job and replaced you with Art." He looked thoughtfully off into space before adding, "In a way I sort of hope they do."

Saxon gave him a quizzical look.

"That's just the politician in me," Foley said with a grin. "They won't, because it would be political suicide. They'll give you the permanent appointment whether they want to or not, because city councilmen who flout the public will get voted out of office."

Rising to his feet, the mayor said, "Stand and raise your right hand, Lieutenant. I'm about to swear you in as acting chief of police for the City of Iroquois."

chapter 3

SAXON CALLED a general meeting of the police department at 4 P.M. to announce his appointment as acting chief. The announcement was greeted not merely with approval, but with an obvious measure of relief, which led the new chief to suspect that the men had been discussing possible successors to his father with some concern. It was rather gratifying to know that they had been afraid he might not get the appointment. He had been aware that he was well liked in the department, but he hadn't suspected the force was so solidly behind him.

If Lieutenant Art Marks felt any disappointment at being passed over, he didn't show it. His congratulations were just as hearty as anyone else's.

As the meeting broke up, Sam Lennox came over and said, "Can I see you a minute, Chief?"

"Sure," Saxon said, leading the way out of the squad room and into the office that had been his father's.

Inside he discovered that he couldn't yet bring himself to sit in the chief's big chair. Closing the door, he sat in one of the guest chairs and waved Lennox to another.

"What's on your mind, Sam?"

The older man nervously shifted his feet. "I was just wondering what I'm supposed to do around here, now that your dad's gone."

Saxon regarded him curiously. "What do you mean? You're still a member of the force."

"Well, you know how it was with your dad. I was supposed to be his driver, but most of the day I just sat around in the squad room. Even when he went somewhere, he really didn't need me. He could have driven himself for all he used the car. You know why he assigned me as his driver?"

"I suppose he figured you'd earned a soft job after all your years of service."

Lennox's red-veined face moved back and forth in a negative. "He wanted his eye on me all the time I was on duty. He knew that some time, somewhere, I'd slip and take a drink otherwise. And after one I never stop. He would have had to board me if he caught me drunk on duty, because he played by the book. But he didn't want to have to. He wanted me to make it to my pension. That's the kind of guy he was."

"I see," Saxon said. "And now you're afraid I'll stick you on a beat, and you'll get drunk and be boarded."

"Are you going to stick me on a beat?"

When you inherit a job, you sometimes inherit with it responsibilities that you hadn't counted on, Saxon realized. If it had been important to his father to see that Sam Lennox reached retirement age without his record being tarnished during the last few years of his service, he supposed that out of duty to his father he was obligated to nurse the old alcoholic the rest of the way.

"For the time being suppose you just continue as the chief's driver," Saxon said. "You show up as usual at nine in the morning."

"Thanks, Chief!"

When the man had gone out, Saxon sat musing for a time on the burdens of his new job. There was an implied responsibility for the welfare of his men both on and off duty which involved a measure of paternalism not very appealing to him. He hoped Sam Lennox would be the only member of the force with a problem requiring special handling.

After a time he roused himself and went out to the waiting room to use the desk phone, having a strange reluctance to use the one on the desk that had been his father's. He phoned the Alstrom Funeral Parlor and asked if the funeral director had as yet heard from the coroner.

He had. The body was to be released the next day. They set the funeral for 2 P.M. Friday, and Alstrom said everything would be ready for friends to call at the funeral home by Wednesday evening.

By then it was 5 P.M. and Saxon hadn't yet found time even to phone Emily. She had gone on duty at three; he called her at the hospital to tell her of the funeral plans and to announce his appointment as acting chief.

Emily received the news with a mixture of pride in him and sadness. "You certainly deserve it, honey," she said. "But I hate to think of what made the promotion possible."

As Mayor Ben Foley had prophesied, Saxon's appointment met with general public approval. The announcement had appeared in Tuesday's *Iroquois Evening Bulletin,* and by the next morning everyone in town knew it. A steady stream of city-hall employees, plus many people from the street, stuck their heads in his door Wednesday morning to offer congratulations. Those whom he hadn't seen the day before combined their congratulations with sympathy for his father's death. It may have helped that the *Evening Bulletin* had run, in conjunction with the news item, an editorial heartily endorsing the choice.

In order to get some work done, Saxon finally left instructions with the desk man that he was to be disturbed only on official business, and closed his office door.

As Saxon was putting on his galoshes to go across the street for lunch, his office door opened and Emily peeped in.

"Hi," she said. "I had to come downtown to mail a stack of wedding-postponement cards, so I thought I'd try to cadge a free lunch."

"I may as well get used to it," he said.

As they walked down the front steps of the city hall

together, a tall, spare man in his early forties who was passing by paused to wait for them. It wasn't snowing at the moment; there was no wind, and the temperature had risen to a crisp thirty-five; but he was bundled to the ears and his thin nose was pink with cold.

Saxon said politely, "How are you, Mr. Bennock?"

Adam Bennock said in a thin, reedy voice, "Sorry to hear about your father, Saxon. Is the funeral date set yet?"

"The day after tomorrow," Saxon said. "Friday at two. It'll be in the paper tonight. Do you know Emily Vane?"

The mayor-elect gave Emily an austere nod and tugged briefly at his hat brim. "We've met. How are you, Miss Vane?"

"Fine, Mr. Bennock."

Bennock said, "I see by last night's paper that you're our new acting police chief, Saxon. Congratulations."

"Thanks."

"Usually it's customary for a lame-duck executive to consult his successor before making new appointments, but Mayor Foley didn't deign to render me that courtesy. He left me to read it in the newspaper. However, no harm's done. I quite likely would have made the same choice."

"Thanks again," Saxon said dryly.

"We'll have to get together right after the first of the year to discuss the general status of the force."

"All right."

"You'll need one new man to replace the vacancy left by your father's death. Have you given that any thought?"

"There are a couple on the waiting list," Saxon said. "Mayor Foley's taking them up with the council tomorrow."

Adam Bennock frowned. "The mayor seems bent on leaving as little as possible for me to do. Does he also plan to fill the lieutenancy vacancy before his term expires?"

"There won't be any until a permanent chief is appointed," Saxon said.

"Hmm. It's gratifying to know I may have some say in that matter at least."

Touching his hat brim to Emily again, he abruptly walked on.

"He's a cold fish," Emily said. "See what comes of staying a bachelor? You'd be like that in another dozen years if I hadn't come along."

"What makes you think I wouldn't have been snagged by some blonde if you hadn't?"

She made a face at him. "I hear he doesn't smoke or drink either. What's he do for amusement?"

"He skates," Saxon said. Adam Bennock's business was the operation of a roller rink at one of the civic beaches, and he had once been a champion skater.

"Well, anyway, I don't like him."

"You're in the minority," Saxon told her. "He got seventy per cent of the popular vote. Let's get over to Hardy's Restaurant before they run out of food."

chapter 4

ONCE THE ORDEAL of the funeral was over, Saxon threw himself into his work. There were no drastic changes he cared to make in the procedures his father had set up, but he did make one minor change.

He found a safe yet more useful role for Sam Lennox than sitting around the squad room waiting for the rare occasions when he was needed as a driver. Since he was around headquarters all the time the chief was there—which was most of the time, inasmuch as a police chief's work was chiefly administrative—Saxon put him on permanent daytime desk duty, thus releasing one more man for necessary outside duty. Lennox still remained under his watchful eye most of the time, and in addition was performing a useful function.

Meantime neither the sheriff's office nor the state police had discovered any new leads in Andy Saxon's murder. It was beginning to show all the dreary signs of an unsolved homicide.

It had for many years been Andy Saxon's custom to allow members of the force assigned to duty over Christmas and New Year's to shift duty with other members who were willing to trade. The new acting chief saw no reason to suspend this tradition. Accordingly, he called a general staff meeting for 4 P.M. on Saturday.

The Christmas Eve and Christmas Day schedules were settled first. A number of swaps were made, matters finally being settled to the satisfaction of everyone concerned. New Year's Eve wasn't as easy to resolve, however, for everyone liked that night off.

It was customary on New Year's Eve to move each shift forward one hour so that the relief change-over wouldn't come just at midnight. Instead of running from 4 P.M. until midnight, the second trick started at 5 P.M. and ran until 1 A.M. This allowed those assigned to the swing trick an extra hour to see in the new year instead of having their celebrations interrupted at the climax of the evening.

The second trick consisted of two radio-car teams, a single foot patrolman in the downtown area, and a desk man. One of the radio-car men got George Chaney to swap duty with him for the usual ten-dollar fee. The other three and the beat cop preferred to save their money. So everyone was satisfied but Art Marks, who was assigned to desk duty that night. Marks wanted off because he and his wife were invited to a house party New Year's Eve. When no one volunteered to swap with him, he raised the bid to fifteen dollars.

There were still no takers.

The expression of disappointment on the middle-aged lieutenant's face was too much for Saxon. He said, "I'll sit in for you, Art."

Everyone in the squad room looked at him in astonishment, for the chief of police wasn't expected to pull desk duty at any time, let alone on New Year's Eve.

"I don't have a thing on," Saxon said. "Emily has to go on duty at eleven P.M., so we'd have to leave anywhere we went by ten, and local parties don't get started until that time. We hadn't planned any celebration in any event, so soon after my dad's funeral."

Art Marks said uncertainly, "Well, if you don't mind, Chief, I'd sure appreciate it." He started to reach for his wallet.

"Skip the fee," Saxon said. "I'll get even by making you do me a favor sometime."

When the meeting broke up, Vic Burns followed Saxon into the chief's office. Closing the door behind him, he stood scratching his right biceps.

"Got an itch?" Saxon asked.

The stocky lieutenant dropped his hand to his side. "That damned bullet burn. It's scabbed over and itches all the time. That was a pretty nice thing you did, Chief. Smart, too."

"Why smart?"

"You must know Art expected the chief's appointment. He hasn't said anything, but you can tell it rankled. Now you've got him solidly on your side."

"I think he was on my side anyway, Vic. I haven't noticed any sign of resentment."

"Oh, he's being a good trouper. But if you'll notice, he hasn't smiled since the day you broke the news of your appointment."

"You're imagining things," Saxon said. "He never did smile much."

"Maybe," Burns said doubtfully. "Still, I've had a feeling all week that Art was brooding over the injustice of being bypassed. I think what you're doing for him may shake him out of it." He turned toward the door. "Just thought I'd tip you off. Morale's important."

"Thanks for bringing it to my attention."

When Burns had gone out, Saxon sat musing for a time. Had the lieutenant been trying to warn him that Art Marks's attitude was something deserving serious attention—that perhaps there was danger of the veteran lieutenant's attempting deliberately to undercut his authority in some way? Knowing the stolid Marks as well as he did, Saxon considered it hardly likely that he would be capable of anything that devious. Nevertheless, the incident left him vaguely disturbed.

During Christmas week Emily was still working the three-to-eleven trick at the hospital, her change-over to the swing trick not coming until Monday, December 29. On Christmas Eve Saxon picked her up when she got off at eleven o'clock, and they had their tree together at her apartment at midnight.

Since Julie Fox had received a few days off to spend Christmas with her parents in Rochester, they were all alone. Saxon brought up the question of their marriage.

"We ought to wait at least until six weeks after the funeral," Emily said. "That's considered proper."

"Who makes these rules?" Saxon inquired. "Old dried-up spinsters who grab at any excuse to delay weddings?"

Emily smiled at him. "Six weeks isn't forever, Ted. How about the first week in February?"

"The original date we picked was the first day of winter," he said. "We ought to pick another special day. It makes anniversaries easier to remember. Let's make it February second."

"Groundhog Day?" she said. "We will not!"

They finally settled on Saturday, February 7.

On Tuesday, December 30, Saxon entered police headquarters at his usual hour of 9 A.M. to find Vic Burns working the desk. The daytime shift consisted of three beat cops and a single one-man car, and Burns was supposed to be working the car.

"What are you doing here?" Saxon asked. "Where's Lennox?"

"He's sick," Burns said a little uneasily. "I pulled one of the beat cops and stuck him in the car so I could take over the desk."

"Sick with what?"

"I don't know. Just sick."

"Did he call in?"

Burns looked embarrassed. "I guess Hanson phoned his house when Sam didn't show up to relieve him. His wife said he was sick."

"He's drunk again, huh?"

Burns made a helpless gesture. "Aw, give him a break, Chief. Your dad's death shook him up pretty bad."

"It shook up the whole force," Saxon said grimly. "But nobody else stays out drunk. I'll be back in thirty minutes."

Going back out to his car, he drove southeast to the small frame house where Sam Lennox lived. Lennox had two sons and a daughter, but they were grown and married, and he and his wife now lived in the house alone.

Nora Lennox was a thin, sad-faced woman of about her husband's age. When she opened the door and saw Saxon, she began to cry. It was a silent, hopeless sort of crying.

"Cut it out, Nora," Saxon said gruffly. "I'm not here to eat anybody. May I come in?"

Silently she stepped aside to let him enter. Carefully wiping his feet, he moved into a small entry hall, took off his galoshes, and laid his hat on a little table against the wall.

"Where is he?"

"In the kitchen," she said in a barely audible voice.

Saxon moved on into a tiny front room, through it into a central hall, and into the kitchen. Sam Lennox sat at the table in his police uniform, except for the jacket, an empty quart bottle and another just opened before him. He badly needed a shave. He made an attempt to rise when he saw Saxon but couldn't quite make it and sank back into his chair again. He was as drunk as Saxon had ever seen anyone.

" 'Lo, Chief," he muttered.

There was no point in attempting to talk to Lennox. Saxon turned to face Nora, who had paused in the doorway. Tears were no longer running down her face, but her expression was one of hopelessness.

"How'd he manage this so early in the day?"

Nora Lennox worked her hands together. "He got up at four in the morning. Said he couldn't sleep. He hasn't been sleeping at all well since your father died. I thought he was just getting a glass of warm milk, like he does sometimes, so I went back to sleep. I didn't know he had any whisky. I know there wasn't any in the house, so it must have been hidden in the garage. When the alarm went off at seven, he wasn't in bed. I came out and found him like this. He'd dressed himself, as you can see, but I couldn't let him go to work. It's grief over your father, Ted. You've got to consider that."

"How do you mean, consider it?"

"It's been months since it happened. I know your

father warned him if it happened once more he'd have to board him off the force. But please give him one more chance. If he loses a third of his pension, what would we do? We're going to be barely able to live on a full pension."

"I'm not going to have him boarded," Saxon said gruffly. "At least not this time. But he's a police officer with definite duties, and it louses up the whole schedule when he pulls things like this. I may as well tell you bluntly that I won't put up with it again."

"It won't happen again," she said eagerly. "I promise. Next time I'll get up with him."

Lennox said in a maudlin voice, "Didn't do no good after all. Might's well let Vic tell the chief last time."

Saxon glanced over his shoulder. "You might as well have let Vic tell the chief what, Sam?"

"When he caught me drunk. What'sa difference ole Andy boards me or you? Mighta known I'd get caught again."

Apparently Vic Burns had caught Lennox drunk at some time in the past and had covered for him by not reporting it to the chief, Saxon thought. Suddenly he remembered an incident a few weeks back when both he and his father had been in city court all morning. When they came downstairs at noon, Lennox was gone and Vic Burns, working the desk, had said he'd had him driven home because he was ill. Lennox, free from Andy Saxon's watchful eye all morning, had probably sneaked out several times to hoist a few in taverns. And Burns, realizing he was drunk on duty, had sent him home.

Saxon could hardly bring himself to blame Vic Burns for the cover-up. Everyone knew that Lennox had been warned that he was through if he ever again drank on duty. Saxon realized that he was now doing exactly what Burns had done on that occasion: letting the old alcoholic get away with it again.

Wearily he said, "See if you can get him sober by tomorrow morning, Nora. I'll expect him to be on duty at eight A.M."

chapter 5

ON NEW YEAR'S EVE, Saxon took Emily out for a single cocktail at 4 P.M., then dropped her at home and reported for desk duty at five.

It had long been the custom in Iroquois for the police to be tolerant of drunks on New Year's Eve. Local drunken drivers were allowed to park their cars and were driven home by police, provided no accident or flagrant violation of the law had occurred. Out-of-town speedsters were usually merely warned and sent on or, if too drunk to drive, were escorted to jail to sleep it off, then were released without charge. Consequently, New Year's Eve was usually a quiet night at police headquarters.

Until nine o'clock there wasn't a single phone call, and the only radio message was from one of the squad cars reporting that it would be out of service for fifteen minutes for a coffee break.

At 9 P.M. Patrolmen George Chaney and Mark Ross came into headquarters hustling between them a lean, knobby-jointed man in his mid-forties. The man had a narrow, ascetic face, a humorless, thin-lipped mouth, and wore steel-rimmed glasses that began to cloud over the moment he came indoors. His overcoat and hat were obviously expensive.

Getting up from his chair, Ted Saxon approached the counter and gave Chaney an inquiring look.

"Forty-five miles an hour on downtown Main Street," Chaney said laconically. He tossed a driver's license and a car-registration form on the counter.

According to the operator's license, the man's name

was Edward Coombs and he lived on Delaware Avenue in Buffalo. The birth date made him forty-six.

Saxon raised his eyes from the driver's license to give Chaney a puzzled look. Coombs showed no indication of being under the influence of alcohol, and it wasn't customary to pull in sober speeders on New Year's Eve.

"We stopped him twice," Chaney explained. "About an hour ago he was speeding south on Main. We warned him and let him go. We just stopped him again going north, and he decided to give us a hard time. He wanted to know why we hick cops weren't off catching criminals instead of bugging law-abiding citizens."

Saxon looked at the motorist. "Well, Mr. Coombs?"

Coombs unbuttoned his overcoat, probed in his hip pocket, and drew out a handkerchief. Removing his glasses, he briskly massaged the lenses and put them back on. Immediately they started to cloud again, though not as badly.

"It's a clear, moonlit night out, Sergeant," he started to say.

"Not sergeant," Mark Ross interrupted. "You're speaking to the chief of police."

"Oh?" Coombs said with a supercilious show of interest, which Saxon and both police officers found irritating. "You always work this late, Chief?"

"Just get on with your alibi," Saxon said.

"All right," Coombs said agreeably. "As I started to say, it's a clear, moonlit night out, and besides, the main street of your one-horse town is brightly lighted. Apparently it hasn't snowed here recently, because the road was clear and dry. Furthermore, there wasn't another car on the street. I feel the speed at which I was traveling was entirely safe under the circumstances."

The man's tone was deliberately provocative, as was his reference to Iroquois as a one-horse town. Nevertheless, because it was New Year's Eve and there was a tradition of tolerance for New Year's Eve celebrants to uphold, Saxon attempted to be patient.

"The arresting officer says you were traveling at forty-five."

"Possibly," the man admitted. "I wasn't watching the speedometer."

"The speed limit on downtown Main happens to be twenty-five."

"Yeah? You run a speed trap, huh? How much cut do you get from every fine, Chief?"

After gazing at him coldly for a moment, Saxon opened the traffic charge book and entered as much of the pertinent data as was available from the driver's license and registration form.

Then he said, "Occupation?"

"Accountant," Coombs said.

"Place of employment?"

"The Upstate Harness Racing Association, Incorporated."

"Oh," Saxon said. "The outfit that wants to build a race track here."

"Yeah. Then it won't be a one-horse town any more. You'll have a stableful."

Saxon silently finished filling out the charge, tore off the original and pushed it, the driver's license, and car-registration form across the counter to Coombs.

"You will appear in City Court on the second floor of this building on Monday, January fifth, at ten A.M., Mr. Coombs. Bond is twenty-five dollars."

"I'm not carrying that much money," Coombs said.

Saxon indicated the phone sitting on the counter. "You may use that to call your family in Buffalo. You'll have to reverse the charges."

"I don't have a family. I'm a bachelor."

"Then I suggest you use it to call either a lawyer or a bondsman."

"I don't believe I'll bother," Coombs said with arrogant cheeriness. "Now what are you going to do?"

Saxon finally lost patience. "Throw you in the can, mister. Empty your pockets here on the counter."

"Sure," Coombs said with a shrug. He started to draw items from his pockets and lay them in a neat pile.

Aside from a wallet, he was carrying a key ring, pen-knife, handkerchief, glasses case, package of cigarettes, lighter, and forty cents in change.

"Take the money out of your wallet," Saxon ordered.

Coombs drew out two one-dollar bills.

Saxon wrote out a receipt listing two dollars and forty cents in cash, one key ring containing six keys, one pen-knife and one cigarette lighter, and one wallet containing personal papers. Tearing off the top copy, he handed it to Coombs, sealed the enumerated items in a manila envelope, and stapled the second copy to the envelope.

"You may keep the handkerchief, glasses case, and cigarettes," he said.

"How about my lighter?"

Ordinarily a mere traffic violator would have been allowed to keep all the items, but the man's attitude had irritated Saxon to the point where he was according him the treatment usual for felony prisoners.

"You can call me when you want a light," Saxon said. "Give your topcoat, scarf, and hat to one of the officers."

Obediently the man removed the items and handed them to Mark Ross, who carried them into the squad room to put them in one of the lockers.

"Shake him down," Saxon said to Chaney.

Chaney ran his hands down the man's sides from beneath his armpits to his ankles, patted his hips, and rose from his stooped position. "He's clean, Chief."

"Take off your belt," Saxon said to Coombs.

The man raised his eyebrows. "Think I might hang myself?"

"If I thought it probable, I'd let you keep it," Saxon said dourly. "Get it off."

Slipping it off, Coombs laid the belt on the counter. Coiling it, Saxon laid it on top of the manila envelope on the shelf beneath the counter.

Saxon lifted the cell key ring from its hook beneath

the counter and tossed it to Chaney. "Stick him in cell number one."

When the prisoner was lodged in the first of the three cells, Chaney and Ross prepared to go back out on cruise. At the door Chaney looked back and said, "Think he's nuts, Chief?"

"He certainly has a defective personality," Saxon said. "He did everything possible to get himself jailed."

"Guess we obliged him," Chaney said with a grin.

He and Ross went out.

It was quiet again for another hour. Twice Coombs called for cigarette lights and Saxon went back to the cell block to hold lighted matches between the bars. Otherwise, nothing at all happened.

At 10 P.M. the street door opened and a slimly built woman of about thirty preceded a man inside. The woman wore a full-length mink coat and a white head-scarf that completely hid her hair but exposed a round, full-lipped, rather attractive face. She was wearing handcuffs.

The man was about forty, well over six feet tall, and with a burly frame. He had a heavy-featured, rather glowering face and his expression suggested that he was in some pain.

Saxon rose and rested his arms on the counter as they approached. The man held out his open wallet to display a Buffalo police badge that read: *Sergeant of Detectives.*

"I'm Harry Morrison of Buffalo's Homicide and Arson," he said in a deep, rumbling voice.

"Ted Saxon, acting chief of police," Saxon said, extending his hand across the counter.

Morrison looked surprised. Clasping the hand, he said, "Glad to know you, Chief. How come you work New Year's Eve? Shorthanded?"

"Just a favor for one of the men who wanted to go to a party. I didn't have anything planned." He looked at the woman with curiosity and she gazed back at him sullenly.

"This is Grace Emmet," Sergeant Morrison said. "I'm bringing her back to Buffalo from Erie. Maybe you read about her."

Saxon had. Grace Emmet had been the purported mistress of Buffalo industrialist Michael Factor, who a month previously had been found shot to death in the apartment he had been maintaining for the woman. Grace Emmet had disappeared. Neighbors' testimony of overhearing a violent lover's quarrel preceding the shooting, plus the fact that someone, presumably the woman herself, had carefully removed from the apartment all photographs of Grace Emmet, resulted in a warrant for her arrest on a homicide charge issued by the district attorney of Erie County.

The case had received considerable sensational coverage as a "love nest" murder, one of its most played-up factors being the woman's cleverness in destroying all photographs of herself before fleeing. A composite drawing based on descriptions by acquaintances had been widely circulated, but Saxon saw that it was only a mediocre likeness of the woman. She possessed the same round face and full lips that he had seen pictured, but aside from that, he wouldn't have recognized her from the drawing.

"She was in Erie all this time?" Saxon asked.

"Yeah," Morrison said disgustedly. "How do you like that? We've had reports of her being seen everywhere from Denver to Miami, and all the time she was less than a hundred miles from Buffalo. The Erie police picked her up last night and she kindly waived extradition. Wonder if you'll do me a favor, Chief?"

"Sure," Saxon said.

"I've been developing a pain in my side ever since we left Erie, and it's getting worse by the minute. I think maybe I have a hot appendix. I'm afraid to risk the last twenty-five miles. Can you stick my prisoner in a cell until I can get looked at by a doctor?"

"Of course. The woman we use as a matron happens to be at a party, but I know where she is. I'll phone her to come over."

"Why pull her away from a party?" the sergeant said. "At least until I'm sure I won't be able to drive on. The prisoner won't have to be searched, because she was searched by a matron in Erie, and I have everything she's not allowed to carry in an envelope in my car. If I can find a doctor, I should know within an hour if it's safe to drive on. If it isn't, phone your matron then."

Rules required that a matron be present at the jail any time there was a female prisoner. As this occurred too seldom to justify a full-time matron, the town's only meter-maid, Jenny Waite, pinch-hit as matron when necessary. As a condition of her employment she had to keep headquarters informed of where she could be reached in emergency. But as the sergeant suggested, it would be a shame to interrupt Jenny's New Year's Eve celebration if the female prisoner was going to be there no more than an hour.

"I guess we can skip regulations this time," Saxon agreed. He said to the woman, "I'll hang your coat in one of the lockers."

"Can't I keep it?" she asked huskily. "I'm still cold from the ride. This dumb cop hasn't got a heater."

"Let her keep it," Morrison said. "Which way do we go?"

Saxon took the cell key ring from his pocket and led the way back to the cell block. The three cells were in a row, the last one having a solid steel wall between it and the center one so that it couldn't be seen into from the others. This was the "women's section."

As they passed the first cell, Edward Coombs said, "Company, huh? Maybe we can have a New Year's Eve party."

No one answered him.

chapter 6

AT THE DOOR of cell number three Sergeant Morrison removed the woman's handcuffs. The barred door was standing open. The prisoner walked into the cell without being ordered and glanced around disdainfully. The place was immaculately clean, but not very homey, containing nothing but a washbowl with a polished steel mirror over it, a screened commode, and a drop-down bunk.

Seeing her expression, Morrison said, "Better get used to it, lady. You're going to be living in one like it for a long time."

She turned to glare at him, then whipped off her headscarf and tossed it on the bunk. Without the scarf she looked more like the composite drawing that had been published, for the short, bleached blonde hair which curled around her face in a poodle cut had been one of the distinctive features of the drawing.

Saxon locked the cell door. "You want anything, just holler," he said.

"Who could want any more than this bridal suite has to offer?" she asked contemptuously.

Saxon turned away without answering. Morrison trailed him back to the waiting room.

Moving behind the counter, Saxon lifted the radio microphone and said, "Control to Car Two. Come in, Car Two."

From the speaker George Chaney's voice said, "Car Two to Control. Go ahead."

"Come on in, George," Saxon said. "I want you to run a patient over to the hospital."

As he hung up the mike, Morrison said, "I could have driven that far, Chief."

"They aren't doing anything," Saxon said. "New Year's Eve is our quietest night of the year."

Picking up the phone, he dialed the hospital and asked for the chief duty nurse. After a few moments' wait a feminine voice said, "Mrs. Forshay speaking."

"Hi, Edna," he said. "This is Ted Saxon. I have a Buffalo police officer at headquarters who thinks he may have a hot appendix. Who's on standby duty?"

"Dr. Harmon."

"Better give him a ring and have him meet the patient in the emergency room. I'm sending him over in a squad car. The name's Sergeant Harry Morrison."

"Will do," Edna Forshay said cheerily. "Happy New Year."

"Same to you, Edna."

Five minutes later the squad car reported in and took Morrison away. Three minutes after that, George Chaney's voice came over the radio to announce their arrival at the hospital and report the car out of service until further notice.

At eleven-thirty Sergeant Morrison phoned from the hospital. "False alarm, Chief," he said. "The doc diagnosed it as indigestion. He was a little sore about being pulled away from his merrymaking."

"Well, I'm glad it was nothing more serious. You'll be going on tonight, then?"

"Uh-huh. But do you mind if I goof off for another half hour? The nurses on this ward are having a quiet little New Year's Eve party. No drinks, just coffee and cake. They've asked me and your two boys to help them bring in the new year."

"Sure," Saxon said. "Let me speak to either Chaney or Ross."

It was Chaney who came to the phone. Saxon said, "What extension are you going to be near, in case of emergency?"

"One eleven, Chief."

"Okay," Saxon said, marking it down. "Happy New Year."

"Same to you," Chaney said.

If one eleven had been the extension of Emily's ward, he would have asked to speak to her, because by now she was on duty; but it wasn't. He contemplated phoning to wish her a Happy New Year, then decided against it. If she wasn't tied up with a patient at midnight, she would probably phone him.

At midnight the fire whistle emitted the prolonged blast with which it annually signaled the start of a new year. A dozen church bells began to toll an accompaniment to it. Saxon went to the door and opened it a crack to listen for the horns and noisemakers of any celebrants who happened to be on the street.

There weren't any, because it was now snowing heavily. When he had come on duty, the streets and sidewalks had been dry, although a foot-deep residue of old snow lay on the ground. But now there was an inch-deep blanket of white on the street.

He closed the door and went back to the cell block, suddenly impelled to have at least some kind of human contact at the moment all the rest of the town was celebrating.

Pausing before the first cell, he said, "Happy New Year, Coombs."

The man gazed at him for a moment before saying sardonically, "Happy New Year to you, Chief."

Walking on to the last cell, he found the blonde seated on her bunk. She had removed her fur coat and it lay folded alongside of her. She was wearing a green dress of expensive cut, but of not very good fit, for it hung too loosely on her.

She must have lost weight since she fled Buffalo a month ago, he thought. He wondered if it had been deliberate, in an attempt at disguise, or if worry over being hunted had sloughed off the poundage.

"Happy New Year, Miss Emmet," he said.

She glared at him. "Are you kidding?"

Saxon returned to the desk and reseated himself. Emily must have been too busy to call, he thought, for the phone didn't ring.

At five after twelve George Chaney's voice came from the radio speaker. "Car Two to Control. We are back in service. Will drop Sergeant Morrison off at headquarters before resuming patrol."

"Control to Car Two," Saxon said into the mike. "Roger."

Five minutes later Edward Coombs called, "Hey, Chief!"

Walking back to the cell block, Saxon said, "Yeah?"

"You better check that woman prisoner. Some awfully funny sounds are coming from there."

Saxon continued on to the last cell. What he saw made him hurriedly draw the key ring from his pocket and unlock the door. The blonde stood on the dropdown bunk. One end of her headscarf was knotted about an overhead water pipe; the other end she was winding about her throat.

As he turned the key in the lock, she quickly unknotted the scarf and dropped it on the bunk. By the time he got into the cell, she had jumped down to the floor.

Saxon paused in astonishment when she took hold of the front of her dress and deliberately ripped it to the waist, also bursting the center strap of her brassiere to bare small but well-formed breasts. Her skirt came up to her waist and she savagely tore at the unglamorous plain white cotton panties she was wearing. The elastic burst and the material split, allowing them to slither down to her knees. She completed their destruction by ripping them right in two and letting the segments fall to the floor.

Then she hurled herself at Saxon, scratching, kicking, biting, and screaming. Fingernails burned one cheek. He made a grab for the clawing hand, missed, and felt her teeth sink into his palm. The toe of a pointed shoe dug into his shin.

Spreading his arms, he managed to pin hers to her

sides by enveloping her in a bear hug. Her pointed toes began to beat a tattoo on his shins and she attempted to get an ear in her teeth. He pulled her over to the bunk, threw her down and held her there by the simple expedient of falling on top of her with the full weight of his two hundred pounds.

Quite suddenly she relaxed.

"You going to cut it out?" he growled.

"All right," she said in an entirely calm voice. "Get up. You're hurting me."

Cautiously he released her arms and started to rise to his feet. At once her legs shot out to encircle his waist and her arms locked about his neck. She gave an abrupt jerk that pulled him off balance and made him fall heavily atop her again.

A voice from the cell door said, "What the hell's going on here?"

Then the woman was pushing against his chest, fighting him away and screaming again. Saxon fell from the bunk to his knees, climbed to his feet, and staggered backward across the room, to back into someone in the doorway. He turned to find Sergeant Morrison glaring at him in outrage.

"She's gone crazy," Saxon said. "She tried to hang herself, and when I came in to stop her, she was all over me like a swarm of hornets."

"Looked to me more like you were all over her," Morrison said in his rumbling voice.

The woman still lay sprawled on the bunk, her skirt bunched around her waist to disclose her bare thighs, her naked breasts heaving. In a flat, unemotional voice she said, "He raped me."

After staring at her for a moment, Saxon walked over and picked up the headscarf. Morrison was still standing squarely in the doorway when Saxon turned back toward the door, a belligerent expression on his face. But as Saxon bore down on him, the expression on the acting chief's face turned Morrison's expression uncertain. At the last instant he stepped aside.

Relocking the cell door, Saxon stalked to the waiting

room, trailed by the silent Morrison. Tossing the head-scarf on the counter, Saxon entered the washroom, leaving the door open, and stared into the mirror over the washbowl. Two raw scratches ran down his left cheek. Rubbing water on them, he patted his cheek dry with his handkerchief, then ran water over his bitten hand and dried that too.

Sergeant Morrison watched silently from the wash-room doorway. When Saxon turned toward the door, again he stepped aside to let him pass. Saxon walked behind the counter. Morrison walked over, leaned his elbows on the counter, and regarded the acting chief steadily.

"You can stop looking at me so accusingly," Saxon said irritably. "I don't know why she pulled that. Maybe she's just got a grudge against all cops."

"Pulled what?" Morrison asked quietly.

"Faked my raping her."

"I saw it," Morrison said in the same quiet tone.

Saxon said hotly, "You saw the tail end of a delib-erate act. She lured me into her cell by pretending she meant to hang herself. Then she ripped her own clothes and jumped me." He came back out from be-hind the counter. "Come with me and I'll prove it."

He led the way back to the cell block and stopped be-fore the first cell. "You couldn't see into the last cell," he said to Coombs. "But you could certainly hear every-thing going on. Tell Sergeant Morrison what hap-pened."

"Sure," Coombs said. "You raped the woman."

chapter 7

SAXON GLARED through the bars at the man, "Quit horsing around, Coombs. This is no joke. Tell the truth."

"I'm telling it," Coombs said calmly. He looked at the sergeant. "The chief here kept going back to the last cell and asking the woman if she wanted a little company. I didn't like the way he asked it, and neither did she, because she kept telling him to get lost. Finally I heard him unlock the cell and go in. I heard her say, 'Leave me alone! Stop it! Are you crazy! You're hurting me!' Not all at once. There were little gasps and cries and suppressed screams, like he was holding his hand over her mouth, in between. A couple of times there was the sound of tearing cloth. It was clear to me he was raping her, but locked in here, I couldn't do a thing about it."

Saxon stared at Coombs with his mouth open. After a long time he said, "Why, you lying punk! You'd go that far to get even for a lousy traffic ticket?"

"You told me to let the sergeant know what happened," Coombs said reasonably. "So I told him."

Saxon strode back to the last cell and looked in. The woman still lay sprawled in the same position. She looked at him with such hate that, in spite of himself, he couldn't suppress a twinge of guilt, immediately followed by a rush of anger at both her and himself for allowing her histrionics to begin to get to him.

Returning to the first cell, he said, "Now that you've had your little joke, Coombs, tell the truth."

"How many times do I have to say it?" Coombs inquired. "You raped her."

45

Saxon looked at Morrison. "Do you believe this guy?" he demanded.

"Uh-huh."

"I told you the way it really happened. Your prisoner deliberately framed me. And Coombs is backing up her story because he's sore about being jailed."

Morrison slowly shook his head. "You're not getting through to me, Chief."

Saxon felt his face redden. "So what do you plan to do about it?"

"I can hardly place a police chief under arrest in his own headquarters," Morrison said tonelessly. "But I'll be damned if you get away with raping a prisoner of mine left in your custody. I want a doctor to examine this woman before she leaves here. And I want your district attorney brought down here to decide what to do about you."

Saxon stalked past him back to the desk, lifted the phone, and dialed the number Jenny Waite had left in case of emergency. It was the private home of a friend of the meter-maid's, and he had no trouble getting her called to the phone.

"Sorry to break up your party, Jenny," Saxon said. "But I need you at headquarters right away."

"Oh, no!" she said. "Tonight of all nights." Then her tone became resigned. "Okay, Chief. Soon as I can get home and change into uniform."

"Skip the uniform," Saxon said. "I want you here fast."

"If it's that important, I'm on my way," Jenny said.

Breaking the connection, Saxon dialed the hospital. When the switchboard operator answered, he said, "Is Dr. Harmon still in the hospital?"

"No, sir," the operator said. "He left about eleven-thirty."

"This is Chief Saxon. What emergency number do you have listed for him?"

"He's at the Elks party, Chief."

Hanging up, he dialed the Elks Club and had Dr. Bruce Harmon paged. When the doctor came to the phone, Saxon said, "This is the chief, Bruce. I need you over at headquarters. Better bring along whatever equipment you need to determine if a woman has been forcibly raped."

"Oh, oh," Harmon said. "Anyone I know?"

"I doubt it. How long will you be?"

"Expect me in twenty minutes."

"Fine. The D.A. happen to be at the Elks party?"

"Nope. He always makes the country club on New Year's Eve."

"Okay. Thanks," Saxon said.

He hung up and dialed again. When a voice behind a background of noise and music said, "Country Club bar," Saxon asked, "Arnold Kettle there?"

"He was in the bar a minute ago. Hold on."

About three minutes passed before a deep voice said, "Hello."

"This is Ted Saxon, Arn. Hate to interrupt your party, but I'm afraid you'll have to come down to headquarters."

"Why? What's up?"

"A female prisoner is claiming forced rape."

"Oh. Can't it wait till morning?"

"You must not have heard me clearly," Saxon said. "I said a female prisoner."

"Huh? You mean while in custody?"

"That's right. In a cell."

"Who did it?"

"Nobody. It's a frame."

"Well, who's she accusing?"

"Me," Saxon said.

"My God!" Arnold Kettle said. "I'll be right down."

Saxon hung up the phone and looked at Sergeant Morrison. "Everything is arranged," he said coldly. "Satisfied?"

"Don't get yourself sore at me," Morrison said. "I didn't rape the woman. You did."

Saxon's face darkened and he started around the counter. The sergeant held up one hand. "Now don't get excited, Chief. I don't want any trouble."

Saxon paused with his fists clenched. Though Morrison was a big man himself, he regarded the width of the younger man's shoulders dubiously. "I don't want any trouble," he repeated.

Saxon pointed at the bench along the wall. "Then sit down over there and keep your mouth shut."

Obediently the sergeant went over to the bench and sat down.

Jenny Waite was the first one to arrive. She came in with a snow-sprinkled headscarf over her head, hung it on one of the hooks near the door, and hung an evening cloak next to it. Beneath the coat she wore a flowered evening gown. She was a slightly built woman in her late thirties with a thin, pixie-like face and an amusing manner of cocking her head to one side whenever she asked a question. She was a widow with four children and had been vaguely "engaged" to a local widower named Joe Penny for the past five years.

"Joe dropped me off and went back to the party," she announced, seating herself on the bench to remove fur-topped boots. "What's up?" She glanced curiously at Sergeant Morrison, seated only a few feet away on the bench.

"Female prisoner," Saxon said briefly. He didn't bother to introduce her to the sergeant.

Jumping up, Jenny set her boots against the wall beneath her cloak and approached the counter. "Keys?"

"She doesn't require searching, and I don't want you in the cell alone with her, because she's a little nuts. You can go take a look, then wait out here until the doctor arrives."

"Oh, she's sick?" Jenny asked, starting toward the cell block.

Saxon didn't reply.

As Jenny disappeared, the phone rang. It was Emily, calling from the hospital.

"Sorry I couldn't phone at midnight," she said. "But a patient picked that time to pull loose an intravenous transfusion needle. Things have quieted down now. Just called to say Happy New Year."

"Thanks," he said. "Same to you."

"Things quiet there, too?"

"Not very. I'd better phone you back later, honey."

"Oh. Well, make it before five A.M., because we start taking temperatures again then."

"All right," he said, and hung up.

Jenny came back into the room and asked, "What's the matter with her? Why's she lying there all exposed like that?"

So the woman still hadn't changed position, Saxon thought. She must be simulating being in a state of shock.

"Guess she's preserving evidence," he said dryly. "She's pretending she was raped."

Jenny's eyes widened. Saxon felt savage amusement when her gaze touched the silent man seated on the bench and her expression indicated she had jumped to the conclusion that he was the accused rapist. Apparently deciding that it wouldn't be tactful to ask any questions in front of the suspect, she seated herself on the farthest end of the bench from Morrison.

Dr. Bruce Harmon arrived at a quarter of one. He was a lean, bouncy man about Saxon's age, who gave the impression of always being in a hurry and usually moved at a gait approaching a trot. Setting his bag on the bench, he quickly hung up his coat and hat, but retained his galoshes.

Briskly rubbing his hands together, he said, "Getting colder out. Hello, Jenny. Where's the patient?" Then he glanced at Morrison with recognition and said, "Hello there. How you feeling?"

"Better," Morrison said.

Saxon laid the cell keys on the counter and said, "Show him, Jenny."

Moving over to the counter, Jenny picked up the keys. "This way, doctor." She led the way toward the cell block.

They had hardly disappeared when District Attorney Arnold Kettle came in stamping.

Arnold Kettle was a plump, red-faced man of fifty-five with iron-gray hair and such an erect stance that his protruding stomach gave the impression that he was leaning slightly backward. He didn't remove either his hat or his overcoat.

After glancing at Sergeant Morrison, Kettle came over to the counter. "Now what's this all about, Ted?"

"Doc Harmon and Jenny Waite are back with the alleged victim," Saxon said. "You'll have to wait until Bruce is finished before you can talk to her. The woman is Grace Emmet."

The district attorney's eyebrows shot upward. "The Buffalo murderess?"

"Uh-huh. Sergeant Morrison over there on the bench was bringing her back from Erie and dropped her off here for an hour in order to see a doctor. This was about eleven o'clock. He thought he had a hot appendix. Turned out he didn't, but while he was gone, the Emmet woman faked a suicide attempt in order to get me into her cell. Soon as I entered, she ripped her clothing, scratched me up a bit, and started yelling rape. Morrison walked in while we were wrestling and jumped to the conclusion that she was telling the truth."

"I know what I saw," Morrison said in his rumbling voice. "I assume you're the district attorney. The chief here isn't introducing me to anyone because he's sore at me."

The D.A. walked over and held out his hand. "Arnold Kettle."

Rising, Morrison shook hands. "Glad to know you, Mr. Kettle. Chief Saxon neglected to mention that there's another witness to the rape. There's a guy in one of the cells. He couldn't see into the woman's cell, but he heard everything that took place. And he verifies the woman's story."

Kettle turned to frown at Saxon.

"Oh, it's a very thorough frame," Saxon said. "The prisoner he's talking about is sore at me for jailing him on a traffic charge. He's corroborating the woman's story just to get even."

"You've got a persecution complex," Morrison said.

"Why the hell would either prisoner want to frame you?"

Saxon leaned his elbows on the counter. "You think you saw the rape actually taking place, don't you, Morrison?"

"I know I did."

"Okay, think about what you saw. The Emmet woman's clothing was convincingly disarranged, but it takes two to tango. Was mine even slightly disarranged?"

"You were on your knees with your back to me for several seconds after she pushed you off the bunk. You had plenty of time to button up."

"For God's sake," Saxon said disgustedly. "I'm beginning to think you're in on this frame." Then his eyes narrowed. "You know, that's a thought, Arn. Maybe he is."

Arnold Kettle gave him a strange look. "Are you suggesting a conspiracy between the sergeant and his prisoner?"

"Yeah," Saxon said slowly. "I don't know why it didn't register sooner. He comes in here with a faked appendix attack and leaves the woman in my custody. He even talks me out of calling in a matron, because that would spoil the frame. I see just how they worked it now."

"Boy, are you reaching out in left field," Morrison said in a tone of disgust. He smiled the slightest smile.

chapter 8

"I HAD CHANEY AND ROSS run him over to the hospital," Saxon said, speaking to the district attorney and ignoring Morrison. "When they brought him back, they just dropped him off and continued on patrol, they didn't come in with him. Before coming in, Morrison must have walked back to the woman's cell window and rapped on the glass to signal her it was time to go into her act. That way they could time it perfectly for him to walk in at the crucial moment."

Morrison laughed aloud. "This guy isn't just a rapist. He must be on marijuana."

"Well, explain your faked appendix attack," Saxon said hotly.

"What's to explain? I got worried over a pain that turned out to be just indigestion. I can demonstrate how silly your story is, though. You're charging that this whole thing was a conspiracy between me and my prisoner, huh?"

"I am."

"Okay, let's kick that around. I was assigned to this case when Factor's body was discovered a month ago, but Grace Emmet had already skipped town when I got it. I never in my life laid eyes on her until I picked her up at the Erie police station at nine this evening. You can check that time with the Erie police. By the time they checked her out and we got going, it was nine-thirty. Are you suggesting that in the hour and a half it took us to drive here, I talked a total stranger into framing you for rape?"

After thinking this over, even Saxon had to admit

it seemed unlikely. Arnold Kettle's expression indicated he considered it impossible.

Morrison said, "Furthermore, I never before laid eyes on you. Why the hell would I want to frame a total stranger, using another total stranger as an accomplice?"

Arnold Kettle cleared his throat. "It does seem that an awful lot of coincidence would have to be involved, Ted. A plot such as you suggest would require considerable advance planning. Assuming just for the sake of argument that there was such a plot, how would Sergeant Morrison know you'd be on duty tonight? Or do you think that for some psychopathic reason he and his prisoner decided to frame just anybody they found on duty?"

"The whole town has known for ten days that I'd be on duty tonight," Saxon said doggedly. "A police chief voluntarily taking New Year's Eve is the sort of story that travels. And you must know how fast news travels in Iroquois."

"I guess that guy in the cell was in on the conspiracy too, huh?" Morrison said sardonically. "I never laid eyes on him before, either."

Saxon studied him from narrowed eyes. "Now that you mention it, he probably was planted here in order to be on hand as a witness. He did his damnedest to get himself jailed." He turned to Kettle. "The boys brought him in about ten o'clock. Twice they'd stopped him for speeding, but the first time they let him go with a warning. He'd probably been racing back and forth all over town hoping to be stopped. The only reason he's in jail is because he deliberately made himself obnoxious. He *wanted* to be jailed."

"Why would all these people go to so much trouble?" the D.A. asked reasonably.

Saxon made a hopeless gesture. "You've got me, Arn. But they all have to be in on it. It's too pat."

"That's true," Kettle agreed. "Almost too pat to be believable. I'd like to talk to this witness."

But questioning of Edward Coombs was postponed

because Dr. Harmon and Jenny Waite came from the cell block at that moment. Jenny handed Saxon the keys as the doctor set his bag on the bench and started to put on his coat.

"Hello, Arn," Harmon said to the district attorney. "How was the country-club dance?"

"Too loud to stand, sober. And you had to put me on a non-alcoholic diet. What's the story on the woman?"

The doctor shrugged. "You can't just look at a woman and tell whether or not she's been raped. Unless it was so violent there's physical damage—which there isn't in this case. Aside from the damage to her clothing, there isn't anything either to prove or to disprove her charge. Her pulse and respiration are normal. Of course, by now she's had time to quiet down. An hour ago she may have been registering a pulse of two hundred for all I know."

"Then you can't say one way or the other?" the district attorney asked.

"Not tonight. Ask me tomorrow when I get the lab report. I've prepared a microscopic slide which should tell the story."

Saxon said, "Bruce, when you examined Sergeant Morrison at the hospital earlier, what did you find?"

"Nothing. He just seemed to be experiencing a touch of mild indigestion."

"Could he have been faking?"

The doctor glanced curiously from Saxon to the sergeant and back again. "I have no reason to suspect he was," he said cautiously.

"But could he have been? It's important."

"If you mean was it possible, of course it was. My diagnosis was based on the patient's description of symptoms, because there weren't any physical symptoms to base it on. When a patient claims pain, I assume there is pain." Glancing at the sergeant, he said humorously, "The only way to tell definitely is to ask the patient. Were you faking?"

"If you'd felt my pain, you'd know I wasn't," Morrison rumbled.

"I guess that settles that," Harmon said, picking up his bag. "I'll phone you the lab-test results some time tomorrow morning, Arn. I assume you'll be home instead of at your office."

"If I'm not, try me here. My office will be closed for the legal holiday."

As the doctor went out at his usual rapid walk, a whole group of police officers trooped in together. In addition to the five members of the second trick, now going off duty, there was the reduced staff of three who would now go on for the swing trick, plus patrolman Verne Dowling, Saxon's desk relief. Glancing at the wall clock, Saxon saw it was just one o'clock.

Naturally, all the officers were curious about the presence of Jenny and the D.A., but Saxon brusquely interrupted their questioning, told the old crew to log out, and the relief to get out on patrol. All of them seemed a little surprised at his brusqueness, but they hurried to comply with his orders. Within five minutes all but Dowling had departed again.

Verne Dowling didn't ask any questions either. Though he had no idea of what was going on, he recognized that his usually amiable acting chief was in a towering rage and discreetly made himself inconspicuous. Storing his overcoat and hat in his squad-room locker, he quietly moved behind the desk and seated himself.

Saxon said coldly, "I'll take you back to talk to the prisoners now, Arn. You can stand by while we question the woman, Jenny. But we won't need you, Morrison."

Morrison agreeably reseated himself on the bench. Saxon led the others back to the cell block.

There was no change in either prisoner's story. When they returned from the cell block. Kettle looked thoughtful, Jenny looked upset, and Saxon was furious. It increased his anger when he saw by the disbelieving expression on Verne Dowling's face that Sergeant Morrison had informed the desk man of what was going on.

Morrison stood up and said, "If you're through with my prisoner, Mr. Kettle, is it all right if I take her on to Buffalo? I'm sure the Erie County D.A. won't object to her being returned as a witness whenever you're ready for her."

"I suppose it's all right, Sergeant. She isn't charged with anything here, and it may be weeks or months before we need her as a witness. You'd better scare up something for her to wear, though. There isn't much left of her clothing."

Morrison said, "I'll bring in her suitcase and let her change."

Saxon asked bitterly, "Am I under arrest, Arn?"

"I don't think you'll run anywhere," the district attorney said equably. "We'll hold off any legal action for the time being. Suppose you meet me here tomorrow morning. Say about eleven?"

"All right," Saxon said stiffly. "Jenny, you stick around until Sergeant Morrison gets his prisoner out of here. We don't want anyone else accused of rape."

Stalking into the squad room, he got his coat, hat, and galoshes from his locker, put them on, and strode out again. As he headed for the door, he threw curt goodnights to Kettle, Jenny, and Dowling. He didn't even look at Sergeant Morrison.

There were now several inches of snow on the street, and snow was falling so heavily that visibility was cut to a matter of yards. Saxon drove the three blocks to Iroquois General Hospital at ten miles an hour.

There was no one in the hospital lobby at that time of night. As he passed the desk, the switchboard operator called, "Hi, Chief," and he gave her a distant nod. He took the elevator to the third floor and walked down the hall to Ward 3-B. He found Emily seated alone in the nurses' alcove marking charts.

She looked up with a surprised smile, then simultaneously saw the twin scratches on his cheek and his expression of controlled rage. The smile changed to a look of concern.

"What's the matter?" she asked.

"We may have to postpone our marriage again. I'll probably be in jail."

She paled. "Why? What's happened?"

"I'm accused of raping a female prisoner in her cell."

She stared at him in astonishment. "You? That's the most ridiculous thing I ever heard."

"You're prejudiced," he said bitterly. "The D.A. thinks I'm guilty. Jenny Waite thinks it. By tomorrow everyone in town will think it."

"Maybe you'd better sit down and tell me about it," she said. "I'll get us a couple of cups of coffee."

Rising, she dropped dimes in a coffee vendor in the corner beyond the desk and filled two paper cups. Setting them on the desk, she reseated herself. Saxon took the extra chair and dropped his hat on the floor next to it.

"Where are the other nurses?" he asked.

"Louise is checking the tents and intravenouses. Beth is sitting with a terminal case. We won't be disturbed for a while."

He took a sip of his coffee. Then he started at the beginning and described the events of the evening. When he finished, her eyes were blazing with anger even greater than his.

"The beasts!" she said indignantly. "Of course all three of them were in on it." Suddenly leaning forward, she cupped his chin in her hands and kissed him fiercely on the mouth. "Poor darling. Why do you imagine they did such a thing?"

He hadn't really expected that Emily would even for a moment have any doubts of his innocence. Nevertheless, her immediate and unquestioning acceptance that it couldn't have been anything but a deliberate frame sent a warm feeling through him. For the first time in two hours he smiled.

"You know you're quite a doll?" he said.

She colored. "Sometimes you make me feel like one. But why have they done this to you?"

Ted shook his head. "I can't even begin to conceive of a reason. When I think about it, it doesn't seem possible that it could be a frame. And I know it was. You can hardly blame Arn Kettle for thinking I'm guilty."

"I can," she said loyally. "He ought to know you couldn't be guilty simply because you're you."

"Your prejudice is showing again," he said with a grin. "I even boggle myself at believing it was a deliberate conspiracy when I think about it too hard. Maybe Grace Emmet planned it alone for some neurotic reason; maybe Coombs wasn't deliberately planted there and only went along with her story to get even with me for jailing him; maybe Sergeant Morrison actually thinks he saw a raping. How could it have been planned so elaborately if Morrison never saw that Emmet woman before he picked her up in Erie?"

"Perhaps he promised her leniency if she co-operated," Emily suggested doubtfully.

"Then you have to assume that Coombs got himself jailed on the off-chance that Morrison could talk her into co-operating during the hour-and-a-half drive from Erie. He couldn't even have gotten in contact with Morrison to find out if he was going through with the plan."

"Perhaps Morrison lied about never seeing her before," Emily said. "Perhaps she was an ex-mistress or something, and he knew she would do as he wished."

"That would be an even more unlikely coincidence." Draining his coffee cup, he picked up his hat and climbed to his feet. "I'm not going to think about it any more tonight. Good night, doll."

"Do you have to leave so soon?"

"You'll get fired, entertaining a boy friend on duty. I'd better get out of here before the chief nurse comes along."

Leaning down, he kissed her lightly, turned, and walked toward the elevator.

chapter 9

ON NEW YEAR'S DAY, Saxon came into headquarters half an hour ahead of his appointment with the district attorney. It was Sam Lennox's day off and Vic Burns was on the desk.

Burns said with obvious self-consciousness, "Morning, Chief."

"You've heard about it, huh?"

"I guess everybody has by now," Burns admitted. "What the devil happened? She lure you on, then scream rape when the sergeant walked in and caught you in the act?"

Ted gazed at him coldly.

"I'm just trying to figure why," Burns said defensively. "Don't look so sore. I thought we were friends."

"So did I. It didn't occur to me that my friends would find me guilty without trial."

The stocky lieutenant looked a little bewildered. "I thought I was putting the best possible construction on it. The way I heard it, there were two witnesses aside from the woman, so something must have happened. Only, knowing you, I figured it must have been just seduction and she decided to yell rape after the *fait accompli*. I figured it was New Year's Eve; maybe you brought a little bottle on duty to have a quiet celebration; and when she gave you an invitation, you fell for it."

Instead of anger, Saxon felt only a vast weariness. If Vic Burns believed him guilty, no one was going to accept his explanation. Continuing to protest his innocence was like trying to fight a roomful of feathers. He decided to save his efforts for the district attorney.

59

Without making any reply, he went on to the squad room and hung up his wraps. When he came out again, he turned through the door leading to the cell block and glanced into the cells. All were empty.

Back in the waiting room, he said, "When was Coombs released?"

"Early this morning before I came on. About six. I guess he phoned some friend in Buffalo and the guy drove down to post the bond."

"Who was it?"

Burns checked the receipt book. "Somebody named John Simmons."

Walking over to the counter, Saxon took a tiny notebook from his pocket and copied down the name and address listed.

"I may as well get everybody while I'm at it," he said. "I assume the D.A. had Dowling take down the addresses of the witnesses before releasing them last night. Know where they are?"

"Sure. Right here in the basket."

Burns lifted a sheet of paper from the wire basket on the desk behind the counter and handed it to Saxon. On it were listed the names of Harry Morrison, Edward Coombs, and Grace Emmet, with home addresses behind them. The woman's was given as Erie County Jail.

Saxon copied all of them in his notebook. Then he went into his office and closed the door.

A sheet of paper beneath the glass top of his desk listed the telephone numbers of all police agencies within a hundred-mile radius. Locating the number of the Erie, Pennsylvania city police, he dialed it direct. When the police switchboard operator answered, he asked to speak to someone familiar with the Grace Emmet case.

After some delay, he was switched to a Detective Everett Cass.

"This is Acting Chief Saxon of the Iroquois, New York police," he told the Erie detective. "Last night you turned Grace Emmet over to a Buffalo detective named Sergeant Harry Morrison."

"Yeah. I was the one who picked her up."

"Were you present when the transfer was made?"

"Sure. Had to be. I work days, but I had to come down to brief the Buffalo officer."

"I see. What time was the transfer made?"

"Morrison showed up about nine P.M. He took off with the prisoner about nine-thirty."

Saxon asked, "Did you get any impression that Morrison knew the prisoner personally?"

There was silence for a moment. Then Cass said, "That's a kind of funny question. What's this all about, anyway, Chief?"

"The sergeant and his prisoner stopped off here en route to Buffalo and there was a little trouble. It's too long a story to go into over the phone. I'd just like to know if you think he was acquainted with the prisoner before he picked her up."

"Neither of them gave any indication of it," Detective Cass said slowly. "What kind of trouble? She escape?"

"No. Far as I know, she's now safely jailed in Buffalo. It was just a wild idea I had. Thanks for the information."

He hung up and sat musing for a few moments. So much for that idea. All he had accomplished was to verify Morrison's story and tighten the web about himself.

There was a knock on the door. When he called an invitation to enter, the door opened and District Attorney Arnold Kettle pushed his large stomach into the room. Unbuttoning his overcoat but not removing it, he seated himself with his hat in his lap and looked at Saxon with an expression of sadness.

"You look as if you had more bad news," Saxon said.

"Afraid so. Doc Harmon phoned just as I was leaving home. The lab test was positive."

Saxon gazed at him with his mouth open. "It couldn't be! They made a mistake."

Kettle slowly shook his head. "Bruce says not. You can't argue with a microscope, Ted."

"But it's absolutely impossible! I never touched the woman."

The district attorney cocked one eyebrow. "Are you accusing Doc Harmon of being in on the conspiracy too?"

Saxon let his wide shoulders slump in defeat. After a long silence he said tonelessly, "So am I under arrest, Mr. District Attorney?"

A look of irritation formed on Kettle's face. "I don't know what you're sore about, Ted. If you weren't the chief of police and a lifelong friend of mine, you would have been in jail last night. You ought to appreciate the way you've been handled."

He was being unfair, Saxon realized. There was no point in taking his resentment out on Kettle, who obviously had no liking for this distasteful job and was performing his duty solely because he had no choice. The man had leaned over backward to make it as easy as possible for Saxon.

"Sorry, Arn," he said wearily. "Hereafter I'll try to aim my temper at the people who set me up. I have another bit of evidence for you to make the case against me even tighter. I just phoned Erie. Morrison told the truth about the time he left there with Grace Emmet. And a detective who witnessed the transfer says he noticed nothing to indicate they had ever seen each other before."

The district attorney regarded him strangely. "Why are you telling me this?"

"Because, good or bad, I want the whole truth to come out. I'm not interested in eventual acquittal for lack of evidence."

For a few moments the district attorney gazed down at the hat in his lap. Without looking up, he said tentatively, "Before I came in here, I stopped to talk to Vic Burns. He has a kind of interesting theory."

"I heard it," Saxon said shortly. "No, thanks."

Kettle raised his eyes to look at him. "Forced rape

is a felony, Ted. Actually, adultery is a crime too in this state, punishable with up to a year in prison, but I never heard of the law being enforced. If you could establish that it was her idea and she only yelled rape because Morrison caught you together, the worst that would probably happen would be a charge of misuse of your office."

"You mean I could resign from the force," Saxon said. "No, thanks. I have no intention of pleading guilty to a lesser offense when I'm not guilty of any. Can't you get it through your head that I didn't do *anything?*"

The district attorney sighed. "Okay, Ted. You don't leave me much choice but to ask the grand jury for an indictment for first-degree rape."

"Then I'm under arrest?"

Kettle moved his head back and forth wearily. "I'm going to stick my neck out. If you run, I'll have to resign as D.A., but I'm sure you won't. We'll hold off formal charges until tomorrow morning, so you'll be free to arrange bail. You be here at headquarters at nine A.M. to be booked. Then we'll immediately go upstairs to City Court for a preliminary hearing. I'm sure the judge will fix bail at the lowest amount he can under the law, because we're all as upset about having to do this to you as you are about having it done. Until a jury finds you guilty, if ever, I see no reason why you'll have to spend a single day in jail."

In view of the fact that everyone seemed convinced of his guilt, he could hardly expect friendlier treatment than that, Saxon thought. He had always been a little impatient with the general belief that the equality of all persons under the law was a myth, but now he was confronted with evidence that it was. There was little doubt in his mind that if he had been Joe Nobody, factory worker, he would already be behind bars and would languish there until trial.

He was a little ashamed of himself for accepting this special treatment, but it would have required a degree of nobility rare in the history of human relations to insist on being jailed simply because others in the same position would have been. Particularly since he knew himself to be innocent.

"Thanks, Arn," he said. "I do appreciate the way you're handling this."

Saxon wasn't supposed to be on duty that day. He had come down solely to keep his appointment with Arnold Kettle. When the district attorney left, Saxon walked into the squad room and put on his coat and hat.

As he started past the desk, Vic Burns said, "Chief."

"Yeah?" Saxon asked, pausing.

"The D.A. says we have to book you tomorrow."

"Uh-huh."

"You're going to need bail," Burns said diffidently. "I only have a couple of thousand salted away, but you're welcome to it."

Saxon's resentment at Burns's earlier suggestion as to what might have really happened in Grace Emmet's cell had left him a little cool toward the man. But now his coolness evaporated.

"Thanks, Vic," he said. "But I'm sure I can arrange professional bond."

He drove to the big lake-front home of outgoing Mayor Ben Foley.

Saxon found Foley and his wife in their bathrobes. They had just finished a late breakfast. Alice Foley excused herself to go upstairs and dress, leaving Saxon alone with her husband in the big front room.

The outgoing mayor looked at him keenly. "Something's wrong, Ted. What is it?"

"You haven't heard?" Saxon asked with raised brows.

"Heard what? We haven't been out of the house."

Saxon told the whole story.

When he finished, Foley regarded him shrewdly. "Have you told Emily?"

"Of course," Saxon said. "I drove over to the hospital last night as soon as I got away from headquarters. She was on night duty."

"How'd she take it?"

"She was madder than I was. Not at me. At the people who rigged this."

Foley gave a satisfied nod. "Then I guess you're as innocent as you claim."

Saxon frowned at him. "Of course I am."

"If you were guilty, you wouldn't have gone near Emily. You would have wanted to hide your face from her. Do you have any idea of the motive behind this frame?"

Saxon shook his head. "Not the slightest."

"Hmm. You want me to handle the legal end of this?"

"That's why I'm here. You're a lawyer, and I certainly need one."

"Okay. You say Arn Kettle's going to push for the lowest possible bail?"

"He implied that."

"Then you forget everything until tomorrow morning," Foley said. "I'll arrange professional bond. I'll meet you at headquarters at nine A.M."

chapter 10

SAXON DIDN'T FEEL like a lonely lunch at home, but neither did he care to patronize a local restaurant where he would run into people he knew. It had stopped snowing during the night and plows had already cleared the main roads, so he drove thirty miles to a roadhouse on the outskirts of Rigby and lunched there. Afterward he watched television in the roadhouse bar.

Because Emily had worked until 7 A.M. and usually slept until 3 P.M. when she was on the third shift, Saxon didn't disturb her until the late afternoon. It was almost four when he arrived at her apartment. He had timed it correctly, for she told him she had just finished showering and dressing.

"Where's Julie?" he asked as he removed his hat and coat.

"She's on three to eleven this week. As a matter of fact, I'm her relief. What did Arn Kettle have to say?"

Sinking into the center of the sofa, he stretched out his long legs and glumly regarded his toes. "I'm to be booked and have a preliminary hearing tomorrow morning. Meantime he's trusting me not to run."

"Will they put you in jail, Ted?"

"Not unless I'm convicted. And the trial may not come up for months. There seems to be a general reluctance to jail the chief of police. I've retained Ben Foley as my lawyer."

"Oh, I'm glad," she said. "He's not only good; he's nice."

"I chose him primarily for the first reason," Saxon

66

said dryly. "Incidentally, he believes in my innocence."

"I told you he was nice."

"It isn't just blind faith. He reasoned it out. He thinks if I were guilty, I wouldn't have run to you for sympathy the minute I got away from headquarters. He says I wouldn't have been able to face you."

After contemplating this, she said, "I suppose he has a point, but I wouldn't have believed you did it even if you had avoided me. I'd figure you were just embarrassed by the charge, not by guilt."

"Boy, are you prejudiced," he said with a grin. "We'll try to get you on the jury. Have you had anything to eat?"

"Toast and coffee when I got up at three. I'm not hungry, but I'll fix you something."

"I had lunch," he said. "I was going to offer to take you out for some. It isn't snowing and the sun's shining. Or was."

"Maybe later on," she said. "Would you like a beer?"

"That sounds good."

As she moved into the kitchen, he walked over to turn on the TV set. Channel 4 was broadcasting the Rose Bowl game, which, because of the three-hour time difference, was just about to start. A marching band filled the screen. Then the station cut in on the preliminary features of the game to give its regular five-minute summary of the four-o'clock news.

At that moment Emily brought in two bottles of beer.

The newscaster turned to local news. The first item was:

A one-car accident at Halfway Creek on Route Twenty just southwest of Buffalo claimed the life of one person and caused minor injuries to another early this morning. Instantly killed when the car driven by Sergeant Harry Morrison of the Buffalo Police Force skidded on snow and went over a twenty-foot bank was alleged murderess Grace Emmet, who was being transported in handcuffs from Erie, Pennsylvania to Buffalo by the police officer. Thrown from the car as it went over the bank, Sergeant Morrison suffered superficial bruises. He was treated for minor injuries at Meyer Memorial Hospital and released. The accident occurred at about 1:45 A.M.

The dead woman, wanted for the month-old murder of Buffalo industrialist Michael Factor, had been picked up by Erie police on December 30 and had waived extradition to New York. Sergeant Morrison was bringing her back to face the murder charge.

Saxon lost all interest in the football game. As the newscaster went on to another local item, he set his beer bottle on the floor, rose, and switched off the set. Crossing to the phone, he dialed Ben Foley's home number.

Alice answered. Saxon asked for her husband.

When the lawyer came on, Saxon said, "Did you happen to hear the newscast just now?"

"I heard it on the two P.M. news," Foley said. "I imagine it's been on all day, but who turns on TV New Year's morning? I tried to phone you, but there was no answer."

"I haven't been home," Saxon said. "How's this affect matters?"

"With the alleged victim dead, I'd say it pretty well kills the charge against you. We'll see in the morning, though. Kettle may insist on pushing it on the basis of the two living witnesses' testimony."

"I see We still meet at nine A.M., then?"

"That's right. But I don't think I'll bother with a bondsman. If things get to that point, we can always phone Jimmy Good and tell him to hustle over."

"Okay," Saxon said. "See you in the morning."

When he hung up, Emily asked, "What did he say?"

"He thinks this will kill the charge. I'm sorry it happened, though."

"Why?" Emily asked in surprise. "The woman was a murderess and she did this terrible thing to you. I can't feel any sympathy for her."

"I wasn't thinking about her. But now she can never retract her charge. I wanted a public admission from her that she lied."

"Oh," Emily said. "I hadn't thought of that. Now how will we ever prove it?"

Walking over to the sofa, Saxon drew her to her feet and put his arms about her. "The important thing is your believing in me, doll. It doesn't really matter what the rest of the world thinks."

"It does to me," she said. "I won't have people thinking badly of you. They'd better not say anything to me if they know what's good for them."

He kissed the end of her nose. "What'll you do, tigress? Bite them?"

"I'll at least kick their shins," she said. She put her arms around his neck. "Oh, Ted, what will we do if we can never disprove this thing? It'll hang over your head for the rest of your life."

"We'll disprove it," he said. But he didn't feel nearly the amount of confidence he put into his tone.

Promptly at nine the next morning Saxon arrived at police headquarters. Ben Foley was already there and Arnold Kettle came along a few moments later. They gathered in Saxon's office to confer.

Foley opened matters by saying, "I don't suppose you'll try to push this with the complainant dead, will you, Arn?"

The district attorney raised his eyebrows. "I can't see that the victim's death changes things much. The fact remains that a crime was committed."

"Is alleged to have been committed," Foley corrected. "How are you going to prove it? Did you take a formal statement from the Emmet woman?"

"Well, no. But she told her story in front of a reliable witness. Jenny Waite was present when I questioned her."

"Hearsay," Foley said. "Try to get it in the record. You know the law better than that."

Arnold Kettle frowned. "We still have the eyewitness testimony of Morrison and Coombs. Plus the lab test."

"What Morrison saw doesn't differ from what my client says happened. It's only his interpretation of what was happening that differs. Ted admits struggling with the woman on the bunk and being pushed off onto the floor by her. He and your witness part company only on the reason for the struggle. Your witness says it was rape; my client says he was trying to subdue an hysterically violent woman. It's one's word against the other. I'll warn you in advance that I'll block any expression of opinion by Morrison when he's on the stand. I'll confine him to describing exactly what he saw—which doesn't differ from what Ted admits happened."

"There's still Coombs," Kettle growled. "He heard the woman protesting Ted's advances."

"Claims to have heard," Foley corrected. "Personally I think he's a liar. But aside from that, he isn't an eyewitness, because he couldn't see into the cell. I can tear him apart on the stand."

"Think you can beat the lab test?" Kettle challenged.

"That doesn't prove rape. It only establishes a physical relationship with *some* man, which may well have been voluntary."

"There wasn't any man but Ted around," the district attorney growled.

"No? Well, for your information, I talked to Doc Harmon on the phone yesterday afternoon. The test would have shown positive if she had been with a man *at any time within the previous twenty-four hours.* How do you know what happened in her cell in Erie?"

"Oh, come off it, Ben," Kettle scoffed. "You'd get laughed out of court."

"I don't think so. It's enough to establish the reasonable doubt that is one of the fundamentals of our legal system. I'll concede that you could probably get an indictment on what evidence you have. But try to get a conviction for rape where the victim's testimony is barred and your only eyewitness's testimony agrees with what the defendant admits, and for which the defendant has a reasonable explanation. *You* would be the one to get laughed out of court, Arn."

The district attorney glanced at Saxon, who had been quietly listening. "I'm not anxious to press this thing," he said grumpily. "Hell, Ted's been a friend of mine for years. But the public raises a bigger fuss when charges are dropped against a public official than they do when we let off some nonentity. They always think there's some kind of cover-up. Next election I'd be voted out of office."

"You'd be more likely to be voted out if you prosecute the case and lose it."

"There's that factor, too," the district attorney agreed unhappily. "I can't really afford to jump either way."

"Suppose we get another opinion?" Foley suggested. "Let's go upstairs and talk to the city judge. He may tell you you don't even have enough for a preliminary hearing."

Kettle seemed relieved by the suggestion. Rising to his feet, he said, "Okay. You stick here, Ted. We'll be back."

They were gone about twenty minutes. Then Ben Foley re-entered the office alone.

Sinking into a chair, he said, "I guess that's that, Ted. Arn has agreed to drop charges."

Saxon emitted a sigh of relief. "That's one hurdle over."

"What do you mean, one? The case is closed."

Saxon shook his head. "Dismissal of charges for lack of evidence isn't acquittal. In the public mind I'll be a rapist until I prove what really happened that night. Maybe Arn considers it a closed case, but I haven't even started my investigation."

Foley pursed his lips. "I've been thinking about the

public reaction. The first session of the new Common Council is this afternoon. I have to be present to turn over the reins formally to our new mayor. Maybe you ought to look in, too."

"Why?"

"Because one of the orders of business will be to consider a permanent appointment as chief of police. And in view of what's happened, I doubt that it's going to be you unless you appear to protect your interests and present an awfully strong case."

chapter 11

DESPITE BEN FOLEY'S SUGGESTION, Saxon did not attend the council meeting. There were a couple of reasons for his decision. One was that since he had already argued his innocence of rape before the proper authority, he had no intention of publicly repeating the performance and, in effect, pleading for his job. Another more practical reason was that he was sure his presence would do no good. Undoubtedly it would inhibit open criticism of him, since he knew all the councilmen personally, but it probably would also prevent any action at all. He suspected that the council would simply table the matter until it could be discussed without his embarrassing presence.

An indication of what was to come was that he wasn't disturbed in his office all day. Ordinarily there would have been a dozen phone calls, and members of the force would have been in and out constantly to make verbal reports, discuss the handling of cases, or ask questions on procedures. Usually there were also a few influential citizens who felt they were above dealing with a mere desk man and came directly to the chief to ask favors or to register complaints. But today there wasn't a single phone call for him, no visitors appeared, and apparently members of the force were resolving their problems without his advice; not even a patrolman entered his office. After Ben Foley left, his only conversation was over the phone with Emily when he called to give her the news that the rape charge had been dropped.

He spent the day getting his records in order so that the new chief, whoever he was, could take over with a minimum of difficulty. He didn't even leave his office for lunch; instead, he phoned Hardy's Restaurant across the street and had a sandwich and coffee delivered.

Apparently it had been a long council meeting, for it was just breaking up when Saxon left at five. If he had left by the front entrance, he would have run into the entire council as it filed down the front stairs, but he always parked his car in the police parking area next to the alley entrance to headquarters. Consequently, none of the councilmen was embarrassed by having to speak to him. He was in his car when he rounded the front corner of the city hall and saw them exiting from the building.

Ben Foley forced the confrontation on the new mayor, however. He and Adam Bennock had just reached the bottom of the city-hall steps when Saxon's car came around the corner. Spotting it, Foley signaled Saxon over to the curb.

Leaning across to crank down the car window on the curb side, Saxon looked out inquiringly. The former mayor took the new mayor's elbow and propelled him over to the car.

"Good thing we caught you," Foley said. "His Honor has something to tell you."

"Hello, Saxon," Bennock said with a peculiar inflection of reluctance in his high, reedy voice. Then he glanced at Foley. "I see no point in making an official announcement in the middle of the street, Mr. Foley."

"You just plan to write him a letter?" Foley asked, retaining his grip on the elbow. "He has a right to be informed face to face."

Saxon said, "I think I know what you have to say anyway, Mr. Bennock. You may as well get it over with."

Bennock cleared his throat and his face took on color, though that might have been due solely to the cold, to which he was inordinately sensitive. There was a muffler wrapped around his neck to the chin. completely hiding his Adam's apple, but Saxon got the odd impression that the throat-clearing caused the knobby organ to bob up and down beneath the muffler.

"Very well, then," the new mayor said. "The Common Council has voted to suspend you from duty pending a thorough investigation of this charge against you."

"I expected it," Saxon said with no indication of surprise or resentment. "The new chief will find all my records in order and a memorandum of all pending matters requiring his attention lying on my desk. I won't even have to come in to brief him. By the way, who is he?"

"Lieutenant Arthur Marks has been appointed acting chief pending the outcome of the investigation."

So they hadn't yet gone all the way and made it a permanent appointment, Saxon thought. They were at least intending to go through the motions of a formal inquiry.

"Art's a good cop," Saxon said, refraining from adding that Marks would make a lousy chief. He had hoped the council would be smart enough to appoint Vic Burns, but he might have known it was a forlorn hope. Burns wasn't a native of Iroquois and Marks was.

Foley released the new mayor's elbow and the man moved on with a jerky nod of good-by. Foley opened the car door, stepped in, and cranked up the open window.

"I couldn't help that," he said. "I suspected the coward was merely going to inform you by letter and I wanted him to have to tell you personally."

"Why'd you get into the car?" Saxon asked curiously.

"Alice took mine this afternoon. I need a ride home."

"Nothing like inviting yourself." Saxon managed a grin.

"You should be grateful that I'm willing to ride with you," Foley told him. "I'm probably the only person in town aside from Emily who's willing to be seen with you today."

His expression became serious. "Actually I wanted to

talk to you, Ted. I had a kind of wild thought while I was in council meeting."

"It was in good company."

"Remember the conversation we had the day I appointed you acting chief?"

"Uh-huh. You mean about wanting to leave an effective chief in office?"

" 'Incorruptible' is the word I used, I think. We also discussed a possible attempt by Larry Cutter to move in and take over the town. I mentioned that in order to accomplish that, he'd have to control both the mayor and the police chief. I suggested that if Adam Bennock was co-operating with Cutter, his probable choice for chief would be Art Marks. And, lo, the day Bennock takes office Art Marks becomes acting chief."

Saxon gave him a sharp sidewise glance. "You think Larry Cutter may have been behind my frame?"

"I've projected my thought even farther than that. Your father's death had all the earmarks of a professional kill."

Saxon's eyes narrowed and his mind began to work so furiously that he nearly missed the turn toward Foley's home. At the last minute he braked and skidded around the corner on the hard-packed snow. He didn't say anything until he reached the big house and swung into the driveway. He leaned back in the seat.

"My frame was part of a deliberate campaign to get the right man in office, you think? First they killed Dad, but you can't go on bumping one police chief after another until you finally get the one you want appointed. It would be so obvious, it would probably bring on a state investigation. So they had to use an entirely different method to get rid of me."

"That's the theory I've been developing. Doesn't it make sense?"

"It fits all down the line," Saxon said slowly. "It even explains how they got Coombs to co-operate. I doubt very much that an investigation of Coombs's background would turn up anything disreputable about him, because they wouldn't use a witness who couldn't stand investigation. I'll bet no one could link him to Larry Cutter. But you know what he does for a living?"

Foley shook his head. "You never mentioned it."

"He's an accountant for the Upstate Harness Racing Association.

A gleam appeared in the plump ex-mayor's eyes. "And Larry Cutter's money is behind that," he said softly.

"Now that we know where to look, maybe we can beat them after all," Saxon said, beginning to feel a surge of excitement. "At least we now have an idea who the enemy is. Up to now I couldn't even begin to imagine why I was framed."

"Don't get too enthusiastic," Foley cautioned. "With the rape charge dropped, you'll have a devil of a time reopening that investigation. You can't put Morrison or Coombs on the stand, because there's no court action pending. How do you plan to start?"

"By heading for Buffalo in the morning," Saxon said. "I have some contacts there who should be able to brief me on Larry Cutter's organization."

"I don't think I can help you there, because I'm a little too old for undercover work. But any other way I can help, don't hesitate to call on me."

"I won't," Saxon assured him.

Climbing out of the car, Foley stood for a moment with the door open. "One thing, Ted. You're not police chief any more. While you're under suspension, you're not even a cop."

"So?"

"You don't have the protection of your police force behind you. And I don't think these people would hesitate for an instant to kill you if you get too close."

"I'll try to keep them from learning it until I'm right in their laps," Saxon said dryly.

Backing out of the driveway, he headed for Emily's to tell her the news.

Emily had news for him, too, but she was sidetracked from immediately announcing it by his story of the day's events. She was indignant over his suspension from the force, elated when he told her of Ben Foley's theory, which finally gave them something definite to get their teeth into; then she became fearful for Saxon's safety when he told her of his plan to go to Buffalo the next day and attempt to uncover evidence that he had been framed. Only after she had run the scale of these emotions and they had discussed every phase of the day's happenings did she get around to making her announcement.

Going into the kitchen, she returned with a copy of the *Iroquois Evening Bulletin*.

"Look at this," she said. "There isn't a word in it about the rape charge."

There wasn't, he discovered on leafing through the paper. This was the first issue in which the news could have been reported, as there had been no paper on New Year's Day, but the *Bulletin* hadn't mentioned it.

Since by now everyone in town had heard of the alleged rape, it could hardly be because the editor was unaware of the story. Saxon could only conclude that he was following the discreet self-censorship policy of so many small town papers, which maintain dead silence concerning scandals involving prominent local citizens.

On his way home from Emily's, Saxon stopped to pick up a Buffalo paper. The story was mentioned here, but only on an inner page, and it was cautiously worded. There had been a similarly cautious item in the Buffalo morning paper that day.

With both Buffalo newspapers having local correspondents in Iroquois, they could hardly have avoided hearing of the rape charge, even though no news release had been issued. Both papers must have checked with some official source, most likely with the Iroquois County district attorney's office. And the printed stories indicated that the response had been "No comment."

The story that a chief of police was accused of raping a female prisoner was too newsworthy an item to be passed up altogether, but without official confirmation it had to be handled carefully. In both papers it was merely reported that acting Police Chief Theodore Saxon of Iroquois was "under investigation" for an alleged mistreatment of a prisoner. Not only was the prisoner unmentioned by name; the sex wasn't even disclosed.

Saxon wondered if he were going to make it all the was through the scandal with no more adverse publicity than that.

He found out the next day that he wasn't.

THE GORDON FRAME

Thus by the time he arrived in Buffalo early next
day morning the whole city knew of his suspension.

chapter 12

THE SATURDAY, January 3 issue of Buf-
falo's morning paper reported Saxon's suspension on its
front page. The new mayor was quoted extensively to
explain the suspension. In part the item read:

Reform Mayor Adam Bennock told the corre-
spondent for this paper that acting Chief Saxon's
suspension was the result of an accusation of rape
made by a female prisoner placed in Saxon's custody on New Year's Eve. The woman was Buffalo's murderess Grace Emmet, since killed in an
automobile accident, who was left at the Iroquois
city jail for a short time on New Year's Eve while
the police officer escorting her back to Buffalo
from Erie, Pennsylvania, was receiving medical
treatment for a minor complaint.

Mayor Bennock said that no criminal charges
were brought against Saxon because the complainant died in the automobile accident less than two
hours after the alleged attack, and the Iroquois
County district attorney's office felt her death left
insufficient evidence to obtain a conviction. However, the Iroquois Common Council is conduct-
ing an independent inquiry to determine Saxon's
fitness to remain in office. Pending the result of the
inquiry, Lieutenant Arthur Marks has been appointed acting chief.

Saxon felt grim amusement at Adam Bennock's
characterization of himself as a "reform" mayor. The
adjective would probably give Ben Foley apoplexy.

Since by the time he arrived in Buffalo early Saturday morning the whole city knew of his suspension, he decided it would be a waste of time to try to get to any information from police headquarters. The past relationship of the Iroquois police and the Buffalo police had always been excellent, and Saxon was personally acquainted with the chief and most of the division heads. But he knew that most cops hold rapists in the same contempt they hold blackmailers, and he could hardly expect a very favorable reception at Buffalo police headquarters if he started inquiring about a woman he was supposed to have raped.

Instead his first stop was the city morgue.

He was a day too late to view the remains of Grace Emmet. A fat, rather unpleasantly affable morgue attendant told him the body had been released to a relative from New York City the evening before.

"Helter and Fork Funeral Home picked her up," the man said. "You could still probably find her there, 'cause they have to embalm her before shipping her back to New York. Shouldn't think you'd want to see her if you were a friend, though."

"Why not?"

"You wouldn't recognize her. It'll be a closed-casket funeral. She hadda be cut out of the car with a torch. When the car went over the bank, it nosed straight down twenty feet. Folded up like an accordion. If it wasn't for her clothes and that mink coat she was wearing, we wouldn't even of been able to tell she was human when they brought her in. She didn't have no face left. And she had short hair just like a man, you know."

"It wasn't that short," Saxon said with a frown.

"You should see some of the men we get," the fat attendant said, grinning lewdly. "Sure it was short. What they call a poodle cut. Bleached blonde. But we get bleached blond men too. Somebody's always bumping off a swish. She was so banged up, they hadda identify her by fingerprints."

"Oh? Where'd they get the fingerprint record to compare her with? She'd never been in custody here, had she?"

"Hadda send to Erie, where she was picked up. It was Grace Emmet all right. That cop with her was sure lucky he was throwed clear."

"Yeah, I guess so," Saxon said. "Well, thanks a lot, anyway."

He decided not to visit the Helter and Fork Funeral Home. Primarily Saxon had gone to the morgue to make sure the body was really that of Grace Emmet. It had occurred to him that possibly her inducement to go along with the frame had been a promise to let her escape, and that Morrison had rigged the accident with some other body in the car to substitute for his prisoner. But if she had been identified through fingerprints, that killed that theory.

It had been a rather farfetched idea anyway, he decided.

From the morgue he drove to a drugstore and checked the phone book for the address of an Anthony Spijak. The man was listed as living on North Street just off Delaware—which was a section of big, expensive homes. Five minutes later he parked in front of a large brick house, followed a winding, freshly shoveled walk to its wide porch, and rang the doorbell.

A dark, good-looking woman of Saxon's age answered the door. She looked at him in surprise. "Why, Ted Saxon!" she exclaimed. "We were just talking about you!" Then her face slowly colored with embarrassment.

"You saw the morning paper, huh?" he said dryly. "Tony home, Marie?"

"Sure. He never leaves until about eleven. Come on in."

Pausing to kick off his overshoes and leave them on the porch, he stepped into a small entry hall off a wide front room which, he could see, was expensively furnished in modern American. Marie Spijak took his coat and hat and hung them in a guest closet, then led the way into the front room.

"Tony!" she called.

A tall, darkly handsome man with black curly hair appeared from the rear of the house. Shirt sleeves rolled to his biceps exposed muscular forearms covered with fine, curling black hair. He too was about Saxon's age.

The man grinned broadly when he saw Saxon. Advancing with hand outstretched, he said, "How are you, Ted, old buddy? I ain't seen you since your old man ran me out of Iroquois."

Clasping the hand, Saxon said with an answering grin, "You have to admit you deserved it, Tony."

"I guess trying to run a wide-open handbook in a place like Iroquois was asking for it," Spijak admitted. "Incidentally, I was sorry to read about your dad. He was a great guy, even if he did roust me out of my home town."

"He certainly lasted in the job a lot longer than I did."

"We've just been reading about that. Sit down, Ted. Like a drink?"

Saxon shook his head. "Too early for me."

"I have beer for breakfast. Keeps me in shape." Seating himself in a chair opposite Saxon's, Tony Spijak said to his wife, "How about a beer for me, hon?"

Marie disappeared in the direction of the kitchen.

Glancing around at the expensive furnishings, Saxon said, "You seem to be doing pretty well, Tony. The bookie business must pay well. I assume you're still in it, aren't you?"

Spijak cocked an eyebrow. "You asking as a cop or as an old buddy?"

"I'm not a cop any more. You read the paper. I wouldn't have any jurisdiction here, anyway."

Spijak grinned. "You sure made the front page. What the hell got into you, anyway? Were you drunk?"

"It was a frame," Saxon said.

Marie returned with a glass and an opened can of

beer in time to hear the last remark. Handing them to her husband, she said, "I told you there was some mistake, Tony. I knew Ted wouldn't do a thing like that."

Spijak poured beer into the glass and set the can on the floor. "Marie used to have a crush on you in high school," he said amiably. "I don't think she ever quite got over it."

"Don't be silly," Marie said, blushing.

"Remember the time your old man caught us skipping school?"

"I can still feel in it the seat of my pants," Saxon said with a rueful smile.

"He was a great old guy. If he was alive now, he'd probably give it to you across the seat of the pants again for this deal. How do you mean, it was a frame?"

"You know Larry Cutter?"

Spijak paused with his beer glass suspended halfway to his lips. "I know who he is," he said cautiously.

"He's looking for a place to land, and I think he's picked Iroquois. He couldn't swing it with Dad in as chief, so I think he had him killed. He couldn't swing it with me in as chief, either. Now they have a good, honest, dumb cop in office who wouldn't know what was happening if Cutter opened a casino at Fourth and Main."

Tony Spijak took a sip of his beer. "Yeah, I saw by the paper they appointed Art Marks. He was walking a beat when we were kids."

Ted said, "You're still in the bookie business, aren't you, Tony?"

"Oh, I've got a couple of spots around. I'm not gonna tell you where, because the Buffalo cops are getting almost as tough as your old man used to be."

"I don't care where they are, so long as they aren't in Iroquois. All I'm interested in is that you're still on the inside of things. You must know the scoop on Larry Cutter."

"I keep my ear pretty close to the grapevine," Spijak admitted. "You have to in this business. What you want to know?"

"First, have you heard any rumors of Cutter planning to move in on Iroquois?"

"Not with any illegal operations. Everybody on the inside knows he's behind this harness-racing business, but that's on the up-and-up. It would make sense, though. He's a got a pretty big organization sitting idle, and he can't open up here. The Buffalo cops are just waiting for him to make a move, and he knows it."

"Ever hear of a man named Edward Coombs?"

After taking another thoughtful sip of his beer, the bookmaker shook his head. "Doesn't ring a bell."

"He's an accountant for the Upstate Harness Racing Association." Taking his small notebook from his pocket, Saxon read off the man's home address.

Spijak shook his head again. "Still never heard of him."

"I doubted that you would have. He was in jail in Iroquois the same night Grace Emmet was. He was one of the witnesses to the supposed rape, and Cutter wouldn't have picked a witness with any underworld connections." He glanced at the notebook again. "How about a John Simmons?"

Spijak gave him a peculiar look. "Hardnose Simmons?"

"I wouldn't know of any nickname he had." From the notebook Saxon read aloud the man's home address.

"That's Hardnose," Spijak said. "What about him?"

"He was the man who posted Edward Coombs's bail."

The bookie grunted. "I guess you were framed by Larry Cutter, then. Simmons is one of Cutter's guns."

Saxon felt a surge of elation. Here was the first actual evidence to support Ben Foley's theory. Larry Cutter had made one stupid mistake in his carefully worked out plan to get Saxon out of office. He had wisely chosen a witness whose connection to him couldn't be traced, then had allowed one of his gunmen to post the man's bail.

He said, "One more question. Do you know a Sergeant Harry Morrison of Homicide and Arson?"

"That creep?"

"You do know him, huh? Is he tied in with Cutter?"

Tony Spijak looked surprised. "Cutter doesn't have any cops on his payroll that I know of. Buffalo's got a pretty clean force. Except for a few two-bit chiselers like Morrison who shoot angles on their own. Every police force has a few bad apples."

"What's Morrison's angle?"

"One that'll get him kicked off the force if they ever catch up with him. He's running protection for a call girl."

"Oh?" Saxon said.

"The rumor is that he steers customers to her, then takes away most of what she knocks down. He's a real nice guy."

"You know this girl's name?" Saxon asked.

"Ann something-or-other. I don't know her personally. I could steer you to somebody who does, if it's important."

"I'd appreciate it."

Draining his beer glass and setting it on the floor next to the can, Spijak rose and crossed the room to a small writing desk. He wrote on a scratch pad, tore off the sheet and carried it over to Saxon. The paper read: *Alton Zek, Fenimore Hotel, Room 203.*

"The guy's a junkie," Spijak said. "Also a stoolie who plays both sides. But he knows everything that goes on in the vice and narcotics rackets. I don't want you to tell him I sent you, because he'll probably run tell Morrison you were nosing around the minute you leave, and I don't want a guy like Harry Morrison down on me."

"How will I get him to talk, then?" Saxon asked.

"Show him a twenty-dollar bill. He won't give a hoot in hell who you are. He'd sell out his mother for a twenty."

"Thanks, Tony."

chapter 13

THE FENIMORE HOTEL was on lower Main Street in the area where Main abruptly turns from a district of sleek modern stores, theaters, and cocktail lounges to one of dives and flophouses. It was a ramshackle frame building of three stories that advertised rooms at a dollar and up.

There was an elderly man with a dirty shirt behind a desk in the lobby. He eyed Saxon warily. It was the sort of place where a seedily dressed stranger would automatically be stopped for questioning about his business to make sure one of the tenants wasn't allowing a friend to bunk in without paying rent. But Saxon's dress passed him, because it was also the sort of place periodically visited by the police. Saxon's clothing was hardly expensive, but it was of a good, solid quality worn by only one type of visitor to the Fenimore. The desk man probably assumed he was a local cop.

There was no elevator. Saxon climbed rickety stairs to the second floor and found room 203.

When he knocked on the door, a hoarse voice from inside said, "Yeah?"

Saxon tried the knob, found the door unlocked and pushed it open. There was an unmade iron bed with dirty sheets, a battered dresser with a washbasin and pitcher on it, a single straight-back chair before a small table, and a soiled and sagging overstuffed chair near the window facing the door. A thin, shriveled man of indeterminate age sat in the overstuffed chair. He wore stained denim pants and a wrinkled O.D. army shirt. He looked up at Saxon's height dully, one cheek twitching.

Closing the door behind him, Saxon said, "Are you Alton Zek?"

"Yeah. But if you're a cop, I ain't done nothing." He dropped his eyes, which were beginning to water with the strain of gazing upward.

"You look as if you need a pop," Saxon said. Taking out his wallet, he removed a twenty-dollar bill, replaced the wallet, and let the bill dangle from his thumb and forefinger.

Alton Zek licked his lips, his eyes on the bill. His cheek gave another twitch.

"I don't know what you're talking about, mister."

"Sure you do," Saxon said. "You've got a monkey riding you so hard you're shaking apart."

Zek said cautiously, "If you're from Narcotics, you're wasting your time. I don't even know what horse means."

"I'm not from Narcotics and I'm not after your pusher. I'm after a different kind of information."

"Yeah? What?"

"You know a Sergeant Harry Morrison?"

The man's watery eyes remained fixed on the dangling bill. "I know of him."

"He has a call girl working for him whose first name is Ann. I want her full name and where to find her."

Alton Zek's gaze climbed to Saxon's face. "You guys finally got wind of that, huh? The damn fool, risking his job over a hustler. You from Internal Affairs?"

"I'm not any kind of cop," Saxon said. "I just want the information."

"Why? Who are you?"

"Do you really care?" Saxon asked. "You can make twenty bucks by answering the question. If you're not interested, I'll go ask somewhere else."

Thrusting the money into his overcoat pocket, he turned and reached for the doorknob.

"Hold it," Zek said quickly. "I didn't say I wouldn't tell you."

Looking over his shoulder without taking his hand

from the knob, Saxon said, "Then tell it fast. I'm in a hurry."

Zek licked his lips again and his cheek was twitching. "All you want is the broad's name and address? You'll give me the twenty for that?"

"Uh-huh."

"You're not gonna drag me before no investigating board to tell what I know about Morrison steering business to a hustler?"

"I told you I'm not a cop. All I want is her name and address. Then you get the twenty, I walk out, and you never see me again."

"All right," the man said. "Let's have the twenty."

"Let's have the name and address first."

"You can trust me," Zek said aggrievedly.

"I'd rather have you trust me."

"Okay," the informer said with resignation. "Her name's Ann Lowry. She lives in an apartment on Bailey just off Main. I don't know the exact address, but it's in the first block west of Main. You can check apartment directories."

"In case she isn't listed, what's she look like?"

"She's a good-looking doll with a nice built on her. About five feet four and a hunnert and fifteen pounds, I'd say. Long red hair down to her shoulders and rolled under, kind of."

"You mean in a page boy?"

"Yeah, that's what they call it. You couldn't miss her. Her hair's real red and it's natural."

Walking over to the chair, Saxon took the twenty from his pocket and dropped it into the man's lap. Zek seized it and thrust it into a side pocket of his denim pants.

"Like to earn another?" Saxon asked.

The informer looked up. "How?"

"You know of any other rackets Morrison is in?"

Zek frowned. "Like what, for instance?"

"Does he have any kind of tie-in with Larry Cutter?"

"Cutter?" Zek said in surprise. "He ain't operating in Buffalo. He's just living here."

"That isn't what I asked. Do you know if Sergeant Harry Morrison has any kind of an arrangement with him?"

Zek shook his head. "Not that I ever heard."

"Then I guess you don't earn the second twenty," Saxon said, starting for the door.

"Wait a minute!"

Turning with his hand again on the knob, Saxon said, "Yeah?"

"I could inquire around. If Morrison's got some kind of deal going with Cutter, somebody'll know about it. Why don't you drop back tomorrow about this time and bring some more money?"

There was a pay phone in the hallway near the stairs, and a tattered phone book hung from a string next to it. Saxon leafed through the book until he came to the Lowrys and ran his finger down the column. There were a lot of them, but none with the first name of Ann and none with addresses on Bailey.

He wasn't surprised, for call girls usually have unlisted numbers that they pass out only to clients.

He went on down the stairs. In the lobby the gaze of the elderly man with the dirty shirt followed him to the door, but again the man said nothing.

Outside he climbed into his car and headed north up Main toward Bailey.

There was a filling station, then a string of small private homes on one side of Bailey in the block west of Main. On the other side were three multiple-dwelling apartment houses. In the lobby of the first he studied the name cards beneath a bank of mailboxes. No Ann Lowry was listed.

In the second apartment building's lobby a card beneath one of the mail slots read *Apartment 6-B* and, below that, *Sandra Norman—Ann Lowry*.

There was a self-service elevator, but Saxon took the stairs to the second floor. Six-B was at the end of a hall. A dark-eyed brunette of about twenty-five answered the door. She was a pretty little thing only about five feet tall, with a prominent bosom she must have been proud of, for she wore a white sweater far too tight for her, which stressed its size by molding itself to the curve of her breasts like an extra coat of skin. She exposed small, even white teeth in a smile of inquiry.

Saxon took off his hat. "You must be Sandra Norman," he said.

"Yes. Who sent you?"

The question momentarily puzzled him until he realized that the apartment mate of a call girl would undoubtedly be a call girl also. Apparently the brunette took him for a customer.

"I wasn't looking for you," he said. "I just happened to see your name on the card downstairs. Is Ann home?"

The smile remained on her face, but the look of interest in her eyes died. "Sorry, but she's out shopping. I expect her back about two."

Saxon checked his watch. It was only eleven-twenty.

"Okay," he said. "I'll come back."

"Is there any message?" she asked.

"No. I just wanted to talk to her."

She looked him up and down calculatingly. "It's a long time until two. I might let you wait inside if you told me who sent you."

The girl wasn't above cutting in on her apartment mate's trade, he thought with amusement. On impulse he said, "Harry Morrison."

"Oh, Harry's introduction is fine around here," she said. "Have you been to see Ann before?"

He shook his head. "Never met her."

"Then how do you know you won't like me as well? Want to come in?"

He was tempted to accept the invitation to see if perhaps Sandra Norman knew anything of Morrison's relationship with Larry Cutter, but he realized that the moment she discovered he wasn't a client, she would become suspicious and it might spoil his later chance of getting in to see Ann Lowry.

"Maybe another time," he said politely. "I don't think Harry would like it if I didn't wait for Ann."

She grinned at him without resentment. "He warned you not to let me sidetrack you in case Ann wasn't here, eh? That's because he doesn't get any cut from me. Okay, Red. I'll tell Ann to stick around until two in case she gets back before then. You can't blame a girl for trying."

"It's all right," he said in the same polite tone. "I was flattered, really."

Turning, he walked back down the hall toward the stairs. He heard the door close behind him.

"Maybe another time," he said politely. "I don't think Harry would like it if I didn't wait for Ann."

chapter 14

IT WAS A COLD DAY, probably about fifteen above, but it was clear and windless, and what snow hadn't been shoveled from sidewalks was hard-packed enough so that walking wasn't difficult. Saxon decided to leave his car in front of the apartment house and walk to a restaurant he knew of only a block down Main Street.

He had lunch, then dawdled at the restaurant bar until one forty-five, carefully limiting himself to two glasses of draft beer. It was five of two when he got back to the apartment house and rang the bell of 6-B.

When the door opened, there was no one in view. Whoever had pulled it open was standing behind it out of sight. Saxon stepped in only far enough to peer around its edge.

A hand thrust the door closed with a gentle bang. Saxon found himself staring into the bore of a forty-five automatic.

The man holding the gun was tall and lanky, with a rubelike face and protruding front teeth. He was dressed with what was probably intended to be quietly expensive taste, but his dark, conservative suit failed to get across the tailor's intention. It must have been meant to lend an executive air to the wearer, but the man possessed such a bony, gangling frame that it succeeded only in making him look like a backwoodsman dressed up for church.

"Just lean your hands against the wall," the man ordered in an adenoidal voice. "You know. Like for a shakedown." He gestured with the gun toward the wall on the opposite side of the door.

After contemplating the gun for a moment, Saxon faced the indicated wall and placed his hands against it at shoulder height.

"Okay, Hardnose," the man called.

Glancing over his shoulder, Saxon saw a heavy-set, gray-haired man in his mid-forties come from a hall that he assumed led to the kitchen. He had a wide, rather pleasant face with a strong Roman nose a trifle too big for it, to which he evidently owed his nickname. He also was dressed in a dark, conservative suit, but in his case the tailor had achieved his purpose. He looked like a successful business executive.

The new arrival also had a gun in his hand, but the moment he saw that his partner had everything under control, he slid it out of sight beneath his arm. Coming up behind Saxon, he ran his hands expertly over his body from beneath his armpits to his waist, patted his hips, then both legs.

Stepping back he said, "He's clean."

"You can turn around now," the rubelike man said. Dropping his hands to his sides, Saxon turned to face the two men. The forty-five automatic remained trained on him.

"Hardnose," Saxon said. "Would that be Hardnose John Simmons?"

"My fame has spread, Farmer," the gray-haired man said with mock delight. "The general public is starting to recognize me."

The man called Farmer said, "You can reach in your pocket for your wallet, mister. Hand it to my buddy. Just keep your movements slow and easy."

Unbuttoning his overcoat, Saxon felt for his hip pocket and drew out his wallet. He held it out at arm's length. Hardnose Simmons reached out the full length of his arm also to take it, staying as far from Saxon as possible.

"Yeah, it's him all right," he said. "Just like Harry figured from the description."

The remark explained to Saxon how the men had happened to be here waiting for him. Tony Spijak had warned him that Alton Zek played both sides. Probably Saxon had no more than left the hotel room when the little informer ran to Sergeant Harry Morrison to sell the information that someone was inquiring about him.

He felt irked with himself for being such easy prey, because he had actually considered the possibility of Zek informing on him. It just hadn't occurred to him that Morrison would get the news so soon. With the shape the little addict had been in, Saxon had assumed he would think of nothing during the next few hours except converting his twenty-dollar bill into heroin and shooting it into his veins.

Simmons tossed back the wallet.

"You can put it away again," Simmons said. "How come you're not carry a gun?"

"I'm not a cop any more. You should know, Hardnose. You had a minor part in framing me out of office."

"Me?" the man said with raised brows.

"Didn't you post bond for Edward Coombs's traffic offense?"

"Oh, that. Just following orders. I didn't even know what it was all about. You can take off your hat and coat, Saxon. We'll be here awhile."

Saxon took off his hat, glanced at the man with the gun for permission, and unhurriedly crossed the room to lay it on the sofa. Shedding his coat, he dropped it alongside the hat, then stooped to remove his overshoes.

The man with the gun said, "You can sit right there on the sofa."

Saxon seated himsel.f "Mind telling me what this is all about?"

"We don't know," Simmons said pleasantly. "We're just following orders."

The man didn't seem to know much about his work, Saxon thought.

He asked, "From Harry Morrison or Larry Cutter?"

"My, my," the man called Farmer said. "He knows lots of names. He's been doing some nosing."

Saxon decided that the remark had been a mistake. There was now no question in his mind that Sergeant Harry Morrison was allied with Larry Cutter, for at least one of these men, and probably both, were hired guns of Cutter's. That was the information he had come here to get from Ann Lowry, and now he had it, though by a different means from the way he had anticipated. Having accomplished his mission, there was no point in divulging how much he knew, for he suspected that if his captors decided he knew too much, he would never walk out of the place alive.

"I really don't know much," he said. "For instance, I don't know if Farmer is your first or last name."

"Neither," the man said with a buck-toothed grin. "It's just a nickname. Farmer Benton."

Saxon said thoughtfully, "Neither of you seems very eager to conceal your identities. Don't you think I'll put in a complaint about being held up?"

"You ain't been held up," Farmer Benton said. "You still got your money, ain't you? You come walking in a strange apartment without invitation, so I put the gun on you until you explain yourself. The cops ain't going to get very excited about that."

"Let's call them and see," Saxon suggested.

"Don't get cute," Simmons advised. "Just sit there and relax." Then his tone became more pleasant. "We may have a long wait. Like a drink while we're waiting?"

"No, thanks," Saxon said with equal pleasantness. "I just had a couple of beers, and I like to keep a clear head when I'm around people who are handling guns. What are we waiting for?"

"A phone call. Until it comes, we don't know no more about this than you do, so it won't do any good to ask questions."

"A phone call from whom?"

"You're still asking questions," Farmer Benton complained.

"Sorry. I'll just ask one more and then shut up. Where are the girls?"

"Ann and Sandra?" Simmons asked. "They took off. They kind of loaned us the place."

Conversation lapsed. Farmer Benton took a chair across the room from the sofa, but facing it, and sat with his gun in his lap. Hardnose John Simmons disappeared into the kitchen. In a few minutes he returned with a clinking glass of whisky.

"The girls stock a pretty good brand of bourbon," he said to his partner. "Want a drink?"

"No. And you better lay off, too. You know how the boss feels about drinking during working hours."

"One little highball isn't drinking," Simmons said.

When Farmer Benton didn't answer, there was another conversational lapse. Simmons carefully circled behind Benton's chair, so as not to cross between Benton's gun and Saxon, seated himself in a chair a good distance from the sofa, and sipped his drink. Benton gazed unwinkingly at Saxon. Saxon simply sat.

After a time Saxon checked his watch and saw it was 3 P.M. An hour had passed since he had entered the apartment.

Then the phone rang.

The phone stood on an end table near Saxon. But when he rose to answer, Simmons went into the kitchen. When the ringing abruptly stopped, Saxon realized the man had picked up a kitchen extension.

Several minutes passed before Simmons reappeared and resumed his seat. His glass was freshly filled and its color was darker than the first time. Farmer Benton frowned at the glass.

"One little highball isn't drinking," he mimicked in his adenoidal voice.

"Neither is two, if you know how to handle your liquor," Simmons said. "That was the boss."

"Yeah? What's the scoop?"

"He's sending over Spider Wertz with instructions. But not until dark."

"Oh, fine," Benton said. "We gotta keep this guy under a gun all afternoon?"

"Well, we could tie him up."

Farmer Benton considered, then shrugged. "Aw, the hell with it. Long as we got to sit here anyway, I'll keep him covered. What's the matter with these girls that they got no TV?"

"The guys who come to see them ain't interested in TV," Simmons said. He snickered.

Benton threw a suspicious glance at Simmons's glass, which was again nearly empty.

Another hour dragged by. Twice Simmons went to the kitchen and returned with a replenished glass, and both times Farmer Benton objected to his drinking.

The first time he said, "You trying to get drunk? Every one of those gets darker."

"You ever seen me drunk?" Simmons demanded.

"I've seen you blotto. You didn't think so, because you never know when you're drunk. You're always talking about being able to handle your liquor, but you get so you can hardly talk."

"That's a barefaced lie!" Simmons said. "I never showed my drinks in my life."

The second time Benton said crossly, "Go ahead and get stupid. You'll be a lot of help if Spider brings word we have a job to do."

Simmons merely gave him a benign smile.

It was a quarter after five and Simmons had made two more trips to the kitchen when the doorbell finally rang. Setting down his glass, Simmons circled behind his partner's chair to answer it, and Saxon noted that he was walking with exaggerated straightness. When he opened the door, Saxon caught a bare glimpse of a lean, mustached man before Simmons stepped out into the hall and pulled the door closed behind him. Saxon was disappointed. He had hoped to hear the instructions brought by the mysterious Spider Wertz.

Some five minutes passed before the door reopened to let Hardnose Simmons back in. Behind him, Saxon saw that the hall was now empty. Simmons again circled behind his partner's chair with studied care of movement and reseated himself. Benton gave him a questioning look.

Simmons lifted his glass from the floor and drained it.

Saxon felt the hair at the base of his neck prickle.

"When do we get started?" Benton asked.

"Soon as it's good and dark. It's already getting there. Spider's waiting out front. He said to come out about a quarter of six."

chapter 15

AT A QUARTER OF SIX Simmons picked up his empty glass and rose to his feet.

"You can put on your things," he said to Saxon, enunciating his words with great care. He moved toward the central hall in an unwavering line, but a little too rapidly, just brushing one side of the doorway as he passed.

Saxon reached for his overshoes and put them on while still seated. When he got up from the sofa, Farmer Benton lifted the gun from his lap and covered him as he shrugged into his coat.

Simmons returned overcoated, hatted, and wearing a pair of rubbers. He was carrying a second coat, hat, and pair of galoshes. Dropping the galoshes on the floor, he tossed the coat and hat onto the chair where he had been seated. Then he produced his gun and held it on Saxon while his partner put his away and got dressed for outdoors.

When Farmer Benton was ready, Simmons took off his hat and dropped it over his gun hand. Again carefully enunciating, he said to Saxon, "I will be right behind you on the way out. If we meet anyone, it will look like I'm carrying my hat, and I would hate to blow a hole in it. Get the idea?"

"Yeah," Saxon growled. "You mean if I try anything, you'll shoot me in the back."

"You understand perfectly," Simmons said with a smile. "You can run interference, Farmer. Go ahead."

Benton frowned at him. "You're pretty gassed, Hardnose. Better let me trail."

"Just get going," Simmons snapped at him.

Benton gave his partner an irritated look, but he didn't argue. Striding over to the door, he opened it and peered into the hall.

"All clear," he announced in a sullen voice.

He stepped out into the hall and Simmons gestured Saxon toward the door, falling into line a step behind him. Simmons paused at the door long enough to click off the light switch next to it and set the spring lock before stepping outside and pulling the door shut behind him. Farmer Benton had already reached the stairway and had stopped there, and Saxon was half-way to him.

"Hold it!" Simmons ordered.

Saxon halted. The man up ahead peered down the stairwell, then signaled them to come on.

By the time Saxon reached the stair landing, with Simmons right behind him, Benton was at the bottom of the stairs. After glancing both ways along the lower hall, Benton again gave the all-clear signal. Then he moved on to the front door.

No one except Benton was in sight when Saxon stepped into the outdoor cold with Simmons still only a step behind. At this time of year sunset came at about four-thirty, so it was quite dark by now. A light snow dimmed the light cast by a nearly full moon. The temperature seemed to have fallen since 2 P.M. Saxon judged it at about zero.

Farmer Benton waited on the front sidewalk for them to join him. When they reached him, Simmons glanced up and down the street. Aside from Saxon's Plymouth, parked directly in front of the building, there were only two cars parked on the block. One was across the street, the other on this side about a quarter of a block back. The windshield wipers of the second were working, indicating someone was in it, though it had no lights on.

It seemed that for whatever reason Spider Wertz had been waiting, it wasn't to furnish them transportation, for after one glance that way, Simmons looked at the Plymouth.

"This your car?" he asked Saxon.

It seemed useless to deny it, for of the only other two cars in sight, one was their friend's and the other, across the street, must have been the one Benton and Simmons had arrived in. Saxon merely nodded.

"Get in from this side and slide over under the wheel."

Taking his keys from his pocket, Saxon unlocked the car door, opened it, and worked his way across the seat to the driver's side. Simmons slid in next to him, lifted the hat concealing his gun, and put it on his head. Without taking his eyes from Saxon, he reached behind the seat with his left hand to unlock the rear door.

Climbing in back, Farmer Benton settled himself in the seat before asking, "What's with Spider back there?"

"He saw us come out," Simmons said. "He'll trail."

"Trail where?" the man in the back seat asked fretfully. "It'd be nice if you'd let me know what the hell the plans are."

"You'll find out when we get there," Simmons said. "All right, Saxon. Head straight east until you hit Route Twenty."

Saxon glanced sideways at the gun. Simmons sat with his back against the door, the gun butt steadied on his thigh and the muzzle pointed unwaveringly at Saxon's midriff. If it happened to go off, he would die rather messily, Saxon realized. He decided not to make any sudden moves that might inspire it to go off, at least until he discovered how lethal the plans for him were. Starting the engine, he switched on his wipers and his lights and pulled away from the curb. After a moment he leaned forward to turn the heater and defroster both to high. In the rear-view mirror he saw the other car's lights go on. The car pulled out to follow.

Despite the cold, by the time they were within a block of Route Twenty, the car's heater had made the interior of the car quite comfortable. Simmons unbuttoned his overcoat.

"Which way on Twenty?" Saxon asked.

"Southwest. You're going home."

This time Simmons's enunciation was not so precise. There was a definite slur in his voice. Saxon wondered if the car heater was having an effect.

Turning right on Twenty, Saxon said, "Why are you accompanying me home? I know the way."

"Wanna make sure you get there. Car following will bring us back."

If it hadn't been for the trailing car, the lights of which he could see only a few yards behind in the rear-view mirror, Saxon would have been sure this was a death ride. But if the men intended to shoot him and dump his body somewhere, there was no point in the second car. They could drive his back to Buffalo after committing the murder and simply abandon it somewhere. Saxon could imagine no purpose for the trailing car other than transportation back to Buffalo for Simmons and Benton. Which was reassuring, even though it was also puzzling.

It wasn't until they crossed the Route Seventy-five turn-off to Hamburg that he began to get an inkling of what Simmons had in mind.

The man said, " 'Bout five miles on there's a bridge across a ravine. Pull over on the shoulder this side of it."

Saxon knew the ravine he referred to, which was only about four miles out of Iroquois. Steep-sided, it was about thirty feet deep. The road was straight there, so there were no guard rails at the approach to the bridge. And except for the ravine, the ground was flat. A car fitted with snow tires, such as Saxon's, with an unconscious man behind the wheel and the throttle wedged to the floor, could be aimed to go off the road just before the bridge, and would have no trouble plowing its way across the few yards of snow-covered ground before it nosed over the thirty-foot drop.

The reason for the trailing car ceased to puzzle Saxon. It was necessary for his captors' transportation back to Buffalo, because his wouldn't be in condition to drive. They planned to leave the Plymouth, with him in it, crushed out of shape at the bottom of the ravine.

Saxon's mind began to race. Once he pulled over on the shoulder and stopped, he knew it would be all over. Probably the man in the back seat would knock him unconscious the moment he set the hand brake. His only hope of escape was to attempt to catch his would-be murderers off balance while the car was still in motion.

With a gun leveled directly at him, this would have been equally hopeless, except for the fact that Hardnose John Simmons was feeling his liquor. Each time the man spoke, his tongue got a little thicker. By all physical laws, the man's rate of reaction in emergency should slow in direct proportion to his increasing difficulty with speech.

The snowfall, which had been light when they started, had steadily thickened. Also, here in relatively open country where there were no buildings to block the wind, gusts periodically tugged at the car in attempts to wrest it off the road. Because of the Thruway, which paralleled it, Route Twenty was never heavily traveled along here, and tonight it was virtually deserted. They had met but one car going in the opposite direction since they had left Buffalo.

To suit driving conditions, Saxon had adjusted his speed from the legal limit of fifty to only about thirty, which gave him extra time to plan a course of action.

He had made up his mind before they were within a mile of the bridge. Having made it up, he concentrated on driving until the near end of the bridge's stone railing hove into sight through the screen of falling snow.

"Pull over here," Simmons ordered thickly.

Saxon took his foot from the accelerator. As the car started to slow, his right hand suddenly left the wheel and slashed sideways, palm down. The hard edge of his gloved hand caught John Simmons squarely above the bridge of the nose.

Saxon's stomach convulsed against the expected blow

of a bullet. Instead, there was a thump as Simmons's gun hit the floor. The man slumped forward to crack his head against the windshield.

Saxon pushed the throttle to the floor and aimed the car at a point just to the right of the stone bridge railing.

Behind him in the rear seat he imagined that Farmer Benton was frantically clawing beneath his arm for his gun, but he didn't have time to worry about that danger. By the time his front wheel hit the narrow, two-foot-high ridge of piled-up snow at the edge of the shoulder, the car was traveling at fifty miles an hour. It plowed right through, although the impact considerably slowed it, then surged forward again as the snow tires bit into the shallower snow covering the ground beyond the ridge.

It was only about fifteen yards from where the Plymouth left the road to the edge of the ravine. Saxon's left hand hit the door handle and his shoulder simultaneously bucked open the door. He left the car in a headlong dive just before it ran over the lip of the ravine.

As he slid along on his face in a foot of soft snow, he heard the agonized shriek of bending and tearing metal from the bottom of the ravine. Inconsequentially he wondered if he had remembered to pay his insurance.

When he climbed shakily to his feet, the car that had been trailing them was parked on the shoulder with its headlights murkily illuminating the scene through the heavily falling snow. And ten yards away, between Saxon and the car, Farmer Benton was scrambling erect. Saxon hadn't even been conscious of the man's jumping from the rear of the Plymouth.

Benton spotted Saxon at the same moment. Jerking off his right glove, he shot his hand inside the front of his overcoat. The headlights of the parked car glinted on the barrel of the forty-five automatic as it came out.

Saxon took three running steps and slid down the

steep bank of the ravine on the seat of his pants. Snow made it a frictionless ride. He sailed down as smoothly as if riding a child's playground slide, landing on his feet at the bottom.

chapter 16

THE PLYMOUTH had hit nose down and rolled over on its back. Both doors on the left side had been torn off and the other two had popped open. The headlights had been smashed, but both taillights still burned and the dome light, which was controlled automatically by the doors, was burning. These threw enough light to show that the snow was littered with shattered glass and bits of metal.

Saxon didn't pause for a careful study of the scene, but he did give it one quick glance. Inside the front of the car he could see the huddled figure of Hardnose John Simmons.

He moved past the car through the foot-deep snow at a lumbering trot, heading away from the road. Despite the falling snow, there was enough moonlight to see where he was going.

Unfortunately there was also enough for him to be seen, too. He was perhaps ten yards beyond the wrecked car when a shot sounded from the top of the bank and a bullet swished past his ear. An instant later he rounded a curve in the ravine which hid him from the sniper.

Apparently there had been no water in the ravine at winter's onset, for beneath the snow there wasn't the smoothness of ice. The ground was rocky and uneven, making progress difficult. Twice as he hurried along, he stumbled over snags concealed by the snow and nearly fell.

Travel along the top of the bank would be easier, he realized. With this thought, Saxon started to look for a way up the opposite side. He spotted it almost

instantly. Just ahead a section of the left side of the
bank had fallen away some time in the past, leaving a
gash which angled upward far less steeply than the
original bank. It was an old landslide, for the bare
branches of bushes which had grown there since thrust
up through the snow.

Using the bushes as handholds. Saxon laboriously
started to work his way up the bank. Halfway to the
top he heard the blast of Benton's forty-five and a
geyser of snow leaped up three feet to one side.

He didn't even pause to glance over his shoulder at
the opposite bank. There was nowhere to go but up,
and no way to make himself less a target. All he could
do was continue to climb and pray.

Fortunately the opposite bank was about seventy-
five feet away, about the limit of accurate range for
the cumbersome forty-five automatic under ideal conditions. In the dark, with falling snow further obstruct-
ing vision and erratic gusts of wind trying to shove
the gunman off balance, firing conditions were far from
ideal for Benton.

Pulling himself upward from one frozen bush to the
next, it seemed to Saxon that it would take him hours
to reach the top of the bank. Another shot boomed
and he heard the bullet plunk into the snow a foot to
his right. When seconds elapsed before the next shot,
he realized the gunman was taking careful aim and
squeezing the trigger with target-range slowness. This
time the bullet plucked at the skirt of his overcoat.

A sudden, minute-long howl of wind swept down
the ravine and raised a blinding fog of snow from the
ground to mix with the falling flakes already in the air;
that reduced visibility to zero. Under cover of the
swirling mass, Saxon managed to climb the rest of the
way to the top and swing himself behind the thick bole
of an elm.

He had hardly settled to one knee, panting from the
exertion of his climb, when the wind died as suddenly
as it had started. Cautiously he peered around the tree
trunk at the opposite bank.

Dimly he could make out the silhouette of Farmer Benton standing there. As he watched, a figure joined him. The man Simmons had mentioned as Spider Wertz had joined the hunt.

Saxon lost the advantage the pursued has over the pursuer at night: the advantage of darkness. Wertz had brought a light from his car. It wasn't an ordinary flashlight. It had a square lens probably four to five inches across and a wide, powerful beam.

The beam probed the bank below Saxon, slowly working its way to the top. When it touched the elm behind which he was hiding, he drew his head out of sight.

The beam lowered again and he took another peep. It was directed downward to illuminate the side of the opposite bank. As he watched, Farmer Benton stepped over the edge of the bank and slid downward on the snow in the same manner that Saxon had previously. Landing on his feet, he plodded across the ravine and started to climb the bank on Saxon's side.

Saxon crawled ten feet back from the bank, rose to his feet and doubled back toward the highway as rapidly as he could. This wasn't very fast, for the best gait he could muster through the steadily deepening snow was a plodding, high-stepping trot.

The taillights and dome light of the Plymouth were still burning when he passed it. He came out on the road on the opposite side of the bridge and started across it toward Spider Wertz's parked car, his hope being that Wertz had left his key in the ignition. Only the parking lights of the car were now burning.

Halfway across he realized he had fallen into a trap. His hunters had anticipated his doubling back, and Benton's descent into the ravine must have been designed to flush him this way. The car's highway lights suddenly switched on, pinning him in their glare.

Turning, he ran back the other way, expecting a bullet in the back at any moment. The only reason he could think of for Spider Wertz's not firing was fear that Farmer Benton might have reached the other end of the bridge by now and might be hit by one of the bullets.

He was nearly to the end of the bridge when the figure of Benton loomed through the curtain of falling snow. The man was plodding along the edge of the ravine toward the road, not more than twenty feet away. Spotting Saxon, he raised his gun.

Making a left wheel, Saxon raced for the opposite side of the road. Four rapid shots rolled out, so closely spaced that they sounded like one long-drawn-out explosion. Saxon's hat lifted from his head and tumbled to the ground before him. Ignoring it, he hurdled the low bank of snow piled up at the edge of the road by snowplows and kept running.

There were no more shots. Altogether he had counted eight from Benton's gun, which would account for one full clip plus one extra in the chamber. Saxon hoped that the bitter cold had numbed the man's hands enough to make reloading difficult.

He continued to flounder across country until he reached the protection of a clump of trees, then stopped to listen. A wind abruptly rose again, filling the air with eddies of fine snow and cutting vision to a matter of feet. He could hear nothing but the roar of the wind and the panting of his own breath.

When the gust died and he could see through the falling snow again clear to the dim outline of the bridge, he could make out the figure of Farmer Benton moving across it toward the lights of the car. Apparently the man had given up trying to locate him in this blinding near-blizzard.

As he watched, Benton reached the car and crossed in front of the headlights to the side away from the road. The highway lights blinked off and the parking lights came on again. Then the square-lensed hand lamp switched on and moved toward the point where the Plymouth had gone over the bank. Belatedly, Farmer Benton and Spider Wertz were going to check on the man who had ridden Saxon's car into the ravine.

Saxon grew conscious of a growing numbness in his ears. Pulling his scarf from around his neck, he shook the snow from his hair, draped the scarf across the top of his head, and tied it beneath his chin.

Then, sticking as much as possible to the protection of trees, he started to walk toward Iroquois, staying back from the road a good fifty feet. The area along here clear to the edge of town was open country, with numerous wooded sections. A good portion of it was state-owned and was reserved for an eventual state park. Nearer town, one side of the road was owned by the Iroquois Country Club, the other by the local conservation club. There wasn't a single private home along the whole four-mile stretch.

The going was difficult because of the foot-deep snow, but he couldn't risk taking the road. If Benton and Wertz came along and spotted him, the chase would start all over again. Back from the road he would have time to run for the protection of some tree if headlights appeared or, if in an open area, simply to fall flat and wait until the lights passed.

Once headlights did appear from the northeast and he froze to immobility behind a tree. They went past slowly—which meant nothing, considering driving conditions. It might have been his hunters or it might not have been.

Fifteen minutes later lights swept by at a higher speed from the opposite direction. This time he was in the open and had to drop flat. He didn't care to chance the first car's having been Wertz's and these lights being from the same car returning.

Periodically the wind rose and surrounded him with a cloud of fine snow, sometimes blowing with such intensity that he struggled to the nearest tree and set himself to leeward of it until the gust died again. The bitter cold seeped through his overcoat and gloves, numbing his body and hands more with each yard of progress. The exercise of having to lift his feet high because of the depth of the snow at least kept his body from freezing. And ever so often he beat his gloved hands together to retain circulation in them. He plodded on at the rate of about two miles an hour.

He heard the city-hall clock strike nine at the same moment that he glimpsed the lights of the country club on the opposite side of the road, which indicated the very edge of town. He could have found sanctuary there, but Emily's apartment was only a quarter of a mile beyond the club, and by the time he had crossed the highway and followed the long, winding drive to the club building, he would have traveled nearly as far as to her place. He decided to go on. He moved onto the road now, for from here on there were houses, the shadows of which he could dart into if headlights appeared.

At nine-fifteen he rang the bell of Emily's apartment.

When she opened the door and saw him standing there laden with snow, his face red with cold and the scarf ridiculously tied beneath his chin as if he were some outsize peasant woman from the old country, she couldn't help bursting out laughing.

"I'm glad I tickle your funny bone," he growled. "You'll roll on the floor when you hear how close I came to being dead."

Her laughter died. "What happened, Ted?"

Inside he walked past her to the kitchen and hung his overcoat and scarf over the edge of the door so that the residue of melting snow could drip on the floor. He came back into the front room rubbing his hands and shivering.

"You need a hot drink," Emily said with concern. "You look half frozen to death."

"About seven-eighths, I think. Got any rum?"

"No, but I can make you a coffee royal."

"I'll settle for that. Julie at work?"

"Yes," Emily said. "She's still on three to eleven. But what happened?"

He walked through the bedroom to the bathroom and ran the washbowl full of lukewarm water. Pulling his sleeves up as far as they would go without removing the jacket of his suit, he plunged both hands into the water. After a few minutes he let some out and ran in more hot. He kept gradually increasing the hot until his hands and wrists were thoroughly thawed and his hands began to redden from the heat. Then he pulled the plug and dried his hands.

When he got back to the front room, Emily said, "I'm making instant because it's faster. That all right?"

"Sure," he said. "The faster the better."

"Ted Saxon, *will* you tell me what's wrong!"

chapter 17

WHILE HE WAS ALLOWING the warmth of
the coffee royal to seep through his body, Saxon told
Emily the whole story.

"This proves your innocence," she said excitedly.
"They'll have to apologize and reinstate you."

"Providing I can prove it," Saxon said dryly. "I
doubt that Benton and Wertz are going to admit taking
me for a ride. They're probably busy establishing alibis
right now. And I haven't any witnesses. It'll be my
word against theirs."

"There's the man left in the car. Do you think he
was killed?"

"I'm sure of it. Nobody could survive a crash like
that."

"Then won't that support your story? If they establish that he was one of Larry Cutter's men, it will prove
you were telling the truth."

Saxon set down his coffee cup. "Of course it will.
I'm not thinking very clearly. I guess my brain isn't
thawed yet."

Rising, he went over to the phone and dialed.
"Police headquarters," Vic Burns's voice said in his
ear. "Lieutenant Burns."

"This is Ted, Vic, " Saxon said. "I want to report an
accident."

"Okay. Shoot."

"It's my car." Saxon reeled off the make and license
number. "You know that bridge over a ravine about
four miles out of town toward Buffalo on Route
Twenty?"

"Uh-huh. The one that marks the county line?"

"That's it. The car's at the bottom of the ravine just west of the bridge. Probably with a dead man in it. His name's John Simmons."

"Jeepers! When'd this happen?"

Saxon glanced at his watch and saw it was nine-forty. He had been at Emily's just twenty-five minutes. "Almost three hours ago. Some time just before seven. I wasn't watching the time."

"Three hours! Why'd you wait so long to call in?"

"I had to walk to town," Saxon said. "There's more to the story, but I won't bother you with it over the phone. It's out of your jurisdiction anyway, because it happened out of town."

"Okay, Ted. I'll pass it along to the state cops for investigation. You all right?"

"A little cold, but I'm thawing out. I wasn't hurt in the accident."

"Good." Vic Burns's voice turned thoughtful. "That name John Simmons rings a bell."

"It should," Saxon said. "He's the guy who posted bond for Edward Coombs."

"That's it! I knew I'd heard it somewhere. What was he doing with you?"

"It's a long story," Saxon said. "Better get on the radio to the state police. I'll see you later."

Hanging up, he immediately dialed another number. When a male voice said, "Hello," Saxon said, "Ben?"

"Yes," Ben Foley said. "That you, Ted?"

"I stirred things up a bit in Buffalo today," Saxon said. "Too much, I guess. I managed to get myself taken for a ride. I think the D.A. would be interested in my story, and I'd like you to sit in."

"A ride? What happened?"

"It'll keep until we get together. Can you get away long enough to see Arn Kettle?"

"Tonight?"

"Sure. He's a servant of the public, supposedly available twenty-four hours a day. Want to call him and see if it's okay for us to come over?"

"Why don't you call him?"

"Because I'd only have to phone you back. I don't have a car, so you'll have to pick me up. I'm over at Emily's. You can make arrangements, then swing by here to get me."

"Boy, the services lawyers have to perform for their clients," Ben Foley said. "Okay. If he's not available, I'll call you back. Otherwise I'll honk out in front of Emily's place. That's the Hawthorne Apartments, isn't it?"

"Uh-huh. Miller 2-1041."

"Got it," Foley said. "Want to give me a hint as to what this is all about?"

"I'd only have to repeat it to Arn Kettle. Let's kill two birds with one stone."

At 10 P.M. a horn sounded outside.

"That's Ben," Saxon said, going to get his coat and scarf from the kitchen. "If it was a little later, we could drop you off at work."

"He'd love that," Emily said, laughing. But she was not laughing when she kissed him.

It was still snowing and blowing when Saxon got outside. As he climbed in Ben Foley's car, the former mayor said, "How come no hat in this weather? Think you're still a college kid?"

"I got it shot off," Saxon said. "You'll hear all about it when we get to Arn's. Have any trouble?"

"No. He's a night owl, too. And he's as curious to hear what you have to say as I am."

District Attorney Arnold Kettle lived in one of the big lake-front homes southwest of the country club, a few blocks almost due west of Emily's apartment. It was only a five-minute drive.

Kettle himself answered the door, a bright-purple smoking jacket encasing his large stomach.

"Joanne's at a hen party," he said. "And the kids are in bed. Come on in."

He took their wraps and hung them on a clothestree in the entry hall, then led them into a broad, old-fashioned front room where a log was blazing in a huge fireplace.

"Drink?" he asked.

"I could stand a little anti-freeze," Foley said. "My ancient bones can't take this kind of weather any more. Scotch on the rocks, if you've got it."

Saxon said he'd have a bourbon and soda. Kettle disappeared into the kitchen and returned with three drinks on a tray. After passing them around, he settled in a chair between the other two men with a highball in his hand.

"Now what's this all about?" he asked Saxon.

Saxon started at the beginning and told the whole story of the day's events, withholding only the name of Tony Spijak as the one who had steered him to Alton Zek. By the time he finished, the glasses were empty. Kettle went to the kitchen to make more drinks.

When he had returned and was settled in his chair again, he said, "This is a pretty incredible story, but I'm inclined to believe it, Ted. It makes more sense than you being a rapist."

"We've been telling you all along he didn't rape that woman," Ben Foley said. "Seems to me there's enough evidence here to have Larry Cutter and his gunmen pulled in and shake confessions out of them."

"First thing, let's check with the state-police barracks," the D.A. suggested. He glanced at his watch. "Ten forty-five. It's over an hour since you reported the accident. They ought to have something on it by now."

He went to the phone. "This is District Attorney Arnold Kettle, Sergeant. Do you have any report yet on that accident at the bridge on Twenty a few miles out of town?"

Some time passed as Kettle merely listened. Then he said, "Yes, that is odd, but I think I know the explanation. He's here now, being questioned by me, so there's no point in his coming out there to repeat the story. You'd only turn his statement back to me anyway, if you think some criminal action is indicated. I'll have him get in touch with you tomorrow."

There was another period of silence, then: "I suggest you have the lab classify the blood type for future reference. I'll ring you again in the morning, Sergeant."

Hanging up, he returned to his chair. "The state cops are all up in the air," he said. "They wanted you down there for questioning right now, but I stalled them off. They say they were told there would be a body in the car."

"Wasn't there?" Saxon asked.

The D.A. shook his head. "Your playmates are certainly cute. There was blood splashed all over the front seat, but no body. There goes your best evidence that Larry Cutter was behind the kidnaping."

Foley said, "Not if the body's recovered and it's established by blood type that Simmons died in the car."

Saxon looked at him ruefully. "You don't know how professional hoods operate, Ben. By now a hole's probably been cut in Lake Erie's ice half a mile from shore and the body wrapped in tire chains and dumped through it. By morning the hole will be frozen over again. And when Farmer Benton and Spider Wertz are picked up, they'll have a dozen witnesses to insist that they were somewhere miles from the scene of the accident. It'll be my word against theirs plus all their alibi witnesses' words."

"You mean we can't do anything about an attempted murder?" the plump lawyer demanded.

"Oh, sure," Saxon said. "We can have the Buffalo police arrest Larry Cutter and his two stooges, set a preliminary hearing, and have charges dismissed for lack of evidence. That about sums it up, Arn?"

"I'm afraid so," the district attorney admitted. "However, I'm willing to try, Ted. I'm completely convinced now that you were framed."

"Let's just drop it," Saxon said. "Why tilt at windmills? It may worry Cutter more if no one even comes around to question him than if we try to throw the book at him. He's used to beating legal raps. At least we now know where to look for evidence. I'll start digging again tomorrow."

"You're going to Buffalo again?" Foley asked with a frown.

"Sure. But tomorrow I'll carry a gun. Am I still legally entitled to, Arn?"

The district attorney pursed his lips. "Technically you're still a member of the force. You've been suspended, not fired. It might be an arguable point, but I doubt that any jury would convict you under the Sullivan law. I'm not going to suggest that you go up against this band of armed hoods with your bare hands."

Grinning, Saxon rose to his feet. "I'm afraid I'd ignore the suggestion if you did. I guess we've accomplished all we can tonight. Let's go home, Ben."

place was not merely a gas station, but also a repair
garage that handled used cars.

chapter 18

SUNDAY MORNING Saxon didn't go to
church. His first act after breakfast, while still in robe
and pajamas, was to phone the state police barracks.

Arnold Kettle had already phoned the barracks and
talked to the lieutenant in charge, he learned. As a result Saxon wouldn't have to come down to make a
formal statement. In a few days he would receive an
accident report form in the mail from the state Bureau
of Motor Vehicles, and would be required to fill it out
and return it. If there was to be any criminal investigation in connection with the accident, he would hear
from the district attorney.

Saxon asked what had been the disposition of his
car and was told it had been hauled from the ravine
and into Iroquois by a wrecker owned by the Fellinger
Repair Garage. He would have to phone the garage to
learn the towing charge. When he phoned the garage,
he learned he owed twenty-five dollars. The man he
talked to suggested that the wreck would bring about
that amount from a junk yard, and offered to call it
even.

"Better leave it there until the insurance adjuster can
examine it," Saxon said. "I'll talk to you again after
he's seen it."

When he hung up, he looked for and located his
auto insurance policy. It was a seventy-five-dollar-de-
ductible policy and he had paid the premium. He made
a mental note to phone his insurance agent first thing
Monday morning.

Then he phoned Bell's Service Station, where he
bought gas, and caught owner Dick Bell on duty. The

place was not merely a gas station, but also a repair garage that handled used cars.

"This is Ted Saxon, Dick," he said into the phone. "I wrecked my car last night."

"Yeah, I heard about it," Bell said. "But the way I heard it, you're not gonna want it repaired."

"No. I'm not calling about that. Do you have anything I can use for a few days until I find out if the insurance company is going to buy me a new one?"

"Sure, Ted. How far away you going to be traveling?"

"Well, I want something that will get me to Buffalo and back."

"Oh. Then I'd better not send you the clunker I had in mind. I thought maybe you wanted something for just around town. I have a five-year-old Dodge here in pretty good shape. I'll have Lenny leave it in front of your house."

"Fine," Saxon said. "Want me to drive him back?"

"Any kid working for me who couldn't walk two blocks I'd fire," Bell said. "The keys will be over the visor. It'll be there in ten minutes."

Hanging up, Saxon went upstairs to shower, shave, and dress. Before putting on his jacket, he snapped the holster of his thirty-eight Detective Special to his belt just over his right hip. When he took his overcoat from his closet, he noticed a torn spot on the bottom hem. Examining it, he realized that it was a bullet hole and remembered the bullet plucking at the skirt of the coat as he climbed up the ravine bank. Saxon, a one-hat man, didn't have a replacement for the one he had lost. His father had owned several, though, and their head sizes had been the same. He selected one from the closet in what had been Andy Saxon's room.

A black Dodge sedan was parked at the curb when he left the house. The storm had spent itself during the night and it was a clear, still day. The tireless snowplows had cleared the streets before dawn and traffic had melted what little snow the plows had left. The temperature hovered just below freezing.

Saxon took the Thruway to Buffalo, on the theory

that it was more likely to have been plowed free of snow than the less-used Routes Twenty and Five. It had been. He made the twenty-five miles in twenty-five minutes, arriving about eleven o'clock.

He got off at the Bailey Avenue exit and drove straight to the apartment house where Ann Lowry and Sandra Norman lived. In the lobby he threw a casual glance at the card beneath the mail slot for apartment 6-B, then did a double take.

The card read: *Mrs. Helen Fremont.*

Going back outside, Saxon glanced both ways at the apartment houses on either side. He had entered the central of the three buildings on the block, all right.

Back inside, he climbed the stairs and rang the bell of 6-B. A plump blonde woman of about forty-five answered the door.

Saxon took off his hat. "I'm looking for Ann and Sandra."

Carefully she looked him up and down, her expression becoming thoughtful when she noted his red hair. "Who?" she asked with rehearsed puzzlement.

"They live here," he explained.

"Not here," she said. "You must have the wrong apartment."

"Well, they did live here," he amended. "Did you just move in here today?"

"I've lived here for three months, mister. All by myself. I never heard of no Nan and Sandy."

If her stagey manner hadn't already given it away, Saxon would have realized by the woman's pretense of misunderstanding the names that she was a plant. He didn't bother to argue with her. Replacing his hat, he turned and walked away without even saying good-by.

Downstairs the first apartment off the lobby, numbered 1-A, had a sign on its door reading MANAGEMENT. Saxon's ring brought a buxom, hard-featured woman in her mid-fifties to the door.

Removing his hat, he said, "You the manager here, ma'am?"

She nodded. "But there's no vacancies, mister."

"I'm not looking for an apartment. I'm looking for the former tenants of 6-B."

A film seemed to settle over the woman's eyes. "Former tenants? The same woman's lived there six months."

The woman herself had claimed only three, but Saxon didn't offer any correction. He decided on another approach. "Larry Cutter sent me," he said.

Her gaze touched his red hair. "Never heard of him," she said stolidly.

His damned red hair and freckles, he thought. They made him to easy to describe.

It was obvious that Larry Cutter had moved fast to make Saxon's story of the kidnaping seem implausible, in case he reported it to the police. The two girls had been whisked out of sight and a different tenant installed in their place. The manager had been bribed to substantiate the new tenant's story of having occupied the apartment for some time. If the police came around to investigate apartment 6-B on Saxon's complaint, they would come away convinced he had nightmares. In case Saxon himself showed up, the new tenant and the manager had been briefed on his appearance so that they wouldn't fall into a trap.

He could, of course, ring the bells of other apartments on the second floor and probably find tenants who recalled seeing the girls. But he doubted that a pair of call girls would have mingled much with their neighbors, so it was unlikely any would know where they had gone. He decided it would be a waste of time.

The same elderly man, wearing the same dirty shirt, was behind the desk of the Fenimore Hotel. Again he said nothing to Saxon when he walked by.

Upstairs there was no reply to his knock on the door of room 203. Trying the knob, Saxon found the door unlocked. He opened it and walked in.

No one was in the hotel room. Nevertheless, Saxon checked. A curtained alcove served as a closet. Jerking the curtain aside, he stared at two bare coat hangers hooked over the clothing rod. He let the curtain drop in place and turned to the battered dresser. Every drawer was empty. There was no sign of human occupancy anywhere in the room.

Downstairs the elderly man eyed him warily as he approached the desk.

"What happened to the tenant in two, oh, three?" Saxon inquired.

"Mr. Zek? He moved out."

"When and where to?"

"Last night. He didn't leave no forwarding address."

"Did he leave alone?"

"No," the desk clerk said. "Some friend came to help him move."

"You know the friend's name?"

The elderly man shook his head. "Tall, kind of skinny fellow with a mustache."

That would be Spider Wertz, Saxon thought. Larry Cutter had lost no time in removing all witnesses who could possibly corroborate anything at all Saxon told the police. He had done as good a job covering up the blunders of his men as he had in framing Saxon.

Stalking across the lobby to the single phone booth, Saxon flipped open the book to the C section. No Lawrence Cutter was listed.

Of course not, he thought furiously. Big-shot hoods, like call girls, had unlisted phones.

He looked up Tony Spijak's number, dropped coins, and dialed. The bookmaker himself answered the phone.

"This is Ted Saxon, Tony," he growled.

"How are you, boy? How'd you make out yesterday?"

"Lousy," Saxon said coldly. "Do you know Larry Cutter's address?"

After a moment of silence, Spijak said cautiously, "Yeah, I know it. Why?"

"Because I want it."

"I don't like the sound of your voice, old buddy," the bookmaker said. "You sound sore. You going to do something foolish?"

"Listen, Tony," Saxon said. "Are you going to give me the address or not?"

"I guess so," Spijak said reluctantly. "But I hope I don't read about your mutilated body being found in a car trunk. Cutter can play rough."

"Just come up with the address," Saxon snapped.

"Keep your pants on, pal. I have to look it up in my little black book."

A full minute passed before the bookmaker came back to the phone. "Apartment 4-C, the Gawain Apartment Hotel," he said. "That's on North Delaware."

"I know the place," Saxon said. "Thanks."

At the Gawain Apartment Hotel furnished apartments were rented for two hundred and fifty dollars a month and up. The bigger ones, such as Larry Cutter probably had, brought six hundred a month. A self-service elevator took Saxon to the third floor. He walked along deep-napped carpeting until he came to the door numbered 4-C. He unbuttoned his overcoat and suit jacket and loosened the gun in his holster before ringing the bell.

A couple of minutes passed before the door opened six inches and the face of Farmer Benton peered out. His face was just beginning to form an expression of startled recognition when Saxon's shoulder hit the door and smashed it wide-open, driving Benton backward several feet. The man recovered his balance and was reaching for his armpit when Saxon swept out his gun and leveled it.

Paling, the buck-toothed gunman hurriedly raised his arms overhead.

Saxon's glance flickered over the room. It was the front room of the apartment. To the right an archway led to a dining room, and the only other door led to a central hall off which Saxon could see into a bedroom. No one except Farmer Benton was in sight.

Saxon moved forward, dipped his left hand beneath Benton's coat and drew out his forty-five automatic.

"I don't know why I bother," he said. "You can't hit anything with it anyway." He tossed it over on the sofa. "Put your hands down. You look silly holding them over your head that way."

Benton slowly lowered his hands to his sides.

A voice from beyond the dining room called, "Who is it, Farmer?"

Saxon had been about to ask where Larry Cutter was, but this answered his question in advance. Grasping the gunman's shoulder, he spun him toward the dining room and said, "Move." Stiffly Benton walked ahead of him through the dining room and to the door of a kitchen.

A powerfully built man of about forty with close-cropped blond hair sat at the kitchen table in bathrobe and pajamas. He had a square, granite-hard face and pale-gray eyes. Across from him sat a vivid, baby-faced blonde in her early twenties. She was wearing a white housecoat over a nightgown. Though it was now past noon, they seemed to be having breakfast. Both had coffee cups before them and were munching sweet rolls.

Saxon shoved Farmer Benton to one side. The gray-eyed man looked up and his eyes narrowed when he saw Saxon's gun. He threw Benton a bleak glance.

"He caught me off balance," Benton said apologetically. "I wasn't expecting nothing, Larry. Nobody's been gunning for you."

Larry Cutter turned his attention back to Saxon. The girl gazed at Saxon wide-eyed, her jaws still mechanically chewing a piece of sweet roll.

"Know who I am?" Saxon asked Cutter.

Cutter contemplated him for a moment before saying, "From descriptions I've heard, I'd guess you were Ted Saxon."

Saxon shook his head. "I never even heard of him." He crooked his left forefinger. "Come here."

Puzzled, the man warily got to his feet. Rounding the table, he neared to within a couple of feet of Saxon and stopped. Saxon looked him up and down. It wasn't necessary to search the man to determine he was unarmed. The only place he could have concealed a gun was in his robe pockets, and they were perfectly flat. Saxon holstered his gun.

Larry Cutter gazed at him in astonishment. "I don't think I understand this."

"You will," Saxon said.

His right fist lashed out in a short, powerful hook which caught Cutter flush on the jaw and drove him clear across the room against the sink. For a moment the man groped at the edge of the drainboard for support, then his face turned blank and he toppled forward. He hit the floor with a crash and lay still.

Benton gave Saxon a buck-toothed gawk.

"I decided it was my turn for a change," Saxon explained.

Tipping his hat to the blonde, he turned, stalked to the front door, and let himself out.

chapter 19

THERE WAS a Thruway service area half-way between Buffalo and Iroquois, where you could gas up or dine without getting off the Thruway. Saxon stopped there for lunch. It was just 1:30 P.M. when he drove back into Iroquois.

Emily having worked until 7 A.M., he knew she would still be asleep. He drove over to Ben Foley's house and found the former mayor home.

When they were settled with drinks in their hands, Saxon said, "I wouldn't ask you to perjure yourself on the stand, Ben, but if there's merely a police inquiry, would you furnish me an alibi for today?"

The plumb lawyer examined him quizzically. "Depends. Who'd you kill?"

"It would only be a forced entry and battery charge. I socked Larry Cutter on the jaw."

Foley looked pleased. "Did he go down?"

"I knocked him colder than a carp. I suppose it was a childish thing to do, but I suddenly got fed up with him. I thought it was time he got pushed back for the way he's been pushing me, then ran up against a rigged alibi if he tried to do anything about it."

"Sounds like poetic justice," Foley agreed. "I wouldn't mind telling a white lie, so long as it's not under oath. Just what happened?"

Saxon told him of the switch of tenants at the girls' apartment and of the disappearance of Alton Zek from the Fenimore Hotel.

"All at once I saw red," he concluded. "Here this strutting two-bit hood who doesn't even know me first deliberately wrecks my career, then orders me killed.

By instructing his hired hands in what lies to tell and bribing others to give false evidence, he arranges things so that if I even make a complaint, the police will think I'm having hallucinations. I found out where he lived and went over there. Farmer Benton, one of the goons who took me for a ride, answered the door. I disarmed him at gun-point and made him lead me to Cutter. Then I socked Cutter and left."

Foley emitted a low whistle. "Forced entry, assault with a deadly weapon, and battery. I guess you do need an alibi."

"I may not. He may not care to risk having me explain in court why I was mad at him. But just in case his resentment overcomes his judgment, I thought I'd better have one lined up."

"You had Sunday dinner with Alice and me," the lawyer said with a disarming grin. "You know, I lay awake half the night thinking about this thing, Ted. And it doesn't quite make sense to me."

Saxon raised his eyebrows. "I thought we had the whole plot pretty well figured out."

"The reason for the rape frame, sure. But why did Cutter suddenly order you killed? From what you told Arn and me last night, I think we can reconstruct what happened something like this: the informer you talked to at the Fenimore Hotel contacted Sergeant Morrison and told him you were en route to see the Lowry woman. Morrison must in turn have got in touch with Larry Cutter. Cutter sent his two gunmen over to get the girls out of the apartment and to wait for you to walk in. Then, as you described it, there was a long wait for instructions. Your two captors didn't even know what plans for you were until the messenger from Cutter arrived several hours later. Spider Wertz was the messenger's name, wasn't it?"

"Yeah. From the desk clerk's description, I think he was also the man who spirited Alton Zek away from the Fenimore."

Ben Foley rose and began to pace up and down, as if addressing his remarks to a jury. "So we have a picture here of indecision. It looks as if when he first heard from Morrison, Larry Cutter couldn't decide what action to take. As an expedient, he sent his minions to get the girls out of sight and latch onto you until he could make up his mind. The long delay before the decision to dispose of you permanently suggests he may have been discussing strategy with someone—probably Sergeant Morrison. But why did they finally decide you had to be killed?"

"You've got me," Saxon said. "I suppose a man like this Cutter automatically thinks in terms of murder as the solution to problems."

Ben Foley looked doubtful. "Cutter's no dummy. He's proved that by the beautiful way he planned your frame, and also by the way he managed to cover up for his hired hands' bungling of your attempted murder. I don't think he'd order an unnecessary murder. And just what danger were you to him? If he wanted to prevent your pumping Morrison's girl friend for information, all he had to do was to have her drop out of sight."

After considering this, Saxon said, "He knew I had linked Morrison to him, because I asked Alton Zek if he knew of any tie between Morrison and Cutter. That sort of gave it away that I knew Cutter was behind my frame. Maybe he was afraid that since I knew why I had been framed, and by whom, I would be able to find evidence to prove it."

"What evidence was there to find? The supposed rape victim is dead. The only way you could possibly prove that it was a frame would be to get Morrison or Coombs to reverse their stories. But you weren't attempting to see either of them. You were merely visiting a call girl to whom Morrison was in the habit of steering business."

Saxon stared up at the lawyer for a long time before carefully setting down his still half-filled glass. He said slowly, "It does seem that they got awfully excited about my seeing that girl. Maybe that's the answer."

"You mean she may know the details of the frame? Perhaps Morrison confided in her?"

"I just dredged up an even hotter idea than that," Saxon said, rising. "I have to run along, Ben. I want to check something."

The lawyer looked surprised. "What?"

"It's such a far-out idea, you'd think I was crazy if I told you. I want to check it out first. I'll either drop back or give you a ring this evening."

The plump lawyer followed him to the entry hall. "All right, if you want to be mysterious. Here, let me help you with your coat."

Saxon took the Thruway to Erie, Pennsylvania, making the seventy-some miles in an hour and fifteen minutes. He got off at the State Street exit and drove straight to police headquarters.

A middle-aged sergeant was on the desk. Saxon asked if Detective Everett Cass was on duty.

"Try the Detective Bureau squad room," the man said.

Saxon walked down the hall to the Detective Bureau. The door opened just before he reached it and a thin, stooped man with a narrow, long-chinned face stepped out into the hall.

"Detective Cass in there?" Saxon asked.

The man said, "I'm Cass."

Saxon held out his hand. "My name's Ted Saxon. I talked to you on the phone from Iroquois on New Year's Day."

The look of polite inquiry on Everett Cass's face faded. Examining the outthrust hand with contempt, he made no move to grip it. "Yeah, we read about you in yesterday's paper," he said coldly.

Flushing, Saxon let his hand drop to his side. In an equally cold voice he said, "You a cop or a judge, Cass?"

The man stared at him.

"You've declared me guilty on the basis of what you read in the paper, have you? Who took you off the force and put you on the bench?"

The detective frowned. "What's eating you, Saxon?"

"Your attitude. That rape charge was a frame, and the reason I'm here is to get evidence to prove the frame. What right have you to look at me as if I were some kind of dirt when you don't know one damned thing about the case?"

After gazing at him for a while, Cass said, "Okay, you've made your point. What do you want?"

Saxon let himself simmer down. In a more normal tone he said, "I assume that when you picked up Grace Emmet here, she got the usual felony-suspect treatment, didn't she? Prints and mug shots?"

The detective nodded. "Both. After she was killed in that auto accident, Buffalo called us for her prints to identify the body, and we sent them a set."

"I know. I'd like to see her mugs."

"Oh? Why?"

"Is there any rule against it?"

Everett Cass shrugged. "I guess not. Come along to Records."

At the Records desk he asked for the mug shots of Grace Emmet. After a search, the clerk brought over a double photograph showing both front and profile views of the woman.

Saxon looked at it for a long time The blonde poodle cut was the same and there was a similar roundness to the face and a fullness of lips. But aside from that, the pictures bore no resemblance to the woman Sergeant Harry Morrison had left at the Iroquois jail for an hour.

Saxon had never before in his life seen the woman who was pictured.

"Can I get a copy of this?" he asked.

Detective Cass looked at him. "What for?"

"Because this isn't the woman I'm accused of raping," Saxon said. "The Buffalo sergeant who picked up Grace Emmet here rang in a substitute when he got to Iroquois. I told you it was a frame."

Cass stared at the picture, then back at Saxon. "You mean the Buffalo cop passed off somebody else as Grace Emmet at your jail?"

"You're beginning to get the picture. How about a copy of the mugs?"

"Sure," Cass said, his attitude suddenly changing to one of puzzled friendliness. "Why'd he pull a thing like that?"

"To frame me out of my job," Saxon said. "It's too long a story to go into. If you'll get me my copy of the mugs, I'll get going back to Iroquois."

They had to wait twenty minutes for a print to be run off from the negative. Saxon got started back toward Iroquois at 4 P.M.

chapter 20

AT FIVE-FIFTEEN Saxon pulled into Ben Foley's driveway. He rang the bell.

"Hello, Ted," Foley said. "Come on in."

Stepping into the entry hall, Saxon removed his hat but made no move to take off his coat. "What time do you eat on Sunday?" he asked.

Foley looked surprised. "Usually not until about seven. Why? You hungry?"

"I just didn't want to disturb your dinner. Get your coat on and we'll take a run over to Arn Kettle's."

Foley's eyebrows shot up. "You must have found whatever it was you rushed off after."

"I certainly did."

They took Saxon's car.

Joanne Kettle answered the door and told them her husband was in his study.

"That's the only quiet place in the house on Sunday afternoons," she said as she took their coats and hats.

Saxon could see what she meant. The Kettles had two teen-age girls, and apparently both had invited over all their friends. A hi-fi was playing in the front room and a dozen teen-agers were doing some kind of tribal dance in which the partners stood apart from each other, in some cases back to back, and shuffled their feet. It wasn't the twist, with which Saxon was familiar. This seemed to be some new craze.

He followed Ben Foley down the hall to the study. Arnold Kettle opened the door at Foley's knock. The noise from the front room followed them inside but abruptly ceased when Kettle closed the door.

"I had this soundproofed," the district attorney explained. "It was either that or get rid of the kids, and nobody will take the monsters. Cocktail?"

Saxon was too impatient to announce his discovery to be interested in a drink. Foley, as curious as Saxon was impatient, declined too.

"All right," Kettle said, settling back in his chair. "What's the big news?"

Saxon laid the front and profile views of Grace Emmet on the desk. Picking it up, the D.A. first read the printing beneath the pictures, then studied the photographs.

He looked up with a puzzled frown. "This says Grace Emmet."

"I know," Saxon said. "I just got it from the Erie police. They mugged and printed her when they picked her up."

"But it isn't Grace Emmet."

"Sure it is, Arn. The woman you questioned in jail wasn't Grace Emmet."

Kettle stared at him. "Well, I'll be damned," he said slowly. "Who in the devil was she?" He handed the double photograph to Foley. "Look at this."

After examining it, Foley laid it back on the desk. "It doesn't mean anything to me. I never saw the woman in jail."

"That's right," Kettle remembered. "But a number of other people did. Jenny Waite, Doc Harmon, Verne Dowling, who was on the desk. We can blow this frame wide apart. Who was she, Ted?"

"I suspect it was Morrison's friend, Ann Lowry," Saxon said. "That must be why they got so excited when I got on her trail. If I had ever seen her, the whole plot would founder. Not only would the frame be uncovered, but Sergeant Harry Morrison would be arrested for murder."

"Of course," Kettle breathed. "The accident that killed Grace Emmet was rigged. It had to be."

Saxon said, "One thing I couldn't understand about the frame from the beginning was how they set it up so quickly. Morrison didn't know until the previous night that Grace Emmet had been captured in Erie, and didn't know until that day that she had waived extradition and he was supposed to go after her. They only had a matter of hours to make plans and line Coombs up as a witness. Yet it was the sort of thing that would require careful advance planning and detailed rehearsal by the actors for it to work."

"I felt that way, too," Kettle agreed. "That's why at first I couldn't see it as a frame."

"I think it was planned days in advance. Ten days beforehand it was generally known around town that I'd be on duty New Year's Day. How the news got from Iroquois to Larry Cutter, I don't know. Possibly from Adam Bennock, if our new mayor is in cahoots with Cutter. At any rate, I think plans were all made and the actors had been thoroughly rehearsed before the Emmet woman was ever captured. I don't believe she was included in the original plan."

Ben Foley said frowningly, "I don't think I follow that."

"It's simple enough, Ben. I think the original plan was for Ann Lowry to come to Iroquois and get herself arrested on some charge. Possibly soliciting in one of the local taverns, since that was her normal trade and a check with Buffalo would probably show a previous record of such offenses. They would want an offense that was plausible, yet would not get her into too much trouble. After she was jailed, Sergeant Morrison would drop in on some pretext just in time to be a witness when she yelled rape. Coombs, of course, would already be in a cell as a second witness. But when Morrison learned he had to go to Erie after Grace Emmet that night, he had a brilliant idea. There weren't any photographs of the Emmet woman, and her features in the composite drawing vaguely resembled Ann Lowry's. Their hair color and styles were totally different, but that was easily remedied. He had Ann cut her long red hair in the same style Grace Emmet wore hers and dye it blonde. I imagine Ann followed Morrison to Erie in a second car. After picking up his prisoner in Erie, Morrison forced her to change clothes with Ann. You know, I wondered about that at one point New Year's Eve."

"About what?" Kettle asked.

"Her clothes. The woman was wearing a mink coat worth several thousand dollars. Her dress was obviously expensive too, yet it didn't fit. At that time I passed it off by guessing she had lost weight, either as an attempt at disguise or from worry over being a fugitive from justice."

Foley said, "They had to switch clothes, I suppose, in case someone just happened to check with Erie to ask what Grace Emmet was wearing when the transfer took place. They wouldn't want their careful plans to fizzle on a small point like that." Then he rubbed his chin. "But how'd they manage to fool Doc Harmon by getting a positive lab test?"

Both Saxon and Kettle looked at him. Saxon said patiently, "Aren't you being a little naïve, Ben? Ann Lowry was a call girl and Morrison was her procurer. They pulled off on a side road somewhere on the way back from Erie."

The plump lawyer turned red. He changed the subject. "Where was Grace Emmet all the time her substitute was in the local jail and Morrison was at the hospital having coffee and cake?"

Saxon said, "Probably bound and gagged in the trunk of either Morrison's or Ann's car. When they started on again, Morrison must have had the two women switch back to their own clothing so that Grace would be properly dressed when her body was found in his wrecked car. He took the precaution of making her face unrecognizable before pushing the car over the bank."

"A hell of a fine representative of law and order he is!" Foley said with disgust.

The district attorney said, "You should be back in office tomorrow, Ted."

"I'd rather not break it just yet," Saxon said quickly.

Kettle looked at him as if searching for a hole in his head. "Why not?"

"What will it get us? Harry Morrison on a murder charge, providing we can find Ann Lowry to help prove our case. Ann Lowry for conspiracy—again providing we ever find her, which is doubtful. While the guy who planned the frame-up goes free."

Kettle said doubtfully, "Morrison might implicate him, once he realized he was in for the rap."

Saxon shook his head. "His best bet would be to deny the whole thing and make us prove it. Which might be tough if we can't turn up Ann. Even in the face of four disinterested witnesses who saw the prisoner in her cell and are willing to testify that she wasn't the woman in this picture, a smart lawyer might be able to establish reasonable doubt if we can't produce the woman who actually was in the cell. You've both seen what a good lawyer can do in the way of discrediting identification in court. In fact, both of you have probably been guilty of it."

"I know what you mean," Kettle said glumly. "All he'd have to do is get one witness to admit the mug shots resembled the woman in the cell, then stress to the jury that police photography is notoriously poor. We'll have to get hold of Ann Lowry in order to build an unbreakable case."

Saxon said, "Cutter already has her under wraps. She'll probably end up at the bottom of the lake if we have Morrison arrested."

"Hmm," Kettle said. "What do you suggest?"

"Let's quietly ask the Buffalo police to hunt down Ann Lowry. And just sit on what we have until she's safely in custody."

"That sounds sensible," Ben Foley said.

"All right," Kettle agreed. "I'll give the Buffalo police a ring. Temporarily we won't take any other action."

Saxon said, "Even if the Buffalo cops manage to

pick her up, I wish you'd discuss it with me before you move against Morrison, Arn."

The district attorney raised his eyebrows. "All right. But why?"

"Even if Morrison breaks and tries to implicate Cutter, I doubt that we could get Cutter on conspiracy to murder in Grace Emmet's case. He could admit the whole plot to frame me and still deny knowing anything of Morrison's plan to kill his prisoner after she had served her purpose. I suspect we'd end up, at most, with my getting a civil judgment against him for defamation of character. And I want him in the electric chair for conspiracy to murder."

"How are you going to get him there? You just argued down your own case."

"Just so far as Grace Emmet is concerned. You forget that Cutter's guilty of arranging another murder."

When Kettle looked at him blankly, Ben Foley said, "Andy, Arn. It's obvious that Ted's father was murdered on Cutter's order."

Saxon said, "Let's not settle for the small fry. I'd rather hold off until we can build ironclad cases against everybody who had a part in both crimes. And that means not only Larry Cutter, but the gunman who actually killed my dad."

chapter 21

ASIDE FROM BEN FOLEY and the district attorney, Saxon discussed the new evidence he had uncovered with no one except Emily. And he impressed on her the need to keep it to herself.

"Don't even mention it to Julie," he said. "You know what a hotbed of gossip the hospital is. She'll impart it in confidence to one of the other nurses, and in twenty-four hours it will be all over town that we know the woman in jail New Year's Eve wasn't really Grace Emmet. The moment Adam Bennock hears it, Larry Cutter will know. And Ann Lowry will probably end up on the bottom of the lake."

"I won't say a word to anyone," she promised.

This conversation took place at her apartment Sunday evening before she went to work. Saxon was nursing a beer and Emily had his overcoat spread across her lap, mending the bullet hole near the lower hem.

"I don't think it will show unless you look close," she said, taking a final stitch, breaking the thread and smoothing the cloth. "Is it all right?"

Setting his beer down, he rose from his chair and crossed to the sofa to examine the job. She had stitched it from the inside with blue thread of the same shade as the overcoat and he had to search closely to detect the small dimple in the cloth.

"A professional seamstress couldn't have done better," he said, leaning down to kiss her on the nose. "Just for that, I'll stay long enough to drive you to work."

"You'll have to," she said, dimpling. "When you phoned that you were coming over, I canceled my taxi."

When he got home at eleven that night, he looked at the mending job again. And suddenly a thought struck him. After he was in bed, he brooded over the thought for a long time.

Monday morning he phoned his insurance agent to report the car accident. Then he drove downtown to police headquarters. Sam Lennox was on the desk.

"Morning, Chief—uh, Ted," the veteran patrolman said.

"Morning, Sam. Art's still keeping you on regular day duty, is he?"

"Yeah, he ain't changed anything yet." Lennox looked a trifle embarrassed. "I never did have a chance to thank you for what you did last week, Ted."

"What was that?"

"Covering up for me that day I got drunk."

Saxon frowned. "I didn't exactly cover up, Sam. I just didn't press it. I told you it was the last time I'd put up with it."

"You don't have to worry about that," Lennox said quickly. "I'm going on the wagon for good."

Saxon studied the man. The veins in his lined face seemed even redder than they had a week ago and his eyes were red-rimmed and bloodshot. If he were going on the wagon, he hadn't stepped on it yet, for he had all the symptoms of a hang-over from the night before.

"Just stay on it during duty hours and nobody will kick," Saxon said dryly. "It would be too bad if you got bounced now and had to take a twenty-year retirement, when you can make full retirement if you hold out two more years."

The door of the chief's office opened and Art Marks stepped out with a sheet of paper in his hand. He looked a little startled when he saw Saxon.

"How are you, Ted?" he asked with a touch of reserve.

"Fine, Art. Beginning to get the feel of things yet?"

Marks emitted a forced chuckle. "It's not as easy as it looks from the squad room. As a plain cop, you can forget this place when your duty trick ends. Nobody told me the chief had to take tomorrow's problems home with him every night." He handed the sheet to Sam Lennox. "Here's the new duty roster, Sam. Type it up and get it on the bulletin board."

Lennox said, "Sure, Chief. Right away."

Marks regarded Saxon contemplatively for a moment, then seemed to come to a decision. "Want to step in the office a minute, Ted?"

"Sure."

He followed the acting chief into his private office and closed the door as Marks rounded the desk to sink into the swivel chair. Saxon took a seat in front of the desk.

Marks cleared his throat and looked past Saxon's left shoulder. "I hope you aren't sore at me for moving into your job, Ted."

"Why should I be?" Saxon asked with raised brows. "You didn't push me out. That female prisoner did."

With effort Marks looked him in the face. "Was that really a frame, Ted?"

"It was a frame," Saxon assured him.

"I kept thinking it had to be. I've known you since you were a kid, and it just didn't make sense for you to go off your rocker like that. Do you have any idea what was behind it?"

"Uh-huh. But I'm not ready to talk about it just yet."

"Oh." There was a lengthy pause before Marks asked, "Think you'll ever be able to prove you were framed?"

"I think so."

Marks looked relieved. "Then you'll be reinstated as chief, I suppose."

Saxon studied him curiously. "What's the matter, Art? Don't you like the job?"

"I think it's a little beyond me," the acting chief said frankly. "I'm no desk cop. But even if I liked it, I think I'd be leaving in a few months. I've got a better offer."

"Oh?" Saxon said in surprise.

"It's contingent on the race-track deal going through. I've been offered the chief security guard spot at ten thousand a year."

Saxon formed his lips into a silent whistle. "How about your pension?"

"I could take two-thirds. All I'd lose is credit for my last four years' service. And I could build up another twenty-year retirement credit with the racing association by the time I reached sixty-five."

Larry Cutter was going to take no chances at all when he moved in to take over Iroquois, Saxon thought. He wasn't willing to settle for a dumb chief who could be hoodwinked into co-operating with a puppet mayor. He wanted a man in office over whom he had absolute control. Andy Saxon had been murdered, his son framed out of office, now Art Marks was being lured out by the offer of a better job.

He thought about whom that left next in line. The answer was no one. Vic Burns *could* be put in as chief and would be accepted by the general public simply because he was the only remaining lieutenant on the force. But not being an Iroquois native and having only seven years' seniority on the local force—less than many of the patrolmen—no one would make an issue of his being bypassed. It would be simple to bring in some outsider with police experience.

Sergeant Harry Morrison, for instance.

"You've decided to take the offer?" Saxon asked.

"How could I afford to turn it down?"

Saxon felt a little sorry for the man. He hated to disrupt his rosy dream of the future, but it wouldn't have been very kind not to let him know there was a distinct possibility the local race track would never develop. He decided to tell Marks as much of the story as Larry Cutter must be aware Saxon knew anyway.

He said, "You know who's behind this race-track deal, Art?"

"Sure. The Upstate Harness Racing Association."

"That's just a front. It's Larry Cutter's money."

Art Marks looked at him blankly. "The guy who was run out of Saratoga Springs?"

"Uh-huh. He's decided to land here. And he wants his own chief in office. Dad would have tied a can to his tail, so Dad was murdered. I would have done the same thing, so I was framed out of office. You're too honest a cop to suit his fancy, so you're offered a better job in order to induce you to resign. Then they bring in an outsider who's in Cutter's pocket. Get the picture?"

Marks stared at him with his mouth open. "You mean the offer to me wasn't serious?"

"Oh, sure. If the track ever opens, no doubt the job will be waiting for you. But don't count on the track's opening." Saxon rose to his feet. "Sorry to throw cold water on your plans, Art, but that's the way it is. A few of us are making plans to keep Cutter out of Iroquois along with both his legitimate and his illegal operations."

Art Marks rose, too. The expression on his face suggested he was still trying to absorb what Saxon had just told him. After a time he thrust his hand across the desk.

"Any way it goes, I hope you clear yourself and come back as chief, Ted. I won't mind going back to lieutenant, if it's under you. I called you in here mainly to make sure there weren't any hard feelings between us."

Outside in the waiting room, Saxon stopped at the desk again. Sam Lennox rose from his chair and came over to the counter.

Saxon said, "I really came in to talk to you, Sam, but Art sidetracked me before I got to the point."

"What's on your mind?" Lennox asked.

"I want to ask you something about the night Dad was killed."

"Sure. Go ahead."

"When this man in the stolen car pulled over at your siren, you parked just behind him. That right?"

Lennox nodded. "That's S.O.P. You always pull in behind instead of in front."

"I know. Then Dad and Vic got out of the back seat? From opposite sides, I assume."

"No. There was a snowbank on the right side. The chief was sitting on the left, so he got out first and waited for Vic. Vic slid over and got out the same side. They started for the car together and the guy opened up."

"How close were they to him?"

Lennox looked thoughtful. "They were about even with me, where I was sitting in the front seat, when he started shooting. The guy was seated in his front seat, so I'd say the range was no more than ten or twelve feet. He could hardly have missed."

Saxon gazed at him for a long time. "That far? Both of them were that far away when he fired?"

"At least. I told you they were right together. Practically side by side. Why?"

"I just wanted to get the picture straight," Saxon said. "See you around, Sam."

"Sure, Ted. See you."

From police headquarters Saxon drove to the county courthouse. He found District Attorney Kettle in his office. The D.A. waved him to a seat and offered a cigar.

Saxon shook his head. "Have you called Buffalo yet?"

"Last night after you left. No kickback so far."

"I have a feeling they won't turn her up," Saxon said.

"Why not? I didn't explain the real reason we wanted her. I was afraid some cop might let it drop while questioning her friends, and it would get back to Larry Cutter."

"What excuse did you give?"

"I told them you claimed you'd been waylaid and taken for a ride when you visited her apartment. That shouldn't get Cutter excited. He must have expected you to make a complaint."

"It may not get him excited, but it isn't going to make him want the cops to get their hands on her. If she isn't already in Canada or dead, Cutter will probably arrange one or the other."

Kettle frowned. "It was your idea to handle it this way."

"I've had some second thoughts," Saxon said. "We're going to have to throw a block into Cutter fast Arn. I just found out that Art Marks has been offered the job of chief security guard at the new track when it opens."

"So?" the district attorney asked puzzledly.

"Marks will be the third chief boosted out of office by one means or another. It leaves the way wide open for Adam Bennock to recommend some experienced outsider to the Common Council. Such as Sergeant Harry Morrison."

After thinking this over, Kettle said slowly, "Yes, I suppose there's no longer much doubt that our new mayor is in cahoots with Cutter. What are you second thoughts?"

"I'd like to try something that might net us everyone involved, including Larry Cutter, providing it works. Will you be party to a frame?"

"A legal one?" the district attorney asked cautiously.

"I wouldn't ask you to risk disbarment even to nail my father's killers. But it's still a frame."

"Turnabout's fair play, I suppose," Kettle said. "Cutter framed you. Just what do you have in mind?"

Saxon spent fifteen minutes explaining his idea in detail.

chapter 22

IT WAS STILL FAIRLY EARLY in the morning when Saxon got back home, only a little after ten. He placed a phone call to Tony Spijak's home in Buffalo.

He caught the bookmaker just as he was leaving the house. Spijak said, "A minute later you'd have missed me. I'm surprised to hear from you. I thought you'd be full of ice-pick holes by now."

"The only damage at our meeting was to Cutter," Saxon said. "And that wasn't much. Just a bruised jaw."

"You clipped him? You never had any sense, Ted. You better keep one eye over your shoulder for a while."

"He isn't all that tough," Saxon said. "What I'm calling about is that I want to get in touch with the man, and he isn't listed in the phone book. I assume he has an unlisted number."

"Yeah, he has."

"Think you can get it for me?"

"It's in my little black book. Hang on."

A few moments passed, then Spijak said, "Maxwell 7-3204."

Saxon jotted the number in his notebook. Then he asked curiously, "How do you happen to have his number, Tony?"

"Why shouldn't I?"

"Are you tied in with Cutter in some way?"

"Nope," the bookmaker said cheerily.

"It's kind of important for me to know," Saxon said. "I was going to ask another favor of you, but I can't if you're on Cutter's team."

"I'm not on his team. I don't give a hoot in Hades what happens to the guy."

"Then how come you're so friendly with him—you have his unlisted phone number?"

Tony Spijak laughed. "If you have to know, he likes to play the ponies. I'm his bookie."

"Oh," Saxon said, surprised that a man whose fortune had been built on the gambling fever of others had a touch of the fever himself.

"What's the other favor you want?" Spijak asked.

"Later tonight I may want you to phone somebody and deliver a message. It'll be some time before I'll know just when I want the call placed, though. Is there any way I can get in touch with you on short notice?"

"Sure. Marie's my answering service. I'll be moving from spot to spot, but she always knows where to reach me. Buzz her and you'll get a call back from me within ten minutes."

"Fine," Saxon said. "Thanks, Tony."

"Any time, old buddy. Keep looking over your shoulder."

"I will," Saxon said, and hung up.

His next call was to police headquarters.

When Sam Lennox answered, Saxon said, "This is Ted, Sam. Is Vic Burns on duty?"

"No. He comes on the second trick."

"On the desk?"

"Nope. Patrol car."

"Thanks," Saxon said. "I'll try his home."

There was no answer at Burns's bachelor apartment. Saxon phoned Lennox back.

"Vic isn't home, Sam," he said. "Will you ask him to call me this evening? Not before eight, because I'm taking Emily out to dinner and won't be home before then."

"Sure, Ted," Lennox said. "I'll tell him."

Saxon spent a good part of the rest of the morning and the early part of the afternoon practicing a voice imitation. When he got to Emily's apartment at four o'clock, he tried out the imitation on her.

"Who does this sound like?" he asked in a thin, reedy voice.

She burst out laughing. "It's pretty close to Adam Bennock."

"Just pretty close? It has to be better than that. Guess I need some more rehearsing."

With Emily as a critical audience, he did some more practicing, adjusting his voice up and down at her suggestion until she decided he was perfect.

"You could fool his own mother now," she said finally. "What's the purpose of all this?"

"A nasty scheme I've dreamed up. Now I have to know if Bennock plans to be home this evening. Have any ideas as to how I could find out and not make him suspicious?"

"That's simple," Emily said. "He's on my list of patrons for the hospital charity ball next month. I'll phone and ask if I can drop off his ticket and pick up his contribution tonight."

When she phoned, the mayor assured her he would be home all evening.

There was nothing further Saxon could do to put his plan in operation until that evening. He took Emily out to dinner, and about seven-thirty stopped in front of Adam Bennock's house long enough for her to run in with his hospital ball ticket. Then he drove her home and got home himself just before 8 P.M.

At exactly eight the phone rang. It was Vic Burns.

"Can you drop over here, Vic?" Saxon asked.

"Sure, Ted. What's up?"

"I have a little police business for you. Tell you when you get here. Who's riding with you?"

"Nobody. We're short-handed tonight, so I'm riding alone. Will this take long?"

"It might. Better tell the desk to phone here if you're needed."

"Okay," Burns said. "See you in about fifteen minutes."

While waiting, Saxon went upstairs and clipped the holster of his short-barreled Detective Special to his belt beneath the suit coat. He was starting downstairs again when he had another thought. Turning around, he went into the room that had been his father's and took a similar holstered gun from the top bureau drawer. Removing it from the holster, he replaced the holster in the drawer and carried the gun down to the basement. He was still there when the doorbell rang.

Slipping the second gun into a side pocket, he went upstairs to let in Vic Burns.

It hadn't snowed now since the Saturday night storm, and the stocky lieutenant wasn't even wearing rubbers. Saxon took the heavy uniform overcoat and gold-shielded cap and hung them in the entry-hall closet. Then he led the way into the front room and offered Burns a chair.

When the lieutenant was seated, Saxon handed him the mug shots of Grace Emmet.

Burns examined the pictures, read the data printed beneath them, and handed the sheet back. "So that's the gal who caused all your trouble, eh? Where'd you get the mugs?"

"From the Erie police."

Burns examined the expectant look on Saxon's face with puzzlement. "You look as if you thought I should show some kind of reaction."

"I forgot you'd never seen the woman in jail," Saxon said. "She wasn't the woman in these pictures."

"Huh?" Burns said blankly.

"Sergeant Morrison substituted another woman for Grace Emmet, Vic." He explained how the frame had been worked and who was behind it.

When he finished, Burns emitted a low whistle. "Larry Cutter, huh? This is big stuff. What do you plan to do?"

"Frame him back. I'll never be able to prove the frame without getting my hands on Ann Lowry. And even then, I doubt that I could tie Larry Cutter to the frame, or prove any collusion between him and Adam Bennock. But if I can get Cutter, Bennock, Morrison, and the Lowry woman to come together voluntarily for a conference and catch them all together, we'll have evidence of the conspiracy."

Burns raised his eyebrows. "How do you plan to do that?"

"You'll see in a minute. Your part will be to arrange the raiding party. But first let's see if we can set up the meeting."

Going over to the phone, he dialed the unlisted number Tony Spijak had given him. A voice he recognized as that of Farmer Benton answered.

In his high-pitched imitation of Adam Bennock, Saxon said, "Mr. Cutter, please."

A couple of minutes passed before Larry Cutter's voice said, "Hello, Adam."

"How did you know it was I calling?" Saxon asked in the same precise, reedy tone. "I didn't say."

Cutter laughed. "You have a kind of distinctive voice, Adam. The Farmer recognized it. What's up?"

"I think we'd better have an immediate meeting. And I think you had better bring along the sergeant and that girl."

"Why?" Cutter asked, his tone suddenly becoming cautious. "What's happened?"

"I don't care to discuss it over the phone. Can't you guess?"

"Yeah, I guess I can," Cutter said slowly. "But why do you want me to bring along the girl?"

"I thought we'd meet at my skating rink. It's right on the beach and the beach is absolutely deserted at this time of year. It seemed a convenient location in the event we have to make a decision."

After a moment of silence, Cutter said, "You might have a point there. I'll phone Morrison right now. I happen to know he's not on duty. Expect us in, say, an hour and a half. It's almost eighty-thirty now, so we'll be there at ten. In case I can't reach Morrison, what's your number there again?"

"I won't be here," Saxon said. "I'll have to get over to the rink to start the place warming up. The heat has been off since I closed for the winter in November. The phone there is disconnected, so you can't call me there."

"Okay. I'll get hold of Morrison somehow. If I can't, I'll just bring the girl. I *know* where she is. See you at ten."

When he hung up, Vic Burns was gazing at Saxon in astonishment. "Even sitting here watching you, I'd swear that was Adam Bennock talking," he said. "I never knew you were such a good mimic."

"Practice makes perfect," Saxon said with a grin. "And I've been practicing."

Lifting the phone again, he dialed Tony Spijak's number. When Marie answered, he asked if she would get in touch with her husband and have him call back.

"Sure, Ted," she said. "Tony told me to expect your call. You should hear from him in a few minutes."

It wasn't more than five minutes before the bookmaker called back.

Saxon said, "I want you to make a phone call to Adam Bennock down here, Tony. Remember him?"

"Sure. Bennock's Skating Rink. He's the mayor now, isn't he?"

"That's right. It's Miller 2-3101. Place the call person-to-person so that he knows it's coming from Buffalo. Tell him you're phoning to deliver a message from Larry Cutter. Tell him Cutter will be down to see him at the roller rink at ten tonight. You don't know why. You're just relaying a message. Don't phone him until nine-thirty, so that Cutter will already be on his way. I don't want Bennock to be able to reach him if he decides to check back. Got that?"

"Uh-huh. Suppose he asks who I am?"

"Make up a name. Bennock can't know all of Cutter's men. Don't pick someone who actually works for Cutter, because Bennock may be familiar with the voice."

"All right," Spijak said. "I don't suppose you want to tell me what this is all about?"

"When I see you," Saxon said. "I really appreciate all the help you've been, Tony."

"What have I done?" the bookmaker asked. "If you feel indebted, you can spring me for a beer next time you hit Buffalo."

chapter 23

WHEN SAXON HUNG UP, Vic Burns asked, "Now what do you want me to do, Ted?"

"Get a raiding party organized and ready to move in at ten o'clock. I figure about six men can handle it. Are there two patroling in the other car?"

"Uh-huh. Chaney and Mark Ross."

"You and I make four. Tell the desk man to call in two off-duty men to report to headquarters at nine-thirty. Chaney and Ross can pick them up there. Meantime you and I will stake out the entrance to Beach Road to make sure everybody's in the trap before we spring it."

"Okay," Burns said. Rising, he went to the entry-hall closet and started putting on his overcoat.

"You can phone the desk from here," Saxon said.

"I'll use the car radio."

"Oh. Wait until I get my coat and hat and I'll go with you."

"I'll be in the car," Burns said, opening the door and going out.

Saxon went upstairs for his coat and hat. When he got out to the police car, Burns was just hanging up the mike.

"Everything's set," the lieutenant said. "The other car will meet us at the entrance to Beach Road with four men at a quarter of ten. Suppose I pick you up at nine-fifteen?"

Saxon slid into the front seat. "That's only half an hour. I may as well cruise with you until then."

"Suit yourself," Burns said with a shrug.

For fifteen minutes they cruised slowly about town. Finally Burns parked in front of a drugstore.

"I need a pack of cigarettes," he said.

"I'll get them," Saxon said, getting out of the car. "What brand?"

Burns was already out the other side. "I'm not crippled, Ted. Stay in the car." He went into the store.

Saxon pushed the car door closed and walked over to the plate glass window. Inside Burns bought a package of cigarettes at the counter, then headed for the rear of the store. Saxon opened the door and stepped inside.

Burns glanced over his shoulder and his stride slowed. He paused at the magazine rack next to the phone booth and looked over the selection. Then he turned and moved back toward Saxon.

"Guess we'd better get going," he said. "I thought you'd stay in the car to monitor the radio."

"It hasn't been more than thirty seconds," Saxon said mildly.

Back in the car they cruised for another fifteen minutes. Saxon finally said, "We may as well get to the stake-out point."

Burns headed the car west toward Beach Road.

Beach Road was only a block long, starting at Lake Shore Drive and ending at the northernmost of the three municipal beaches. A quarter of a block down the street from its entrance, on the opposite side of the street, was a filling station, now closed for the night and with only a single night light burning inside it. When Burns parked behind it and cut his lights, they were shrouded in darkness, yet they could see headlights approaching from either way along Lake Shore Drive. As there was a street lamp at the intersection of Lake Shore and Beach Road, they would also be able to get a clear look at any cars that turned in there.

Saxon drew his father's Detective Special from his pocket and handed it to Burns butt first.

"Stick this in your overcoat pocket," he suggested.

"Then you won't have to unbutton your overcoat to get at your service revolver."

"What are you going to use?" Burns asked.

"I have mine. That's Dad's old gun."

"Oh." The lieutenant switched on the dome light long enough to break the gun and examine the bases of the shells in the cylinder. All six were filled. Switching off the light again, he flipped the cylinder back in place and shoved the gun in his side pocket.

At a quarter of ten a car came along Lake Shore Drive from the southwest and turned down Beach Road. By the light of the street lamp Saxon got a glimpse of the mayor's lean face.

"There goes Bennock," he said.

Burns said nothing.

Five minutes later Saxon said, "Wonder what's holding up our reinforcements?"

"They'll be along," Burns said.

But the other patrol car still hadn't arrived when, at five minutes to ten, a car came along Lake Shore Drive from the northeast and turned down Beach Road. By the street lamp Saxon could see two men in the front and a woman and man in back.

"There's Cutter and his group," Saxon said. "Where the devil are those other four cops?" He picked up the dash mike and pushed the button. "Car Two to Control."

There was no response from the speaker. Saxon didn't expect any. He could tell by the sound of his own voice in the microphone that he was speaking into a dead instrument.

"That's great!" he said, hanging up the mike. "Your radio's dead. We'll have to move in alone. They'll take off in all directions the minute they find out they've been tricked."

Burns immediately shifted into drive and pulled out into the street. Without lights he drove the quarter block to Beach Road and turned into it. Where the road ended and the beach began there was a large parking area. At its near end was a refreshment stand, all boarded up for the winter. At the far end stood the barnlike roller-rink building. Two cars were parked alongside it.

Burns pulled the squad car behind the concealment of the refreshment stand, cut the engine, and got out. Saxon got out the other door. Quickly he started toward the roller rink with the lieutenant right behind him. Snow covered the lot, but it had partly melted, then frozen to form a hard, crunchy surface. Saxon could hear Burns's footsteps following only a pace behind.

The only windows in the roller rink were high up, and they couldn't see into the building from outside, but lights shone through the high windows. As they neared the door, Saxon drew his gun. At the same moment he felt a gun muzzle press into his back.

"Drop it, Ted," Burns said quietly. "Fast, or I'll shoot."

Saxon stared over his shoulder. "You gone crazy, Vic?"

"Drop it!" Burns snapped.

Saxon let the gun fall to the snow.

"Open the door and walk in," Burns ordered.

Saxon pushed the door open. It led into a short hallway where there was a ticket window, then another door. Saxon went past the ticket window and pushed open the second door. Burns crowded right behind him.

The second door led into a huge, barnlike room. To the left was a refreshment counter, to the right a locker room and skate-rental desk. There were several rows of benches before an iron railing, and beyond the railing was the roller rink proper. It was nearly as cold in the building as it was outside.

Five people standing in front of the refreshment counter turned to stare at them as they came in. They were Adam Bennock, Larry Cutter, Sergeant Harry Morrison, Farmer Benton, and the women who had posed as Grace Emmet on New Year's Eve. All had their coats and hats on against the cold. Morrison and Benton had guns in their hands, but they let the muzzles droop when they saw the gun in Saxon's back.

"Saxon set this thing up," Burns announced generally. "It was him talking to you on the phone, Larry, pretending to be Bennock. I couldn't get to a phone to tip anybody off, because he's been sticking to me like a leech."

"Are there more cops out there?" Cutter asked sharply.

Burns shook his head. "Relax. Saxon left it to me to organize the raiding party, and I forgot to do it. I gimmicked my patrol-car radio so he couldn't check on it."

Morrison and Benton put away their guns. Saxon looked Adam Bennock up and down. "You're in pretty fine company, your Honor. How's it feel to sell out your own town to a bunch of murderers?"

Bennock said nervously, "I'd better get out of here and let you handle this, Cutter. I don't want to be witness to a murder."

"Sure, run along home to bed," Saxon said. "You didn't mind when your partner, Larry Cutter, planned the murder of my father and of Grace Emmet, but you don't want to watch a killing, do you?"

Bennock didn't answer. He merely walked to the door and went out.

Saxon looked at the woman. In place of the mink she had worn New Year's Eve she wore a cheap dyed-rabbit coat. Her hair was still in a poodle cut, but had been dyed back to its natural red.

"How are you, Ann?" he said casually. "Did you know the reason Cutter brought you down here was so you'd be handy in case they decided to kill you?"

Her eyes widened and she looked at Larry Cutter. He paid no attention to her.

Saxon gazed sorrowfully at Vic Burns. "I hoped you weren't in on this, Vic, but I was afraid things would turn out like this. You were the one slated to end up in the chief's job, weren't you? You killed my father."

"What do you mean, you were afraid things would turn out like this?" Burns asked with a frown.

"Farmer Benton put a bullet hole in my overcoat

last Saturday night. While looking at it, I suddenly remembered the hole in your coat the night Dad was killed. The cloth had been singed. You don't get a burn like that from a ten- or twelve-foot range. Sam Lennox held the gun close to your arm when he fired, to be sure only to nick you. I suppose you got poor old Sam to go along by threatening to tell Dad he was drunk on duty, and he would be losing his pension. Sam's wife told me how you had covered for him the day he got drunk on duty."

Burns said in a tone of disbelief, "If you had all that figured out, why'd you walk into this trap with me?"

"Oh, I'm not in a trap," Saxon said. "You are. The state cops bugged this place this afternoon so that they could get all the conversation on tape. There are concealed mikes all over the joint. Adam Bennock didn't go home, incidentally; he walked into the arms of the state cops outside. Their signal to move in was when you and I walked in the front door."

Farmer Benton and Sergeant Morrison both started to reach for their guns. Saxon took two fast steps and smashed Benton in the jaw. As the man went down, Saxon wheeled toward Morrison. Morrison's gun was just appearing when a left hook caught him flush on the chin. At the same moment Saxon's right hand snaked out and plucked the gun from his hand.

A small pop similar to the noise made by a cap pistol sounded, then two more in quick succession. Vic Burns stared down blankly at the gun in his hand, then let it fall to the floor when Saxon covered him with Morrison's gun. Apparently Larry Cutter was unarmed, for he had made no move to draw a gun.

Saxon said, "I took the bullets and powder out, Vic. Those were just percussion caps going off. Everybody over against the wall with hands against it." He gestured with the gun.

Slowly Vic Burns walked over to the wall and leaned his hands against it. Cutter followed suit. Morrison and

Benton didn't hear the order because they were stretched out on the floor unconscious.

"Me, too?" Ann Lowry asked in a small voice.

"You, too," Saxon affirmed.

They were all leaning against the wall when the state police walked in.

Saxon was smiling.

A ROOM TO DIE IN

Cast of Characters

CHAPTER 1

Ann Nelson taught second grade at Mar Vista Elementary School in San Francisco's Sunset district. She lived in a third-story apartment at 6950 Granada Avenue, ten blocks from the ocean.

Arriving home one afternoon early in March, she noticed a large, rather shabby Buick parked at the curb. In the driver's seat sat her mother. Ann's first impulse was to drive quickly on, but Elaine had seen her and was purposefully jabbing out her cigarette.

Ann pulled into the parking area. Elaine got out, gave her girdle a tug, and marched briskly toward her. She was a short, not unattractive woman of forty-three—eighteen years older than Ann—plump as a robin, with a swaggering air of self-reliance. Her hair, tinted an impossible auburn-bronze, was teased into hundreds of tight curls. She wore a blue silk suit with large white buttons, a frivolous white hat, and spike-heeled blue pumps.

Ann was taller, with casual brown hair. By contrast, she looked cool and uncomplicated.

They greeted each other with perfunctory pecks; then Ann led the way upstairs. Elaine talked continuously. ". . . Say what you like about Frisco—sooner I get back south the better. My teeth haven't stopped chattering since I got here, the damn fog *and* cold *and* wind ... Last winter I was in Florida; that's God's country. I had the most *marvelous* house trailer, but I had to sell it. Wouldn't you know! ..."

She stood in the middle of Ann's living room and assessed every object in sight with a panoramic glance.

"Sit down," said Ann. "I'll fix you a drink."

Elaine perched on the edge of a chair. "With a job like yours," she said gaily, "I'm surprised you keep liquor in the house."

Ann smiled grimly at the ancient taunt. "Scotch or bourbon?"

Elaine wasn't sure. Ann showed her the bottles, which she had picked out of a bin at the supermarket. Elaine read the labels and winced. "I'll stick to the Scotch; it's safer."

"I'm not all that particular," said Ann.

"Don't get me wrong," protested Elaine. "I know as well as the next one that a schoolteacher's salary doesn't extend to Jack Daniel."

"I make out well enough."

"I envy you your fortitude. I'd go stark raving mad the first day. The first *hour*."

Ann's smile was becoming brittle. "It's not all that bad. Second-graders are pretty amenable."

"On the rocks with a squeeze of lemon. Or bitters, if you have any."

Ann brought ice from the refrigerator. Elaine jumped to the window and looked out into the street. Then she walked over to the counter that separated living room from kitchen and eased herself up on a stool. With quizzical eyes she watched Ann squeeze lemon juice into her glass. "I thought sure I'd find you married. At least going through the motions."

Ann made no comment. She handed Elaine a glass and poured soda into her own. Elaine drank, ruminated a moment, then turned wry eyes on Ann. "My feelings are hurt. It's been *three years* since I've seen you. And you don't even say you're glad to see me!"

"It's certainly been a long time," said Ann. "What have you been doing?"

"Oh ... taking care of myself. I get the most dismal streaking headaches. Honestly, nothing seems to help. I've spent hundreds of dollars on every kind of treatment imaginable. I've been to three of the best doctors in Los Angeles. They look wise, give me some pills, and send a big bill. But night after night it's the same old story—as if somebody hit me with a hammer. Right here." Elaine rubbed her temples.

"Will you have more Scotch?" asked Ann.

Elaine shook her head. "I think not." She primly pushed her glass aside. "I suppose you never see Larry?"

Larry was Ann's ex-husband, an oboist of some reputation. "I think he's in Cleveland, playing with the Symphony."

Elaine screwed up her face. "The awful sounds that man used to make!"

Ann gave a noncommittal shrug. It was her conviction that Elaine, motivated partly by dislike for Larry, partly by sheer deviltry, had broken up the marriage. Ann could now recall the situation with dispassion, even a kind of humor. Larry had displayed a ridiculous tendency toward breast-beating; she probably had lost very little. Still, at the time ...

Elaine absently reached for her glass. Finding it empty she twitched her mouth in a *moue* of surprise. Ann politely poured more Scotch. "I suppose you're still married to what's-his-name ... Gluck?"

"I see Harvey off and on," Elaine acknowledged. "He wants me to move back to Glendale, but"—she gave her head a sage shake—"uh-uh. I've had it with

Harvey, unless he gives up those vile kennels." She sipped the Scotch. "Do you ever see your father?"

Years of practice had schooled Ann in the most subtle shadings of Elaine's voice. She asked, "What do you want with him?"

"You haven't seen Roland, then?"

"About a year ago I had dinner with him and his wife. Then, let's see—in August?—July or August I happened to be in Sausalito and I ran into him on the waterfront. He and Pearl were separated, and Roland was living out in the country. I don't know what he's doing now."

"You lack all sense of duty toward either Daddy *or* Mommy," declared Elaine.

Ann laughed grimly. "I certainly lack something. If it hadn't been for Grandmother, I'd have lacked a lot more."

Elaine sniffed. "Well, it's not kind to say so, but you must know you were an accident. Heavens, I was just a kid. And after your father and I separated ... well, I had my career to think of."

"Career? What career?"

"I've tried everything."

"That's a fact."

Elaine rose, smoothing the blue suit over her torso. Years ago, at Santa Monica High, she had been a cute redhead, full of mischief, ginger, and zip. She had been cheerleader, jitterbug champion, general hell-raiser. How and why she had ever cast her lot with Roland Nelson—scrounger, iconoclast, bum, and sometime chess player—was a mystery Ann had never resolved.

Elaine had decided to sulk. "I must say I expected you to show a little more *warmth*. You've got every bit of your father's egotism. Here I've come all the way north, groped my way through this miserable city ..."

Ann could think of nothing to say. Above all, she must be careful to avoid the slightest proffer of hospitality. Elaine was deft at converting a halfhearted "look in on us sometime" to three weeks in the master bedroom.

"Well," snapped Elaine, "what is your father's address? I want to talk to him."

"Why?" Ann was surprised enough to ask.

Elaine smiled. "If the truth be known, dear Bobo has come into money, and I want what he owes me—which is plenty."

"How in the world would Daddy come into money?" Ann asked, bewildered.

"Haven't you heard? His wife died."

"No!"

"Yep. What was her name . . . Pearl? Anyway, they were never divorced, and he inherited. As easy as that."

"I'm sorry," said Ann. "I liked her." She gave Elaine a puzzled look. "Where did you learn all this?"

Elaine laughed brightly. "Don't you worry; I keep my ear to the ground. You *do* have his address?"

"When I spoke to him he was living in Inisfail. No telephone. He'd become a hermit of sorts."

"Where in the world is Inisfail?"

"Cross the Golden Gate Bridge, keep on the freeway into San Rafael. Then ask or check a map, because it's off the main highway. Toward the ocean. The address is five sixty Neville Road."

Elaine noted it on the back of an envelope. Ann watched her write. "You're just wasting your time."

"What do you mean?"

"Roland won't be anxious to share his wealth with you. Or me. Or anyone."

Elaine pursed her lips in a thoughtful smile. "I

think he will. In fact, I *know* he will. Or I'll make his life so utterly unbearable—"

"You've got a point," said Ann. "But I don't think it'll work."

"We'll see." Elaine drained her glass. A moment later she left. Ann watched from the window as her mother crossed the sidewalk and got into her car. She looked up before she shut the door, flipping her hand in jaunty farewell. The engine started with a burst of blue exhaust.

The car lurched off, around the corner, and out of sight, and Ann was left in a mood of dark depression.

CHAPTER 2

A month later, out of long habit Ann sent her mother a birthday card, addressing it "828 Pemberton Avenue, North Hollywood." Motivated by a mixture of malice and curiosity, she wrote at the bottom *Any luck with Roland?*

In due course the envelope came back, stamped *No forwarding address*. Ann tossed it into the wastebasket.

A week later she passed her own twenty-sixth birthday. Before she knew it she'd be thirty. Unmarried, a schoolteacher to boot. Unpleasant visions of loneliness began to take shape in her mind. But she mustn't panic; that would be the surest way to frighten off the few eligible bachelors she knew.

What she needed was a change, Ann decided. Scenery, friends, profession, outlook—everything! A completely new life ... Easier said than done, however. She had no talent for frugality; her savings were modest. Enough to take her to Mexico, or perhaps even Europe for a couple of months, since her teacher's salary continued through the summer. But returning to the apartment, to the second grade at Mar Vista—what a dreadful anticlimax! ... Of course, there was always the Peace Corps. Ann gave the idea serious consideration. But was she really that dedicated? Probably not.

About this time she met Jim Llewellyn at a party and fell madly, instantly, in love. There were problems, naturally. Jim was married. His wife was hell on wheels, Jim said; they had occupied separate bedrooms now for two months. The only consideration that deterred him from divorce—and he meant it, he said—was the two kids. There was an affair that persisted until Jim's wife wife telephoned Ann and wistfully asked if they could have a talk. Ann said, "Yes, of course," in a tremulous voice; and presently Dorothy Llewellyn appeared—an obviously decent woman whose basic deficiency seemed to be her looks: she was as homely as a coal scuttle.

Ann was stricken ·with guilt, and felt a fool as well. Not only a fool, but a cheap, vulgar, common little tramp. She assured Dorothy Llewellyn that the episode was at an end. The woman sadly confessed that this was a yearly task, this herding Jim back to the fold. "I know I'm not pretty—but he begged me to marry him, and I did. I've kept my part of the bargain. I suppose in time he'll get over this—this . . ." She hesitated over the word.

"Philandering," said Ann.

Dorothy departed, and Ann's depression became more acute than ever. Jim Llewellyn never called again.

During May, Ann definitely decided not to renew her contact with the Mar Vista Elementary School. Or *almost* definitely.

On the evening of Thursday, May 30, Ann had barely arrived home when her doorbell rang. She answered, to find in the corridor a serious young man in a dark blue uniform. The insigne on his arm read *Deputy Sheriff, County of San Francisco*.

"Miss Nelson?"

Ann nodded.

"May I come in?"

Ann stepped back; the deputy entered. He seemed ill at ease. "I've come on a very unpleasant errand," he said, looking everywhere but at Ann.

"Oh? What have I done?"

"Nothing, far as I know. The fact is, I'm the bearer of bad news."

Ann waited.

"It concerns your father."

"Oh? He's had an . . . accident?"

"Worse than that."

"He's dead?"

"I'm afraid so, Miss Nelson."

Ann went thoughtfully to her kitchen cabinet. "Can I pour you a glass of sherry?"

"No, thanks." He added earnestly, "But by all means have one yourself."

Ann smiled in wan amusement. "I'm not about to collapse. I usually have a glass of sherry when I come home."

The deputy raised his eyebrows a trifle. "I see." It was obvious that he didn't.

Ann returned to the living room. "How did it happen?"

"I don't have the details. I understand he was shot."

Ann stared. "Shot? With a gun?"

"So I understand."

"You mean . . . an accident? Or did somebody murder him?"

The deputy shook his head. "I honestly don't know. If you telephone Inspector Thomas Tarr, at the Marin County sheriff's office, he'll give you the details. The number is Glenwood 4-4010."

Ann went to the telephone. "Are you sure you won't have some sherry?"

"No, thanks." He was no longer solicitous. He said in a formal voice, "If everything's all right, I'll be going."

Ann said, "I'm not cold-blooded; it's simply that my father and I weren't at all close."

"I'll be going along, then."

He departed. Ann dialed GL 4-4010 and asked to speak to Inspector Thomas Tarr. An easy, rather husky, voice said, "Tarr speaking."

"This is Ann Nelson. I've just heard about my father."

Tarr's voice turned grave. "Oh, yes, Miss Nelson. A very bad business."

"What happened?"

"This morning your father was found dead at his home. We haven't completed our investigation yet, but the circumstances seem to indicate suicide."

Ann stared unbelievingly at the telephone receiver. "Did you say *suicide?*"

"Yes."

"I don't believe it."

"There doesn't seem to be any other explanation."

"I still don't believe it. When did it happen?"

Tarr's voice became cautious. "I don't have a definite report. He's been dead several days, at least."

"It's fantastic," said Ann. "Anyone who knew my father . . . it's *incredible.*"

"He never spoke of suicide?"

"Never. Although—"

"He did mention it, then."

"No." Ann's voice took on an edge. "When I last saw him I thought he seemed preoccupied. But this was months ago, and he'd just separated from his wife."

"He was depressed?"

"Not to the point of suicide. He said something about being in a state of 'transition,' but I don't pretend to understand what he meant."

"He seems to have been a strange man."

"He was."

"You're his closest blood relative?"

"His only blood relative. I suppose I'd better do something. Arrangements, and so on."

"I guess it's up to you. We'll also want an official identification."

"Oh, heavens. Must I?"

"I'm afraid so."

"Tonight?"

"No, that's not necessary. In fact, I'm about to go off duty. But if you'll telephone in the morning, or meet me here at, say, ten o'clock?"

"I'll be there at ten."

"I'll see you then."

Ann rose slowly, stood for a moment in the middle of the room, then poured herself another glass of sherry and sat down again. Shock had worn off; something like awe took its place. Suicide! Inspector Tarr had been definite; she would have to accept it, unbelievable as it was.

She thought of her father as she had known him over the years: a man of protean complexity, tall and spare, with assertive aquiline features and a ruff of thick, prematurely gray hair. Many times Ann had tried to puzzle out the rationale by which her father lived. Always she had arrived at the same conclusion. Roland Nelson—stating the case in its crassest form—cared not a thistle for anyone's good opinion but his own, and often was driven to makeshifts that might have demolished the dignity of a man less assured. She thought of their meeting the previous summer. She had chanced upon him in an art shop, where he had just placed a number of "non-objective" sculptures cynically welded from oddments of junk. Obviously squandering his entire capital, he had taken Ann to lunch at the best restaurant in town.

Over coffee he mentioned, as an item of no great importance, that he and his second wife had come to a parting of the ways.

Ann, accustomed to capricious, apparently self-defeating acts on the part of her father, was not surprised. She expressed mild disapproval. "You were lucky to find someone as nice as Pearl."

"No question but she's nice," Roland agreed. "Too nice. And she worked hard. Too hard. I'm not used to having my every wish anticipated. Especially when I might not have been planning to wish in the first place."

"It wouldn't have taken her long to learn. You've only been married six months."

"Going on seven. But it's over with. *Kaput.* I'm now in a state of transition."

"What do you mean by that?"

"I'm making rearrangements. Shifting the internal furniture. It takes a while."

"Where are you living?"

"Out in the country, near Inisfail. I don't see anyone for weeks on end. It's remarkably pleasant."

"I suppose your art makes heavy demands on you," said Ann, in ironic reference to the *avant-garde* "sculptures."

Roland smiled his harsh, uneven smile and called for the check.

A week or so later, at eleven o'clock of a rainy night, Ann's telephone had rung. At the other end was Pearl. She apologized for calling so late in the evening; Ann assured her that she had been reading a book; and they discussed Roland for half an hour. Pearl was melancholy but philosophical. She had married Roland Nelson fully aware of his peculiarities; things simply hadn't worked out. "Roland is a very obstinate man, especially where women are concerned. He won't believe that someone can say no and mean it. It may take him a while to come to his senses."

"You're probably right," said Ann, uncertain of what Pearl was talking about. Only later did she speculate that Pearl might have been referring to someone other than herself. And soon afterward Pearl had died. Ann wondered what had caused Pearl's death.

A new thought occurred to her, a startling, exciting thought that burst in her head like fireworks. Roland had inherited from Pearl; Ann would presumably inherit from Roland—and apparently a great deal of money was involved. Unless Roland had left a will making other provision—which she doubted. How strange! Money, originally the property of a total stranger, would now become hers! Ann could not restrain a thrill of joy at the prospect. She instantly scolded herself for rejoicing in a situation which had cost two lives. And she thought of her mother, who would certainly expect a share of the inheritance. Elaine would first hint, then supplicate, then viciously demand. It might be wise to move to a new address, thought Ann.

Tomorrow was Friday, a workday. She telephoned the principal at Mar Vista, and explained the situation. Mrs. Darlington expressed sympathy and said of course take as much time as necessary.

In the morning Ann dressed in a dark-gray suit and drove across the Golden Gate Bridge, through the hills of Marin County, to San Rafael. Inspector Thomas Tarr proved to be a man in his early thirties, of middle height, unobstrusively muscular, wearing gray flannel slacks, a jacket of nondescript tweed, and a tie selected apparently at random. He had mild blue eyes, an undisciplined crop of sun-bleached blond hair, and an air of informality that Ann found disarming.

He greeted her with gravity. "Sorry I have to bring you here on such an errand, Miss Nelson. Shall we get the worst of it over? Then we can relax?"

He ushered her down a flight of steps, along a brightly lit corridor, into a chilly, white-tiled room. He slid out a drawer; Ann peered gingerly down into austere features, now blurred. She backed away, shuddering. Tears that she had never anticipated came to her eyes.

Inspector Tarr spoke in a sympathetic voice. "This is your father, Miss Nelson?"

Ann gave a jerky nod. "Yes."

They returned upstairs, Ann drying her eyes and feeling a little embarrassed. Tarr was understanding itself. He led the way to a small private office and seated Ann in a worn leather chair. "It's a job I never get used to."

"I don't know what came over me," said Ann with vehemence. "Certainly not grief."

"You weren't close to your father?"

"Not at all."

"I'm glad for your sake, Miss Nelson." Tarr rolled a pencil between his fingers. "Can you think of any reason why your father should have wanted to kill himself?"

Ann shook her head. "It's hard to believe that he did."

"There's not the slightest doubt."

"Couldn't it have been an accident? Or an act of violence?"

"Definitely not. You saw him last when?"

Ann gave Tarr a frowning inspection. Something in his manner suggested that he knew more than he was telling. "Toward the end of last summer. I believe it was August." Ann described the episode, trying to convey its special flavor. Tarr listened with polite interest. When she had finished, he reflected a moment, staring at the pencil. "You don't believe, then, that he was broken up by his separation from his wife?"

"I've just finished telling you he wasn't."

"I'm sorry," said Tarr with patently spurious humility. "I'm sometimes a trifle dense. You know dumb cops."

Ann said with dignity, "I think he liked and respected Pearl, but apparently she got on his nerves. I wouldn't be surprised—"

"If what?"

"If there might not be another woman involved."

Tarr lounged back in his chair. "What makes you say that?"

"Something Pearl told me over the telephone."

"You don't know the identity of this other woman?"

"I wouldn't have the faintest idea. Even if there was another woman."

Tarr looked thoughtful. "According to his landlord, he's been living like a hermit. Going nowhere, seeing no one. Was that the way he usually lived?"

"He had no usual way of life. I think he just decided to live in the country. Since he had no friends, the result would be the life of a recluse."

Tarr reached into a drawer, brought out a wallet, and tossed it on the desk. "This is the extent of what he had in his pockets. I haven't gone through his papers yet."

Ann looked through the wallet. There were four ten-dollar bills, three fives and several ones. One compartment contained a driver's license, a pink automobile-ownership certificate for a 1954 Plymouth, a receipt issued by Apex Van and Storage acknowledging responsibility for "Rugs and household effects as itemized," with an appended schedule.

A second compartment contained several business cards: *Martin Jones, General Contractor,* with a San Rafael address and telephone number; *Hope, Braziel and Taylor, Stockbrokers; The California and Pacific Bank, Mr. Frank Visig, Investment Management Department,* both of San Francisco; and to Ann's astonishment three snapshots of herself, at about the ages of four, ten, and sixteen. On the back of the latest, her current address and telephone number had been scribbed in pencil.

"You were pretty little girl," remarked Tarr, watching her.

"I can't imagine where he got these pictures," Ann exclaimed. "Unless my grandmother sent them to him. Dear old Granny, such an innocent thing." She looked through the other compartments. "Is that all?"

"That's all. Your father apparently belonged to no lodges, clubs, or organizations."

"Small chance of that."

"Didn't he have any close friends?"

"None I know of."

"What about enemies?"

"I wouldn't think so. But I really don't know."

Tarr laid the pencil carefully on his desk. "There's an indication that Mr. Nelson was being blackmailed."

"*What!*"

He clasped his hands, surveying Ann with the blandest of expressions. "I'll explain the circumstances. Your father's landlord, Mr. Jones, found the body. Jones came to collect the rent, which was past due. . . . Otherwise your father might have lain there dead God knows how long. Jones rang the bell and, receiving no answer, looked through a window. He saw your father, obviously dead. He telephoned the sheriff's office, and I came out with another officer.

"The room, a study of sorts, was locked from the inside. The window looked the easiest way in. I broke a pane, cranked open the casement, and crawled through. Mr. Nelson was certainly dead, and I radioed for the coroner.

"While waiting, I made certain observations. As I mentioned, the room was a study. Mr. Nelson had apparently been shot by a thirty-eight revolver which lay on the floor; the laboratory has confirmed this. The door leading from the study into the living room was locked and bolted from the inside. There is no access to the study other than door and window, and both were locked. It has to have been suicide." Tarr glanced at Ann as if to guage her reaction. But Ann said nothing, and he continued. "There's a fireplace in the study. Among the ashes I found a crumpled sheet of paper—I can't show it to you just now; it's at the laboratory. But"—he consulted a notebook "—the message reads like this: 'I've been too easy on you. I want more money. From now on fifteen hundred dollars each and every month.' " Tarr replaced the notebook in his pocket. "It was made up of letters cut from newspaper headlines and pasted to a sheet of cheap paper. There were some fingerprints on the paper, all your father's. The implication is clearly blackmail." He leaned forward. "Do you know of anything in your father's background for which he might have been blackmailed?"

Ann laughed scornfully. "I don't think my father *could* be blackmailed."

"Why do you say that?"

"He had no shame."

"Well, if he'd committed a crime—"

"I don't think so. Because ... well, let me put it this way. My father was a very good chess player. You can't cheat at chess. Or rather, you can, but you don't. Because if you win, you haven't really won; if you lose, you've lost double."

"So?"

"My father wouldn't commit a crime for the same reasons he wouldn't cheat at chess. He was too proud."

"Nice if everyone thought like that," mused Tarr. "Except that I'd be out of a job. I wonder if the crime rate among chess players is below average.... Well, back to your father. You can't conceive a basis on which he could be blackmailed?"

"No."

Tarr flung himself back almost impatiently. "Your father seems to have been ... well, extraordinary. Even peculiar."

Ann felt a prickle of something like anger. Now that Roland Nelson was dead, she felt a need to defend him, or at least to explain the workings of that splendid, reckless, sardonic personality. "It all depends on what you mean by 'extraordinary' and 'peculiar.' He was certainly independent. He never adapted to anyone. You had to adapt to him or go your own way."

Tarr moved in his chair, as if the idea were a personal challenge. He brought out his notebook. "Your mother's name is what?"

"Mrs. Harvey Gluck."

"Where does she live?"

"In North Hollywood. Do you want the address?"

"Please."

Ann looked in her address book. "Eight twenty-eight Pemberton Avenue. I'm not sure she's still there. In fact, I know she's not. I wrote her a card which was returned by the post office."

Tarr made a note. Ann noticed that he wore no ring on his left hand. "How long have your mother and father been divorced?"

"Years and years. When I was two they took off in different directions and left me in Santa Monica with my grandmother. I saw very little of either of them after that."

"Did your father contribute to your support?"

"When he felt in the mood. Not very often."

"Hmm. Now let's see. He married Pearl Maudley ... when?"

Ann studied him a moment. "If you're so sure he committed suicide, why are you asking these questions?"

Tarr grinned as if Ann had made a joke. To her surprise, he tossed the pencil in the air with one hand, caught it with the other. Detectives were supposed to be grim and incisive. Tarr said, "There's still the matter of blackmail."

"He and Pearl were married a year and a half ago. She was a widow with a good deal of money—which may or may not have persuaded him."

"Were you at the wedding?"

"No."

"But you did meet the new Mrs. Nelson?"

"About a month after they were married she invited me to dinner. They had a beautiful apartment in Sausalito. After meeting Pearl, I felt that my father was very lucky."

"But they separated. When she died—since there was no divorce and she had no close relatives—he came into her estate. Is that correct?"

"So far as I know. I wasn't even aware Pearl was dead till my mother told me."

"And how did she find out?"

"I have no idea. It's something I wondered about myself."

Tarr leaned back, his eyes quite blank. "And now you'll inherit."

Ann laughed humorlessly. "If you're suggesting that I killed my father for his money . . ."

"Did you?"

"Would you believe me if I said I did?"

"I'd like to know how you arranged it."

"Just for the record," said Ann with a curling lip, "I did not shoot Roland."

Tarr asked carelessly, "You weren't blackmailing him?"

"I neither murdered nor blackmailed my father."

"What about your mother?"

"What about her?"

"Do you think she might have been blackmailing him?"

"No. I really don't."

Tarr frowned, put the pencil definitely aside. "You saw her when?"

"The early part of March—the first or the second."

"Which would be shortly after your father came into the estate. Did she tell you of her intentions?"

"She wanted money from him. I told her she was wasting her time, but she paid no attention."

"Wouldn't that suggest that she had some sort of hold over him? In other words, blackmail?"

"It seems utterly fantastic."

"You have the same reaction to the idea of suicide," Tarr pointed out, "which is demonstrable fact."

"It hasn't been demonstrated to me yet."

"Very well," said Tarr. He rose. "I'm going out to Inisfail now to check through your father's papers.

You can come along if you like; in fact, I'd appreciate your help. I believe I can also demonstrate the fact of suicide."

"Very well," said Ann with dignity. "I'll help in any way I can."

CHAPTER 3

Tarr conducted Ann to an official car and gallantly assisted her into the front seat. He drove out of town by the Lagunitas Road, which took a preliminary dip to the south, then wound westward over the flanks of Mount Tamalpais, eventually meeting the Pacific at Horseneck Beach.

"I spoke to your father's landlord last night," said Tarr. "He hasn't been too happy. Your father apparently failed to do some work he had promised."

Ann made no comment. The fact was of no interest to her.

Tarr glanced at her sidewise. "What do you do for a living?"

"I'm a schoolteacher."

"You don't look like any of my old school teachers," said Tarr. "I might still be in school."

"You don't look like any of mine, either," said Ann wearily.

After a moment Tarr asked, "Since you're Miss Nelson, you're not married?"

"Not now."

"I guess we all have our problems," said Tarr—a remark over which Ann puzzled for several minutes.

San Rafael fell behind. The road passed through a scrofulous district of housing developments, then

28

veered off across a rolling countryside of vineyards, copses of oak and eucalyptus, and old clapboard farmhouses. The hills became steeper and wilder; fir and pine appeared beside the road.

Ten miles out of San Rafael the road swung across an ancient timber bridge and entered the village of Inisfail. The main street housed the usual assortment of business enterprises; there were three or four tree-shrouded back lanes lined with spacious old dwellings. At the edge of town Tarr turned right, into Neville Road, which after a turn or two led down the middle of a long, wooded valley.

Tarr pointed ahead to a ranch-style house overpowered by four massive oaks. "That's where your father lived."

Ann, suddenly aware of an unpleasant sensation—expectancy? tension? oppression?—had nothing to say.

Tarr turned into the driveway and parked under the largest of the oaks. Ann got out slowly, the unpleasantness becoming ever more acute. She shut out of her mind the recollection of her father's dead face and, forcing herself to relax, looked around her. The house was neat and innocuously modern, quite devoid of character; it might have been a transplant from one of the tracts near San Rafael. The front wall was dark brown board-and-batten, the side walls bisque stucco. There was a shake roof, a used-brick chimney. The garden consisted of a straggling laurel hedge, a patch of lawn, and a line of new rosebushes. In the garage stood a battered green car, evidently the 1954 Plymouth of the ownership certificate.

If Tarr was aware of Ann's state of mind, he ignored it. Matter-of-factly he took several keys from his pocket, sorted through the labels, selected one, unlocked the front door, and stood aside for Ann to enter. She marched into the house, prepared for ... what? The odor of death?

The air was fresh.

Cautiously Ann relaxed. Her apprehensions were overfanciful. This was only a house, a sorry, ordinary house lacking even the echo of her father's personality. She looked around the living room. It seemed a trifle stuffed. The furniture, like the house itself, was impersonal and characterless, except for a large bookcase crammed with obviously expensive books. At one end of the room, beside the bookcase, a door led into another room, evidently the study where Roland Nelson had died. This was on her right hand. To her left were the dining area and kitchen; in the wall opposite, a sliding glass door opened onto the patio; behind her, a hall led to bedrooms.

Ann said tentatively, "It's not the house I'd expect to find my father living in."

"It's a pretty big place for one man," Tarr agreed. "I guess he liked plenty of room." He walked into the study. Ann followed gingerly.

The study was not large, the longest dimension corresponding to the width of the living room. To the left stood a brick fireplace. The single window, opposite the door, consisted of a pair of aluminum casements, each with six panes, each equipped with a detachable screen. One of the panes had been broken and the screen slit: the means Tarr had employed to gain entry. The wall separating the study from the living room was finished in mahogany paneling; the other three walls were textured plasterboard. A large bookcase stood back to back with, Ann judged, the bookcase in the living room, and was equally heavy with luxurious books. The other furnishings were an inexpensive metal desk on which sat a portable typewriter, two chairs, and a pair of card tables against the right hand wall supporting four chessboards with games in various stages of development.

Ann asked, "Where was my father when you found him?"

Tarr indicated the chair behind the desk. "The gun was on the floor."

Ann turned, closed the door, opened it, closed it again. It fitted the frame on all sides snugly. She said grudgingly, "I'll have to admit there's no conceivable way a string or wire or metal strip could have been worked through a crack."

Tarr looked at her quizzically. "Why do you say that?"

"I'm not convinced that Roland killed himself."

Tarr closed the door, shot a heavy bolt into place, and locked the bolt in place with an old-fashioned harness snap. "This is how I discovered the door. I can swear to it, and so can Sergeant Ryan, who was with me. Notice the bolt. It's fixed to the wall, not the door. Unusual, but more secure. This harness snap"—he demonstrated its action—"pins down the bolt. It is impossible for the door to be bolted shut except through the agency of someone standing *inside* this room. Then, for what it's worth, the door bolt was in the lock position—which in itself would very adequately secure the door."

"Then why the extra bolt? Doesn't it seem peculiar?"

"Yes. I suppose you'd say so."

"I thought detectives worried about odd, unexplained details?"

Tarr grinned ruefully. "I have worries enough with simple, ordinary details. The bolt is peculiar, yes. So I asked Martin Jones about it—the landlord. He didn't know it had been installed. This is a new house; your father was its first tenant. Jones was as annoyed as the devil."

"Why would Roland want a bolt on the door in the first place? It seems so strange."

Tarr shrugged. "I've seen a lot stranger things than that. By the way, notice that the hinges are here on the study side, too, and that the pins are as tight as they could be."

Ann went to the fireplace, stooped, peered up the chimney.

"I checked that, too," said Tarr, watching her. "There's a patent metal throat with a slit about four inches wide when the damper is open. The damper was closed, as it is now, with the handle firmly seated in a notch. Outside there's a barbecue grill, with about six inches of brick between." He stamped on the floor. "Under the rug here there's vinyl tile, and then a concrete slab. The walls, the ceiling"—he looked around—"they're ordinary walls: plywood, plasterboard. A ghost could get through without leaving a mark, nothing else. The window?" He motioned to Ann. "Look. When I push down this handle, a hook clamps the sash to the frame. Not even air can seep through the crack. In addition, the screen was securely screwed into place from the inside, as it is now."

"What about the glass? Could a pane have been broken out and replaced?"

Tarr shook his head. "Go outside and check for yourself. All the putty is uniform and several years old."

"Several years? I thought you said this was a new house."

"It's inconsequential. Jones might have had the window on hand. Or it might have been a used window. Or the supplier might have had it in stock for that long. The basic fact is that the putty is old and undisturbed. Until I broke the pane, of course." He turned, considered the chair behind the desk. "Do you know if your father owned a pistol?"

"No, I don't know."

"He was killed by an S and W thirty-eight revolver—little snub-nose job. It was lying on the floor under the fingers of his right hand. Don't tell me he was left-handed."

"No. He was right-handed."

"So it has to be either accident or suicide. The case for accident is weak to the vanishing point. It consists of the fact that there was no farewell note, and that you consider your father temperamentally incapable of suicide. Still, not all suicides leave notes, and every year thousands of people surprise their relatives by bumping themselves off."

"But *why?* Why should he do something so foolish? He had everything to live for."

"The fact that he was living out here like a hermit might indicate . . . well, moodiness, instability."

Ann laughed scornfully. "You never knew Roland, or you wouldn't say that."

"Well, I mentioned the very strong indication of blackmail."

"Perhaps so. Still—"

"You're not convinced?"

"I'm absolutely confused. I don't know what to think." She turned away, went to look at the card tables. Beside each of the four chessboards lay a stack of postcards. Ann glanced at the postmarks. "Amsterdam . . . New York . . . Albuquerque . . . Leningrad. Correspondence chess."

"He did that as a usual thing?"

"As long as I can remember." Ann thought back along the avenue of her life, recalling the infrequent occasions when it intersected with her father's existence. "He was a very talented chess player. Five years ago he placed second in the California Masters Tournament. He might have done better if he had studied more."

Tarr turned to the desk, moved the portable

typewriter to the side. "Let's get to work." He pulled up a chair for Ann; then, seating himself, he tried the drawers on the right side of the desk. They were unlocked, and he opened them one after the other. "Not much here." He returned to the top drawer, brought forth a sheaf of check-sized green papers. "Rent receipts. Eighty-five dollars a month, paid on the"—he looked through them—"well, toward the first of the month. There's one reason why he liked the house. Cheap rent."

Ann examined the receipts. They were standard printed forms, signed in a neat square hand *Martin Jones*. "The first is dated August forth of last year— just after he and Pearl separated." She ran through the forms, one after the other. "The last is dated April fifth. There's no receipt for May."

"Your father didn't pay his rent. If he had, we probably wouldn't have found him for another month. . . . Let's see what else we've got. A bankbook. Account opened March fourth. First deposit: sixty-eight thousand five hundred and twenty-five dollars. Nice chunk of cash. Rather unusual form for an inheritance."

"It might have been a savings-and-loan account," Ann suggested.

"March fourth. That would be six months after his wife died. The court apparently appointed someone else as administrator of the estate. Otherwise he would have had control of the money sooner."

"I wonder why he didn't pay his rent?" Ann mused. "With all that money . . ."

"That's when people get tight-fisted," said Tarr dryly. "Look here now. On March fifth, a withdrawal: twenty thousand dollars."

Ann reflected. "That would be about the time my mother visited me. Somehow she'd heard about his coming into money."

"Would Mr. Nelson be disposed to give your mother twenty thousand dollars?"

"Not likely." Ann laughed. "He was an easy man to irritate—and she's an irritating woman, to say the least."

"How long did they stay together?"

"Off and on, three or four years. It was never a very stable association."

Tarr returned to the bankbook. "Withdrawals on the first of April and the first of May, a thousand dollars on each occasion—which confirms the existence of blackmail. I'll have to inquire at the bank to see how he took the money." He wrote in his notebook. "A blackmailer would naturally want cash."

Ann snorted. Tarr ignored her, studied the bankbook a moment longer, then laid it aside. "What else do we have?" He sorted through the papers. "Nothing of consequence. Three books of blank checks, no stubs. And no checkbook in current use. It wasn't on his person, either. Just a minute." He jumped to his feet and left the room. Three or four minutes later he returned, looking puzzled. "No checkbook in his bedroom or clothes . . . Oh, well. It'll show up. What's that you're looking at?"

"An address book." She handed it to him; Tarr leafed through the pages. "Hmm. Here's a local address: *Alexander Cypriano. Thirty-two Melbourne Drive, Inisfail.*"

"I've heard that name before," said Ann. "Something to do with chess, I think."

Tarr continued to go through the book. "These all might be chess connections. There's not another local address."

"I think you're right. Some of the names I half recognize."

"You're a chess player, too?"

Ann shook her head. "But because of my father

I've always been interested. Once when I was, oh, eight or nine, he took me to a tournament in Long Beach. I was very much impressed." She looked over Tarr's arm into the drawer. "There's the card I sent him last Christmas."

Tarr examined it. " 'Merry Christmas, Ann.' Not what I'd call effusive."

"I never felt effusive."

"But he kept the card. He also carried your photographs. Out of sentiment?"

"I wouldn't know."

"Still, you stand to inherit from him, unless a will providing otherwise turns up."

"Whatever's left after blackmail and taxes."

Tarr considered the bankbook once again. "There should be at least thirty thousand cash. A comfortable sum. There's another twenty thousand represented by that withdrawal. I'd like to know where it went. If your mother got it, she'd naturally claim it was a gift. Unless threats or duress could be proved, that's the last you'd see of it."

"She can keep it, as far as I'm concerned."

"I'll certainly want to talk to your mother."

He opened the bottom drawer. There was nothing in it but a ream of typing paper. On the left side of the desk was a single drawer that proved to be locked. Tarr brought the keys from his pocket and unlocked it. He withdrew a bulging nine-by-twelve-inch manila envelope and opened it. "Stock certificates issued to Roland Nelson." He sheafed through them. "Kaiser Aluminum, a hundred shares. Lockheed, two hundred shares. Pacific Gas and Electric, fifty shares. No, here's more—two hundred and fifty. U.S. Rubber, five hundred. Sinclair Oil, Southern California Edison, International Harvester, DiGiorgio Farms, Lykes Steamship, Koppers, National Cash Register, Fruehauf Trailer ... there must be a hun-

dred thousand dollars here. Good heavens, woman—
you're wealthy!"

Ann tried to keep her voice even. "Unless there's a
will."

Tarr reached into the drawer and brought out a
long white envelope, from which he withdrew two
sheets of typing paper. "Speaking of wills ..." He
read to himself with what seemed maddening delib-
eration. Ann forced herself to sit quietly, though her
heart was pounding and she felt hot, stupid and
greedy.

"Speaking of wills," said Tarr once again, "here it
is. Holographic." He handed the will to Ann. Her
eyes raced across the handwritten sentences:

Inisfail, California
March 11, 1963

LAST WILL AND TESTAMENT

I, Roland Nelson, being of sound mind, good
health, and in a noteworthy state of sobriety, de-
clare this to be my last will and testament. I bequeath all the property of which I die possessed
to my daughter, Ann Nelson, and I nominate
her to be executrix of this will, subject only to
the following exceptions and provisions:

1. She must pay all my legitimate debts;

2. I bequeath my corpse to any medical or ed-
ucational institution which will accept said
corpse. If such institution is not conveniently to
be found, I direct my executrix to dispose of
said corpse by the least costly method consistent
with the laws of California, without the inter-
cession of participation of priest, dervish, witch
doctor, seer, shaman, professional mourner,
monk, fakir, exorcist, musician, incense-swinger,

or other religious practitioner, or cleric of any sect, cult, or superstition whatsoever;

3. She must by all lawful and practical means retain in her personal and immediate possession for a period of at least twenty years from the date of my death that article of medieval Persian craftsmanship presented to me by Pearl Maudley Nelson on or about February 2, 1962;

4. She must pay to Mrs. Harvey J. Gluck of North Hollywood, California, the sum of ten cents per annum, at the demand of the said Mrs. Harvey J. Gluck, for the duration of the life of the said Mrs. Harvey J. Gluck;

5. To each of all and any other claimants upon my estate, I bequeath the sum of one cent.

In witness whereof, on this eleventh day of March, 1963 I subscribe my signature:

ROLAND NELSON

This instrument, having been signed and declared by Roland Nelson to be his last will and testament, in our presence, on this eleventh day of March, 1963, in the presence of Roland Nelson and each other, we subscribe our names as witnesses.

RAYMOND SANTELL, *465 Linden Way, Inisfail, California*
MARTIN JONES, *2632 13th Street, San Rafael, California*

Ann replaced the will on the desk.

Tarr said, "That makes it official. You're rich."

Ann said, in a voice she tried to keep calm, "I'm surprised he went to all this trouble."

"It indicates," said Tarr, in what Ann thought a rather sententious tone, "that he had death on his mind."

Ann dissented. "It indicates that for the first time in his life he had property to worry about. If you'll notice the date—"

"I noticed. March eleventh. Immediately after he took possession of the estate." He sheafed once more through the stock certificates. "What'll you do with all your money?"

"Well, I've got obligations. There's ten cents a year to my mother—"

"If she asks for it."

Ann smiled. "He had fun writing the will."

"What about this article of medieval Persian manufacture?"

Before Ann could answer, the doorbell rang. Tarr jumped up and crossed the living room at a lope. Ann followed more slowly. Tarr opened the door. There stood a tall, slender woman, dramatically beautiful. She wore a dark umber skirt and a black pull-over sweater. She had pale-bronze skin, jet-black hair, clear hazel eyes. She wore no make-up; gold rings in her ears were her only jewelry. Her age was unguessable.

In a car, barely pulled off the road, a plumpish man watched attentively. His face was shrewd, shaped like an owl's; he had a choppy beak of a nose and a fine ruff of gray hair.

The woman seemed surprised at the sight of Tarr. She peered over his shoulder at Ann and spoke in a soft voice. "Is something wrong? We were driving past and noticed the police car. We naturally wondered . . ." Her voice dwindled.

Tarr looked from the man in the car back to the woman. "You're friends of Mr. Nelson's?"

"We live nearby, although we haven't heard from him for months. But seeing the police car . . ." Again her voice trailed off. She half turned, irresolutely, toward the watching man in the car.

"Mr. Nelson is dead," said Tarr.

"He's *dead?*"

"I'm afraid so. May I have your name, please?"

She looked back once more at the man in the car.

"Mr. and Mrs. Cypriano."

"First names?" Tarr brought out his notebook.

"Alexander and Jehane."

"How do you spell that last?"

The woman spelled her name, then turned and called to the man. "Roland is dead."

The man gave no visible sign that he had heard.

Tarr asked, "How long have you known Mr. Nelson?"

"Years. Since . . . well, it's been at least five years."

Ann spoke. "Your husband is a chess master, isn't he?"

"Yes," said Jehane Cypriano quickly, as if Ann had offered her unexpected support. "He's been California champion twice."

From the car Alexander Cypriano suddenly called, "How did he die?"

"Gunshot," said Tarr.

"Who shot him?" Cypriano might have been asking who won a chess game.

"Nothing is definite yet," Tarr called out.

"He probably deserved it."

His wife said, "Don't pay any attention to my husband. He likes to shock people."

Ann asked casually, "Do you know why Mr. Nelson chose this place to live? It seems such a big house for one person."

Jehane examined Ann with careful attention. "I really couldn't say. I haven't spoken to him since shortly after his wife died. He was living in a different house then." She pointed up Neville Road to a gray cottage just visible in a copse of oaks, horse chestnuts, and eucalyptus.

Tarr reflected a moment. "There's some indication that Mr. Nelson committed suicide," he said. "Have you any idea why he might have done such a thing?"

Jehane Cypriano's face became stony. "I find it very hard to believe."

Tarr once more opened his notebook. "May I have your address? I'll probably want to talk to you further."

"Thirty-two Melbourne Drive. The other side of Inisfail, up Blue Hill Road."

Another car turned up into the parking area, a green pickup, with *Martin Jones, Building Contractor*, painted on its side. Jehane Cypriano, at the sight of the pickup, returned to the car. Her husband immediately started the engine, and they drove away.

"That was fast," Tarr remarked. He put away his notebook.

Martin Jones got down from the pickup—a compact, sunburned man with a square face in which things rippled and twitched as if of their own accord. If Jones's temperament were as bellicose as his appearance, thought Ann, it was not surprising that he had clashed with her father. The man favored her with a single glance, which nevertheless seemed to encompass instantly every detail of her face, figure, and clothing.

Tarr said, "This is Miss Nelson, Mr. Nelson's daughter. Martin Jones."

Martin Jones acknowledged the introduction with a curt nod that dismissed her. He gave his entire attention to Tarr. "Find anything?"

"Nothing much. There's one or two points I'd like to clear up. Nelson was in this house how long?"

"Since February or thereabouts. Before that he rented the old family place up the road. I had a chance to sell it; this house was empty, so I moved him in here."

"I see. Another thing. You witnessed his will?"

"I did."

"You didn't mention it when we spoke yesterday."

"You didn't ask."

"Who is Raymond Santell, the other witness?"

"The mailman."

"What were the circumstances?"

"I came out one day to find him talking to a man; in fact, they were having a hell of an argument. I didn't pay any attention, started to load the stuff I had come for. Pretty soon Nelson went into the house, leaving the other man outside. About five minutes later he came back out with a sheet of paper. He called me over and asked if I'd witness a will. I said I would. Then Nelson asked the other man if he'd also witness the will. The man said, 'What's in it?' Nelson grinned and let him read it. The man got even madder than before. He just turned around and stomped to his car and drove off. Just about this time Santell came past on his mail route. Nelson asked him if he'd be a witness, and Santell agreed. So Nelson signed, and Santell and I signed, and that's all there was to it."

"This other man—did you hear his name?"

"No. He was about fifty, I'd say—big soft guy in fancy clothes, with a trick mustache. Drove a black Mercedes sedan."

"You didn't hear what they were quarreling about?"

Jones gave his head a shake. "I couldn't have cared less."

"Anything else out of the ordinary ever happen that you recall?"

The building contractor considered. He said in a grudging voice, "Nothing particular. In fact, nothing. He was a queer customer, a loner—wouldn't have anything to do with anybody. He played chess by mail—an egghead."

Ann decided that she disliked Martin Jones with great intensity. A boor, a cultural barbarian, and probably proud to be both.

Jones looked over Tarr's shoulder into the house. "When do you think you'll be through around here, Inspector?"

Ann said distinctly. "To what date is the rent paid, please?"

Martin Jones seemed surprised to hear her speak; he examined her once again before replying. "If he's dead, his tenancy is over. In any case, he hasn't paid the rent."

"He paid in advance?"

"Usually."

"So he actually owes you a month's rent?"

"That's right."

"It runs to the first of the month?"

"To the fourth."

"I'll see that you're paid. In fact, I'll write you a check right now—and you can come back on the fourth of June."

"In that case, skip the rent. I want to put the place on the market."

Tarr asked in an easy voice, "You're not going to rent any more?"

"No, sir. It's been nothing but a headache. Nelson got the place for peanuts because he said he'd put in a garden." Jones chuckled. "He planted those rose-bushes and that was it." He said it without resentment, as if this sort of conduct were only to be expected from Roland Nelson. Ann's irritation swelled.

The man looked around the yard. "I've got a lot to do around here." He moved off across the lawn to the rose-bushes, examined the leaves, then without a backward glance returned to his pickup and drove away.

Ann glared after him. "There goes my candidate for most unlovable man of the year."

Tarr grinned. "You rubbed him the wrong way."

"I rubbed *him* the wrong way!"

"He's no diplomat, I'll say that." He took Ann's arm and steered her back into the living room. Ann pulled her arm free, stalked to the big bookcase, and pretended an interest in the titles. It presently became genuine.

"These must have been Pearl's books. I can't imagine my father's investing in books like these. They're all special editions."

Tarr pulled one out. *"Phaedra's Dream,* by Richard Maskeyne. Who's he?"

"I've forgotten, if I ever knew." Ann took the book. "Published in nineteen thirty-two. . . . Look at these illustrations. Even in nineteen thirty-two it must have cost ten or fifteen dollars. Now it would cost double that."

Tarr squinted along the shelves. "Not a paperback in the lot." He took the book back from Ann. "Eight inches wide, ten high, an inch and a half thick—a hundred twenty cubic inches. For convenience, let's say it's worth twelve dollars. That's ten cents a cubic inch. This bookcase now. It's just about six feet tall, eight feet wide, something less than a foot deep. . . ." He calculated on the back of an envelope. "Call it thirty-six cubic feet. Substract six cubic feet of air— thirty cubic feet . . ." He looked up with an expression of shock. "That's more than five thousand dollars stacked into just this one case! And there's a case just like it in the study!"

Ann said fatuously. "There's probably more than six cubic feet of air. And many of these books aren't that expensive."

"So knock off a couple of thousand bucks. It's still a lot of money."

But Ann shook her head. "If Roland could have sold them for half of that, they'd be gone." She couldn't believe her good fortune.

They went into the study again. Tarr seated himself behind the desk and picked up the bankbook. "Twenty thousand dollars paid out in a lump, then a thousand a month ... Did your father have any other income?"

Ann shrugged. "Sometimes he'd sell a so-called sculpture or non-objective painting. He had a knack for things like that. He tried writing, but I don't believe he ever got anything published. He'd work at odd jobs if he had to. By his own standards he managed to live pretty well. Meaning he had leisure to do what he wanted."

Tarr studied the bankbook. "This twenty thousand dollars. It's just possible he gave it to your mother."

"Mother and the blackmailer may be the same character," said Ann dryly. "I'm sure you've considered the possibility. If you haven't, you'd better."

"What could she know that would induce your father to pay her off?"

"I can't imagine."

"We'll certainly want to ask your mother some questions." Tarr gathered the papers together, rose. "That's all for today. Next comes the hard part—leg work."

"To find the blackmailer?"

"Yes."

"I still find your suicide theory incredible."

"Well, unless you can demonstrate otherwise ..."

Ann made a slow survey of the study. "I'd love to."

"If only to make me look a chump," Tarr laughed. "Be my guest."

"Ann went to the study bookcase. On the lower shelf, along with two or three large books lying flat, lay a large leather case. She pulled it out and, taking it to the desk, unfastened the snaps and raised the lid.

"What is it?" demanded Tarr.

Ann read the tarnished silver plaque fixed to the red plush interior.

Presented to
PAUL MORPHY
of the United States of America
in appreciation of his magnificent achievements
and to commemorate his notable triumphs
in competition against the most eminent chess masters
of Europe and the world
at the
GRAND MASTERS TOURNAMENT
Geneva Switzerland
August 23, 1858
by the patrons.

Ann lifted out a chessboard. The base was of carved rosewood, two inches thick; the playing surface was an inlay of black opal and mother-of-pearl. At the bottom of the case, fitted into appropriate niches, were the chess-men. Half the pieces were of carved ebony, on gold bases; the other half were of white jade, on silver bases. The black king carried a ruby in his scepter, the white king a diamond.

"That looks like a mighty valuable toy," muttered Tarr. "How long has he had it?"

"I've never seen it before. Perhaps it was Pearl's,

too." Ann suddenly shut the case. "I think I'll take it home."

"Better let me take charge of it," said Tarr. "Technically the estate is still unsettled." Tarr's informality evidently ended where regulations began.

"For all I know," he went on, *"you've* been blackmailing your father."

"Which is why he left me all his property," Ann said tartly.

"You could have worked it anonymously."

"Go ahead and prove it," said Ann; and she marched out to the police car.

They drove back to San Rafael in silence. Ann considered how best to carry out her father's instructions about the disposal of his body; Tarr presumably was sifting the discoveries of the day for hidden conclusions.

Tarr parked in front of the courthouse, in the section reserved for official cars. He switched off the ignition, but made no move to get out. Instead he swung around to face Ann. "There's something I want to say to you."

"What?"

"I'd like to take you to dinner. No ulterior motives. Just a social evening."

Ann was not altogether surprised. Tarr wore no wedding ring; apparently he was not married. Should she?

But just then a blond woman in a red coat alighted from a long tomato-pink hardtop parked two or three spaces away. Tarr saw her and sank low in his seat. The blond woman marched up. She wore heavy eye make-up and her hair was twisted high in the most extreme of styles; Ann thought she looked inexpressibly vulgar. The blonde stooped to look in at Tarr.

"Well, Luther?"

Tarr looked thoughtfully through the windshield, rubbing his nose. He turned to Ann. "Excuse me a minute—" he began in an embarrassed way.

"Excuse *me*," said the blond woman, acidly sarcastic. "I'm *sorry* if I've interrupted something. I thought you might like to know I've been waiting over an hour."

"A case came up. I just couldn't get away . . ."

The woman gave Ann a sugary smile. "Of course. I understand perfectly. I waited to tell you how terrible it is how they overwork you. And also—"

"Look."

"—and also, go to hell." The woman straightened up. "There. That's that." She sauntered to her pink car, backed out into the street, and sped away.

"Unfortunate," mumbled Tarr. "I forgot about her. She's just an acquaintance. Met her in a dark bar."

"Why 'Luther'?" inquired Ann in a silky voice.

"My middle name. I'm Thomas L. Tarr. Born in Tacoma of respectable parents, destined for the ministry, where I still may end up. A hundred seventy-five pounds of sheer decency. I wear white socks, don't smoke or curse, and I put out crumbs for the birds. Now, about us . . ."

Ann let herself out of the car. "I think not, Inspector Tarr. Thank you, anyway."

Tarr heaved a morose sigh. "Oh, well. You're going home?"

"Yes."

"If you hear from your mother, Miss Nelson, please let me know."

"I'll do that."

CHAPTER 4

Ann's apartment, so often her haven of peace, seemed drab when she got home. The sun, hanging low, shone under a reef of cloud, producing a strange watery light, the color of weak tea. Ann felt cross and restless.

She mixed herself a highball and, dropping onto the couch, stared out the window. She almost wished that she had accepted Tarr's invitation. Though, considering the circumstances ... Inspector Thomas Tarr—Ann curled her lip, half in amusement, half in disdain—a blond, affable, woman-chasing lout. Though the affability might be only an act to lull wrongdoers. And suspects. There was no use deceiving herself. Until the whole truth about her father's death was known, she was a suspect—of blackmail, at least.

She ruminated upon the events of the day. Tarr had refused to consider any other possibility than suicide. Ann conceded that his case looked unshakable. It would be gratifying to prove him wrong, or at least to demonstrate that suicide was not the only possibility. She reviewed in her mind the various locked-room situations of which she had read. None of the devices, illusions, or gimmicks seemed applicable. The door and the window could not be manipulated from the outside. Walls, floor, and ceiling were unquestionably sound. No one could possibly have been hidden within the room, to make his exit after Tarr arrived. The fireplace? Ann tried to imagine a long mechanical arm lowered ingeniously down the chimney, thrust across the room, finally to fire a bullet into Roland Nelson's brain. Fantasy ... Here was a startling idea: suppose Inspector Tarr, Sergeant Ryan, and Martin Jones had banded together to kill Roland Nelson! As Sherlock Homes had pointed out, when the possibilities had been eliminated, what remained, no matter how improbable, must be truth. Still—Ann told herself regretfully—suicide looked like the answer. Accident? Of course that was always possible.

Ann put aside her conjectures. They were fruitless as well as tiring. Let Tarr worry about it; he was paid to do so. Except that Tarr was too amiable to worry—in notable contrast to the boorish Martin Jones. Ann wondered if Jones was married. If so, God help his wife! ...

That made her think of her own marriage to the hypersensitive Larry. A mollycoddle. Though, to be sure, her mother had brought out the worst in him. A more virile man—Martin Jones, for instance—would very quickly have set things straight with Elaine.

The thought of Elaine prompted Ann to reach for the telephone. She dialed Operator and put in a call to Mrs. Harvey Gluck, at 828 Pemberton Avenue, North Hollywood. A peevish voice answered the ring: Mrs. Harvey Gluck was no longer residing there. She had taken off several months before, leaving no forwarding address. Ann shifted the call to Mr. Harvey Gluck, in Glendale. The connection was made, the phone rang. No answer.

Ann replaced the receiver and went back to staring out the window. The sun had dropped from sight; the underside of the clouds burned with gold, deepening to persimmon as she watched. The room dimmed. Ann rose, switched on the lights, and mixed another highball.

She thought of dinner, but the idea of cooking ... Now, as a wealthy woman, she could call a cab and dine at any restaurant in the city. If she chose. She did not choose; it seemed a sordid thing to do, so soon after her father's death—the source of her good fortune.

She had never really been fond of her father, aware always of his subsurface streak of cruelty. "Cruelty" was not the word. "Callousness" was better—though it still failed to describe Roland Nelson and his devil-take-the-hindmost attitude. He had asked no quarter from life, and he gave none: a mocking, cynical man, austere, flamboyant, disliked by some women, irresistible to others ...

Jehane Cypriano. Ann's subconscious tossed up the name. She sipped her highball reflectively. Roland Nelson would be attracted. But what of the woman's husband? He looked like a tyrant. What of Jehane herself?

The telephone rang. Telepathy might well have been at work, because, lifting the receiver, Ann was sure that she would hear the voice of Jehane Cypriano.

"Hello?"

"Ann Nelson?" She had been right! "This is Jehane Cypriano. I haven't disturbed you?"

"Not at all. I was actually thinking of you."

"I couldn't speak to you today. It was such a shock to hear of your father's death."

"I was surprised, too, Mrs. Cypriano. Especially with the police convinced that he killed himself."

"It's very strange. Couldn't it have been an accident?"

"Inspector Tarr doesn't seem to think so."

"What do you think?"

"I don't know. I suppose it must have been suicide. Although I still can't believe it."

"I can't either." Jehane went on, rather hurriedly: "I wonder if you'd come to lunch tomorrow? There's so much to talk about, and Alexander is anxious to meet you."

Ann could see no good reason to refuse, although the invitation evidently was prompted by something other than the charm of her personality. She said, "I'd be glad to come."

"Good. Twelve o'clock? The address is thirty-two Melbourne Drive, off Blue Hill Road." She gave directions, which Ann noted on a scratch-pad, and the conversation ended.

Ann went into the kitchen and fried bacon and scrambled eggs. She ate, tried to read; but finding that her mind wandered, she took a hot shower and went to bed.

So many things had happened in the last few days. Her father's death, the sudden change in her economic status. Thomas Tarr, his effortless charm, his floozy girl friend in the red coat. Luther? Lothario was more apt, Ann told herself with a sniff. Then there was the odious Martin Jones: like Tarr physically attractive, even magnetic, with an air of repressed hostility in his every word and gesture . . . She fell asleep.

At nine thirty the next morning Inspector Tarr telephoned. His voice was unembarrassed, official. "I can't locate your mother, Miss Nelson. She's no longer at the address you gave me—hasn't been there for months. Can you think of anyone who would know her whereabouts?"

"Only her husband. He lives in Glendale. He's a dog trainer."

"I'll try him."

"Incidentally," said Ann, "Mrs. Cypriano telephoned me last night."

"So?"

"She invited me to lunch."

"You're going?"

"Certainly. Why not?"

"No reason. But call me afterwards, will you? I like to know what's going on. I'll be at the office until three or four."

Ann agreed in a voice of dignified reserve.

She dressed with more than usual care, in a white sleeveless frock and light gray coat, and at eleven o'clock set forth. The day was sparkling and sunny with a cool breeze carrying the salt scent of the Pacific across the city. Ann could not help but feel an elevation of spirits.

She drove up Lincoln Way to Nineteenth Avenue, and turned left into Park Presidio Boulevard, which took her through Golden Gate Park, the Richmond district, the gloomy forest of the Presidio, to the Golden Gate Bridge. Sailboats wandered the bay; San Francisco's skyline rose as crisp and white as sugar icing. To the left the baby-blue ocean spread smooth and glistening, except for occasional cat's-paws. The hills of Marin County loomed ahead; the freeway swung through a tunnel and slanted down past Sausalito to San Rafael, where Ann turned west out Lagunitas Road, toward Inisfail.

Just before the timber bridge, she came to Blue Hill Road, a narrow lane twisting up a hillside heavy with fir trees. Melbourne Drive presently veered off to the left, a lane even narrower than

Blue Hill Road. At the mailbox marked *Cypriano,*
Ann turned up a steep driveway and came out on a
graveled parking area below a tall house that was all
dark wood and glass.

She was early; it was ten minutes to twelve.

Jehane Cypriano appeared on the terrace, waving.
She descended a flight of wide stone steps. The
woman wore black slacks and a short-sleeved beige
sweater; her step was as light as a young girl's.

She seemed genuinely glad to see Ann. "Did you
have any trouble finding the place?"

"I followed your directions, and here I am."

"Apparently I got them right for once." Jehane
led Ann up to the terrace, which was being extended
or repaired. There was a fine view to the west over
low hills and forested valleys, with a gray glint of
ocean far beyond. They entered the house through a
heavy oak door that opened into a vast high-ceil-
inged room built on three levels. The lowest served as
a lobby or foyer, the second as a living room, the
highest as a dining room. To the right, a half-octago-
nal rotunda running from floor to ceiling overlooked
the view. The walls were paneled in dark wood,
with details, accents, draperies, and rugs in uncon-
ventional colors: black, scarlet, mauve, purple,
black-green.

A decidedly unorthodox house, Ann thought, like
no other house she had ever seen.

She said as much, and Jehane seemed pleased. "I
designed it myself for friends. Then two years ago
we bought it from them."

"I think that's wonderful."

Jehane said, "When I was a girl I decided to become an architect. Ridiculous, of course; there simply aren't women architects. But I went to architec-
tural school, anyway. This is what resulted."

"It's a beautiful house," said Ann. "It has a romantic, impractical feel to it. Like a fairy castle. I don't mean," she hastened to say, "that it's *really* impractical."

"Oh, it probably is," said Jehane. "I'm both romantic *and* impractical. And who wants a house that's dull? As a matter of fact, I designed it for Rex and Pearl Orr. They were romantic and impractical, too. When Rex died, Pearl wouldn't live here.... But let me mix you a daiquiri. I've just acquired an electric ice crusher, and I love to play with it."

Ann accompanied her to the top level and into the kitchen.

"Alexander's still in bed," said Jehane. "Sometimes he gets up before dawn; sometimes he stays in bed till two. He'll never get up at a normal hour."

There was the faint far sound of a toilet flushing. Jehane listened, her head at a birdlike tilt. "Alexander is greeting the day. He'll be with us shortly."

Fresh lime juice, Cointreau, rum went into a shaker with a cup of shaved ice; Jehane gave the mixture a stir and served it in champagne goblets.

"Mmm," said Ann. "I suddenly see that I need an ice shaver."

"It's a foolishly expensive gadget. But it's fun."

"Foolish things are always the most fun," said Ann.

"Yes, the things in my life I regret the most are the wise things I've done."

After a moment Ann asked, "Is Pearl Orr the Pearl my father married?"

Jehane nodded. "Roland met her here after Pearl sold us the house. I think she half regretted it—the sale, I mean, not meeting Roland, because she was always visiting."

"I don't blame her. If I ever build a house, you can be the architect."

Jehane shook her head with a wistful laugh. "I

don't think I'll ever design another. You can run into the most frightful headaches. There's zoning, building inspectors, headstrong contractors—heaven knows what-all."

Ann had a sudden flash. "Was Martin Jones the contractor?"

"Yes. How did you know?"

"I didn't. But when he appeared yesterday, you left, and rather abruptly."

Jehane nodded slowly. "He built it."

"He's a surly brute. Good-looking, though."

Jehane made a neutral gesture. "He goes on the defensive with attractive women."

"He's not married, then."

Jehane shook her head. "There's quite a story about Martin. He was engaged to an Inisfail girl—I think they'd been sweethearts in high school. He built the house—where your father lived—for himself and his bride. Last winter the girl flew to San Diego to visit her sister, met a naval officer, and married him the next day. The sister gave Martin the news over the telephone. So now he loathes all women. The prettier they are, the more he hates them."

"I should be flattered," said Ann. "He practically snarled at me. Although, in a way, I can see his point."

Jehane shrugged. "Alexander can't bear the sight of him."

She raised her head. Ann, listening, heard languid footsteps. "Here comes Alexander now," said Jehane.

Alexander entered the room: a heavy-shouldered man with thin flanks, short legs, and a magnificent head. His hair was thick, dove-gray; his eyes were large, coal-black; his mouth and chin were small and almost dainty; his nose was a small parrot's beak. He wore dark-gray slacks and a shirt of maroon gabardine.

Not a man to inspire instant liking, thought Ann.

She wondered why Jehane had chosen to marry him. Still, the match was no odder than dozens of others she had wondered about.

Jehane performed a casual introduction, then said, "I suppose I should see to lunch."

Alexander nodded. "Exellent idea. It seems to be a beautiful day. Miss Nelson and I will go out on the deck." His voice was slow, deep, resonant. "Perhaps you'd bring us another round of drinks?"

He ushered Ann through a pair of French windows out to the second-level deck, which was cantilevered alarmingly over a rocky gulch.

"It's quite safe," said Alexander in a patronizing tone. "But I agree the first sensation is apt to be unpleasant." He drew up a chair for Ann and settled himself in another. The view was even more dramatic than from the terrace, with the full bulk of Mount Tamalpais looming to the south. "Do you smoke?" asked Alexander.

"No. I'm one of those annoying people who never acquired the habit."

Alexander fitted a cigarette into a long holder. "Jehane doesn't smoke, either. I must say that I derive an ignoble satisfaction whenever a nonsmoker contracts lung cancer.... I don't believe your father smoked."

"Not to my knowledge."

"A peculiar man. In many ways an admirable man. I suppose I knew him as well as anyone alive."

"I've heard him speak of you. In fact, five years ago, at the California Masters Tournament—"

"Alexander chuckled, a deep, fruity croak. "I remember that very well. Your father made one mistake—one little mistake. It was enough. Six moves later he resigned. It was a hard game, though to be honest I never found myself in serious difficulty."

Alexander Cypriano seemed more than complacent about it, thought Ann—pompous, actually.

"I've given up active competition. In fact, I rarely play these days. Chess is a young man's game, though of course a number of older men have played superbly. Steinitz . . . Lasker. Do you play?"

The suddenness of the question caught Ann off guard. She stammered, "I know the moves . . . Yes, I play. I've played a few games with my father. Naturally, he won."

"Your father was highly competent—a beautiful tactician. He played a resourceful end game, where most chess players are weak. My own end game is entirely adequate, and my opening game considerably sounder than your father's. When we played I usually won." He peered quizzically at Ann. "I hope I don't seem vain?"

"Not at all," said Ann, thinking, "Oh, don't you?"

"It's often hard to distinguish vanity from simple honesty. We played many an interesting game, your father and I. He exhibited three characteristic faults. First, he refused to study the openings, and often embroiled himself in a line which a more profound student would have avoided. Second, he loved the spectacular combination—he loved to astound, with lunges and sorties, gallops along the edge of a precipice, cryptic exposures of his king . . . These tactics were likely to outrage and confuse players of average ability, but a man maintaining the grand view could usually refute such gasconades. His third fault was his most singular and, I would say, paradoxical. I don't know how to describe it. Indecisiveness? At a crucial moment, when it came to administering the *coup de grâce,* he would falter, veer, temporize. Inexplicable. He lost otherwise brilliant games that way. By the way, my appraisal of your father's character does not include soft-heartedness. I would judge Roland to have been a man quite cold and merciless where his own interests were involved."

Ann, listening with only half an ear, and wondering why she had been invited to lunch, was brought back to reality by the hardening of Alexander Cypriano's tone.

Rising, the man went to the edge of the deck. He took a long, slow sip of the daiquiri that Jehane had quietly brought out on a tray, and looked out toward the far gray sheen of the Pacific.

Ann could think of nothing to say.

Alexander swung around. "But enough of chess. To a nonplayer nothing is less interesting than the maunderings of an addict."

"I'm interested in anything that concerns my father," Ann said politely. "We weren't close, but now that he's dead . . ." She laughed in embarrassment. "I wouldn't call it remorse, because the neglect came from him, not from me—but, after all, he did name me his heir."

"He wrote a will, then? Odd."

"I'd say he had some motive other than simple practicality."

Alexander seemed fascinated. "What makes you say that?"

For no well-defined reason, Ann chose to be evasive. At least until she found out why she had been invited to lunch. "Oh, the general tone of the will. Certain of the bequests."

Alexander inquired humorously, "I take it I wasn't mentioned?"

"No."

He pursed his lips.

"I understand you knew my father's second wife well," said Ann after a moment's silence.

"Yes, she was an old friend of Jehane's. An impulsive, warmhearted woman."

"That was my feeling, although I met her only once. I never did hear how she died, except that it was in an automobile accident."

"To be blunt, she was driving while drunk and simply ran off Blue Hill Road."

"Oh." Ann hesitated. "This may sound like an extraordinary thing to ask. Is there any possibility that my father could have been involved?"

"Involved?" Alexander shot her a sharp glance.

Ann said steadily, "I mean, could he have been responsible?"

"I wouldn't put it past him," said Alexander in a brand-new tone. "But I don't see how he could have managed it. In the first place, Roland could have had no idea she was here. Why should the question occur to you?"

Ann reflected before answering. Alexander Cypriano clearly regarded Roland Nelson as a rival—possibly in more fields than chess—and seemed to relish any information to Roland's discredit, even after death. But if information was to be obtained from the man, Ann would have to prime the pump. So, reluctantly, she said, "The truth is, there's some indication he was being blackmailed."

"Blackmailed!" Alexander seemed genuinely startled. He turned as Jehane came out on the deck to announce that lunch was ready. "Miss Nelson tells me that Roland was being blackmailed."

Jehane became as still as death. "That's hard to believe. What could he possibly be blackmailed for?"

"In everyone's life there are dark corners," said Alexander. "There are one or two things about myself I wouldn't care to have known. And don't forget, Jehane, we haven't seen him for months. Anything might have happened."

"It's silly," said his wife abruptly. "Let's have lunch."

She had set a table on the cool eastern terrace with a green checked cloth and dishes decorated with green leaves. In the center stood a tall green bottle of white wine.

Lunch was as Ann had expected: simple, ample, beautifully prepared. There was a salad of shrimp and avocado; then breasts of chicken in individual iron skillets, swimming in a piquant buttery sauce, served with small round potatoes and watercress; then a dessert of strawberries and vanilla ice cream, with black coffee. Conversation was desultory. Alexander apologized for the clutter of lumber, saw-horses, reinforcing steel, and mesh. He pointed out the extent of the new terrace and indicated where repair work was being done on the foundations. "If the contractor had done his work properly to begin with," he grumbled, "all this mess could have been avoided."

The reference, thought Ann, was to Martin Jones.

After a second cup of coffee, Alexander slapped his hands down on the table. "Since you're interested in chess, I imagine you'd like to see my den."

Ann looked at Jehane, but her face was completely neutral.

"I'm a collector or sorts," Alexander went on. "I believe I have the finest set of chess portraits and photographs extant."

Ann dutifully rose to her feet. Alexander nodded to Jehane. "A delightful lunch, my dear." Ann hastily echoed the compliment. Jehane smiled faintly.

Cypriano led Ann to his den, a large room at the rear of the house. One wall was covered with drawings and photographs of chess masters of every age and physiognomy. There was Sammy Reshevsky perched on a high stool; the autocratic Dr. Tarrasch; Paul Morphy, leaning languidly over a piano like a young Oscar Wilde. Capablanca, suave and handsome, faced a brooding Alekhine; Frank Marshall stared off to the left; Tchigorin peered to the right. There were dozens of group photographs, including a two-foot by three-foot enlargement depicting the participants of the great AVRO tournament, with autographs beside each figure.

Alexander darted back and forth, pointing, declaiming, expounding. When he had exhausted the wall photographs he drew out albums of classic scores, autographed by the competitors. In a cabinet he drew Ann's attention to a group of trophies, cups, and medals. "My own small achievements." Another case held books in six languages.

"Can you read all these?" asked Ann in wonder.

"Oh, yes. I know German, Russian, French, Italian, Spanish, Portuguese, Greek, Serbian, a smattering of Chinese and Arabic—I'm what is known as a natural linguist."

Ann expressed her astonishment, and Alexander nodded his massive head in satisfaction. "I was trained for the bar," he said, "but I have always preferred music and chess. Hence"—he held out his hands—"you see me. No pauper, but by no means a rich man. Luckily I have a shrewd head for investments."

He took Ann to another cabinet, which contained perhaps two dozen sets of chessmen, in a number of styles and materials: wood, stone, ivory, pewter. "Notice these," said Alexander, "... Hindu, of the eighteenth century. And these, once used by Ruy Lopez himself. Which reminds me ... yes, before I forget. Among your father's effects you will find a handsome set of chessmen, which at one time belonged to me, and which he acquired under circumstances that are irrelevant. I'd like the set back, and I think he would want it so. I am naturally willing to pay any reasonable valuation you put upon it."

Could this have been the motive for the invitation? Why else? Ann temporized. "I'm still not in charge of my father's estate."

Alexander's eyes snapped. "Your father's possession of the set came as the result of a joke."

"I really can't make any commitments," said Ann. "I'm sorry, Mr. Cypriano, but so far I haven't had time to think."

He marched to the door of the den; the conducted tour was over. He had clearly hoped for an affirmative answer. After escorting Ann to the living room, he excused himself, saying that he had an important letter to write.

Even with Cypriano gone, the atmosphere seemed to cool in a manner Ann could not define. Jehane was as charming as ever, but the cordiality was gone. Ann presently took her leave. Her hostess accompanied her to the car and expressed the hope that Ann would call again. Ann proposed that she should telephone her on the next occasion she found herself in San Francisco. Jehane Cypriano promised to do so, and Ann drove away.

In her rearview mirror she caught a final glimpse of the woman looking after her: wistful, fragile, lonely.

Ann drove down the hill slowly. At Lagunitas Road she paused, then turned left, and drove into Inisfail—for no active reason other than her vague conviction that there was still much to be learned about her father's death.

She turned down Neville Road. Her father's nearest neighbor, she noticed, occupied an old white stucco house in a flourishing vineyard. The name on the mailbox was Savarini. Ann weighed the idea of calling at the house. But what could they tell her? That her father was unfriendly, eccentric, a recluse, without visible means of support, of dubious morals and questionable politics? All this she already knew.

A car was parked at her father's house. Drawing near, she saw the car to be the green pickup. Martin Jones was in the front yard, guiding a roto-tiller. Ann turned into the driveway. Jones ignored her. He started the clattering machine on another furrow.

Ann compressed her lips. "Mr. Jones!" she shouted.

Martin Jones glanced at her sharply and frowned. He turned off the engine. The silence was sudden and vehement.

"Well? What am I doing that's so damned humorous?"

Ann shrugged. "You're working so intently."

"What of it?"

"There's no need to shout, now that the roto-tiller is off."

Martin Jones blinked. "If you've come to clear out the house, I'll let you in."

"The thought hadn't entered my mind."

"As I told you yesterday, the sooner the better."

"I'll have to wait till I have the authority to act."

"When will that be?"

"I don't know. Monday I'll see an attorney, who I believe must have the will probated. I don't know very much about these things."

The builder grunted and reached to start the engine. "I've just had lunch with the Cyprianos," said Ann.

"So?" His hand hovered and stopped.

"Since I was in the neighborhood I thought I'd drop by."

He studied her for a moment, the muscles in his flat cheeks twitching. "You knew the Cyprianos before?

"I never saw them until yesterday."

"What do you think of them?" His voice was sardonic.

Ann considered. "I don't know. They're rather puzzling people."

Martin Jones nodded, smiling grimly. Once again he made as if to start the engine.

Ann blurted, "I just can't believe my father killed himself."

This time he leaned on the handle. "What do you think happened to him, Miss Nelson?"

"I don't know. But he just wasn't the suicide type. He had too much vitality."

Jones gave a snort of amusement. "In certain ways, no doubt about it."

"What do you mean by that?"

"This garden, for instance. Nelson gave me to understand he was the world's most enthusiastic gardener. He painted a glowing picture—flowers, shrubs, hedges, lawn—"

"Oh, come now," Ann scoffed. "I *know* he never promised you all that."

Jones had the grace to grin. "Well, he said he'd put me in a nice garden. Otherwise I'd have charged him more rent. I could get a hundred and thirty for this house any day of the week."

"How did you happen to rent to him in the first place?"

"He was working for me and needed a place to live. I let him have the old shack down the road."

"He was working for *you?*"

"That's correct."

"As what?"

"A laborer. Union scale is over three bucks an hour. Last year I didn't do that well myself." He straightened up, looked impatiently at the roto-tiller. "Roland Nelson wasn't much of a laborer, ei-

ther. He didn't have enough 'vitality.' I fired him."
He reached for the starting cord to the motor, gave
it a yank. The motor caught. The blades spun, kicking up a shower of dirt. Ann jumped back, yelping
her indignation. But Martin Jones either did not
hear or did not care to listen.

Ann drove back to San Rafael seething. What an
abominable man! Small wonder that his fiancée had
chosen to marry someone else at the first opportunity.

CHAPTER 5

In San Rafael, Ann pulled into a service station, phoned the sheriff's office, and asked for Inspector Tarr.

Tarr's easy voice issued from the receiver, and into Ann's mind came an image of his solid body lounging at his desk. "This is Ann Nelson. You asked me to call you."

"Oh, yes." Tarr's voice took on a different note. "Where are you now?"

Ann told him.

"Wait," said Tarr. "I'll be right there. And if you're not too proud, I'll buy you a cup of coffee."

Ann returned to her car, of half a mind to drive off. Tarr's assurance was almost as infuriating as Martin Jones's boorishness. But she waited. Tarr, after all, was investigating her father's death.

Tarr took his time. Five minutes became ten, then fifteen. Ann's mood darkened. Then the detective appeared in the police car, parked, and jumped to the ground in great haste. "Sorry, Miss Nelson, but I got hung up on the telephone. Some tiresome old idiot. There's an ice-cream parlor just around the corner. Faster to walk than drive."

Ann got out of her car, ignoring Tarr's proffered hand.

At the ice-cream parlor she refused his suggestion of a fudge sundae, primly accepting a cup of coffee. To her surprise, he brought out his notebook. "I haven't been able to locate your mother. Harvey Gluck says that to the best of his knowledge she's still in the San Francisco area. States that he hasn't communicated with her for several months. He's indefinite as to the exact date. I'm wondering if you can give me any leads."

Ann shook her head. "I wouldn't have the slightest idea."

"Does she have any relatives? Sisters, brothers, cousins, aunts, uncles?"

"She has a married brother in New Jersey and some cousins in North Carolina, but I don't know their addresses."

"What are their names?"

Ann told him, and Tarr made note of them.

"What about friends? Any old cronies, school chums?"

Ann considered. "I don't believe she had any special friends, although I don't know for sure. Harvey Gluck would know better than I."

"He gave me some names, but they weren't any help. One of these people said that she'd been talking about Honolulu."

"That should be easy enough to check," said Ann. "She hated airplanes. Try the Matson line."

Tarr made a note. "Anything else?"

Ann said, "She was a hypochondriac. Belonged to the Disease-of-the-Month Club, as my father expressed it. She took her astrology pretty seriously, too."

"That doesn't help much." Tarr tucked the notebook back in his pocket. "How did your lunch with the Cyprianos come off?"

"Very nicely. I think it was at Mr. Cypriano's instigation. He wants that chess set—it belonged to him at one time, he says. He's got practically a chess museum in his house."

"Are you going to let him have it?"

"I suppose so. It means nothing to me. Incidentally, Martin Jones wants me to clear out my father's belongings."

"He'll have to wait. I'm not finished there yet. When did you see him?"

"Today. I drove out past the house."

Tarr frowned. "If I were you . . ." He paused.

"Well?"

"I don't want to alarm you, but remember that a crime has been committed. A blackmailer usually isn't vicious or violent, but there are exceptions."

The warning startled her. Roland Nelson's death, though puzzling, had seemed remote. The thought that she might personally be in danger was shocking. Ann said in a subdued voice, "I guess I've led too sheltered a life. Do you mean that I shouldn't ever go anywhere alone?"

"If you'd like round-the-clock police protection, I could arrange it." At Ann's look, Tarr said with a grin, "I've got a two-week vacation coming up. I can't think of any way I'd rather spend it."

Ann finished her coffee. "For a minute I thought you were serious."

"I am," said Tarr, still grinning. He was an *idiot*.

"I'm going home," snapped Ann. "Martin Jones is a misogynist, and I'm a misanthropist."

"You two would make a good pair!"

Ann rose, marched to the counter, put down fifteen cents, and departed.

On her way back to San Francisco, Ann wondered why Tarr's gibe had got under her skin. It was so really inane. She wasn't a misanthropist; she merely disliked males who leaped at every female they met.

'(An accusation that certainly could not be leveled against Martin Jones!)

Shortly after she got home her telephone rang. Ann told herself that it would surely be Tarr to apologize for his rudeness, but the voice was a stranger's.

"Miss Nelson?"

"Yes?"

"Glad to find you home. My name is Edgar Maudley—I'm the late Pearl Maudley Nelson's cousin. I wonder if you'd allow me to call on you. It's a matter of some importance."

"Now?"

"Now preferably, but of course if it's not convenient—"

"Now is as good a time as any, Mr. Maudley."

"Wonderful. I'll be there very shortly. From your address I gather that you live in the Sunset district?"

"Yes. Ten blocks from the beach."

"It shouldn't take me more than half an hour."

Twenty-six minutes later Edgar Maudley arrived. He was a large, pale, luxurious man smelling of lilac hair tonic. His hair was silver gray, precisely brushed; he had a regimental mustache, and altogether he looked urbane and distinguished.

Ann took his Tyrolean hat and burberry and indicated a chair. Edgar Maudley settled himself decorously.

"I was on the point of making a pot of tea," said Ann. "If you'd care to join me?"

"Oh, excellent," said Edgar Maudley. "This is so very kind of you."

"It'll be a minute or two. The water's only just starting to boil."

Edgar Maudley cleared his throat. "You no doubt are wondering why I'm calling on you."

"I suppose you're curious, or resentful. After all,

I'm inheriting money which was originally Pearl's, and that makes me something of an interloper."

"Not at all. You are who you are—an obviously intelligent young lady. The circumstances that occasion our meeting certainly are not your responsibility."

"Excuse me," said Ann. "I'll make the tea." She went into the kitchenette and busied herself with teapot, teacups, tray, and gingersnaps.

Edgar Maudley continued to speak in his cautious voice. "First of all, let me offer condolences on the loss of your father. I do so with complete sincerity. Although I *am* given to understand that you and your father were not close."

Ann set the tray on the counter and returned to the living room. "Who gave you to understand this?"

Maudley touched his mustache. "I hardly remember ... Village gossip, most probably. Your father, you must be aware, was something of a *rara avis*. He kept to himself—lived alone, saw no one."

"Antisocial, but not disreputable. Did you know him yourself?"

Maudley nodded briskly. "I met him several times. I won't conceal from you that I tried to dissuade Pearl from the marriage. She was my only cousin; and, like Pearl, I have neither sister nor brother. She took the place of a sister, and I was very, very fond of her. I considered your father much too ... undisciplined—shall we say?—for a woman who was actually inexperienced and naïve."

Ann wordlessly poured tea. Edgar Maudley took a lump of sugar and a slice of lemon, but refused the gingersnaps. He sipped, then sat back in his chair. "Perhaps I should tell you something about the Maudleys, Miss Nelson. My grandfather arrived in San Francisco in 1880 and began to publish *The Oriental Magazine*—now a rare and valuable collector's item. He had two sons, my father and Pearl's father. In 1911 the brothers organized The Pandora Press, specializing in the printing of limited editions. I may say that they prospered—both became quite wealthy. When Grandfather died they sold *The Oriental*, which merged with another magazine and lost its identity. My father died in 1940, Pearl's father five years later. Neither I nor Pearl cared to continue The Pandora Press, and we sold it.

"This is beside the point. What is to the point is that, when her father died, Pearl naturally came into possession of a large number of heirlooms: books, pictures, ivories, vases, *objets d'art*. Many quite valuable."

Ann said, "I was admiring my father's books yesterday."

Edgar Maudley winced. "Legally, of course, they were his—just as, now, legally they're yours."

Ann nodded in profound understanding. "And you want me to turn these objects over to you, Mr. Maudley. Is that it?"

Maudley said in a vibrant voice, "Many of these articles have a deep, a very deep, sentimental value to me. Certain of the books are unique—not of vast monetary value, but I'd loathe seeing them pass into the hands of unappreciative strangers, or end up in a secondhand bookshop."

"That's quite natural."

"When your father came into the estate, I paid him a visit and made more or less the same representations to him that I am making to you. He was by no means so sympathetic."

"Do you drive a Mercedes?"

"Yes. How did you find out, may I ask?"

Ann smiled. "Village gossip, most probably."

Her visitor forced himself to smile. "In any event, you now understand the motive behind my visit."

"Not really. Just what is it you expect me to do?"

Maudley raised his eyebrows. "I thought I had made myself clear, Miss Nelson. By a set of unusual circumstances, you are now in possession of a number of Maudley heirlooms."

"Including some sort of medieval Persian artwork?"

"Including a set of medieval Persian miniatures in a carved ivory box inlaid with cinnabar, jade, lapis lazuli and turquoise."

"You want me to give you this item?"

"I would willingly offer you money. But I find it hard to put a price on sentimental attachment."

"My father, I understand, refused this request."

"He was not sympathetic at all."

Ann pictured Edgar Maudley expostulating with her father, and smiled. Edgar Maudley sipped his tea. Ann said, "I'd like to be fair about this. I can't give you any definite answer now, Mr. Maudley; I'm not yet in a legal position to say 'yes' or 'no.' Anyway, while I don't want to be mercenary, these are apparently articles of considerable value. There doesn't seem to be any reason why I should make a gift to you of what will be legally my property."

Maudley grew slightly excited. "But, Miss Nelson, the value of certain of these objects—the Persian miniatures, for instance—is incalculable. The miniatures have been in the family since 1729, when Sir Robert Maudley was in Persia."

"Unfortunately, it is precisely the miniatures which I can't let out of my possession."

He seemed puzzled. "How so?"

"Weren't you at my father's house when he wrote his will? I understand that he asked you to witness it."

"Oh, that. I refused to read the will. I knew it contained abuse or disparagement, and I did not care to be insulted. To be quite frank, I never thought that your father, as a sensible man, would go through with a document composed in such haste and high feeling."

"He was angry, then?"

"I would say so. My requests appeared to irritate him."

"I can't tell you anything more until I've looked through the estate. Certain of the books I'm sure you can have—those dealing with metaphysics and Oriental religion, for example, which don't interest me in the least."

Maudley worked his lips in and out, as if he wanted to say more but was not sure of the wisdom of saying it.

"Let me pour you another cup of tea," said Ann. She felt a little sorry for him.

"Thank you." He spoke with the stiffish dignity of a man unfairly put upon.

"You knew my father well?" Ann asked.

"No. We had little in common."

"You must be acquainted with the Cyprianos."

"Oh, yes. Pearl thought very highly of Mrs. Cypriano. Girlhood chums, and all that. She sold the Cyprianos her lovely home for far less than its market value. I assume they've kept up the payments." His tone was half-questioning

"'Payments'?"

"Yes. They paid eight thousand dollars down, I believe, and Pearl held a mortgage on the balance, about thirty thousand dollars. The mortgage would naturally be part of your father's estate."

"I haven't come across it," said Ann. "Thank you for mentioning it."

Edgar Maudley set his cup down and rose. "Well, I must be on my way. I'm sure we can work something out, Miss Nelson. If I were a rich man—which, alas! I am not—I could offer you what these articles are worth to me, although, as I mentioned, sentiment and value are incommensurable."

"Exactly. So if any of these articles should change hands between us, we'll have them appraised by an impartial authority. Will that be satisfactory?"

Maudley took his hat and coat. With a bitter smile he said, "I did think you might feel the slightest bit uncomfortable, coming into possession of an estate which, strictly speaking, was your father's by sheer chance."

"Not at all," said Ann. "It's the nicest thing that ever happened to me. And since my father had to die in any event, I'm glad I was able to profit by it."

Maudley seemed horrified. "I must say . . . Well, it might be wise not to count your chickadees before they're hatched."

"What do you mean, Mr. Maudley?" Ann asked very distinctly.

The man seemed sorry he had spoken. "Nothing, nothing at all," he said hurriedly. "Thank you for the tea, Miss Nelson. Here is my card, in case you should change your mind." He departed. Ann looked down at the card with a curling lip and tossed it aside.

She took the teacups to the sink thoughtfully. Edgar Maudley's visit had solved one mystery—the identity of the man who had quarreled with her father—but it posed another: Where was the mortgage to the Cypriano house? It had not been in the desk, where her father had kept his other important papers.

On Sunday Ann notified Mrs. Darlington that various contingencies associated with her father's death would prevent her coming to work until the middle of the week. The principal pointed out with just a trace of tartness that since school ended Friday, she might just as well not bother. Ann said that if she possibly could, she would return to work, although perhaps it did seem a trifle foolish under the circumstances.

On Monday she engaged an attorney to deal with her father's will. She also learned that cadavers were no longer in short supply at medical schools. Only after diligent effort was she able to place the body of Roland Nelson with the Stanford Medical Center.

On Tuesday she signed various affidavits, obtained the signature of the Marin County Coroner, and arranged transportation of her father's remains from San Rafael to Palo Alto.

On Wednesday Ann returned to work at Mar Vista, and on Wednesday evening Edgar Maudley telephoned. He was anxious to learn what she had decided regarding the matters they had discussed. Ann informed him that she had not been able to give the situation much thought.

When might he expect her to reach a decision? Probably not before Saturday, Ann replied. This was the earliest she would find it convenient to sort through her father's effects.

Edgar Maudley said that he would make sure to be on hand, if only to assist her. Ann thanked him for offering to help, but said it might be better if she conducted the preliminary survey by herself.

Maudley made a noncommittal sound, something like "Hmm, hmm, hmm." Then he said, "Incidentally—and I ask from sheerest curiosity; it's no affair of mine—have you learned what disposition your father made of the Cypriano mortgage?"

"Not yet. I haven't checked things over."

"They didn't mention the mortgage?"

"No."

"Strange."

"There's probably some simple explanation," said Ann. "We spoke of other things." The thought came to her, was this the reason she had been invited to lunch? It seemed unlikely, since the mortgage had not been mentioned. No, it was about the chess set.

Maudley said, "I'll give you some advice, young woman, and that is—be businesslike! Your father and the Cyprianos were friends of long standing, but don't let this fact influence you. I hope you don't regard me as meddlesome."

"Of course not." Edgar Maudley apparently did not like the Cyprianos. Ann wondered why. Because Jehane had introduced Pearl to Roland Nelson?

Maudley reiterated his intention of helping Ann on the coming Saturday. Ann discouraged him once more, and the conversation ended.

On Thursday morning, as she left for work, she found a letter from her mother in the mailbox. It was postmarked Tuesday, June 4, at Beverly Hills. She read it, went back to the apartment, telephoned the Marin County Sheriff's Office, and asked for Inspector Tarr.

Tarr was not in, reported the clerk. Was there any message?

"No, said Ann, it was important that she speak to Inspector Tarr personally. She had important information for him.

The clerk promptly gave her a number at which she might be able to reach Inspector Tarr.

Ann dialed, listened. Finally, a woman answered. "Hello?"

Ann spoke in the most formal of voices. "May I speak to Inspector Tarr, please?"

"Who's calling?" The woman's voice sounded suspicious.

"Ann Nelson."

"Ann Nelson." The woman repeated the name, then grudgingly said, "I'll see if I can wake him up."

Several minutes passed. Ann, with not too much time to spare, was on the point of hanging up when Tarr's drowsy voice sounded in her ear. "Tarr speaking."

"This is Ann Nelson," said Ann, very distinctly. "I'm sorry to disturb you—"

"Not at all," said Tarr. "It's my day off. I'm at my sister's house."

"Oh?" Ann tried to convey in a single word the extent of her utter indifference—and disbelief. "I've received a letter from my mother. I thought you ought to know about it as soon as possible."

"A letter from your mother?" Tarr seemed puzzled and surprised. "Where was it mailed?"

"The envelope is postmarked June fourth, Beverly Hills."

"Can you read it to me?"

Ann read aloud:

My dear Baby Ann:

I have just learned of your good fortune, so to speak, from a person who chooses to remain nameless. For some reason he is interested in you, and also me, and is asking delicate questions about the past.

As you know, I am having a tough time financially as well as being miserably unhappy with my health. I have a practically continuous migraine which gives me *hell!* I hope that you will see fit to share your good fortune with me. I really need a stroke of good luck to boost my flagging spirits.

I plan to come north in a day or so and will drop in on you. I am sure we can come to a mutually happy settlement.

As ever,
ELAINE

After a short silence Tarr asked, "Do you recognize the handwriting, Miss Nelson?"

"It's definitely her handwriting."

"Is the letter itself dated?"

"No. She just starts writing."

"What does she mean: 'delicate questions about the past'?"

"I don't know."

" 'A person who chooses to remain nameless'—now who could that be?"

"I haven't the faintest idea."

"What about that 'Baby Ann' bit? Is that her usual salutation?"

"It might be almost anything: 'Snooks,' 'Toodles,' 'Brat.' I've seen 'You miserable little ingrate!' on occasion. Anything, in fact, but 'Dear Ann.' "

"This is certainly interesting. She doesn't give her address?"

"No."

"What about the envelope?"

"There's no return address. She just printed 'Ann Nelson, sixty-nine fifty Granada Avenue, San Francisco.' That's all."

Tarr grunted. "Do you consider that typical?"

"With my mother nothing is typical."

"I see ... I definitely want to examine that letter. How about tomorrow?"

"Tomorrow is the last day of school; I should be finished about noon. If it's convenient I'll drop by your office. There's another matter about which I'd like your advice."

"So long as it's not about investing your money. I'm the lousiest businessman in the country."

Ann did not deign to notice Tarr's facetiousness. "It will probably be close to one by the time I arrive."

"I'll expect you at one."

On Thursday evening the attorney called to notify her that the Marin County Probate Court had issued a decree naming her executrix of her father's estate, and that he had also obtained an authorization for the transfer of the various stocks and securities to her name. There were papers to be signed, an inventory of possessions, assets, and obligations compiled and filed with the court. Ann made an appointment to meet him Monday.

On the following morning Ann took unusual pains with her clothes: this might well be the last day of her teaching career. Also, she'd be leaving directly for San Rafael. In spite of her disapproval of Tarr, his hypocrisy, and his lechery, she refused to appear at a disadvantage compared with his vulgar girl friends. Vulgar and *blowsy*. Perhaps he liked them vulgar and blowsy. So what? Tarr's tastes were of no concern to her.

Ann dressed in a spanking dark-blue and white frock with white accessories, an outfit in which she knew she looked her best.

The morning passed quickly; the pupils trooped home at noon. There was still a certain amount of paper work, which Ann would take care of next week. She bade her fellow faculty members goodbye and drove across the bridge to San Rafael.

Tarr greeted her with formality. She saw by his glance that the pains she had taken with her clothes had not been wasted. He escorted her into the little office where he had taken her before, and without preamble said, "Let's see the letter."

Ann produced the envelope. Tarr scrutinized it closely. Then, extracting the letter, he pored over it for several minutes. Ann finally became restless. "Well?"

Tarr said in a colorless voice, "May I keep it?"

"If you like."

He laid the letter with exaggerated care upon the corner of his desk, leaned back, and inspected Ann quizzically. "What do *you* make of the letter?"

"What do I make of it? It's self-explanatory, isn't it? Elaine wants in."

"Her prospects, I gather, aren't very good."

Ann smiled faintly. "I'm required to pay her ten cents a year."

Tarr nodded. "Don't you find it odd that your mother asks for money, but doesn't let you know where to find her?"

"No. According to the letter, she plans to see me in a few days. There'll be a flaming quarrel; she'll have hysterics; and she'll run from the apartment screaming that I'll never set eyes on her again." She watched Tarr, daring him to show disapprobation. But Tarr only lurched erect in his seat, once more examined the letter, again put it to one side. "I'll send this to the lab. There's one or two points ..." His voice trailed off. Then he said, "I've found out where your mother stayed during her visit last March: the Idyllwild Motel on Highway 101. She arrived about seven o'clock and checked out the next morning. The proprietor's wife remembers her because your mother priced a house trailer they had for sale, talked about Florida and Honolulu, and burned three cigarette holes in a pillowcase. Another item of information, a rather peculiar one: your father's nearest neighbors live about two hundred yards up the road."

"The Savarinis."

"Correct. Simple people, but far from stupid. About two weeks ago they heard three shots. I wish they could be sure of the date, but they can't. The time was midnight; they remember that well enough. They had just turned off the TV and gone to bed."

"Three shots?"

"Three shots, at intervals of about a minute, from the direction of Roland Nelson's house. Mr. Savarini is positive that the sounds were shots, not backfires or firecrackers. He owns six guns and he insists that he knows what a shot sounds like. That's about all there is to it. Three shots at midnight, about the time your father died."

"Odd."

"I agree. Damned odd. Roland Nelson was killed by a single shot; we found a single empty cartridge. It's possible that someone totally unconnected with the case may have fired the shots, but it's certainly stretching coincidence. . . . Well, it'll all come out in the wash." He stretched lazily. "You mentioned a problem."

"I suppose it's a problem. Pearl's cousin called on me the other night, a man named Edgar Maudley. Incidentally, he's the man who refused to witness my father's will." Tarr looked at her reproachfully. "I suppose I should have telephoned you."

"For two days Sergeant Ryan has been out flagging down black Mercedes sedans, interviewing dealers, checking registrations—"

Ann said hurriedly, "He wanted some of Pearl's belongings, which he described as heirlooms. He tried to get them from my father, but had no luck." She described Edgar Maudley's visit in detail.

"Edgar Maudley has a grievance," mused Tarr. "If it hadn't been for Pearl's marriage to Roland, he probably would have inherited. Still, that's not your problem. . . . By the way, what *is* your problem?"

"It's something Maudley mentioned. In addition to cash and securities, Pearl also seems to have held a first mortgage on the Cyprianos' house—presumably part of my father's estate. Where is the mortgage? It wasn't among his papers. Did Roland have a safe-deposit box? If so, why didn't he keep his stock certificates there?"

Tarr shook his head. "He rented no safe-deposit box in any local bank. I've checked. In addition, I've accounted for all his keys, so it's unlikely he had a box elsewhere. But in the matter of the mortgage, why not ask the Cyprianos?"

"I could, I suppose—but, oh, I don't know—it would make me seem avaricious."

Tarr pushed the telephone toward her. "Call right now. Maybe they paid the mortgage off. Better find out one way or another."

Ann reluctantly dialed the Cyprianos' number. Jehane answered. Ann said brightly, "I've been trying to find the mortgage my father held on your house, and it's in none of the obvious places. Inspector Tarr suggested I call you."

Jehane was silent for several seconds. Then she asked, "Where are you now?"

"In San Rafael."

"Can you drop up to the house? Alexander is in San Francisco today with the car; otherwise I'd come into San Rafael."

"I'll be glad to stop by."

"I'll see you shortly, then."

Ann hung up the telephone. "She wants to talk to me."

Tarr rose to his feet. "I'll come along for the ride."

"I don't think she expects you," said Ann dubiously.

"I'm investigating a crime. It makes no difference whether she expects me or not."

Ann shrugged. "By the way, what crime are you referring to?"

"Blackmail, naturally," said Tarr. "Has there been another?"

"I wish I knew."

"Don't wish too hard," said Tarr. "You might wish yourself out of a hundred thousand dollars."

Ann started to ask his meaning, then, like a coward, decided not to.

They went out into the street. "Let's go in my car," said Ann. "It looks so brutal, arriving in that police car."

Tarr laughed.

All the way out to Inisfail, Ann pondered the implications of Tarr's remark, and arrived at 32 Melbourne Drive in a rather unsettled state of mind. It *would* be terrible to lose a hundred thousand dollars now that she'd become accustomed to the idea of inheriting leisure and independence. . . .

She drove up the steep driveway to the parking area. As before, Jehane came out on the terrace; seeing Tarr, she swiftly became gracious.

Ann steeled herself for what could only be a difficult interview. At Jehane's invitation she entered the house, with Tarr, apparently oblivious to atmospheres, coming behind.

Jehane took them up the stairs to the middle level and arranged chairs. She asked, rather uncertainly, if they'd like a glass of sherry.

Feeling a pang of sympathy, Ann said, "Yes, please." Tarr echoed her. Jehane poured, then seated herself on a sofa, legs tucked beneath her.

There was an awkward pause. Ann could think of nothing to say.

"You asked about the mortgage," began Jehane with a shaky laugh. "I've tried to work out some simple way of telling you, without going into all the complications. But it's impossible. So I'll tell you everything. The exact truth."

CHAPTER 6

When Pearl Maudley Orr sold her house to the Cyprianos, she took a down payment of eight thousand dollars and a first mortgage on the balance—that was true enough. The mortgage, however, was at Jehane's insistence, she said. Pearl had been quite willing to sell for the eight thousand. "We're by no means wealthy people," said Jehane. "I have a small income, and Alexander a bit more, and he also does fairly well on the stock market. That's where he is today."

After the Cyprianos moved into their new house, Roland Nelson became a frequent visitor. He played an occasional game of chess with Alexander, but more often they would dispute the tactics of long-dead chess masters in the classic games. They would argue with great dash and vehemence; out would come the board, the pieces would be arranged, each would seek to demonstrate the accuracy of his judgment. Alexander generally got the better of these arguments. He had the more meticulous mind, and he played the careful positional game of the modern Russian masters. Roland's style being swash-buckling and adventurous, Alexander predictably won most of the games they played. On other occasions Alexander might be off on business, whereupon Jehane and

Roland would discuss their own affairs. Here a pinkness came into Jehane's cheeks.

Pearl, returning from a trip to Mexico, had met Roland at the Cypriano house. She was at first repelled, then by successive stages curious, interested, fascinated, infatuated. Jehane did nothing either to advance or discourage the situation. Roland's attitude was equivocal. No one could avoid liking Pearl: she was generous, modest, and not unattractive; though, beside Jehane, she looked like an English schoolgirl.

Jehane could not be certain which of the two put forward the idea of marriage; she speculated that it might well have been Pearl. In any event, the marriage took place. Pearl was quite aware that her money was the main attraction, Roland making no pretense, but she was naïvely sure that she could make it a successful marriage. And the marriage was far from unsuccessful. The Nelsons rented an apartment in Sausalito; Pearl did her best to avoid smothering Roland, who on his part could hardly have failed to recognize her virtues.

Edgar Maudley, Pearl's cousin and confidant, wholeheartedly disapproved of the marriage. He and Roland held contrary opinions about everything, and each detested the sight of the other. Whenever Edgar found the opportunity, he would hint to Pearl that Roland would do well to secure employment—"to make something of himself," as Edgar put it. Edgar himself was a quasi-professional bookdealer who bought and sold when the price was right. His resentment of Roland was enhanced by the fact that valuable books and art objects, originally the property of his grandfather, and subsequently divided between his father and Pearl's father, were now more or less in Roland's control. To put a final touch to the situation, Pearl gave Roland as a wedding token the set of Persian miniatures.

Thinking only to demonstrate her trust and affection, Pearl had handed them to Roland wrapped in white tissue paper and tied with a pink ribbon. Edgar Maudley could scarcely contain his fury.

For several months after the marriage the Cyprianos saw nothing of Roland and Pearl. They were having troubles of their own, chiefly connected with their new house. The spring had brought heavy rains to Marin County, and the downhill corner of the house, under which there was a certain amount of compacted fill, had begun to sag. Alexander, investigating, found a crack in the foundation which caused him great concern. He wanted to complain to Pearl, but Jehane would not hear of it. Pearl, after all, had been more than generous about the mortgage, the interest being a mere nominal 3 per cent. Alexander had groused and sulked and spent the rest of that day in his study.

About this time, Roland showed signs of restiveness. Pearl was working too hard at keeping him happy. She had bought him a white Jaguar roadster as a surprise, conceiving it to be exactly the sort of car Roland would enjoy owning, and she was astounded and hurt when he showed no enthusiasm for it, referring to it, through some perverse logic of his own, as the bird cage. Pearl was an excellent cook. She devoted a great deal of effort to the concoction of imaginative meals, accompanied by the right wines. Roland took polite note of her efforts, but again and again he hurt her by wolfing down half a loaf of French bread with a can of sardines or a chunk of cheese an hour or two before dinner.

But Pearl had redoubled her efforts. It was evident, for example, that Roland enjoyed informality. Pearl bought a gay red-checked tablecloth, a pair of saucy ceramic candelabra in the form of roosters, and milkglass goblets; and she served him a dinner the *pièce de résistance* of which was duck stuffed with wild rice, raisins, and glacé fruit, the whole garnished with oranges. Roland made no comment, but during dinner he appeared more than usually thoughtful. The next day he announced that he was going off by himself for a week or two.

Pearl was too stunned to expostulate. She pretended understanding. Roland departed and never came back.

About this time Alexander Cypriano, making another survey of the foundation, discovered that the crack in the foundation had widened. He probed with a hacksaw blade and could find no reinforcing steel in the concrete. This was too much. He strode into the house and, before Jehane knew what he was up to, telephoned Pearl and told her of the sorry state of the building. Pearl agreed in a dreary voice that of course she took complete responsibility for the soundness of the house, and she had driven out to Inisfail, inspected the crack, and said she would see that appropriate repairs were made. She stayed for dinner, and in her state of depression drank a great deal more than was usual for her. Jehane wanted her to spend the night, but Pearl insisted on leaving. On the way down the hill she ran off the road and was killed.

She died intestate, and Roland automatically inherited. After the death of her late husband, Rex Orr, Pearl had entrusted her investments to the Property Management Department of The California and Pacific Bank; and the Probate Court, taking cognizance of this fact, as well as of the circumstances of Pearl's marriage, appointed the bank administrator of the estate. Hence six months would have to elapse before Roland Nelson could assume complete control.

If Roland felt guilt or grief, he gave no indication, though he attended the funeral decently dressed in a dark suit. Alexander took occasion to mention the faulty foundation and the fact that Pearl had undertaken to set matters right. Roland pointed out that as yet he had no title to the estate, that he was without financial resources of any kind—in fact, he was penniless. He ascertained the name of the contractor—Martin Jones—and said he would see if an adjustment would be made.

Roland kept his promise. He spoke to Martin Jones, but the sole result was that Roland went to work for Jones as a laborer.

To this point Jehane had been speaking in a soft unaccented voice, with an air of detachment. Now she became uncomfortable, twining her fingers, frowning out the window. "These are things I do not like to talk about. I'm sure you've suspected that Roland and I . . . well, frankly, we had been lovers. I use the word in a general sense, because I have no idea what emotion, if any, Roland felt. He never told me, and I never asked. I'm not even sure what kind of emotion I felt." Jehane pondered a moment. "The relationship was confused, and yet perfectly simple. I'm sure I was no more than a superficial incident in his life." She shrugged, and made an attempt to return to her previous detachment.

"The thing started when I first met Roland five years ago. You're wondering, what of Alexander? How is it that I obviously feel no guilt—that I can talk about it this way to perfect strangers? The fact is, Alexander and I have no physical relationship. We never have had. Before we were married he explained his . . . well, views, and I made no objection.

I think I was even relieved. I had been married once before, to a ... well, I'll merely say that I agreed to Alexander's proposal. And our marriage hasn't worked out too badly. I'm a sister to him, an aunt, a mother. Psychologically, perhaps physically, he is not virile. I hasten to say that he has no peculiar inclinations; it's just that sex means nothing to him. I suppose the situation seems remarkable. Anyway, Alexander was fully aware of my relationship with Roland, and made no complaints."

Jehane's voice took on a tone of sad amusement. "Eventually, for some mysterious reason, Alexander became annoyed. It may be because Roland and I were too casual about our affair. In any event, Alexander insisted that the relationship come to an end. I obeyed him, at least until I decided whether or not to stay married to him. Roland just shrugged.

"A month or so later he married Pearl, and I saw very little of him—although he telephoned, asking me to meet him. Naturally I refused. When Roland left Pearl, he called me again and asked me to go to Ireland with him, of all places. Why Ireland? Who knows? Anyway, I said 'no,' and Roland became angry. He'd already written off his marriage to Pearl, and he thought of Alexander as a petulant child. There was no arguing with him. I simply refused.

"Pearl was killed," Jehane went on, "and Roland became moody. He rented an old house from Martin Jones and cut himself off from everyone. His whole life seemed to be in flux; he was determined to make some sort of change, but hadn't decided exactly how to go about it." Jehane laughed wryly. "Perhaps I'm projecting my own feelings into Roland, because this was exactly the frame of mind I was in. Why didn't I leave Alexander and go to live with Roland? First, there was Alexander; second, I was afraid. I'm sure Roland would have become bored with me, just as he became with Pearl. And this takes us back to the cracked foundation and the mortgage. . . ."

Alexander had become preoccupied with a book he was writing—a critique of ancient Hindu chess—and seemed to forget the cracked foundation.

In March, Roland came into control of Pearl's estate, including the mortgage on the Cyprianos' house. The event prompted Alexander to make another inspection of the foundation; the crack had widened still further. Alexander at once composed a formal letter to Roland. He stated that the house had been bought with a warranty of sound construction, that Pearl had undertaken to honor this warranty, and Alexander now called upon Roland to perform in like manner. Jehane expected that Roland would throw the letter away.

But Roland appeared at the house on the evening of the day he received the letter. Alexander showed him the foundation, Roland took a cursory look, and they returned inside. Roland took the mortgage from his pocket, slapped it down on the table. "I'll play you a game of chess," he told Alexander. "I put up the mortgage—if you win, you can have it and make your own repairs."

"And what do I put up? If I lose?"

"Jehane."

Alexander's eyebrows rose. *"Jehane?"*

"Exactly. She's nothing to you but a housekeeper. If you lose, you can get yourself another."

Alexander had snorted; then, contemplating the mortgage, he massaged his chin and gave an excited laugh. "Very well. I agree to your terms."

Jehane, standing to the side, had turned slowly and gone out on the deck to stand in the gathering dusk. Through the window she could look down into the living room. Alexander brought forth the

Morphy Presentation set—a sign that he regarded the game as highly important. The two men seated themselves, the beautiful old pieces were set up. Alexander held out his closed fists, Roland touched one of them. He drew White.

Alexander Cypriano waited placidly while Roland Nelson considered his opening. If Roland played his usual game, it would be the Ruy Lopez, a King's Gambit ,the ancient Evans's Gambit, perhaps the Colle System, or some nameless dramatic irregularity which Roland might attempt on the spur of the moment. Alexander had few fears for the outcome. Whenever he concentrated on his close, careful game he defeated Roland; he expected no other outcome now.

Roland studied the board for two minutes. Alexander sat quietly. The chess pieces facing each other had come to life, each with its distinctive personality.

Roland played knight to KB3; Alexander smiled faintly and played pawn to Q4. Roland played pawn to QKt3. Alexander shrugged, played pawn to QB4. Roland played pawn to K3; Alexander, knight to QB3; and Roland fianchettoed his bishop.

Alexander finally made a comment. "I see you have advanced in your thinking by perhaps sixty years."

"When I play chess for fun, I play my game," said Roland. "When I play to win, I play your game."

"We shall see."

The game proceeded, infinitely cautious. Alexander exchanged pawns, and presently knights, but the game stayed even. Alexander maintained an imposing pawn mass in the center, while Roland's pieces had greater mobility. Jehane watched from the deck for perhaps half an hour; tension seemed to ride the

hunched backs of the two men in the room below.
She turned suddenly and looked out toward the Pacific, where a peaches-and-cream sunset had faded to
afterglow. Up the dark slopes of Mount Tamalpais
there were occasional twinkles of light; out across
the valley twinkled others—snug homes, and
farmsteads, and a wan cluster where Inisfail lay.

Jehane turned back to the chess game. Alexander
was reaching out; he made a move in his ponderous
way, which somehow conveyed remorseless inevita-
bility. He seemed calm and confident. Roland
brooded.... A crisis was imminent: this Jehane
could see, and it seemed to augur badly for Roland.
Jehane turned away again. Her emotions could not
be defined, or perhaps they constituted a single emotion that had never before existed.

She walked down the deck and went into her bedroom.

The game proceeded. Alexander with almost contemptuous disdain postponed castling in order to
maintain his momentum—a strategy that yielded
fruit when he forced an exchange of bishops, leaving
Roland's king-side defenses in precarious balance.
Then Roland suddenly thrust forth his queen.

"Check," he said.

Alexander studied the situation. The threat was
not particularly alarming. In fact, it seemed point-
less. He advanced a pawn, blocking the critical di-
agonal and attacking the queen. But Roland, rather
than retreat his queen, moved out his knight. If
Alexander took the queen, Roland would fork king
and queen. Alexander chewed his lower lip and
prudently moved his queen. Roland checked with
his knight, and on the next move won a pawn that
Alexander's retreat had left unguarded. The crisis
eased. Roland was a pawn up, but the advantage was

balanced by Alexander's king's rook, which had seized an open file.

Jehane, in her room, tried to read. The words blurred. Her ears strained for sounds from the living room. She went back out on the deck. From what she could see of the board, the game seemed even. Looking down at the two men, she felt a great pity for both. Each in his own way was a helpless child, as helpless as one of the pieces on the chessboard, which now breathed such a defiant imitation of life.

She wandered down into the living room just in time to see Roland move a pawn forward and lean back in his chair, tension gone.

Alexander stared down at the board. He reached, his hand heavy. When he moved, Roland almost casually nudged his queen forward. Alexander's jaw dropped; he glanced at Roland in utter disbelief. He took the queen with a pawn, and Roland moved a knight. "Check." The black king fled. Another knight's move. "Check." The black king stood at bay, isolated from its queen by the pawn that had captured the white queen. The black king backed into the rook's square, and again the white knight loped forward.

"Checkmate."

Alexander's face was a pale mask of fury. He seized the black king and hurled it across the room. Then he jumped to his feet and turned on Jehane. "Pack your clothes," he snarled. "I've lost the game."

Jehane, standing in the shadow, shook her head. She spoke in a slow, calm voice. The words seemed to hang in mid-air. "I'm not yours to give. If either of you had asked me, this silliness would never have been played out."

Nothing more was said. Jehane's husband sat stunned; her lover seemed exhausted. Cypriano slowly packed the chessmen into their compartments. He picked up the black king, brushed it with his sleeve and stowed it away with the others. Then he shut the case and handed it to Roland.

Roland took the case, expressionless. He went to the door, where he turned. He then tore the mortgage into eight pieces and laid the scraps gently on a table. And departed.

Alexander Cypriano from that moment had played no more chess. "And," said Jehane, "never again did I set eyes on Roland."

CHAPTER 7

"That," said Jehane, "is the story of what happened to the mortgage. I'm sorry it took so long, but I could hardly explain it any other way. . . . If you will examine the black king, you'll notice that the crown is bent."

"I noticed," said Ann.

Jehane made a gesture toward their glasses. "Sherry?"

Ann and Tarr both accepted.

"Roland was a strange man," said Jehane. "I'm sure I did what was right. Neither of us would have gained—though Roland might still be alive, which I suppose could be considered a gain. Things happened as they had to happen. Now that he's dead, I notice the gap he leaves, but I feel no grief. Certainly not as much as Pearl would have felt."

"Out of sheer curiosity, Mrs. Cypriano," asked Tarr in a peculiarly respectful voice, "what are your plans?"

Jehane smiled. "Perhaps you'll think me perverse, but I have an urge to go to Ireland. I don't know what I'll find there, but I think I'll be going soon."

"With your husband?" asked Ann.

"No."

Ann rose. "Thank you for being so honest."

"I had no choice. You would have thought us thieves otherwise."

In San Rafael, Tarr lured Ann into a coffee shop. He ordered two hamburgers and a milkshake, explaining that he had not yet had lunch. Ann ordered coffee, in spite of Tarr's insistence that she eat. "Have a sandwich, or a sundae, or pie. Shoot the works. It's on me."

"No, thanks. I'm not hungry."

"You're dieting?"

"Not at the moment."

"I'm relieved. It would be a terrible mistake. Every one of your pounds is important. There's not one wasted."

"I suppose you intend that as a compliment," said Ann. "Thank you."

"You're welcome. I'm not the heavy-handed lout I seem."

"You don't seem heavy-handed," said Ann. "Just light-headed."

Tarr grinned and ate his hamburgers. Presently he said, "Now you know what happened to the mortgage."

Ann shuddered. "If I were Jehane I'd have *hated* him."

"And Alexander wants his chess set back—which is rubbing it in."

"He's willing to pay for it, or so he says."

"Everyone is so fair," said Tarr cynically. "But somewhere among the group is a blackmailer."

"Why 'among the group'? It seems to me it might have been practically anyone."

"The blackmailer took great pains to conceal his identity—which argues that he, or she, is someone your father knew well. I'd certainly like to talk to your mother."

"You probably can in a day or so."

Tarr looked up. "How come?"

"Her letter said as much."

"Oh, the letter." Tarr seemed to lose interest. He leaned back in the booth. "You're a wealthy gal now. A poor slob of a cop doesn't stand much of a chance."

Ann laughed. "Which slob did you have in mind?"

"I was referring to Inspector Tom Tarr. I have scruples, but luckily they don't stand in the way of living off my wife."

"My father tried it," said Ann. "He didn't seem to like it."

"I'm of a different temperament. More independent."

"*More* independent?"

"Certainly. Your father couldn't figure out how to adapt."

"You're confusing 'independence' and 'hypocrisy.'"

"There may be a difference," conceded Tarr. "Still, it all seems simple enough to me. Pearl served roast duck with oranges, admittedly a vile concoction, when he wanted bread and cheese. Why not tell her so in a nice way, instead of suffering so dramatically? He'd have had his bread and cheese; his wife would be happy. It seems to me your father was being unnecessarily difficult."

"He was a hard man to live with, no doubt about it."

"Now me, I'm not. If I wanted bread and cheese, everybody within twenty miles would know it, including my wife."

"That's not so good, either, unless you're married to somebody like Pearl."

A short, paunchy man came into the coffee shop. "My lord," muttered Tarr, "here's Cooley."

Cooley wore heavy black-rimmed eyeglasses; black hair rose in a tuft from a narrow forehead. "Hey, there, Tom!" he called cheerfully. "Out feeding the missus on the taxpayer's money, I see. That's the spirit! Show no mercy."

Tarr said to Ann, "This is Ben Cooley, photographer with the city police. Until they canned him."

"I never thought they'd do it," said Cooley without embarrassment. "*Nichevo.* I took the wrong kind of pictures of the wrong kind of people."

"Cooley put enterprise ahead of discretion," Tarr told Ann.

"In my business, enterprise is what counts," said the photographer. "Now what would you do? I ask you, Mrs. Tarr. Here's the situation. Picture a naked man running down the street, with a dog chasing him. You've got your camera ready. Would you take the picture or wouldn't you?"

"If I could hold the camera steady, I'd certainly take it."

"So did I. Turns out the man was visiting the home of a friend, and the friend arrives unexpectedly. So the man jumps out the window. I won't mention any names—that's not my style—but it turns out he's one of the big shots in the Police Department. I should have recognized him, but without clothes he didn't look the same. One thing led to another, and I was allowed to resign."

"Dirty shame," said Tarr.

"I'm through with this damned city. As soon as the Civil Service exams for the county go up, I'll try for special investigator, or maybe photo-lab technician. Who knows, Tarr? Maybe I'll ease you out. You've been on the gravy train long enough." He winked at Ann. "Except that I'd get in dutch with your wife."

Tarr rolled his eyes toward the ceiling. "This is Miss Nelson."

"Oh. Excuse me. You sure look like Mrs. Tarr. Same build. Even the face—"

"Here now!" expostulated Tarr. "There isn't any Mrs. Tarr! Hasn't been for four years!"

"Oh, come *on*, Tom. I saw you two at the department picnic last month. In fact, I've got pictures to prove it. One where she was standing on the beer keg on one leg, and another during the Charleston contest. Unless maybe it was Miss Nelson?" Cooley looked questioningly at Ann, who had risen.

"It must have been Mrs. Tarr," said Ann. "I don't have a very good sense of balance. Goodbye, Mr. Cooley. Goodbye, Inspector Tarr."

"Wait!" said Tarr.

"Don't go on my account," said Cooley.

But Ann went, clicking along on staccato heels.

"Cooley," said Tarr, "I ought to beat you up."

"Nice-looking number," said Cooley. "What is she, friend or criminal?"

"She might be either . . . or both."

"You always come up with cute ones," said Cooley.

"Just a natural talent, I guess." Tarr heaved to his feet. "I've got to get back to headquarters."

Ann arrived home in late afternoon. The apartment seemed unnaturally quiet. She made a pot of tea and sat down in the big chair by the window, wondering what to do with herself for the evening. Dinner downtown? A movie?

She snatched the telephone and dialed Hilda Baily, who taught fourth grade at Mar Vista. There was no answer; Hilda was probably celebrating the end of the term. While she was considering whom next to call, the phone rang. Ann lifted the receiver and heard a careful baritone voice. "Miss Nelson? Edgar Maudley here. Please don't think me a nuisance, but I've been wondering if you've come to any decision."

"No. Wait, let me think. Tomorrow is Saturday. Maybe I'll go over tomorrow and check through things."

"About what time will you be going?" inquired Maudley.

"I'm not sure. Probably in the morning."

"I'd be glad to help you. It's quite possible—"

"*No*," said Ann. "I want to look things over by myself."

There was a moment of silence. Then Edgar Maudley said with dignity, "Certainly."

"I'll call you tomorrow evening, or Sunday, and we can make whatever arrangements need to be made."

"Very well, Miss Nelson."

Ann replaced the receiver. Perhaps she should have accepted Maudley's offer of assistance. There would be a great many books to move. Well, she'd manage. Inspector Tarr still had her father's keys; she should have taken possession of them. But Martin Jones could let her into the house. She ascertained Jones's number from Information, and called him. He grumbled but agreed to be on hand to open the house. So much for that.

The evening still remained a void.

Ann phoned two more of her friends, suggesting dinner downtown. Each was committed.

She showered, changed into a black cocktail dress, drove downtown, and dined alone at Jack's. The evening was still young; the Fairmont Hotel was nearby; the cocktail lounge was a dim sanctuary. Ann relaxed. Inisfail seemed far away; the circumstances of Roland Nelson's death were remote, and she was able to consider them with detachment.

The entire course of her life had been changed. She had not yet reckoned the total of her new riches, but it surely would exceed a hundred thousand dollars, even after taxes. With twenty-two thousand dollars still unaccounted for—the loot of the blackmailer. Or such was Tarr's contention. He also continued to espouse the suicide theory. One was as bizarre as the other, but Ann was forced to admit the lack of any convincing refutation. Her father had been found dead in a foolproof locked room; suicide was the only rational explanation. The note rescued from the fireplace, the withdrawal of twenty-two thousand dollars from the bank, as clearly indicated blackmail. Against facts and logic Ann could only oppose her conviction that Roland would never have paid blackmail or killed himself.

She took an envelope from her purse, wrote on the back: *Questions.* Gnawing on her pen, she sought to recall the various occasions she had been puzzled, surprised, mystified. Gradually she composed a list:

How did Elaine learn that Roland had inherited money?

Why was she so sure of collecting from him? Had she been really sure, or only optimistic?

Why had Roland put such secure locks on his study door?

While Roland was short of money, he paid his rent regularly (evidenced by the rent receipts). When he came into the estate he fell behind. Normal relaxation? Or other reasons?

Where had Elaine spent the time since March? Where was Elaine now?

Why had Elaine written so indefinite a letter,

without a return address, without information of any sort other than that she wanted money?

If Elaine had received $22,000 from Roland, why was she now complaining of financial stringency?

The Elaine questions suggested an answer as unthinkable as Roland's blackmail and suicide. Yet Ann was forced to admit that the three incredible ideas formed a plausible unity.

Suppose Roland had done violence to Elaine? Suppose someone knew of it and blackmailed Roland? Suppose Roland, half crazy with guilt, worry, or fear, had then decided to kill himself? In a burst of illumination, Ann realized that these were the premises on which Inspector Tarr was working. It was an obvious point of view for someone who did not know Roland Nelson. No wonder Tarr had been so skeptical of the letter!

Nevertheless, facts were facts. The letter *had* been written by Elaine, and postmarked only last Tuesday—evidence of Elaine's continuing existence. Why was she being so elusive? Was she afraid? Of whom? Of the blackmailer? Of whoever had told her of Roland's inheritance? Of the law?

Questions, questions, questions. So very few facts . . .

Ann ordered another drink from the cocktail waitress. Dance music floated in from the ballroom like smoke.

She threw up her hands. Suicide, accident, murder, blackmail . . . what difference did it make?

For five minutes she sat in blissful relaxation. No more school. No more second grade. Travel . . . Italy would be fun. Venice, Positano, Taormino: places she long had wanted to visit. Paris, Copenhagen, Vienna. Or Ireland, which must be charming. Ann toyed with the thought that she might run into Jehane Cypriano on some Dublin street. . . .

The thought of Jehane reminded Ann of Alexander Cypriano and the Paul Morphy Presentation chess set by which he set so much store. In turning the set over to Roland, Cypriano symbolically, if not actually, had cut himself off from chess, the wellspring of his existence. And in tearing up the mortgage, Roland in effect had compensated Alexander for the long-term use of his wife. Not a nice gesture, but then, Roland had not been a nice man.

Ann was tapping her fingers to the music from the ballroom. She drank some more, feeling a little giddy. Another drink, and she would become reckless, perhaps flirt with one of the men at the bar. Wiser to go home and to bed . . . But she found herself in no hurry to leave. Here were color and shimmer and music, all to the tinkle of ice. The apartment was lonely.

Suddenly Ann recalled something Tarr had said about danger, danger to herself. Presumably he had not been talking idly. Ann considered the questions she had noted on the back of the envelope. Suppose, for the sake of argument, that she chanced upon a clue that would lead to the identity of the blackmailer. Then there might be danger indeed.

A frightening possibility existed that she was already in possession of the clue, and that the blackmailer knew it. The apartment seemed lonelier than ever. . . . She didn't have to go home. She could take a room for the night here at the Fairmont. But no, she told herself in a sudden reversal of mood, it was ridiculous; why should anyone want to injure her? She paid her check and left.

She drove out Geary Boulevard toward the Pacific.

Fog drifted across the street lamps. Ann began to wish that she had given in to her fears and remained at the Fairmont.

She crossed Golden Gate Park, turned right into Judah Street, then left into Granada Avenue. She drove slowly past her apartment building. She saw nothing unusual. Making a U-turn at the corner, she returned, parked, locked her car, then gave way to nervousness and ran at full speed up to her apartment. Looking over her shoulder, she fumbled with the key, unlocked the door, snapped on the light, and slipped inside, with panting relief. The apartment was exactly as she had left it.

Nevertheless, she checked bedroom and bathroom, and tested the lock of the service door, angry at herself for her childishness.

She hurried into the bedroom and could hardly shed her clothes fast enough and dive into her bed.

She awoke to find sunlight streaming into the room. Her fears of the night before seemed absurd. How could she ever have got herself into such a state?

It was almost nine o'clock; she would have to hurry. She dressed in blue jeans, a yellow polo shirt, and sneakers; scrambled an egg, made toast and a cup of instant coffee; and, taking an orange to eat on the way, Ann ran down to her car.

She was in the best of moods. On this sparkling day the job ahead of her seemed not too formidable. Martin Jones? More bark than bite, no doubt highly sensitive underneath his glowering façade. She'd be especially nice to him. And she'd let Edgar Maudley have his darned old books . . . maybe.

She laughed.

Ann did not arrive at the house on Neville Road

until twenty minutes past ten. Martin Jones was already here, raking the area he had cultivated the previous week. In his pickup lay flats of dichondra. He greeted her almost with civility. "I see you've come to work. What are you going to do with the stuff?"

"Sort everything into three piles. For myself, for the Salvation Army, and for Edgar Maudley."

"Maudley?" Jones gave a contemptuous snort. "Why Maudley?"

"Oh, he has an understandable desire to retrieve a few odds and ends. After all, he was my father's wife's cousin."

"Your father told him to go to hell."

Ann changed the subject. "How much garden are you going to put in?"

"Not much, just enough to make the place look nice. Your father wasn't much of a gardener. . . Who's this?"

"It looks like Edgar Maudley," said Ann.

"He's sure come prepared," Martin Jones observed.

Into the driveway swung a glossy station wagon, towing a trailer in which were nested a number of cardboard boxes.

Maudley climbed down from the car. He was dressed informally, in tweed trousers and an old tweed jacket. "Good morning, good morning," he called cheerfully. "I see you're here."

Ann eyed him coldly. "I thought I'd made it clear ι . ." Then she shrugged. It was too nice a day to wrangle.

"I decided I could be of help," said Maudley, "so I came along. Clear the whole thing up in one fell swoop, you know."

Ann turned toward the house. "Is it open?" she asked Martin Jones.

Jones nodded and, going to the front door, threw it open. "The desk in the study goes, also the two big bookcases. The rest of the furniture belongs to the house."

CHAPTER 8

The house smelled warm, dusty, and stale. Ann left the front door open and slid back the living-room door that opened to the patio. A pleasant current of air flowed through the room.

Edgar Maudley looked frowningly around the room. "Yes, there are the books. Some of them. I wonder what happened to the rugs."

"They're in storage."

"Indeed. Just as well. Certain of them are quite good, notably the two Kashans." He surveyed the walls, and said gloomily, "There's the Monet."

Ann had not previously noticed the painting, a little confection of pink, blue, and green. "A real Monet?" She went over to look at it.

Maudley seemed to regret having spoken. "You hadn't known of it?"

"No."

"Uncle Dan bought it in Paris in 1923."

"Your family seems to have run to collecting."

"I'm afraid so. Shall we start? I'll bring in boxes, then I can point out the books not specifically part of the Maudley collection ..."

Ann decided to establish a position immediately. "You certainly may bring in the boxes," she said. "Then I'd like you to sit down somewhere while I sort through things. That way there'll be no confusion."

Maudley assumed a stiff stance. "I can't see how confusion can result—"

"Also, I want to work at my own speed—which I'm afraid means slowly."

Maudley glanced at his watch. "The more reason for us both to pitch in and separate the Maudley books from Rex Orr's, which I don't care about."

"Please, Mr. Maudley, bring in the boxes. We'll do this my way. If any of your father's books are among those I don't care to keep, I'll be happy to let you take them."

Pearl's cousin swung on his heel and went out to his car, exuding unhappiness. Ann resolved not to let his avarice influence her decisions, though it was impossible not to sympathize with him. In his place, she supposed, she'd feel the same way.

The books, she found, could be divided into five general categories. First, children's books, for the most part with Christmas and birthday inscriptions: *To little Pearl, on her fifth birthday; may she learn to be as brave and pure as the little girl whom this book is about. Love, Aunt Mary.* Second, volumes dealing with metaphysical subjects: mysticism, Oriental philosophy, spiritualism, the Bahai and the Rosicrucian doctrines, telepathy, clairvoyance, even hypnotism. These books apparently had been the property of Rex Orr. Third, luxuriously bound and illustrated uniform editions: Shakespeare, Robert Louis Stevenson, Alexandre Dumas, Goethe, Balzac, Flaubert, many others. Fourth, a potpourri of books printed by The Pandora Press of San Francisco: genteel erotica, flamboyant works by obscure authors, volumes of poetry, collections of graphic art, *belles-lettres* of various lands. Fifth, standard modern works, those normally accumulated by the literate upper- and upper-middle-class families: Proust, Joyce, Mann, Cary, assorted best sellers of the past two or three decades.

The entire group seemed to include no volumes of extraordinary value or even special antiquarian interest. The children's books Ann decided not to keep; they exhaled memories of a childhood of happier times. They were keepsakes that meant nothing to Ann. She packed them for Maudley in a box.

The second category, expounding the occult and the doctrines of the Orient, Ann likewise put aside for him. She had no interest in yoga or the powers conferred by hypnotism. A thought wandered through her head: Could chess-playing ability be enhanced by hypnosis? From somewhere her father had dug up the resources to beat Alexander Cypriano. Had he been benefiting from a study of Rex Orr's books?

The third category, the uniform editions, she decided to keep. Maudley, who with saintly patience had composed himself on the couch, uttered a feeble bleat when he saw Ann's intention. Ann ignored him.

The books from The Pandora Press posed the most serious problem. Some of them she wanted to keep, and Maudley was watching like a distraught mother. Ann could not restrain her guilt pangs. To him these books represented irreplaceable treasures. An unpleasant dilemma. Ann wondered, were their positions reversed, how generously Maudley would have dealt with her. But this was a sterile line of thought.

The front door opened and Martin Jones peered in. He clumped into the living room, staring first at Edgar—composed with glacial self-discipline on the couch—then at Ann. His grin comprehended everything. He asked Ann, "What are you planning to do with the bookcases?"

Ann inspected the living-room bookcase dubiously. Like its twin in the study, it was a massive mahogany piece resting on six short legs. Two beautiful pieces of furniture, but far too big for her apartment. "I don't have any particular use for them."

"I'll take them off your hands," said Jones, "provided the price is right. The fact is, I don't want them very much."

Ann shrugged. "Twenty dollars apiece?"

"That's high."

"Oh, hell, I'm not going to haggle with you. They're worth lots more. You keep them. They're yours. No charge."

"That's all they're worth to me. I own three books," Jones said calmly, "the telephone directory, a Sears-Roebuck catalogue, and the Marin County Building Code"

"You must plan to acquire a lot more directories and catalogues."

He inspected the bookcases sourly. "I don't intend to use them for books."

"What else can you use them for?"

"Storage. Tools, nails, hardware, things like that."

Behind them, Maudley shuddered. Ann stared in horror. "I won't let you have them. It's *desecration.*"

Martin Jones was not abashed. "To put something to honest use? Look at those books. Do you suppose Nelson read them? Do you think *anybody* ever read them? I'll bet a hundred dollars most of them weren't opened more than once. If at all."

Ann was momentarily silenced. She probably would have lost the bet, she thought.

"Books," intoned Edgar Maudley, "are a repository of knowledge, of ideas, of inspiration, which otherwise would be lost."

Jones grinned. He picked up one of the books, turned to the title page. "*Stones of Venice,* by John Ruskin." He flipped some pages, and read a passage aloud in a nasal, mincing voice:

And well may they fall back, for beyond those troops of ordered arches there rises a vision out of the earth, and all the great square seems to have opened from it in a kind of awe, that we may see it far away;—a multitude of pillars and white domes, clustered into a long low pyramid of colored light; a treasure heap, it seems, partly of gold and partly of opal and mother-of-pearl, hollowed beneath into five great vaulted porches, ceiled with fair mosaic and beset with sculpture of alabaster, clear as amber and delicate as ivory,—sculpture fantastic and involved, of palm leaves and lilies, and grapes and pomegranates, and birds clinging and fluttering among the branches, all twined together into an endless network of buds and plumes; and in the midst of it the solemn forms of angels, sceptered and robed to the feet, and leaning to each other across the gates, their figures indistinct among the gleaming of the golden ground—

He broke off. "Doesn't this guy ever run out of breath? He must have written when ink was a penny a quart."

After a pause, Ann said, "You might use the cases to hold your collection of comic books and *TV Guides.*"

And Edgar Maudley said, "Ruskin wrote to a cultured and discriminating audience who, whether they agreed with his ideas or not—and most of them did not—at least had the grace to recognize the felicity of his style."

Jones angrily tossed the book down. "What burns me about you people is that first you invent a club, then you pull the plug on anybody who doesn't want to join. I'm not interested in walking around with a lily in my hand, or sobbing over a dead mouse."

"Neither were the Neanderthals," retorted Ann. "All they cared about was cramming food into their gullets and bashing other people with clubs."

"Not entirely apropos," said Maudley primly. "You probably mean Zinjanthropus or Eanthropus."

"What it boils down to," growled the contractor, "is that you're calling me an ignorant peasant—which bothers me not one bit, coming as it does from a schoolmarm whose biggest decision is whether to play blind-man's-bluff or tic-tac-toe with the kiddies. But—"

"My word, you're an offensive man," declared Maudley. "I think you should apologize to Miss Nelson."

Martin Jones laughed. "Sure. If she apologizes for calling me an ignorant peasant."

"First convince me otherwise," said Ann, tossing her head.

"That would involve reading a lot of stupid books about pomegranates and angels' wings. I'd rather remain ignorant."

Ann took up *The Stones of Venice.* "Read this book, and I'll give you the bookcases."

Jones's flat cheeks twitched sardonically. "You already gave them to me."

"I took them back, Mr. Jones."

"It would be nice," said Jones. "But I don't have the time."

"Just turn your TV set off two hours early tonight," suggested Ann. "That should get you well started."

"TV? I don't have one."

"What do you do with your spare time?"

"Lady, I don't have any spare time. I'm running a big construction job. I have thirty-eight men on my payroll. I'm fighting architects, building inspectors, subcontractors, the bank, four unions, the planning commission, and the customers. When I have a minute I figure new jobs. And now you want me to recline in a hammock reading about angel wings?"

"You've got time to come over here and putter around the garden."

Jones chuckled. He hefted the book. "It's a lot to ask for two beat-up old bookcases. Still . . . why not? Maybe you'll make a cookie-pusher out of me yet."

Ann often amused herself by imagining an adult as he must have been as a child. She now saw Martin Jones as a handsome, rebellious little boy, perhaps in fear of a heavy-handed father, but stubbornly defiant, who grew up to remain defiant of authority, in much the way Roland Nelson had defied social dicta. Then his abortive love affair. She wondered what the girl was like. A tramp, probably. Oh, well, it was no affair of hers.

She went into the study to the companion bookcase and emerged with several dozen chess manuals, texts, compendia—her father's own books, which she would keep. Edgar Maudley no longer occupied the couch. Ann assumed that he was visiting the bathroom and continued with her work. . . . Edgar came out of the hall leading from the bedrooms, and stalked out to his car. He walked, so it seemed to Ann, rather stiffly.

He returned and resumed his seat on the couch.

With both cases empty, Ann considered the Pandora Press Books. Maudley frowned as Ann sorted through the books, putting to one side those that attracted her, perhaps one in three. He could no longer restrain himself. "May I ask what you are doing?"

"Picking out the books I want from the ones I don't."

Maudley became almost tearful. "Do you realize that The Pandora Press was my grandfather's creation? That these books are extremely rare, that with them I would have a complete file of Pandora publications?"

Ann nodded. "I won't give them to you outright, but I'll sell them to you. This pile goes for, say, five dollars a book. *This* pile, the books I'd like to keep, I'll let you have for twenty dollars a book."

Martin Jones had returned. "You're letting him off cheap," he told Ann. "Those books ought to go for three times that."

"No such thing!" exclaimed Maudley. "Merely because they're rare doesn't automatically make them valuable."

"*Some* of these books are valuable," said Ann. "And you're getting them cheap. Do you want them?"

"Oh, I want them, all right."

"All of them?"

"Yes."

"Very well, you can take them out to your car, and I'll figure out what you owe me."

To Ann's surprise, Martin Jones assisted. While the two men carried out books, Ann calculated. There were forty-six books at $5 each and nineteen books at $20 each—a total of $610. Not bad, thought Ann spitefully.

The two bookcases were now empty. They were really handsome pieces of furniture. What a shame if Martin Jones did use them to store tools and hardware. He could not have been serious. . . . She wondered about him. Perhaps he had been teasing her—

perhaps he occupied his spare time reading. His vo-
cabulary was good; his outlook seemed broad. He
was an interesting man, she thought—a tough,
uncompromising fighter. Roland Nelson had been
tough and uncompromising, too.

She wandered back into the study. In that chair
her father had died. She tried to imagine the scene:
Roland Nelson somberly gazing out the window,
then raising the revolver, holding it to his head,
pulling the trigger. Unthinkable. But how else?
Ann's brain raced, seeking an answer. The floor?
Concrete. Ceiling? Without mar or scar. Door? Window? Almost hermetically tight. Fireplace? A mar-
moset might have gained entry—if the damper had
been open, as it had not been. Walls? Sound as the
ceiling, everywhere that she could see, unmarred,
unbroken, unsullied. The single area not yet investigated was that section of the paneled wall separating
study from living room, between the back-to-back
bookcases. Ann returned to the living room and
called to Martin Jones. "Would you do something
for me?"

"What?"

"Nothing contrary to your principles, like reading.
I'd like you to move this bookcase away from the
wall."

Jones approached warily. Ann snapped, "I won't
bite you. Just move the corner of the bookcase out
into the room."

"Why?"

"Look, Mr. Jones, either do it or don't."

Edgar Maudley came into the living room. Two
boxes of books remained, a large and a small. He
scowled, lifted the small box, gave a pitiful groan,
and staggered out the front door. "What's wrong
with him?" Ann asked. "He seems angry."

Jones chuckled. "He's sore because I didn't carry

out that big box." He put his shoulder to the bookcase, eased it three or four feet out across the vinyl tile that covered the floor.

"Thank you." Ann peered behind the bookcase.

Martin Jones watched her curiously. "What's the reason for all this?"

"I had a fantastic idea that someone might have broken through the study wall, pushed the bookcase aside, shot my father and got back out the same way."

"A good trick," said Jones. "Especially since the bookcases loaded with books weigh a ton or so apiece."

Ann frowned. "I just can't *imagine* my father shooting himself. He wouldn't do it."

"A man sometimes chooses his own time and place to die. Why be conventional and die of cancer? Everybody has to die sooner or later."

"Preferably later," said Ann. "I'm conventional."

"I've noticed that. 'Read a nice book, Mr. Jones. Be cultured like me and Mr. Maudley.'" But the mockery was good-natured, and Ann felt no obligation to retort.

"You can push the bookcase back if you like. No, wait a minute." She got down on her knees, looked at the floor. "That's strange."

"What's strange?"

"The dents in the vinyl tile where the feet of the bookcase rested. It has only two legs, but there are three dents."

"'Two legs'? Six legs."

"I mean the two at this end. And there are three dents from the middle pair, too." Ann crawled to the other end of the case. "And three here as well."

Edgar Maudley came back into the room. He said in a peevish voice, "Mr. Jones, I'd be obliged if you'd help me with the big box. I've got a weak back—"

"Sure. Just a minute."

Maudley came over to where Ann was examining the floor. "What now?"

"These marks in the tile," said Ann. "Notice the three sets of feet on the bookcase. Each pair is about nine inches apart. See where they've dented the vinyl? But notice that between each two there's the print of a third foot. How can that be?"

"The things women bother their heads about," said Maudley. "What are you charging me for these books?"

"It comes to six hundred and ten dollars."

He winced. "For my own books!"

"They're not your books," said Ann acidly. "They're my books. You don't have to take them."

Edgar produced his checkbook and carefully wrote out a check. "There," he whined. "Six hundred and ten dollars. I don't have any choice."

"I won't thank you," said Ann, "because the books are probably worth two or three times that."

"Conceivably," said Maudley. "In any event, the deal is consummated, and I'll say no more about it." Martin Jones seized the box that Edgar had found too heavy, hoisted it without effort, and carried it outside.

Ann made a last puzzled inspection of the impressions in the tile. There was undoubtedly some pedestrian explanation, but what it was she couldn't fathom.

She took stock. The books were sorted; Martin Jones would take care of the bookcases; and she decided to give him the desk in the study. Maybe she'd insist that he read another book to earn it. It was fun to tease him, the surly brute.

Where was that "article of medieval Persian craftsmanship" presented to Roland by Pearl, which Ann had been enjoined to keep? She inspected a china closet in the dining area, which contained a few inexpensive dishes. They could stay with the house. There was no other storage area in the living room.

She went to inspect the bedrooms.

The first bedroom was starkly empty; the second contained little more than a bed and dresser. In the wardrobe hung two or three men's suits, a jacket or two. The dresser held underwear, socks, handkerchiefs. The barest minimum of personal belongings. Roland Nelson all over.

The Persian miniatures were nowhere to be found. She went outside. Martin Jones was setting out dichondra. "All through?"

"Almost. You've been through the house, of course."

Jones's eyes narrowed. "I cleaned up the kitchen, straightened up here and there."

"Did you notice a set of Persian miniatures? In a carved ivory box?"

"It's in the bedroom, on the dresser."

"It's not there now."

He frowned and led the way to the bedroom. He pointed to the top of the bureau. "That's where the thing was. I saw it only this morning."

Ann swung around and marched ouside. Edgar Maudley was preparing to leave. Ann said evenly, "I don't seem to find the miniatures, Mr. Maudley. Have you seen them?"

Maudley said in a lofty voice, "If you're referring to an item which since 1729 has been a prized heirloom of my family—"

"And which is going to be a prized heirloom of *my* family. Where is it?"

"As you can see, I don't have it on my person."

"Very funny. Let's look in your car."

"I don't enjoy the implication. And I don't care to have you prowling through my car."

"I think I'll prowl anyway. Those miniatures were in the bedroom; you went in there, then you went out to the car carrying something under your coat. You swiped those miniatures."

"Think what you like. The subject, so far as I am concerned, is closed."

Ann walked to his car. The doors were locked. Ann swung around. "Please unlock your car. If you don't have the miniatures I'll apologize. If you do, I want them back."

"My dear young lady, I must insist that you drop the subject. In any event, I remind you that by every moral right they're my property—that they passed into the possession of Roland Nelson only through the misguided generosity of my cousin Pearl."

Ann turned to Martin Jones. "I want you to witness this, Mr. Jones. I have reason to believe he has the miniatures in his car . . ."

Jones eyed Maudley with dislike. He stepped forward, held out his hand. "Let's have the key, Maudley."

Maudley eyed him nervously. "You'll get no keys from me, sir. Stand aside."

Martin Jones gave his head a slow shake. "I could take them away from you. But it's easier to break a window."

"You do that, sir, and I'll charge you with vandalism."

"If the miniatures are there," declared Ann, "I'll charge you with theft."

White with fury, Maudley reached in his pocket for the car keys, unlocked the door, opened the glove compartment, and brought forth an ivory box, which he thrust at Ann. "Here you are. I let you have them under protest. And I assure you your possession will be only temporary."

"Oh?"

"You have no right to *any* of this. *Nor* the money. I've been a gentleman so far, but no longer! The money, the books, the rugs, the miniatures belong to *me*, not *you*, and I intend to recover! The estate should never have gone to Roland Nelson in the first place."

"And why not, pray?"

"Why not? I'll tell you why not! *Because the marriage of Roland Nelson to Pearl Maudley was not valid.*

Ann was astonished. "How so?"

"Because," snapped Maudley, "he never divorced your mother."

Ann leaned back on the fender of Maudley's car. She controlled her voice. "Where did you hear this?"

"Never mind where I heard it."

"At last," said Ann, "it becomes clear where my mother got her information."

"You don't deny it, then?" Maudley asked in a triumphant blat.

"Deny what?"

"That Pearl Maudley never was the legal spouse of Roland Nelson?"

"Certainly I deny it."

"How can you? He never divorced your mother."

Ann could no longer control her laughter. "Why should he? He never married her."

Maudley started to speak, clamped his mouth shut. His face was red. Finally he stuttered, "This is not the situation as I understand it."

"Where did you get your information? From my mother?"

"Yes, if you must know!"

"Where is she?"

"Where is she? How should I know? Los Angeles, I suppose."

"How long has it been since you've seen her?"

"Several months. Why do you ask?"

"Inspector Tarr has been trying to locate her."

He chewed his lip. "She made no mention of non-marriage to your father. In fact, she gave me definitely to understand . . ." His voice trailed off.

"How much did you pay her?" Ann asked gently.

He chose to ignore her question. Instead, he said pompously, "You know, of course, that a murderer can't inherit from his victim."

"What of it?" Ann instantly perceived the drift of Maudley's thoughts.

"There's a line of investigation which in my opinion the police have neglected."

Ann pretended to be puzzled. "Investigation of what?"

"The death of my cousin Pearl. From Roland Nelson's point of view, she could not have died more conveniently."

Ann's voice blared her contempt. "He didn't see her the night she was killed. She died on her way down the hill from the Cyprianos."

"Oh? He lived nearby. Suppose she had called on him, mentioned where she'd been? He had only to knock her unconscious, drive back up the hill, run the car off the cliff, and walk home—a matter of twenty minutes."

"You," said Ann, "have a dirty mind!" She walked back toward the house. Edgar Maudley drove off with a jerk, the trailer groaning and rumbling at his bumper.

At the door Ann paused to take her first thorough look at the Persian miniatures. They were contained in two intricately carved ivory trays, hinged to form the box. A silver filigree emanating from the hinges divided the exterior into medallions, inside which the filigree branched and elaborated into a thousand twining tendrils, and these were garnished with leaves of turquoise, flowers of lapis lazuli, cinnabar, and jet.

The miniatures themselves were cemented to the interior of the trays. They depicted a garden on a hillside overlooking a city: in the bright light of noon on the one side, in the blue dimness of midnight on the other. In the daylight garden a warrior prince walked with four advisers. A Nubian slave proffered sherbet; on parapets stood stiff men-at-arms. In the night garden the prince reclined with a languorous odalisque. She wore diaphanous trousers; black hair flowed over her shoulders.

Ann unfolded a slip of paper: *Garden of Turhan Bey: Behzad of Herat. 1470-1520.* Ann closed the box and carried it over to her car. A beautiful, authentic treasure; she could well understand Edgar Maudley's covetousness.

She went back into the house. Martin Jones stood in the middle of the living room. Ann saw that his mood had changed; he once again had become hostile. Because they were alone? Was he afraid of her? Or of women in general? She picked up an armload of books and took it out to her car. With surly grace Jones helped her. When the books were loaded, Ann packed the four chessboards and the chessmen, feeling a twinge as she broke up games that would never be finished. She must remember to notify the four chess-playing correspondents of her father's death.

She made a final survey of the study, the desk, the empty bookcases. Nothing she wanted to keep. She returned to the living room, warm and tired. Jones asked curtly, "What are you planning to do with the clothes?"

"Give them away."

"Leave them here. One of my laborers is just about your father's size."

"What about Roland's car—would he take that, too?"

"I imagine so."

"I'll mail the ownership certificate to you." Ann felt reluctant to leave, though now there was nothing to keep her. "I'm making you a present of the desk," she said.

"Thanks." Jones had not forgotten. "Since I agreed to read that idiotic book, I will. But I don't have to like it."

"It'll do you good. You might even want to visit Venice. Or, heaven help us, read another book."

He grinned his sour grin. "Fat chance."

"You can mail me the book when you're finished with it."

"I don't have your address," he growled.

"Sixty-nine fifty Granada Avenue, San Francisco."

He made a note of it. "Don't expect it for about three months. I might want to read it backwards to see if it makes more sense."

"I'm sure you'd find it so. Oh, and thank you for your help, Mr. Jones."

Jones seemed about to say something catastrophic. Instead, he turned on his heel and re-entered the house. Ann could have kicked him.

She strode over to her car and drove away fast.

CHAPTER 9

Ann arrived in San Rafael shortly before three, ravenously hungry; she stopped at a drive-in for a sandwich. No question but that she should report the events of the day to Inspector Tarr. Tarr, in his vanity, would of course assume that infatuation had induced her to call him. The notion irritated her. Let him assume anything he liked.

At a service station she freshened up, then telephoned the sheriff's office. Tarr got on the phone and said yes, he would like to see her. Could she stop by the office? Or would she prefer to meet him elsewhere?

The office was perfectly satisfactory, Ann said in a tone she hoped would put the Don Juan of the force in his place.

But when she arrived at the sheriff's office, Tarr seemed anything but abashed. He took her into his cubbyhole and seated her with gallantry. "I've been in communication with the Los Angeles County authorities. No sign anywhere of your mother. Harvey Gluck says he knows nothing. He hasn't seen her for two months and professes great concern."

"What about Beverly Hills?"

Tarr looked puzzled. "Beverly Hills?"

"That's where the letter was mailed from."

"Oh, the letter." Tarr pursed his attractive lips. "It might have been mailed by almost anyone. A friend, a mailing service, even the postmaster. The postmark doesn't mean much."

"Do you think something happened to her?"

He ran his fingers through his blond hair. "Anything might have happened. We can't rule out illness or accident. Hospitals report negative, there's no police information, but she'll turn up. Don't worry about that."

"It seems she's been working in cahoots with Edgar Maudley."

"How's that again?"

Ann told him what Maudley had said. "She sold poor Edgar on the idea that she could prove Roland's marriage to Pearl invalid—in which case Edgar would have inherited as next of kin."

"Could she do it?"

"I don't see how. Though, when I saw her," said Ann, "she seemed pretty sure of herself."

Tarr was unimpressed. "Unless she had irrefutable proof that Roland Nelson had made a bigamous marriage, she couldn't pressure him."

"How could he have married Pearl bigamously?" asked Ann. "He wasn't married to my mother."

"Unless he'd married still another woman, whom he hadn't divorced—I mean, between your mother and Pearl."

"I don't know of any such woman. Of course, that doesn't mean she doesn't exist."

"Still, suppose this hypothetical in-between woman was also putting pressure on him," suggested Tarr, "so that he had to pay off two women instead of one. This would explain the bank withdrawals. Twenty thousand to one of them, a thousand a month to the other."

Ann shook her head skeptically. "Not that I have

any better explanation . . . Oh, I've run into another mystery."

"What mystery?"

Ann drew on a sheet of paper:

0	0	0
0	0	0
0	0	0

"This line represents the wall separating the living room from the study. The top and bottom marks are where the feet of the living-room bookcase rested before the case was moved—about nine inches apart. Between is the dent of an extra foot, in the position I've indicated, about five and a half inches from the front leg."

Tarr examined the drawing intently. "What about the other bookcase, the one in the study? Did that show a similar set of dents?"

"No. I looked."

"It's certainly a queer one. . . ." Tarr kept staring at Ann's little diagram. He seemed far away. Then he shook his head violently. "I'll have to think about this. Oh, before I forget, Miss Nelson. I'll release that fancy chess set to you, also your father's wallet." He scribbled on a form. "Sign here."

Ann signed, and Tarr brought the chess set and wallet from a cabinet. She opened the case and took out the black king with its dented crown. "Poor Alexander Cypriano."

Tarr chuckled. "Losing that game probably hurt him more than the prospect of losing his wife. Speaking of wives, that fool Ben Cooley, the photographer—don't pay any attention to what he said. There is no Mrs. Tom Tarr. There was one in the dim past, and I mean dim. The way Cooley talks you'd think I'm running around with five women at a time."

"I don't know why you think it concerns me." She rose. "I'll have to be going."

Tarr said with engaging boyishness, as if the thought had just occurred to him, "Oh, what about having dinner with me next week?"

"I don't think that would be wise, Inspector."

"Come on, now . . ."

But Ann took the chess set and wallet, and departed.

Back in her car she scowled down at the chess set; she supposed she ought to return it to Alexander Cypriano. It meant another trip to Inisfail. She sighed, started her car, drove west on Lagunitas Road, and presently turned into the driveway of the house on Melbourne Drive.

Ann walked up the stone steps to the front door and rang the bell. The door opened slowly; Jehane, pale and serious, looked out from the gloomy interior.

Ann held out the leather case. "I brought the chess set back to your husband."

Jehane stepped back quickly, as if the box were infected. "Come in, please," she said in a pale voice. "I'll call Alexander."

Ann reluctantly went up with her to the second level. Jehane disappeared down the hall, and Ann heard her rapping at a door, then the mutter of conversation.

Jehane returned. Her face was expressionless. "He'll be out in a moment." After a pause she said, "I'm afraid Alexander feels that I never should have told you and Inspector Tarr what happened to the mortgage." She broke off as Cypriano appeared in the hallway. He wore a red satin dressing robe with black lapels, and black leather slippers. His hands were in his robe pockets. He glowered at Ann from under threatening eyebrows.

Ann said, "I've brought you the chess set."

"I see." His voice was supercilious. "And what price have you set on it?"

"Nothing. I'm giving it back to you."

Cypriano's eyes went yellow. He seized the case, ran out on the deck, swung his arm. Far out over the rocks flew the leather case, sailing, spinning, disappearing into the gulch.

CHAPTER **10**

As Ann crossed the bridge into San Francisco, a wall of fog was building up at the Golden Gate. The fog overtook her at the Presidio and she was forced to slow down to a crawl. Somewhere unseen, far to the west, the sun had set, and an eerie, monochromatic twilight had fallen over the city. The fog grew thicker, blearing vision; the mercury lamps above the freeway glowed sullen lavender, with a scarlet corona.

At her apartment the fog was almost a drizzle; little cold drops with the tang of the ocean brushed her face. A cab groping along the street stopped by the curb, and a short, plump man got out.

Ann, starting up the steps, paused as the man approached. She recognized him. "Harvey!"

"Bless my soul," said Harvey Gluck. "Am I glad to see you! I was wondering if you'd be home. I telephoned from the airport, but there was no answer. I took a chance, and here I am."

"I'm glad to see you, too," said Ann, with an enthusiasm totally unfeigned. She had always considered Harvey Gluck, whom her mother had so patently hoodwinked and exploited, the most patient and harmless of men. His devotion to Elaine Ann found incomprehensible; it was as uncritical and undemanding as the love of one of Harvey's dogs for Harvey.

"Come on up," said Ann. "I'll mix us a drink and find us something to eat."

"Well." Harvey looked back at the waiting cab. "I thought you could tell me where to find Elaine."

"I've no idea. Don't you know?"

"No. A while back she told me she'd come into money, and that's the last I've seen of her." A trace of uncharacteristic bitterness crept into her voice. "Actually, Elaine and I are washed up. She can't stand my dogs. When I first met her she was the world's greatest dog lover. Goes to show how people change."

"Why are you looking for her, then?"

"If she's come into money, I want what she owes me—which is thirteen hundred bucks. But I didn't come here to bother you with my troubles. What do you say we go to Chinatown? I'll buy you an oriental dinner."

"In these clothes? I'm filthy."

"You look just fine to me."

"I'd love to, Harvey. But let me change."

"Okay. I'll tell the cab to wait."

"Of course not! We'll go in my car."

He looked relieved, and trotted across the sidewalk; money changed hands, and the cab blinked away through the murk and was gone.

They climbed the steps. Ann said, "I was wondering what to do with myself; it's such a dreary evening. You appeared just at the right time."

"I'm Johnny-on-the-spot where the ladies are concerned," said Harvey gallantly. "What's this I hear about your father?"

"It's a long story." Ann unlocked her door. "The police are calling it suicide. Maybe it is, but I don't believe it."

"I never knew him," said Harvey. "Elaine was always talking about him. Sometimes what a great hero, but mostly what a heel."

Ann sighed. "He was both. But I can't understand what's happened to Elaine. Hasn't she written you?"

"Not one word." Harvey surveyed the apartment. "Nice little place you've got here."

"It's a place to live." Ann shivered. "Doesn't it seem cold? Almost as if the fog has seeped in through the windows."

Harvey hunched his plump shoulders. "It does seem a bit nippy."

"I'll turn up the heat. How about a highball?"

"Don't mind if I do." Harvey looked around. "Excuse me, but where is it?"

"The bathroom? Through the bedroom, to the right."

Harvey slunk out. Ann went into the kitchenette, brought out her bottle of bourbon, two glasses . . . She turned her head. Had Harvey called? She took a step, listened. From the direction of the bathroom came a peculiar bumping, scraping sound. "Harvey?"

The bumping, scraping sound diminished. There was silence. "Harvey?" called Ann in an uncertain voice. She peered across the dark bedroom at the line of light under the bathroom door.

The light snapped off. The door opened, very slowly. In the darkness loomed a shape darker than dark. Ann's knees wobbled; she gasped, whirled, and ran for the front door. Behind her pounded footsteps. She clawed for the door handle; the door opened at last, and she ran screaming out into the hall—and, screaming, tumbled down the steps, and, screaming, picked herself up to hammer at the door of the manager's apartment on the ground floor.

He was maddeningly deliberate in answering his door. Ann kept watching over her shoulder, trembling all over. No one appeared. She held her finger on the button, knocked, thumped.

The door opened. The manager looked guardedly out. "Miss Nelson! What's the matter?"

"Call the police," Ann cried. "There's someone in my apartment!"

The manager, an ex-Marine named Tanner who had left an arm on Guadalcanal, said, "Just a minute." He went to a cupboard, brought out a large black automatic pistol. "Let's go look, Miss Nelson."

He bounded upstairs.

Ann's door was shut. She said in a terrified whisper, "I left it open. I'm sure I did."

"Stand back." Holding the gun between his knees, Tanner brought out his passkey, unlocked the door fast; then snatching up his gun he thrust the door open. Once more warning Ann back, he peered into the living room.

Empty. On the kitchen counter was the bottle of bourbon and the two glasses.

"Be careful," breathed Ann. "There's something terribly wrong." Her voice caught in her throat. Whatever had happened to Harvey would have happened to her. . . .

Tanner sidled into the bedroom. He reached in with the hook of his artificial arm, switched on the lights. Ann's neatly made bed sprang up, the dresser, the night table. Tanner peered under the bed, looked suspiciously at the wardrobe. Holding the gun ready, he slid aside first one of the wardrobe doors, then the other. The wardrobe contained only shoes and clothes.

"Stand back, Miss Nelson," he said quietly.

The bathroom door was ajar. The light from the bedroom shone on a polished black shoe, a plump ankle in a black and red silk sock.

Tanner backed slowly off, spoke over his shoulder.

"There's a man's body in the bathroom. Call the police."

Ann fled to the telephone. Tanner went into the kitchen and looked out on the service porch. After a moment he returned, waiting till Ann finished. "He's gone. Broke open the back door to get in, probably took off the same way. What happened? Who's the man in the bathroom?"

Ann sank into a chair. "My mother's husband. We'd just come in. He had to go to the bathroom. It was someone who was waiting for me." The full horror of what had happened to Harvey Gluck—and almost to her—struck her like a blow.

"Easy now," said Tanner. He stood alertly contemplating the door into the bathroom. Someone might still be lurking there in the dark, undecided whether to make a lunge through the apartment or essay the twenty-five-foot drop from the bathroom window. Better to wait out here, he decided, with the gun trained on the doorway.

A few frozen moments later sirens began to moan, first faintly, then growing in volume, finally dying down outside. A pair of officers appeared from the stairway, burst into Ann's living room. Tanner briefed them in a low voice, motioned with his one arm toward the bathroom. One of the officers tiptoed over and, covered by the gun of his mate, reached in and jabbed on the light. Then he ducked back. Using a mirror from Ann's dresser they surveyed the bathroom.

Its sole occupant was Harvey Gluck. Harvey lay on his back with bulging eyes and protruding tongue. In his neck there was a bloody crease, where a wire had jerked tight.

Detective Inspector Fitzpatrick presently descended to the manager's apartment, where Ann sat cuddling a cup of coffee she did not want. Fitzpatrick brought forth his notebook and spoke in a bored voice. "Name?"

"Ann Nelson."

"Married?"

"No."

"Employed where?"

"I teach school. Mar Vista Elementary."

"The deceased is who?"

"My mother's husband. His name is Harvey Gluck."

"Tell me what happened."

Ann described the events of the evening. Fitzpatrick took one or two notes.

"Why had Mr. Gluck called on you?"

"He was looking for my mother." Ann hesitated, then said, "Perhaps you had better get in touch with Inspector Tarr at the Marin County Sheriff's Office."

"Why?"

"My father died a week or so ago. Inspector Tarr has been in charge of the investigation."

Fitzpatrick's black eyes snapped. "Homicide?"

"You'd better ask Inspector Tarr," said Ann. Then with a trace of cheerless humor she said, "He thinks it was suicide."

"And what do you think?"

"I don't know what I think. Except that someone was waiting to kill me." Ann bit her lip to keep it from trembling.

"Easy now, Miss Nelson. How do you know Mr. Gluck wasn't the intended victim?"

"How could he have been?" Ann asked wearily. "He'd only just arrived in town. No one knew he'd be here. But they knew I'd be home, and alone.... Poor Harvey. When he went into the bathroom, whoever was there had to kill him to keep him quiet." Then the tears came.

Fitzpatrick asked permission to use the Tanners' telephone. When he hung up he turned back to Ann.

"If it's any comfort to you," said the detective, "Mr. Gluck never knew what struck him. That kind of garrote works like greased lightning.... By the way, was he friendly with you?"

The implication was too clear to be ignored. "What do you mean?" said Ann with as much indignation as she could muster.

Fitzpatrick was not daunted. "Just what I asked."

"Yes. He was friendly with me."

"How friendly?"

"I liked him. He was a kind, generous man."

"He ever make a pass at you?"

"Certainly not."

Fitzpatrick nodded without interest. "Has he ever been here before?"

"No"

"What about your mother? Where is she?"

"I don't know."

"You don't know?" Fitzpatrick's tone was incredulous.

"I haven't seen her since early March."

The telephone rang; Fitzpatrick answered as a matter of course. The conversation continued for several minutes. Then he hung up and said to Ann, "That was Inspector Tarr. He's on his way." He considered a moment. "Where are you planning to spend the night?"

"I don't know. I hadn't thought."

"A friend's house?"

"I'll go to a hotel."

"She can stay right here," said Mrs. Tanner.

Ann thanked her. She would have preferred the impersonal calm of a hotel, but she was too upset to argue.

Mrs. Tanner said, "You tell me what you'd like; I'll run upstairs and get it for you. And you can be taking a nice hot shower."

"That sounds wonderful, Mrs. Tanner; you're very kind," said Ann. "If you'd just bring some pajamas and my bathrobe."

When Ann emerged from the shower, Mrs. Tanner had a bowl of split-pea soup and a grilled cheese sandwich waiting for her. Ann remembered that she had eaten neither lunch nor dinner. She suddenly felt famished.

While she was eating, Inspector Tarr arrived. She heard his voice in the living room and felt an almost frantic sense of relief. Tarr looked in at her. "Good evening, Miss Nelson." Ann looked up in surprise. His voice was as coolly indifferent as Inspector Fitzpatrick's had been. She flushed with resentment. What a hypocrite! Trying to make a date with her one moment, the next speaking to her as if she were some whore picked up in a raid!

Tarr sat down beside her. Ann moved away. "This is a very serious matter," he said.

Ann made no reply.

"Assuming someone broke into your apartment—"

Ann demanded angrily, "Is there any other possibility?"

"Of course. You might have garroted Harvey Gluck and faked a break-in at the back door. A woman could easily do the job. Once that wire gets snapped tight, it's all over."

Ann curled her lip in ridicule. "Why should I want to hurt poor Harvey?"

"I don't know." And Tarr added blandly, "Incidentally, if you plan to confess, please confess to me. I'm bucking for promotion, and I could use any help at all."

Ann sipped her tea, too outraged and emotionally limp to react.

"Assuming," Tarr went on, "that someone broke into your apartment, planning to attack and kill you, the question is, Why?"

"I can't imagine."

"Any jealous boy friends?"

"No."

"How about your ex-husband?"

Ann smiled wanly at the idea. "He's in Cleveland."

"We'll check to make sure. Anyone else sore at you?"

"Not seriously."

"So we're back where we started—in Inisfail. You're a threat to someone, or someone profits by your death, or someone hates you. Who?"

"I can't imagine."

"The blackmailer?"

Ann shrugged.

"Who would stand to inherit from you?"

"My mother."

"You haven't written a will?"

"No. It seems—seemed—premature."

"Who stands to inherit from Harvey Gluck? Your mother again?"

"Harvey has nothing except two or three dozen dogs, which Elaine has always hated."

"Suppose your mother were dead, who would inherit from you then?"

"Some cousins, I suppose. People I hardly know. Do you think Elaine is dead?"

"I don't think anything. The fact is, we can't find her."

"What about the letter?"

"It's interesting," said Tarr, "but inconclusive." He got to his feet. "You'd better try to sleep while you have the chance. Fitzpatrick may or may not want to question you some more tonight. He'll certainly put you through the wringer tomorrow."

"Should I tell him about my father?"

"Of course."

Ann cowered in her bathrobe. "I wish I'd never been born."

Tarr surprisingly patted her head. "Oh, come now; it's not as bad as all that. Life goes on."

"Not for poor Harvey. If I'd gone into the bathroom first—or come in alone—it would have been me. He was killed in my place, and I feel as if I am to blame."

"I don't see how you could have saved him. Unless you did it yourself."

Ann glared up at Tarr, uncertain whether he was serious. She read nothing from his face and returned to her tea. Tarr patted her head once more and departed. Ann looked stonily after him.

Mrs. Tanner, who had been in the kitchen, not quite out of earshot, poked her head in. "What a funny policeman!"

CHAPTER 11

A few minutes after Tarr left, Inspector Fitzpatrick returned and, taking Ann to the privacy of a bedroom, interrogated her at length. Rather to Ann's surprise, he seemed primarily interested in Elaine and her previous romantic attachments, and in Ann's own history. Ann repeated that Harvey Gluck's visit was totally unexpected; she spoke of the circumstances of her father's death. After about an hour and a half Fitzpatrick rose to leave. "What are your plans now? Are you going to stay on here?"

Ann shook her head decidedly. The mere thought filled her with revulsion.

"Where are you going, then?"

"For a week or two, to a hotel. After that ... I don't know."

"Which hotel?"

"I haven't thought. Downtown somewhere."

"Take my advice," said Fitzpatrick. "Don't tell anyone where you're going. And I mean *anyone*. With the exception of the police, of course."

"I won't."

"Because," Fitzpatrick went on matter-of-factly, "if someone has it in for you, there's nothing to prevent him from giving it another try."

The next morning Ann engaged a pair of neighborhood boys to unload the books from her car and carry them up to her apartment. Meanwhile she packed a suitcase and telephoned the St. Francis Hotel. Then she set off downtown.

After unpacking at the St. Francis, she telephoned the Marin County Sheriff's Office. She was irritated to learn that Sunday was Inspector Tarr's day off; somehow she had pictured him at his desk waiting anxiously for her call. She left a message and petulantly hung up. Tarr was probably off at another picnic, enjoying himself in the company of his newest paramour.

She lunched at the Blue Fox, wandered along Post Street window-shopping, then returned to the hotel. There was no message for her. Feeling neglected, she went to her room, changed into an afternoon frock, and returned to the lobby. She bought a magazine, leafed through it, watched passers-by, went into the bar for a cocktail, and absently rebuffed the gambit of a handsome young man with white teeth and a suntan.

The afternoon passed, by and large pleasantly, or at least uneventfully. The night before seemed a nightmare; indeed, she was unable to think of it as having actually happened.

She dined, lingered over her coffee, visited the cocktail lounge for a liqueur, fended off a lingerie salesman from New York, and presently went up to bed.

The next day was Monday. Ann breakfasted in her room, wondering what to do with herself. As she was dressing her phone rang. Inspector Thomas Tarr asked, "How are you this morning?" His voice was cautious and subdued.

"Very well, thanks."

"No incidents?"

"None."

"You haven't told anyone where you're staying?"

"No one at all."

"Good. Just sit tight for a while."

"For how long?"

"I don't know." Tarr spoke with a harshness Ann had not heard before. "Sooner or later there'll be a break."

"Do you still think Roland committed suicide? After last night?"

"I haven't any reason to think otherwise."

"Then you must think it was the blackmailer who killed Harvey."

"It seems to follow," Tarr admitted. "Assuming, of course, that you were the intended victim."

"But why? I've been racking my brain. Why should anyone want me out of the way?" The words brought a sudden return of the nightmare. Ann's voice blurred; she looked fearfully about the room. "Who could do such a thing?"

"We'll find out," said Tarr in a soothing tone. "Eventually. In the meantime—"

"I know. Don't walk along the edge of any cliffs."

"With anybody. Inspector Fitzpatrick seems to think it was some thief who panicked, but I don't."

Ann laughed nervously. "It would be a shame to be slaughtered by chance."

"Sit tight and you won't be slaughtered at all. I'll keep in touch with you."

Ann hung up and sat still for a few minutes. She felt stifled and frustrated. What a detestable mess! She had no responsibilities; she should be off and away—anywhere but where she found herself now. . . . She sat down by the phone and telephoned Mrs. Darlington.

"I won't be back at Mar Vista next fall," said Ann. "I thought I should let you know now."

Mrs. Darlington's voice softened. "I appreciate your thoughtfulness in notifying me now. We shall miss you, of course; but under the circumstances it's undoubtedly the best and wisest course for all of us."

With a shock Ann realized that Mrs. Darlington had been casting about for some means, preferably polite, to achieve this very end. She wanted none of her staff involved in murders. "Naturally you can look to me for references," said Mrs. Darlington. "I'm sure that with your competence you'll have no trouble—"

"I'm *not* resigning because of the death of Mr. Gluck," said Ann.

"Of course not, certainly not; but under the circumstances . . . well, the school has an image to live up to, and we can't let it be tarnished. By the way, did your mother get in touch with you?"

"My mother?"

"Yes. I told Operator that I had no idea as to your current address. You'd better leave it with me in case—"

"Exactly what happened, Mrs. Darlington?"

"Last evening there was a person-to-person call for you—here, to my home, of all places. I gave Operator your address on Granada Avenue, but she said that you weren't there, that your mother wanted to get in touch with you, and did I know where you could be found. Naturally I said I had no information."

"You didn't hear anyone's voice but the operator's?"

"No."

Hanging up, Ann immediately telephoned the Marin County Sheriff's Office. Inspector Tarr was out, but he would call back as soon as he returned.

She dressed and descended to the hotel lobby, her brain seething with conjectures. She had planned to spend the morning shopping, but perhaps she had better wait for Tarr's call. Half an hour passed. She became restless and went out into Powell Street.

It was a typical San Francisco summer morning. The air was cool, fresh, lightly salt; the sunlight tingled. Over Union Square pigeons fluttered; a cable car clattered past on its way up Nob Hill. In this same bright world, thought Ann, lived the animal who had skulked in her bathroom, waiting to kill her!

She spent an hour or so window-shopping, then telephoned San Rafael, only to learn that Inspector Tarr had not yet returned. She lunched on a sandwich, returned to the hotel, and once again failed to reach Tarr. Twenty minutes later, hearing herself paged, she went to the telephone. It was Tarr.

"I understand you've been trying to get in touch with me."

"Yes." (Ann wondered about his voice, which sounded very grim.) She described her conversation with Mrs. Darlington. Tarr uttered a soft cluck, as if the news corroborated some expectation of his own.

"You don't sound surprised," said Ann.

"Who do you think was calling you?" asked the detective.

"My mother, I suppose. Unless . . . Do you think . . ."

"I don't think, I know. I found your mother."

"You found her! Where?"

"*Dead?*"

"For about three months."

Ann could not restrain a sudden flow of tears. As in the case of her father, she felt neither grief nor remorse, but there was a sundering of *something*, a loss . . . "How did she die?" Her voice sounded strange to her own ears. They had had no relationship at all, and yet . . .

"Wire around her neck. Indications are that she was struck on the head first. I'm sorry I have to sound so brutal."

"She was murdered, then. Where did you find her?"

"To the north of San Rafael a concern called the Guarantee Auto Wreckers has a field full of old cars waiting to be junked. Elaine's car was driven onto the field and parked among the junkers. The tires were deflated, the windows rolled down. The mehanics, if they noticed the car at all, thought it had been acquired in the usual way. The proprietor wasn't aware of its existence. It might have sat there a year. Except that this morning a customer came in wanting a part for a Buick. The owner couldn't find the part in stock. A mechanic named Sam said, 'What about that old Buick out back?' The proprietor investigated, and in due course we were notified."

"Was there anything else? Money? Luggage?"

"Her suitcase and handbag. We're still not absolutely sure, of course, that the woman we found is Elaine Gluck. We'll need you to identify her."

"*I can't!*"

"Someone who knew her has to do it. Your father is dead, Mr. Gluck is dead." His voice grew quite soft. "I'm sorry."

"Must I?"

"I'm afraid so, Miss Nelson."

Ann breathed deeply, once, twice. "I'll be right over."

CHAPTER 12

The room swam before Ann's eyes. She managed to say, "It's my mother."

"It's easy to make mistakes in a case like this," said Tarr. "You're sure this is Elaine Gluck?"

Ann shuddered. "Yes."

Tarr took her upstairs to his cubbyhole. Ann collapsed in a chair.

"It must have happened just after she saw me."

"Within a few days. Probably the next day."

"But that letter . . . It was certainly her handwriting; it was certainly her signature!"

"The report on that letter came in just after I spoke to you. About an inch had been cut from the top of the page, probably to remove the date and the sender's address. The salutation had been altered. Originally it read 'Dear Bobo.' The two *o*'s had been carefully changed to *a* and *y*, and your name was added: 'Baby Ann.' Quite simple."

" 'Bobo' . . . of course," said Ann. "One of Elaine's politer names for Roland."

"So it appears that the letter was originally addressed to your father."

"But why send it to me?"

"Apparently to preserve the illusion that your mother was alive. Did she own property?"

"Property? My mother?" Ann shook her head. "She was chronically broke."

"What about your grandmother? Is she alive?"

"No." Ann, comprehending the direction of Tarr's inquiry, became frosty. "If you think I strangled my mother and somehow beguiled my father into shooting himself"—her voice trembled in indignation—"you can think again."

"I made no such accusation," said Tarr. "Consider my job, Miss Nelson. Naturally, we've got to consider every possibility."

"In that case consider the possibility that I did *not* strangle my mother and Harvey Gluck."

"Oh, I have. Harvey Gluck's death is the monkey wrench. If it hadn't occurred, we could reasonably suppose that Roland Nelson strangled Elaine Gluck, was seen doing it by a person we shall call X, and was blackmailed by X until in desperation Nelson killed himself." He ignored Ann's mutter. "The death of Harvey Gluck creates no end of complications. Fitzpatrick leans toward the theory of a chance intruder or a sex criminal. I don't think so. I see X, compelled by some urgent reason, breaking into your apartment intending to kill you, but by a stroke of fantastic bad luck being forced to kill Harvey Gluck instead. This seems the most logical explanation, but brings us face to face with a blank wall: Why? Have you come up with any ideas?"

"No. None of it seems real."

Tarr looked at her quite unprofessionally. "It's real enough. I have to repeat—you mustn't take any chances."

She shivered. "I don't plan to. . . . I don't really know what to do with myself."

"Don't you have a friend you could visit? Somebody completely unconnected with this business?"

Ann considered. "There's Barbara Crane in Sonoma. I might drop in on her."

"Try to be back before dark," said Tarr. "I don't want to frighten you or limit your freedom, but facts are facts. Somebody went to considerable trouble to try to kill you. He might try again."

Ann turned north on Highway 101, toward Sonoma, a town twenty or thirty miles away. After a few miles her interest in visiting Barbara Crane began to dwindle. Barbara taught sociology at Sonoma Junior College; she would demand a detailed explanation for Ann's presence, which would lead to hours of hashing everything over. Martin, Barbara's husband, taught geology and was inclined to absolute judgments. The visit lost its attraction.

She turned off the freeway and drove westward, over a gently rolling landscape, once placid and rural but now blotched with housing developments. Meanwhile "Martin Crane" had suggested "Martin Jones." Or perhaps the housing developments had worked to this end; whatever the cause, Ann found herself occupied with the image of that dour individualist engrossed in Ruskin's *Stones of Venice*.

Perhaps she should have been surprised, but it seemed quite natural to come upon a sign reading:

PLEASANT VALLEY ESTATES
Top Value for Discriminating Home Buyers
A MARTIN JONES Development

Ann slowed and halted. From the road she could see two dozen houses in various stages of construction, with as many more lots in the process of being graded. On one of these she spied the contractor, sighting through a transit toward a young man in carpenter's overalls who held a surveyor's rod.

Ann watched for several minutes. Then Jones straightened up, jotted something on a clipboard, called to the rodman—who drove a stake, wrote on a label, and tacked it to the stake—and moved on to another location. Martin Jones bent once more over the transit and the process was repeated.

Ann backed her car into the driveway. Martin Jones spotted her, scowled, and returned to his transit. "Five inches low!" he called to the rodman. "That's all for now." He walked over to Ann.

"What brings you out here?"

"I was driving past, noticed your name, and stopped."

His attention was distracted by a pickup loaded with doors pre-hung in their frames, and he jerked as if he had been struck with a pin. "Hey, Shorty, not *there*! Does that house look like it's ready for doors?"

"It's where Steve told me to bring them," the truck driver said defensively.

"Where? House fourteen? Or house four?"

"It might have been four."

"You bet your life it was four. What good are doors here? The roof isn't even framed yet. Use your head!" The pickup moved on; Jones turned back to Ann. "You got to watch these guys every minute. About one in ten knows what he's doing."

"You're busy," said Ann politely, "so don't let me keep you."

"I'm always busy," he growled. "I'd go broke in a week if I weren't." He glanced up and down the street. "I've got to make the rounds. Come along if you like," he said, looking everywhere but at Ann. "I'll show you around."

"If you're sure you can spare the time."

"No time lost. I'd let you know."

"I don't doubt it." Ann climbed out. The sunlight was bright; the new lumber smelled clean and fresh; the clatter of hammers, the whine of power saws, made cheerful sounds. Ann found it impossible not to relax.

Martin Jones seemed to sense her mood and became almost cordial. "Let's walk down this way. I'll show you the whole thing, from beginning to end." He led her to a lot where a loader was scooping up two tons of red-brown earth at a thrust. "Incidentally," said Martin Jones, "I read your book. Or most of it."

"How did you like it?" He *had* read it!

"Hard to say. He writes like somebody building one of the old-time houses, full of stained glass and gingerbread. If you like that kind of thing, I suppose it's great."

"Do you like it?"

Jones's smile turned sheepish. "Parts of it are interesting. About the tides, for instance, and the mud flats. If they were just a bit different there wouldn't be any Venice. . . . The tide flats along Black Point aren't much different. They'd cost a lot to build on when you figure in a causeway, dredging, piles. It could always be worked into overhead, I suppose. The houses would sell; that's the main thing. . . ."

They moved on to another lot, where carpenters were setting foundation forms, while laborers laid out reinforcing steel for the concrete. The sight of the steel reminded Ann of the cracked footing at the Cypriano house. She said, "I understand you built the Cypriano house."

He nodded shortly. "I did. While I was still young and easygoing."

"They're having trouble with the foundations," said Ann sweetly. "They seem to blame you for the trouble."

"They blame *me?*"

"So I understand."

"That's a laugh."

"How do you mean?"

"Blame Rex Orr, not me. He wanted a forty-thousand-dollar house on a twenty-thousand-dollar budget. I told him I'd have to cut corners awful close. He said to go ahead, just so long as it didn't show. I used all utility lumber in the framing. The house stands up, but the floors squeak here and there. No harm done. Wherever I dared, I cut down on reinforcing in the footings. If the ground is solid, it makes no big difference. If the ground settles, though, there's trouble. I explained this to Orr, but he gave me the green light. I guessed wrong. After the rains the ground began to go. I don't feel too bad. I took a beating on that house."

"Don't the building inspectors check on things like that?"

"Sure. But there's angles you can work. You put the steel in the forms, the inspector looks, signs the permit. As soon as he leaves you yank out the steel and pour concrete. Nine times out of ten you're in business, with no harm done. But once in a while there'll be trouble. I don't have any remorse. Orr asked for a jackleg job where it wouldn't show and he got it. The Cyprianos tried to make me the goat; in fact, Cypriano got nasty. He was going to bring out the building inspector, but Mrs. Orr backed me up.

"Do you know something? Cypriano is a kook. I was sitting out there talking to him; he gave me a drink and then, sitting across the table, he began letting his keys swing back and forth. Slow and easy. And he'd say, 'My, but it's a peaceful day. How calm it is. How peaceful. Don't you feel sleepy?' " Jones gave a bark of savage laughter. "The so-and-so was trying to hypnotize me! Then he'd convince me that

I should fix his house. I just laughed at him. He slammed off into one of the back rooms."

Ann listened in surprise and amusement. The taciturn Martin Jones was talking as if a dam had broken. They walked on to where a truck was discharging concrete into footings. Martin Jones became abruptly silent; stopping, he ran his eye along the forms that delineated the outer edge of the house-to-be. He called, "Hey, Pete!" But his voice was inaudible over the rumble of the concrete truck, and he strode off, beckoning to one of the carpenters, pointing to the offending form. Ann, sighting along the edge, saw that it was just a trifle crooked.

While the contractor watched, the carpenter drove a stake with a sledgehammer, and wedged in a brace to straighten the form to Jones's satisfaction.

He rejoined Ann. "As I say, you've got to watch these guys every minute."

"It seems like an active life," smiled Ann.

"I don't get bored. Ulcers, yes. Boredom, no."

"Do you really have ulcers?"

He grinned, shaking his head. "It's the building contractor's occupational disease. But I'm too ornery for ulcers. Ask one of these carpenters what they think of my disposition." He stopped abruptly to face Ann. "Let's go somewhere tonight. A show . . . opera . . . circus . . . dog races . . . public library . . . you name it; I'll take you."

Ann was so astonished she almost permitted herself to show it. Martin Jones asking for a date! He *did* have a potential. She was pleased, very pleased. More than very pleased. "Oh, I'd like to, but darn it, I can't, not tonight."

Martin Jones's mouth twisted at the corners. "Okay."

"Next week, perhaps," Ann said hastily. "The police don't want me going anywhere until they clear up these deaths."

"That might take a long time if that fellow Tarr's running things."

"Just for a week or so." Ann wondered if she was sounding overanxious, so she composed herself and became interested in the next lot. Here a crew of carpenters worked on the concrete slab, laying down redwood two-by-fours along the line of the eventual partitions, fixing them in place with a device which, after being loaded with a cartridge and a heavy nail, shot the nail through the wood into the concrete.

"All four-bedroom houses," said Jones, noting Ann's interest. "Four bedrooms, two baths, play-room, and dining area. They should go fast. I won't be a millionaire, but I'll be out of the woods."

"You're going to sell the Inisfail house?"

"As soon as a buyer shows up."

"And your old family house, too?"

"That shack." He pursed his lips. "I don't know. Maybe I'll remodel it."

"I like it better than the new house."

"Your father liked the old place better, too.... What's so interesting?"

Ann had been watching the carpenters, conscious of a vague tickling at the back of her head. A laborer approached Jones, one hand aloft, blood streaming down his black wrist. "What happened to you?" asked Jones in disapproval. "You trying to cut your hand off?"

"Just a scratch; some of that sharp wire went and dug me. I thought I'd better get a bandage."

"Right. If you don't and you catch blood poison, there's no insurance. Come along to the shack; I'll fix you up." He turned to Ann, and for once his expression was boyish, almost wistful. "Can I telephone you?"

The word "insurance" had triggered a new set of thoughts. Ann said vaguely, "I'm moving; I don't know where I'll be. Perhaps I'd better call you. I think I'd better be going."

Martin Jones nodded brusquely. "Come along, Joe."

Ann returned to her car. Insurance ... The answers to one or two questions could illuminate the entire case. Though now she knew—or thought she knew—how her father had been murdered.

In San Rafael she stopped at a pay telephone and dialed the Cypriano house. Jehane's voice came languidly over the wire.

"Forgive me for bothering you," said Ann, "but do you know if Pearl carried insurance?"

"What kind of insurance?"

"Life insurance."

Jehane considered. "I don't know. It's possible, I suppose."

"When she owned your house she undoubtedly carried fire-and-theft."

"Yes, certainly."

"Do you know the name of her agent?"

"Arthur Eakins, in San Rafael. We just took over the policy. Why do you ask?"

"It's something connected with my father's death."

"Oh. Incidentally, have you seen the afternoon papers?"

"No. And I don't plan to. Are they ... bad?"

"Not yet. But I advise you to stay out of sight if you don't want reporters descending on you."

"That's a good idea. Thanks."

Jehane said, "I'd offer you the use of our guest room if I thought you'd accept. Would you?"

"That's nice of you. But I don't think I'd better."

"You're not still at your apartment?"

"No."

Jehane's voice became thoughtful. "You could stay with us. Alexander really isn't so awful. He's been all morning crawling around over the rocks gathering up the chess set after his grand gesture."

"It was wonderful. But I do think I'd better stay where I am, at least for a while."

"Just as you like." She sounded brusk.

"Goodbye."

Ann looked up the address of Arthur Eakins in the telephone directory and drove to his office. Eakins proved to be an energetic little man with round, earnest eyes and a button nose. When Ann introduced herself, he became guardedly cordial. Yes, Pearl Maudley Orr had insured with him, both before and after her marriage to Roland Nelson. Roland Nelson had done likewise. He supplied particulars, and an opaque window blocking Ann's perception was smashed.

There was now very little about the case that she did not understand. She knew how her father had been murdered. She knew why. She even understood the reason for the abortive attempt on her own life; and she could guess the motive for the strangling of her mother.

Leaving Eakins's office, walking toward her car, she thought: What a simple, ingenious plot! And how evil, how selfish the perpetrator! She looked uneasily over her shoulder, thrilling with a sense of danger.

She gained the comparative security of her car and sat thinking. There should be a graphic way to demonstrate her conclusions. After a moment a possibility suggested itself. In a nearby drugstore she once again consulted a telephone directory and located the office out of which the building inspectors worked.

A three-minute walk took her there. At a counter she inquired if blueprints to all new construction were kept on file. The clerk admitted that such was the case. Ann asked to see those prints relating to the house at 560 Neville Road, near Inisfail, and was informed that such plans were not available for public inspection.

Using the office telephone, she called Inspector Tarr, who expressed surprise at finding her still in San Rafael. "You'd better be sticking to home base till we tie this business up," he warned her. "You had one pretty close call, remember? It could happen again."

"I don't think anything is going to happen where I am now which is at the Building Department."

"What in the world are you doing there?"

"Doing your work for you. Detecting."

"Well, well," said Tarr. "And what have you detected?"

"If you'll meet me here, I'll show you."

"Well, well, well," said Tarr. "I'm not proud, lady. I'll be right over."

Five minutes later Tarr appeared in the doorway. Ann rose from the bench where she had been waiting. "What's this all about?"

"I had an idea," said Ann. "I came here to verify it, but the clerk won't help me. Perhaps you have more influence."

"Influence to what end?"

"To look at some blueprints. Specifically those to the house on Neville Road."

"Why this sudden interest in architecture?"

"I think I can explain the death of my father. If I'm right, the blueprints will prove it."

Tarr stared at her, then went to the counter, and flashed his credentials. The blueprints were promptly forthcoming.

He spread them out on the counter. Ann bent forward, peered closely, and gave a choked laugh of mingled triumph and tragedy. Her theory was now demonstrable fact.

"Well?" asked Tarr.

Ann pointed. "Look there."

Tarr frowned. "I must be dense. What are you trying to prove?"

"First, how a bookcase with six legs can show nine dent marks. Second, how my father was murdered in a locked room."

Tarr ran his fingers through his hair. "Are you still on that kick? Look, no one has any murder motive but you. And if you did it, why aren't you soft-pedaling the matter?"

"I didn't kill him. But Arthur Eakins, the insurance agent, can tell you who did."

"I hate to feel like a chump," said Tarr. "Why not explain in words of one syllable?"

Ann did so. Tarr's expression shifted through disbelief, skeptical interest, reluctant conviction, and finally disgust at his own stupidity. "Now I can't claim any credit for breaking this case," he said.

"Do so anyway, by all means," said Ann. "Personally, I just feel sick."

Tarr glanced at his watch. With sudden energy he said, "Let's go get Eakins. It's two o'clock. With any luck we can clear this thing up right now."

CHAPTER 13

In the conference room adjoining the sheriff's private office they had been assembled by ones and twos: first Ann with Arthur Eakins; then Edgar Maudley and Martin Jones, who exchanged glances of mutual detestation; then Alexander and Jehane Cypriano. The room was long, with dark oak wainscoting and a high ceiling, from which hung two frosted glass globes—a formal room incorrigibly ugly. Pushed against one wall was an oak table of institutional solidity at which sat a pair of uniformed deputies. The laity sat on straight-backed chairs ranged along the walls. There was little conversation. Edgar Maudley leaned toward Jehane once or twice to utter an earnest remark, to which Jehane responded politely. She wore a sheath of beige wool with a coat the color of black coffee; gold loops in her ears were her only jewelry; as usual she looked dramatically, wanly beautiful. Alexander Cypriano wore a dark-blue blazer with a scarf of maroon foulard knotted at the neck. Martin Jones had not bothered to change from his work clothes: tan whipcord trousers, a green windbreaker over a white shirt. He sat sulkily aloof, favoring first Edgar Maudley, then Alexander with bitter glances.

The door from the sheriff's office opened; into the

room came Sheriff Metzger with Robinson, the district attorney; then Inspector Tarr and a young bespectacled assistant to the district attorney. The deputies straightened in their chairs.

District Attorney Robinson and his assistant took seats at the table. Tarr pulled a chair away from the wall, seating himself like a boxer awaiting a bell.

Sheriff Metzger leaned against the table and spoke, looking at no one in particular. "I apologize for assembling you in this rather dramatic fashion. I assure you it's not our customary procedure in cases of this kind."

"Cases of what kind?" demanded Edgar Maudley, who apparently had resolved beforehand to put up with no nonsense.

Metzger examined Maudley with detachment. "I refer to the death of Roland Nelson, and also"—he consulted a list—"the deaths of Elaine Gluck, Harvey Gluck, and Pearl Nelson, which I hope will be clarified. To this end I'll appreciate the help of all of you. Inspector Tarr has been in charge of the case, and he has a few questions to ask." The sheriff settled into a seat beside the district attorney, who muttered something to him. The sheriff nodded.

Tarr consulted some notes he had scribbled on a piece of paper. He rose to lean on the back of his chair.

"This thing starts with the marriage of Pearl Maudley Orr to Roland Nelson. It was not a successful marriage; it lasted only a few months. Shortly after the separation, Mrs. Nelson died in an automobile accident. I think everyone here is familiar with the circumstances, and I'll say no more except to point out the obvious fact that Roland Nelson profited greatly by her death. He inherited money and securities worth more than a hundred thousand dollars, as well as valuable books, rugs, and art objects.

"Mrs. Nelson died intestate; The California and Pacific Bank, which managed her affairs, was appointed administrator of her estate, and an interval of six months elapsed before Roland Nelson came into his inheritance. During this six months Mr. Nelson had very little cash. He rented an old house from Mr. Jones, and he also worked for Mr. Jones. I understand that he was not a very satisfactory employee. Right, Mr. Jones?"

"Right," said Martin Jones.

"You fired him?"

"Correct."

"How did this affect your personal relations with Mr. Nelson?"

"No difference. I got along with him just as well after I fired him as before. He wasn't making any money for me, and he knew it."

"You rented him your old family home for eighty-five dollars a month."

"Correct."

"During this time you completed the house at five sixty Neville Road and allowed Mr. Nelson to move in?"

"Correct."

"Why did he want to move?"

Jones shrugged. "I didn't give him any choice. I wanted to sell the old place. He had no complaints; I let him have the new house for the same rent."

"Do you know if he had any visitors during this period?"

Jones grinned. "While he was still at the old house I think he once conducted a séance, or something of the sort. Mr. and Mrs. Cypriano were there. I watched for a few minutes, but nothing much happened."

Tarr turned to Alexander Cypriano. "Do you recall such an occasion, Mr. Cypriano?"

"Naturally." Alexander was clearly uncomfortable.

"What happened?"

"Very little. Mr. Nelson, after reading certain books belonging to his wife, had become interested in psychic phenomena. The occasion Mr. Jones refers to was not a spiritualistic séance, but an experiment to see if a person's natural telepathic powers are enhanced by special conditions."

"What sort of special conditions?"

"Hypnotism."

"Who was the subject?"

"My wife."

"Were your experiments successful?"

"Not to any significant degree. My wife is not a good hypnotic subject."

"How long did these experiments continue?"

"On this single occasion. None of us was more than superficially interested. In fact, I'd forgotten the incident until Mr. Jones just recalled it."

"This experiment took place in the first house Mr. Nelson rented from Mr. Jones—the old house?"

"That's right."

"Did you ever visit him in the new house?"

"No."

"How about you, Mrs. Cypriano?"

"No. Never."

"Mr. Maudley?"

"I visited him once," said Maudley with dignity, "in an attempt to arrange an equitable division of Mrs. Nelson's property."

"Did you actually enter the house?"

"No. Mr. Nelson was insulting and offensive, and we remained outside. We did not come to any understanding. At any rate, no understanding satisfactory to me."

"In fact, to emphasize his position he wrote out a will and showed it to you?"

"He had the insolence to ask me to witness it. The effect, of course, was to cut me off completely from my cousin's property."

"Which you had hoped to inherit?"

"Naturally. Mr. Nelson practically gave my cousin's house to the Cyprianos, though it was as much a liability as an asset because of faulty construction."

Martin Jones said gently, "That sounds like slander to me. You asking for a bust in the nose?"

"Slander?" Edgar Maudley snorted. "Truth is a completely adequate defense against a charge of slander. Only an incompetent or worse would omit reinforcing steel from the foundations."

"Those were my instructions."

"Nonsense. There was no need to skimp. My cousin was a wealthy woman. Mr. Orr, her husband at that time, was not only wealthy but a cautious and conservative man."

"Who studied ghosts and mind reading and hypnotism. He was a screwball."

Tarr broke into the exchange. He asked Alexander Cypriano, "When Mrs. Nelson learned of the faulty foundation, what was her attitude?"

Cypriano darted a quick, malicious look at Jones. "She was surprised and angry. She said that she would see that repairs were made. After she died, Mr. Nelson and I came to an understanding, and I agreed to perform the necessary repairs."

Tarr examined his notes. "On March third, Elaine Gluck visited Roland Nelson and disappeared. On May twenty-fifth, approximately, Roland Nelson died. He was discovered on May thirtieth in circumstances strongly suggesting suicide. During my investigation I found evidence of blackmail. It crossed my mind that Nelson might have murdered Mrs. Gluck—a notion that was reinforced when we eventually found Mrs. Gluck's strangled body. I might say here that Miss Nelson"—he nodded toward Ann—"insisted from the first that her father would neither pay blackmail nor commit suicide. I could see no alternative theory.

"On the evening of Saturday June eighth, Miss Nelson, arriving home, encountered her mother's husband, Harvey Gluck, who had arrived unexpectedly from Los Angeles. They went up to her apartment together. Mr. Gluck had occasion to use the bathroom and was garroted by someone waiting there. Under the circumstances it's clear that Miss Nelson was the intended victim. But why should anyone wish to kill Miss Nelson? Well, she is now a girl of considerable wealth. Who would inherit from her if she died? She has no close relatives; her mother and father are both dead. Her nearest kin live in North Carolina. The money cannot revert to the Maudleys. So gain is not a credible motive.

"It would seem, then, that Miss Nelson is a threat to someone. Remember that she has never accepted the theory of suicide in connection with her father's death, even though no other theory presented itself. The study in which Mr. Nelson died was almost hermetically sealed. The door was bolted securely, the windows clamped shut, the damper in the chimney fixed in the 'shut' position. Murder seems impossible. In fact, I'll go so far as to say this: to shoot someone and leave the room in the condition in which I found it *is* impossible.

"Could Mr. Nelson somehow have been persuaded to raise a pistol to his forehead and pull the trigger? There are conceivable circumstances where this might be the case—an elaborate practical joke to astound someone watching through the window, perhaps. But surely Mr. Nelson would have checked and double-checked the gun to make sure he was in no danger of shooting himself.

"In any event, whatever the plot—if such a plot existed—the fact that Miss Nelson was a victim of attempted murder makes it appear that she either suspected or was in a position to suspect it. Hence, by a kind of backward reasoning, we must take very seriously the idea that Roland Nelson was indeed murdered.

"What did Miss Nelson learn? What was she about to learn? In the first place, she was baffled by a series of peculiar events and circumstances. One was the three shots heard by Mr. Nelson's neighbors, the Savarinis, about the time or shortly after Mr. Nelson died—never satisfactorily explained. Another was: Why hadn't her father paid his rent when he had ample funds?

"She was also puzzled by the fact that the bookcase standing along the wall that separated the living room from the study—the case facing into the living room—had made nine dent marks in the vinyl flooring, although it had only six legs—three sets of two each, the two in each set being nine inches apart from back to front. The extra dent marks were approximately five and a half inches from the front legs, between the front and back legs.

"Obviously, that bookcase had once stood in a different position. Away from the wall—further out into the room? But in that case there should have been *twelve* dents in all, not nine—two sets of six. So it couldn't have been that."

Tarr fixed them with a glittering eye. "That the bookcase had once stood in a different position had to be, from those extra three dents. But if it wasn't because the bookcase stood *away* from the wall, it had to be because the bookcase extended *into the wall.* Obviously, that's impossible . . . *unless there hadn't been a wall there.*

"The solution came to Miss Nelson this morning,

when she noticed carpenters fastening two-by-four partitions to concrete slabs using a stud driver—a kind of tool, almost a gun, which shoots nails through wood into concrete. The sound of the shots suggested her father's death—the three shots heard by the Savarinis. *Could it be that the three shots had been not the reports of a gun but the reports of a stud shooter? Somebody building something? A wall?"*

Tarr glanced at Ann with unabashed admiration. "Miss Nelson pictured the dents the bookcase had left in the flooring. She eliminated the further-out-into-the-room theory because it would have left three more marks than were actually there. She embraced the back-into-the-wall theory because that's the only theory that explains those three extra dents where there should have been six—*the wall stood where the missing three marks lay.* In other words, again, somebody had built a wall. That wall, the wall that turned the end of the living room into apparently a second room, the study. And for the wall to be built, the bookcase in the living room obviously had to be shifted the thickness of the wall, out further into the living room, where it now stands."

Tarr was all business now; Ann had never seen him so cold and inevitable-looking.

"I consulted a carpenter an hour ago. He tells me that a wall like the one in the house where Nelson lived would typically consist of framing three and five-eighths inches in thickness, with half an inch of plasterboard on one side, a quarter inch of plywood on the other, and two baseboards half an inch thick—adding up to five and three-eighths inches ... in other words, just about the distance between the front dents and the extra dents in the vinyl tiling.

"So it now becomes clear—thanks to Miss Nelson— how her father could have been murdered in such a way that suicide seemed the only answer. That living room was originally a single room; *there was no study*. Nelson was shot; then a wall was constructed across that end of the living room *to create a study*, sealing him in.

"According to my carpenter consultant, the wall would have to be braced upright. The study side would be finished, the plywood varnished, the door hung and bolted securely. Then the inner baseboards—those on the study side of the wall—would be nailed to the floor, along the line the wall would eventually occupy, and molding would similarly be attached at the ceiling line.

"Next, the killer would clean the study carefully, sort through Roland Nelson's papers, leave a note suggesting blackmail. He would shift the study bookcase back to the wall line. He would slip around the edge of the wall to the living room side, shove, slide and pry the wall into place, so that it fitted squarely across the room, tight against the moldings and baseboard inside the study. He would then nail the studs at each side into the living-room wall; and then, to secure the bottom plate, he would use a stud driver. One shot to the right of the door, two shots into the longer section to the left of the door would be necessary. He would then apply plasterboard, tape the joints and the angles where the new wall met the ceiling and side walls, paint the plasterboard, install a length of baseboard. Lo and behold, the corpse of Roland Nelson would thereupon repose in a room that was truly locked."

Tarr looked around the room from face to face. "Incidentally, this is not just speculation. Today Miss Nelson and I examined the original blueprints of the house on Neville Road. These blueprints show no study—only a long living room. When Roland Nelson came into possession of his wife's books, he arranged the bookcases back to back to function as a kind of partition, thus creating a sort of open-face study. This fact may have planted the locked-room idea in the murderer's mind. And he sure succeeded! He created a true locked-room, without gimmick, illusion, sleight of hand—without person or agency concealed in the room." Tarr gave a slow nod of respect for the still unnamed craftsman's ingenuity.

He again consulted his notes. "I asked my carpenter consultant how long such a job would occupy a man, and I asked how the noise could be muffled—because if a chance passer-by, or the Savarinis, heard sounds of hammering and sawing, the game would be given away.

"An expert craftsman, I was told, could probably complete the job in three or four days, working hard. By precutting the lumber, by predrilling nail holes, and driving home the nails with a rubber mallet, he could both speed up the job and reduce the noise to nearly nothing. Only the sound of the stud driver driving nails into the concrete would have to be heard.

"After the wall was in place only two jobs remained: to move the living-room bookcase back against the new wall—and to arrange for the corpse of Roland Nelson to be found. Because Mr. Nelson lived a very secluded life, he might have remained locked in that 'study' for years."

Tarr's voice had been easy, pleasant, pitched at a conversational level. Now he leaned forward, and his look lost all its geniality. "Miss Nelson was faced with another puzzle: *Why* was her father killed? Well, something turned up to satisfy all the conditions. A chance word supplied the key to the puzzle: *insurance*.

"Miss Nelson paid a visit to Albert Eakins, the

gentleman sitting to my right. Mr. Eakins, did Roland Nelson ever call on you?"

"He did," said the insurance man.

"What was the purpose of his visit?"

"He wanted to take out a comprehensive policy: fire, flood, vandalism, public liability—the works—on a house he had just bought."

"Did you visit the house?"

"I happened to drive past one day and found Mr. Nelson in the front yard planting rosebushes. I stopped to chat a moment. Mr. Nelson asked me what I thought a fair price for the house would be. I told him probably thirty thousand dollars. He told me that he had bought it for twenty-two thousand because the owner was in financial difficulties. I assured him he'd made an excellent buy and could certainly sell the house at a profit."

"So there was never any blackmail, you see," said Tarr. "Roland Nelson had merely bought a house." He turned to Martin Jones. "That's our case, Mr. Jones."

Martin Jones rose. "I've heard all I'm going to hear. I've got to get back to my job."

"I don't think so," said Sheriff Metzger pleasantly.

Martin Jones darted toward the door. Tarr sprang after him, and Jones whirled and knocked Tarr down. As the deputies jumped forward, Jones, his back to the door, flashed a heavy clasp knife, the steel as brightly cold as his eyes. "Anybody want to get cut?"

Sheriff Metzger got ponderously to his feet. "Here, put that thing away. You're likely to hurt somebody." He lumbered over to the contractor and simply took the knife.

Ann's abiding image of Martin Jones was to be that of a sullen small boy discovered in an act of mischief by a stern and sorrowful father.

The deputies seized Jones's arms.

"Lock him up," said the sheriff. "Or maybe you'd like to make a statement first?"

Martin Jones said dully, "All right, I confess. I'm only sorry I didn't get *her*." He nodded toward Ann. "She's been in my hair ever since I first laid eyes on her."

Tarr was wiping blood off his lip. "How did you talk Roland Nelson into giving you twenty thousand cash and a thousand a month? He could as easily have given you twenty-two thousand cash."

Martin Jones's mood of co-operation had departed. "It's your story, not mine. Tell it any way you like."

"Here's a guess. You gave him a deed, but asked him not to register it for a few months. Perhaps you admitted that you'd used the house as collateral on a loan and needed twenty thousand to clear title, or you gave him other security for his money. In any event, you asked Nelson to keep the deal secret. Nelson agreed—though naturally he had to tell the insurance agent."

Arthur Eakins said in a deeply solemn voice, "Mr. Nelson asked me to say nothing about the situation."

The deputies tugged at Martin Jones's arms. Jones took a deep breath and for a moment seemed to exude his old air of sullen purpose. Then his shoulders sagged, and he was led away.

CHAPTER 14

After the Cyprianos and Maudley left, Ann, torn by a dozen conflicting urges, went to sit in Tarr's office. An hour later he came in and flopped into his chair. He showed no surprise at Ann's presence.

"Did he say anything more?" asked Ann.

"He talked. He's a queer one—doesn't seem to give a damn. He hasn't even asked for a lawyer."

"He's probably worried more about his men loafing on the job than anything else. Did he say anything about Elaine's murder?" Ann's hands twisted.

Tarr nodded. "He called at the house on Neville Road, he says, which he'd just sold to your father. He found Elaine sitting at your father's desk going through his papers, including the bill of sale. Mr. Nelson apparently was in San Francisco on business connected with his stocks. Jones had been brooding about money, and he'd already formulated his plans to make your father appear a suicide. But Elaine had seen the deed, so she had to go.

"Jones also saw that he could embellish his original idea with blackmail. He talked to Elaine a few minutes, then knocked her out, strangled her with a length of wire, stuffed her in the trunk of her car, and drove it to the old family house, where he parked it in the garage. There it stayed for almost three months, until Jones collected the final payment, whereupon he shot your father.

"Jones had his preparations all made. He went through Mr. Nelson's papers, leaving only those that were meaningless or misleading. Naturally he burned the deed. He prepared the blackmail note, half-charred it, and wrote false rent receipts for the months of March and April—all this with the corpse of Roland Nelson sitting in the chair." Tarr shook his head in wonder. "Then he started on the wall. He had pre-cut his material during the day, then brought it in at dusk and worked all night. He hung the door with special care, fitting it tightly—almost too tightly—to emphasize the locked-room illusion. The extra bolt was an afterthought. He didn't realize it would have the effect not of calming suspicion but of arousing it.

"Finally he drove your mother's Buick to the wrecking yard and ditched it. That was all there was to it—until you noticed the extra dents in the vinyl under the bookcase."

"What about Pearl?"

"He denies killing her, and I believe him. He couldn't have foreseen that her death would help him. Pearl probably died by accident."

"And Harvey Gluck?"

"Jones only said two or three words which I won't repeat. He saw that you were fascinated by the prints of the bookcase. Edgar Maudley, who was also there, hardly glanced at them, so he was safe. But Jones was afraid you'd work the thing out, and he decided you had to go, and right away, before you could tell me about the dents."

"Poor Harvey," said Ann. "Poor mother. Poor daddy." It was a sort of requiem.

"It's been a long day." Tarr glanced at his watch.

"The few loose ends can wait till tomorrow." He reached over and took her hands. "What about it? Let's have a few drinks and forget this thing. I'll even take you to dinner."

"All right," said Ann listlessly. "I can use some relaxing."

"I'm just the man to relax with," Tarr declared.

"Yes," said Ann, coming to life. "We must call your friend Cooley and have him take photographs.... Oh, well. What difference does it make to me? Thank the Lord I'm not married to you."

"You think that's such a bad idea?" said Tarr. "I've always yearned for a rich wife."

"Is that a proposal?" asked Ann tartly. "If so, it's as disgustingly casual as the rest of you."

"I'm a casual guy," said Inspector Thomas Tarr. "But that doesn't necessarily make me a heel. Where do you want to go, Miss Millionbucks?"

"I don't care. As long as it's quiet."

"I know just the place."

"You would!"

Then a peculiar silence fell. And something happened. How it happened, why it happened, almost to whom it happened. Ann was never afterward able to pin down precisely. All she knew was that she was swept up by a sort of hurricane in a pair of strong male arms, and that a delicate but vigorous kissing game began, and whoever was playing it was enjoying it very, very much.